The
Ladies of
Managua

❧

Also by Eleni N. Gage

North of Ithaka
Other Waters

The Ladies of Managua

Eleni N. Gage

ST. MARTIN'S PRESS
New York

THE LADIES OF MANAGUA. Copyright © 2015 by Eleni N. Gage. All rights reserved. Printed in the United States of America. For information, address St. Martin's Press, 175 Fifth Avenue, New York, N.Y. 10010.

www.stmartins.com

Designed by Kathryn Parise

The Library of Congress Cataloging-in-Publication Data is available upon request.

ISBN 978-1-250-05864-5 (hardcover)
ISBN 978-1-4668-6300-2 (e-book)

St. Martin's Press books may be purchased for educational, business, or promotional use. For information on bulk purchases, please contact the Macmillan Corporate and Premium Sales Department at 1-800-221-7945, extension 5442, or write to specialmarkets@macmillan.com.

First Edition: May 2015

10 9 8 7 6 5 4 3 2 1

To Emilio and Amalía, who exposed me to Nicaragua
and to countless other new worlds as well

We are volcanoes; when we women offer our experience
as our truth, as human truth, all the maps change.
There are new mountains.

—Ursula K. LeGuin

When your country is small, your dreams for it are large.

—Rubén Darío

1

Maria

Revolutionaries make bad husbands," my abuela always says. I don't think that's fair, really. It's not like my papi was such a terrible son-in-law, such a bad husband to her daughter for the brief time my parents were married. His only mistake, as far as I can tell, was being in the wrong hall at the wrong time, opening the wrong door. Like a game show contestant on *The Price Is Right* choosing door number two; my Bela used to watch that every afternoon when we lived in Miami, before I went off to college and my grandparents returned to Nicaragua. Only this wasn't a game, it was a revolution, and choosing the wrong door meant that my father was shot and killed. He died because of a choice he made, I see that, but it was all a mistake. It's not like he opened the door in order to hurt my mother, to abandon us. It hardly seems fair to hold his death against him.

But my abuela would say he shouldn't have been there in the first place, in that general's mansion in Managua, playing at being a soldier, trying to change the world. Not when he had a baby at home, and a baby girl, at that—to my Bela, it makes a difference.

And I see her point, I do. There's a little hubris involved there, sure. But if no one ever tried to do the impossible, there would be no real change anywhere in the world. Mostly it's pretty noble, I think, to see something wrong and try to set it right. Besides, his whole generation tried to reform their country, to change everything. And they did, in some ways. They didn't like the way Nicaragua was being run as Somoza's personal playground, the way the dictator and his government stole and celebrated while most people lived in poverty. My parents didn't like it, even if they didn't really count as "most people." Fomenting revolution, spreading reform—it's what people their age did back then, try to turn the world upside down. The same way my Bela and all her friends try to shore it up, to write letters, to look decorative, to conform to society instead of changing it. When I think about it, both my parents and my grandmother are just followers of trends. Although maybe I should give them more credit; maybe I'm the follower and, really, they're more trendsetters.

How many Christmas parties have I been to on holiday trips "home" to Nicaragua where some tipsy woman my mother's age trips over her Ferragamo heels on her way to tell me how she fought in "la Revolución," how she trained and battled in the mountains of Matagalpa before deciding to help the movement in other ways, press relations, consulting on the rebranding effort? She'll slip me a fuchsia-and-turquoise business card with the words CRISTIANA, SOCIALISTA, SOLIDARIA on it, a little reminder that her rebranding effort has succeeded in making the Sandinistas a religiously affiliated political party, garnering them the support of the Catholic Church, and Daniel Ortega a win in the last elections. And then she'll step a little closer, so I can smell the ronpopo on her breath, and whisper, "Your parents were like movie stars to us when we were all young; so beautiful, so tragic." She'll touch my face, and say something maudlin and semi-unintelligible: "Your father, he was so . . . ," she'll start, but she'll never finish her sentence.

I always want to scream, "What? He was so *what?*" I was four months old when my father died; I never knew him. And ever since I can remember, if I ask about him, Madre fusses with her scarf or studies her nail beds as if looking for clues before changing the subject. So I stop asking. When I was little, I stopped because I wanted to please her. With me living in Miami with my Bela and my abuelo, and Madre in Nicaragua, rebuilding the newly free country, I knew too well that her visits were precious; I didn't want to ruin the time we had together. She'd swoop in like a Very Special Guest Star in an episode of my favorite TV show, and I thought if I behaved, and I didn't upset her by making her talk about my papi, she'd return sooner. Maybe she'd become a series regular. I liked my friends, my school, so I didn't want her to take us back with her to Managua, but I thought if I could keep her happy the whole time she was visiting, maybe she'd decide it was a good idea to stay in Miami with all of us.

By junior high, I realized that she was never going to move in with us. Our apartment on Key Biscayne was too small, not in size but in scope. In Nicaragua, she was raising a young country, and therefore, reshaping the world. How could bringing up one not-very-interesting daughter compete with that? After my epiphany, I made myself stop asking about Papi, out of spite. Everyone else might act as if the Revolution was so fascinating, as if in talking to Madre they were interviewing some sort of female action hero, Jane Bond. But I wasn't everyone else, or I didn't want to be in her eyes. Let her ask about my life, for a change.

Now that I'm an adult, officially, anyway, I like to think I'm less stubborn. Most of the time now, I'll ask about my papi if the timing seems right, if we hear a song that makes Madre say, "We used to sing this during the Revolución." But when I do, she still flushes and looks away and mutters something that reveals nothing at all, even if I can manage to make out the actual words she's spoken. And I don't press the issue. I can tell she's upset, and I'd like to say that I stop asking because I don't want to sadden her. But that would be a lie. I just don't want to push her so hard that she blurts out what I suspect is the truth: that it's not simply too sad for her to talk about Papi, it's too painful for her to talk about him to me. That it hurts her to tell me about his death because I haven't properly honored his life. Because while she's carried on his work in his memory all these years, I've done nothing but resent her for the absence her efforts required. And that's not a truth I'm ready to hear.

So when I'm visiting Managua at Christmas and a (festively, never inappropriately) drunk woman caresses my face and intimates that she knew my father, knew him well enough to tell me something real about him, I can't help but stare. And she'll see the searching look in my eyes and recover with something like, "And your mother, so strong at such a young age. And so impressive now. We look up to her in the Movement, all of us women. How lucky to have such a strong mother."

And once again I've learned nothing more about my father, and I regret having revealed how desperate I am for information. Because all that I've gotten out of the conversation is a reminder that it's not just my parents, but their whole generation, who are amazed by how unlike them I've turned out to be, what a pale, torn copy.

I thought I'd avoided all that this year by spending the holidays with Allen and his mother at their house in the Berkshires, curled up by the fire, watching snow fall outside. I expected it to be everything Christmas in Managua isn't. Cozy. Quiet. A little boring. No listening to strangers' boozy reminiscences by the professionally decorated, artificial tree. It turned out that Christmas in the Berkshires was like the end of *It's a Wonderful Life*, neighbors caroling, bells ringing, angels getting their wings. A much larger cast of extras than I had anticipated. I had thought Allen and I would have time alone, to walk in the snow, to talk in front of the fire, to make plans for the future, to plot it out, making it seem manageable rather than frightening. But the house has been in his mother's family since before her own mother was born. The cottage, I mean—she called it a cottage, as if we were living in a fairy tale. So Allen's aunts and uncles kept stopping by, both real relatives and people who had just known him since he was a little boy vacationing with his parents, who stand across from him once a year, gin and tonic in hand, and ask about his painting and what's going on in his life, which, for Allen, is pretty much the same thing.

I was right about the coziness, and the tree—we were the ones who decked it with silver snowflakes and the ancient plaster handprints that I suppose we could auction off now as Allen's earliest artworks. But I was wrong about the quiet; apparently boozy strangers are inevitable at Christmas the world over.

I decided to relax and try to enjoy the nice long weekend, not to bring up anything important and possibly upsetting until Allen and I returned to New York, life got back to its normal state of controlled chaos, and the black-and-white glow of Christmas in the mountains faded. Which happened faster than I thought possible. By the time we were crossing the bridge into the city, all I could think of was how different this new year was going to be than last January, when Allen and I had been together only six months and were still blissfully floating along. A year later, I knew it was time to focus on our future, on our separate lives, and if we'll be building one life together, somehow.

While I couldn't wait to get back to New York to start making plans, Allen was just as eager to return to his paintings. As the short winter days passed, I got so worn out from trying to get Allen to focus, to look at me instead of the canvas in front of him, that by the time we'd been back in New York a week, all my senses felt dulled, as if I were a pencil in need of sharpening. Suffocated by my winter coat, I dragged my feet through the slushy streets, consoling myself with the thought that at least I hadn't gone home for Christmas and New Year's. At least I wasn't in Managua with Madre and my Bela, trying, and failing, to put on a happy face so as not to worry them, when in fact, the whole time I'd be wondering what my life will be like next Christmas, and if Allen will be a part of it. They'd each pick up on my anxiety and Bela would rage on about Allen not deserving me if he was making me suffer so. And worse, Madre would listen in judgmental silence before asking a probing question that made me realize I was overreacting, getting so worked up over something as trivial and bourgeois as a relationship. She'd pin me with that look, what seemed like concern shining in her big, brown eyes until I realized it was pity. Pity for me that I'm not like her—strong, confident, and consumed only by love for her country, her people. That I was so obsessed by my relationship with one petty little man. As long as there was no one to notice my anxiety—no, my fear—as long as I wasn't pierced by their questions or weakened by their sympathy, I knew I'd be fine. And then Abuelo outsmarted me, bringing me home anyway.

After what the doctor had said on his last visit to Miami, Abuelo's death was no surprise. I was sad that he's gone, but it was a selfish sadness, for myself, not him. "It's okay, niña," he'd said at Mt. Sinai, staring out at Biscayne Bay, after he told me he'd decided not to have another procedure. "I'm ready." And I knew he wasn't talking about going to lunch.

What's shocking is that I still feel surprised. By the normalcy of it all, the way my Bela's voice sounds the same on the phone, the way Managua still looks oddly, impossibly green as the plane swoops toward it. And by the timing, that he got me to come when my Bela wanted me here, despite my determination to have my own, uneventful holiday, followed by my own, quiet crisis.

At least Abuelo waited until January. With the holiday parties over, I'll be spared my mother's colleagues' tipsy reminiscences.

Do I sound callous? Making light of my grandfather's demise? Mocking people who are friendly when they see me standing alone at a party, whose only sin is wanting to relive their courageous youths? I don't mean to make fun of them, not really. When my college friends and I get together we rattle on and on about our younger days, too, even though it's only been a decade and change. In our case, we're yammering on about boys we'd kissed and shouldn't have, trips we took, lies we told. I admire my mother's friends and colleagues, I do. I don't know many people my age who would literally risk their lives to fight for something they believed in; I may not know any, really. But still, it would have been nice to have a mother whose world orbited around me occasionally. And to have had a father at all. I know it's selfish. But I'm tired of pretending that I don't feel that way. I do. Knowing more about where I came from, about the man who helped create me, it might help me figure out what to do now.

Occasionally my Bela will offer some scrap of information about my papi—that he's where I got my dark hair, when I could have been "even more beautiful," she'll say, "with chestnut-colored hair like your mother's." I know what he looked like from the few snapshots I've seen: Madre in a long dress like something out of *Little House on the Prairie*, and Papi luxuriously mustachioed, her clutching a Rojita and him a glass of whiskey at their wedding reception in my grandparents' yard.

"Don't raise your eyebrows at me; it makes you look just like your father," my Bela said once, when I was silently questioning her mandate that you can't wear shoes made of fabric during the day. "As if you think you know something I don't." That was interesting, because I wasn't aware I had raised my brows at all; it must have been an involuntary tic, a genetically coded response brought out by repressed skepticism.

It's from my Bela that I've managed to get all the basic information over the years—where my papi went to high school; that he had one sister who now lives in Honduras; that, even though he was an economics major at the Universidad Nacional Autónoma de Nicaragua, he once won a prize for an essay he wrote about Rubén Darío's poetry. But whenever my Bela and I are finally alone, when I visit from New York and am sitting on her bed next to her while she strokes my too-dark hair, and I ask her straight out, "Tell me something I don't know about my papi," she always has the same answer.

"Your papi was a revolutionary," she says. "And revolutionaries make bad husbands."

They don't make great mothers, either, I want to answer. But I don't.

2

Isabela

Revolutionaries make bad husbands. That's what I tell my granddaughter, my beautiful Mariana. She doesn't like it when I say that, she thinks I'm criticizing her papi, her mysterious, martyred papi. But to me Manuel was just a greasy-haired, black-eyed boy who charmed a stubborn girl and married above himself. My advice has nothing to do with her papi. Or, at least, not quite as much as she thinks.

Like all my advice, that warning comes from the knowledge I've gained over the course of my life. And my Mariana's the only one who wants to hear my hard-won wisdom, such as it is. Ignacio, God rest his soul, he never wanted to hear it, perhaps for good reason. And even if he had, it's too late now. It's thanks to him that I'm sitting here in the backseat while Don Pedro circles the airport, waiting for Mariana to appear like a vision, like the angel to the shepherds keeping watch over their flock in Bethlehem.

An angel in blue jeans—that's funny. I wouldn't have thought of angels, perhaps, if the nacimientos had been taken down already, if there weren't angels and camels and wise men of all races lining the highway that leads to the airport. I'd like to take a closer look at the nacimientos, but these popular neighborhoods, they're not always safe, not like when I was a girl. The side of the highway is not a place for someone like me, with bad knees and expensive jewelry. Still, part of me envies the too-young mothers in too-short skirts holding their babies up for a closer look at the Nativity. I'd love to see for myself how each artist depicts the Virgen, staring at her Child. It reminds me of when my girls were young. Not that I am comparing myself to Her, of course not. It's just that no mother can look at the Nativity and not remember the intensity of her feelings, what it is to love an infant, a being who depends on you for everything, who gazes at you as if you were the stars in the sky. Even Ninexin, with her camouflage fatigues, and, later, her expensive pantsuits, even Ninexin softens each time she sees the nacimiento I have the housekeeper place below the tree. I know because I saw the same expression on her face when she looked at Mariana when she was a baby, when she looks at her still, although both of them would deny it.

My Mariana may not be wearing blue jeans anyway. She's so ladylike these days, ever since she started working at the gallery. When I visited her in New York, she trotted around the city in the sundress she had worn to work earlier the same day, "but with a blazer on top, Bela, of course." I wasn't sure exactly what a blazer was, but I wasn't about to let on.

Maybe my Mariana will be wearing black, for her grandfather. She told me she couldn't come for Christmas, that she had promised to spend it with a friend. Who is this friend? I asked, but she said she had to run and then scurried off the phone. I'll find out now.

Perhaps this is Ignacio's final gift to me, that if he had to die, he was thoughtful enough to do it in January, making sure my Mariana would come back to me at the start of the new year, even though she hadn't planned to do so. The love he couldn't show me while he was alive, he made sure I'd receive it from the person I love the most, as a result of his death. And what a death! After so many dramatic problems, the trips to Miami for stents and open hearts, the agonies of worry he put me through, to have his heart stop beating quietly as he rested in his chair, simply to sleep and never wake up. It was Gladys, the housekeeper, who noticed. He normally snored so much it scared the cats who wander in from the garden, but he was suddenly so quiet that Gladys went over to look at him, and that's when she realized. It gave her quite a shock, really. Snoring aside, Ignacio died a fine death. My mother was right in the end: he was a man with dignity.

I can see that more clearly, now that I no longer have to face the sharp side of that dignity, to see him judging me every day, assessing how I've been spending his money and why, tossing my *Vanidades* magazine onto the coffee table as if he were dropping a piece of rotted fruit into a waste bin. Wondering why I couldn't be more like Ninexin, then blaming me for her stubbornness when she went too far, because I chose her name, the name of a Mayan princess. He wanted to name her Milagro, for his mother, but I lost so much blood in the birth, I was so weak afterward, he couldn't really refuse me, and I remembered the name of the princess in a book I had read long ago, back when I was a schoolgirl at Sacred Heart in New Orleans. One of the other boarders had lent it to me, Concepción. She was from Mexico, and we called her Connie, even I did, although all of us Ibero-American girls would whisper to each other in Spanish when the nuns weren't paying attention. And everyone called Dolores, my sister, Dolly. I still do over a half-century later. So much has stayed with me from those years at Sacred Heart. I remember certain things so clearly and sharply. And not just important things! I could describe, down to the ribbons and fake cherries, every one of the hats Connie wore my first year there. She's the one who lent me the forbidden book with the princess in it. We were close then, young girls together in a city so full of postwar pride that New Orleans was even more jubilant than usual. We felt so grown-up without our parents around, despite the nuns, the chaperones, and, in my case, my older sister, watching us all the time. To be away from Granada, where everyone knew my father, knew us, knew if I stepped into the street with a ladder in my stocking or the cockade crooked on my hat, to have escaped all that, it felt like freedom.

I came back from New Orleans with more wisdom than I would have liked. I had learned things. And I don't mean music and elocution and the proper way to get out of a cab, although I learned those things too. Ninexin laughs at the idea of wasting time on such frivolous lessons; even my Mariana smirked like her father, turning up just the left corner of her mouth when I tried to show her how to exit the backseat of a car, ankles first, knees locked together. But those things are important—they tell the world who you are, how you feel about yourself.

Still, that's not the kind of knowledge I'm talking about. Now that I'm inching toward eighty, it's funny, and a little sad, to think that the most important events in my life happened in the first quarter of it. Is that why I remember those years so vividly, why I can see the bright blue of the sky and the darker blue of our uniforms when I close my eyes, hear the laughter of the children and the scraping of the local boys' shoes dancing on the street corner under our windows until the nuns shooed them away? Or does everyone remember their youth long after they've forgotten what they had for lunch yesterday? Is it that the memories are so important they're seared into our souls, or were we just so malleable then, so easily marked?

I'm not sure that I care. I just know I remember those days so sharply that it sometimes shocks me that the only place they exist anymore is in my head. My Mariana says that if I'd give her Connie's married name, she could find her on the computer, get in touch with her, that maybe I could see pictures of her children, her grandchildren. People display photos on the computer now; my Mariana has shown me. It's how she keeps track of Rigobertito and his kids, although she wouldn't have to keep track of her cousin if she visited more often. But I don't want to see pictures of Connie now. I would rather remember her as she was then—golden and sparkling. More important, I'll admit, I would rather have Connie remember me that way, too, full of the secret, surprising knowledge that the world is an exciting place. I don't need the computer to remember.

I just need someone to want me to remember. Ninexin used to love my stories of New Orleans when she was little, until she took up with Manuel and the others and became concerned with more important things. She went to New Orleans a few years ago, for a free-trade investment conference. Delegates from all over Central America were there. She liked the food, she said, but the city was almost as dirty as Managua, and it smelled worse on some streets. She wanted to take the streetcar up to Sacred Heart, she told me, but she was too busy with the conference, with her meetings, her presentations.

But my Mariana, she never stopped wanting to hear my stories. And so I keep telling her, I tell her everything I discovered in New Orleans, all that I lost when I left, and everything I've learned in the long years since. I tell her on the phone, I write her cards on the holidays, sometimes I even talk to her when she's not with me. Not out loud, of course, I just imagine what I would say to her if she were here. But now she's coming. Don Pedro is slowing down, maybe he sees her; he's nearly as old as I am but since his cataracts operation, his eyesight is almost as good as when he first came to us. My Mariana knows my wisdom is worth something; she wants to know what I think. And so I tell her everything, even the things she doesn't want to hear, even that revolutionaries make bad husbands. Not that Ignacio, God rest his soul, was much of a spouse either. I tell her because I want my Mariana to learn from my mistakes, and from her mother's. I suppose that's one thing Ninexin and I have in common.

3

Ninexin

Revolutionaries make bad husbands," my mother always says, although usually when she thinks I'm not listening. I don't know why she goes to the effort of trying to be discreet; I couldn't agree with her more. Revolutionaries do make bad husbands. Maybe that's why I never remarried. Handling foreign press for the Sandinistas, all I meet are revolutionaries. Or journalists, who would be revolutionaries if they weren't scared of physical activity. Over the years they may have shaved off their Che-like sideburns, grown a bit of a paunch, but all the men I deal with, deep in their souls, still think they're setting the world on fire. Where am I going to meet a nice physics teacher or accountant in my line of work?

Of course that's not really why I've never remarried, but it sounds good to those who worry about me, if I blame circumstance rather than crediting choice. That's what my mother would say if someone were to ask why her daughter never remarried—the fault, dear sirs, lies in her stars, not in herself. Mama firmly believes in fate versus personal responsibility, just as she believes in always depending upon the kindness of strangers. Mama's no fool, although she'd like you to think she is, if it means you'll do what she wants and that she's going to get her way without directly asking you for help or exerting any effort of her own.

Papa was always the one who made the decisions in our family. Even when I was little and I'd ask permission for something Mama didn't want me to do—to go to the park without my nanny now that I was twelve, or to a friend's house after school—she'd tell me, "Ask your father," hoping he'd be the heavy. Was she afraid of me even then? The irony is that Papa would usually say yes. He trusted me even when he shouldn't have.

And yet, when I wanted him to say no—that he and Mama wouldn't move to Miami, that it would be wrong to take Mariana with them—he didn't, arguing that a war-torn country was no place for his granddaughter to grow up.

Now that he's gone I want to think he didn't fail me on purpose, that he thought the move was what I wanted, too. That he really believed, when I agreed to Mama's plan, that I meant it, that I was glad Mariana would be far away and safe. After all, I was the one who warned Celia that it wouldn't be very long before her son, my nephew Rigobertito, would be in danger of being drafted to fight in the war against the contras, who were trying to destroy our fragile new democracy. I was working my way up in the new government at the time, but I rushed to her house right after one of our meetings when it became clear that universal draft would soon be mandated. Two years of service in the Sandinista army would be required by all men ages sixteen to twenty-four, but kids much younger were already getting caught up in the conflict. The war with the contras was intensifying, and more manpower was needed.

I knew it was important to keep things quiet until the announcement was made, to avoid fueling the conflagration of rumors. And to keep people who could from fleeing the country. But I couldn't not tell my sister that Rigobertito would be in danger. I knew how much she loved her son; I did, too. And I owed it to her. Celia was always the good daughter, who did what my parents asked, what they expected. But she was a good sister, too. She told me once that she admired me, even if she wasn't like me. I wonder if she knew how important those words were, especially to a twenty-year-old who still looked up to her older sister with the straight hair and the slim waist. So I had to tell her. Rigobertito was turning fifteen and the conflict showed no sign of wrapping up. What destruction it took to improve our country!

I knew that if I told Celia it meant she would leave, and she did, the very next week. I didn't know that when Celia moved to Miami, our mother and father would go, too. It made sense for Celia to move—she'd been to college at the University of Florida, and her husband had investments he wanted to protect outside of volatile Nicaragua, and a friend with a car dealership who would guarantee him a job. But that my parents would go, too, and bring Mariana with them? That was so preposterous, it couldn't be anything but a fantasy Mama, and later, Papa, tossed around, spoke out loud to hear how it sounded. I fought the proposal from the start. I told Mama that my child belonged with her mother. But then my father said, "I know you want to honor Manuel's memory. And you should! But you'll never forgive yourself if this Revolución harms someone else you love."

He was right. Even though I stormed out of his house, the door slamming behind me, threatening to knock Mama's porcelain shepherdesses off the side table, he was right. Manuel was more alive than anyone I'd known, but he was prepared to die for the Revolución. It was a risk he took willingly. "At least my death would mean something," he told me when I found out I was pregnant and asked him to turn down the more dangerous assignments. "If I die, it would be to make a better country for this baby. Besides, I'm fast, and moving targets are too tricky to kill. And I'm lucky! After all, I have you."

Remembering our conversation always makes me cringe so completely that I feel I might throw up; even my intestines are contorted in shame. If I didn't feel so guilty, I might at least appreciate the irony of his words. But knowing that I cost him his life, and Mariana her father, I had to keep fighting in his place, to try to keep his death from being a waste. Besides, how would it look if the widow of Manuel Vazquez abandoned the Revolución and moved to the United States, a country that had refused to help us in our struggle? It would tarnish his sacrifice, shame him even in death. I had always been a valuable compañera, one of the generals told me, one of the most reliable members of the Frente Sandinista de Liberación Nacional. After Manuel's death, I became even more: a symbol of sacrifice and struggle, triumph after tragedy. Whether I liked it or not, this was how people saw me now. I could use the role that had been assigned to me to help our country, or I could slip out of the ill-fitting halo I now wore and turn my back on the new nation Manuel died to create. It wasn't a choice, really.

And I couldn't honestly tell my parents that Mariana's life wouldn't be at risk in Nicaragua. She was a seven-year-old girl; she wasn't in danger of being drafted. But the war was being fought all over the country. It was possible that she'd get caught in the crossfire, or worse, be harmed in a mission that targeted me. Children had been dying since before the Revolución, when Somoza's army killed kids as young as ten; it was after the death of one of them, Luis Alfonso Velasquez, that my involvement with the Frente intensified. Manuel and I wanted to make the country safer for our future children. We had toppled Somoza, and Manuel had died in the process, but war still raged in Nicaragua. Everyone I had left who loved me was insisting the best way to keep my daughter safe was to send her away.

The war had to end at some point, I reasoned. When it did, we would be together again. But even though I walked back into my parents' home calmly, righted the one shepherdess that had slipped, and agreed to their plan with my mind and my voice, in my stomach, deep in my body, I couldn't believe that this was actually going to happen, that my daughter would be separated from me. Logically, I knew it was the best thing for Mariana. But emotionally, I felt it was an impossibility. I thought someone would have to intervene. I don't know who that would have been—Papa? God? The ghost of Sandino? But I was sure some higher power would stop this impossibility from taking place. And yet, it did take place. A second time, an unimaginable thing happened as I stood and watched in disbelief. And even though Papa assured me that this was the only way to protect the person I loved most in the world, and I still believe he was right, that knowledge didn't make things any easier when I lost her.

All along, Mama swore it was the best thing for Mariana. And I tell myself that she's right, it was. She was so young, at that age where a butterfly or a vial of bubble stuff makes you happy to the core. I hardly saw Mariana as it was, even when we were all in Managua, my mother argued, among all my meetings, my consciousness-raising efforts for the Luisa Amanda Espinosa Nicaraguan Women's Association, and my work setting up the new government, the councils that would turn into the foreign ministry, where I've worked ever since, going from office worker to minister.

Even before we ousted Somoza, I spent half my time in hiding, working from outside the country, recruiting supporters to the cause:

Honduras, Mexico, Cuba. Some of the postings were long enough that I was able to take Mariana and a nanny with me, which was great cover as I posed as a graduate student at the local universities, getting to know my fellow students' political leanings and abilities. That was fine when Mariana was little, Mama said, but she was about to start first grade and needed consistency. Celia enrolled Rigobertito in the public high school on Key Biscayne, and Mariana could go to the grade school, Papa said. Most of the kids there spoke Spanish, and she was smart; I knew she'd learn English so fast. Mariana loved her grandparents, her cousin. If they were leaving the country, she'd have no one but a nanny and me. And I'd be busy, distracted. Maybe, if my history with Manuel proved anything, destructive. So I let Mariana go, telling her that she was going on a great adventure with her abuelo and her Bela and that I'd visit very soon. I swore to myself it was just until her summer vacation, when we would all meet in Mexico, where I'd be seeking support for the new government. Even though I knew I'd most likely have to come back to Nicaragua alone after that, I told myself I would bring Mariana home as soon as the war ended and the situation stabilized.

I didn't think the war would take so long. Or that by the time it ended and things stabilized in the year or two that followed, Mariana would be thirteen, old enough and opinionated enough to say that she wanted to stay at her school, with her friends, in the country she had come to know best. Even then I had hope. Papa and Mama returned to Nicaragua after Mariana graduated high school, as the country rebuilt. And young people here live at home until they're married. Mariana could have moved into my flat near the office after high school, or stayed with my parents, even, in the house in Las Colinas, where there was plenty of room. But there was college and in the breaks there were always internships and summer sessions and friends' and boyfriends' families to visit, so except for a few weeks here and there, she seldom slept under the same roof I did. We saw each other quite often, of course we did. She's a good daughter, a dutiful daughter. But we never lived together again.

I watch the young women Mariana's age who work in the press office with me, I see how confident they are, how radiant, even the ones who aren't beautiful. They're lit with the energy of possibility: trying to make the best of the options open to them a reality, or steeling themselves against disappointment when an opportunity disappears—a job goes to someone else, a lover leaves, a parent insists they choose a more suitable career than politics, or settle down and get married. These girls talk to me as if I'm just a few years older, a big sister or a trusted aunt. Should she take the offer in Colombia, even if it means leaving her aging parents behind? Will he ever stand up to his mother and propose to her? What should she do next to ensure that she'll end up like me—strong, successful, admired?

And as I talk to each one I wonder, what are the questions my daughter is busy turning over in her mind as she stands in line to get her coffee to take a quick break from the gallery? And who does she talk to about them? Who does she admire? Who has access to her soul? Because I am fairly certain that Mariana spends a significant amount of time wondering what she should do next to ensure that she won't end up the way she sees me—hard, cold, alone.

I parked in the lot next to International Departures, so as I walk toward the VIP area, I have to pass the statues of women representing the earth's different nations and peoples. I know some of the models the sculptor used. I've written press releases about these statues, about how Augusto C. Sandino International Airport is the most modern in Central America, and how these all-female statues are inspiring for visitors of all races and countries, and especially for those of us who live here in what is still a machista culture. But the truth is, I hate walking past them. They're carved out of black stone and the eyes have no pupils or irises, no definition. Their eyes are empty, but if I walk past them too slowly, I feel as if they're watching me, judging me, finding me wanting. As if they know what I did. As if I've disappointed them more than they thought possible.

Revolutionaries make bad husbands, Mama says. And she's right. But as I rush past the statues of idealized women to meet my daughter, I have to wonder how revolutionaries shape up as wives, as mothers. I don't want this to be true, but I suspect it's an even harder trick to pull off.

4

Maria

I thought I was going to make it through the airport without interference, but just as I rolled my carry-on up to the customs line, a bashful teenager appeared at my side. I smelled the kid before I saw him, soap, and underneath that, anxiety. He's actually probably in his twenties, married, most likely, with a baby or several children, so he's more of an adult than I am in the eyes of the world, someone who is responsible for the livelihood and happiness of others. But he looks like a teenager dressed up for Halloween in his French-blue-and-navy security uniform. He wouldn't call it French blue, of course. Sky blue, maybe. Celestial. Such a beautiful word for a color that is meant to enforce, to intimidate. This boy is anything but intimidating, stammering as he introduces himself. His name is José. Or Juan; I couldn't quite hear over the hum of the airport.

"Señorita Vazquez," he says, and when I nod, adds, "follow me," and whisks me off to the VIP lounge. Although they're socialists—maybe because they're socialists—Nicaraguans are obsessed with VIP areas; they even have them in movie theaters. This usually amuses me, but today it's just annoying. I'd packed light, hoping to roll through Customs and Passport Control with my twenty-inch bag, out to the curb where I knew my Bela would be waiting with Don Pedro, the only man left who has yet to abandon her. I'm ready to slide into the frigid backseat of the Accord, to lean against the bulk of her warmth and show her what I've brought. It's in my pocket still. I didn't even entrust it to the carry-on; what if all the overhead bins in my row were taken and I had to slide the bag farther back? Or if they insisted on checking my carry-on at the gate, and it was raining as they unloaded, and it got wet and ruined? It's not supposed to rain in January in Managua, in more certain times my Bela would say it *never* rains in January in Managua, but now she's a widow and there's global warming and I have no idea what to do next. All I know is that I have to protect the envelope in my pocket, because if I can put this right, if I can give fate the little push it needs to resolve things that remain unfinished in my Bela's life, then maybe fate will be a bit more straightforward with me in return, and I'll know what to do. I'll be strong and confident and sure. For once, I will take after my mother, walking the right path instead of bumbling into the wrong hallway, like my father, with tragic results.

But José/Juan is steering me softly to the VIP area, his firm, gentle hand on my elbow, and this means that there will be no leaning into my Bela's warm shoulder and Shalimar-scented neck to unveil my secrets. My mother will be collecting me in the VIP and we'll glide past legions of flunkies nodding in obeisance to her as we make our way to the car. And then I'll have to sit in the middle of the back-seat between my mother and grandmother, talking about my flight and my work, splitting my attention evenly between them, like a mother pouring out equal glasses of milk for her twin daughters, making sure no one cup has more than the other or there will be whining all through dinner. This afternoon will be difficult enough without me slipping and hurting one of them, giving them a smaller, sharper pain to focus on instead of the deeper loss of Abuelo.

There she is, looking both brisk and majestic in a black pantsuit with a pink-and-turquoise scarf at her neck. The black is for Abuelo and the pink and turquoise are for Daniel, the president; when the Sandinistas rebranded, they swapped their militaristic red and black signature colors for these friendlier, candy-colored hues my mother would otherwise never wear. It's revolution by Lilly Pulitzer, I once joked, but that was a mistake; I had to listen to hours of research that the branding consultants had delivered which absolutely proved that turquoise is the perfect combination of blue, which has a calming effect, with green, which symbolizes growth, and that fuchsia is eye-catching and would appeal to women. Okay, it wasn't hours, more like minutes, but one thing my mother hates is wasting money—or any other resource—so she did expend a fair amount of breath and energy trying to convince me that the consultants were right and the reason Daniel won the last election was thanks not to the newfound support of the Catholic Church but to the mass appeal of these pop art colors.

Although the scarf may be silly, she looks anything but, and I feel dirty and rumpled in my black wrap dress, which seemed so sophisticated when I bought it yesterday in advance of the flight. It can go anywhere, the saleswoman had promised, and I planned to wear it all weekend. I tug it straight—my mother is looking at her iPhone and hasn't seen me yet, a fact which both pleases me, making me feel as if I have the upper hand, and annoys me—after having me dragged to the VIP room, why isn't she watching for me to arrive?

Then she looks up and grins and I glance down at my bag before smiling back. When I look up again, she's staring at me with a smaller, confused smile on her face, like she used to when I was five or six and I'd wander into her office when she was on the phone, lift my arms up to her, and call out "Mama." It always took three or four shouts before she noticed me, and although she inevitably blew me a kiss or dropped to her knees to give me a hug before putting her finger to her mouth and motioning to my Bela or my nanny or her assistant to get me, there was always a moment where she looked at me like she couldn't quite place who I was or what I was doing there.

"Thank you, Joaquin," she says to the boy, who is not, it turns out, named José or Juan, and I am reminded, again that my mother is a better person than I'll ever be. "Is your daughter's fever down?" He nods and grins and mutters his thanks and then she is hugging me, hard and quick, before grabbing the handle of my rolling suitcase. "Come on, then," she says. "Don Pedro is waiting."

And even though I'm sure I must be the first person off our flight to walk out into the humid air, I feel as if I've made everyone late, and it is all my fault.

"We'll go straight to the calling hours," she says. "Since you're dressed for it. Mama is ready, too."

"And so are you, Madre," I say. And then, because even though I'm an adult woman with a life of her own, I can't help myself, I add something more: "Nice scarf."

5

Isabela

How are you holding up, Bela?" she had asked me last night on the phone, and the enormity of it all hit me again. We weren't Romeo and Juliet, it's true; no one knew that better than my Mariana, who knew all about New Orleans, and who had grown up watching us live our lives, our separate but not equal lives, as I used to joke when the children were young. Ninexin hated it when I said that, she said it was in terrible taste, but it was true. Ignacio had his life, full of money-making endeavors and tales of business coups shared with his friends, who one by one left this world until the only person left to listen to his stories of brilliant investments was Don Pedro. And now Ignacio has followed his friends into the next world. Poor Don Pedro.

And poor me, too. We weren't Romeo and Juliet, but still, we lived together for over fifty years—worked together, him in his law practice, always with some about-to-change-our-lives investment on the side, while my business was raising our daughters, an impossible task when one of your children is as headstrong as Ninexin. And then came Rigobertito and Mariana, our grandchildren, and, more than that, our family's future: the next generation, a new crop to love and lament and worry about and gloat over. At Mass once in Miami—it must have been Christmas or Easter because Ignacio was with me—we bumped into an old client of his, another one who had sold his cattle ranch before the Sandinistas could force him to gift it to the war effort, and moved to the U.S., but not before acquiring a new wife, younger than his first, just a few years older than his daughters; the youngest one had made her debut the same year as Celia. The new wife—Ignacio recognized her; she had been the secretary who had done the books at the man's cattle finca—was holding a little boy by the hand, and the man had a little girl in his arms, one you'd assume was his granddaughter unless you knew better.

"With my older kids, I was always so busy," the rancher told Ignacio when he thought I couldn't hear. "I never knew parenthood could be so much fun." As if he were recommending a restaurant: *Parenthood—try it, you'll like it!*

Ignacio had other women, too. I knew it. They all did in those days. But his work was his great passion, so none of those women really mattered. We knew at our wedding ours was not a love match. And that helped, knowing where we stood. At least I thought it did. It helped me know what to expect, to accept that at twenty, my best years were behind me. Still, I don't think Ignacio ever quite forgave me for knowing that.

No, we weren't Romeo and Juliet, but we shared the same space for fifty-five years. His was the face I saw every day. And now I won't anymore. And what will I do instead? I know what I'll actually, physically, do, on a daily basis. I'll oversee the staff in the kitchen, in the laundry room. I'll have lunch with my friends during the day and I'll call my Mariana at night. Rigobertito will visit with my great-grandchildren, and there will be Christmases with him and my Mariana, and Easter sometimes, too. If I feel up to it, I'll visit my Mariana. Not all the way to New York again, but maybe we'll meet in the middle, in Miami, where that sweet girl she lived with in college has settled, and where my Mariana attends more and more art shows each year. In between there will be distractions, my telenovelas, *Vanidades, Ser, Hola!* Princes and princesses will keep getting married, actresses will keep wearing less and less. The world will continue without Ignacio, as it will without me someday.

I know what I'll do on a daily basis. But what will I feel like? What will my life be like? Some widows expand. They glow like they were supposed to as brides. But others wither and shrink once their husbands die, and soon they're gone, too. And it's never the ones you expect, you can't tell what will happen to whom.

Imagining the future frightens me. I won't be able to avoid it later, at the calling hours, or tomorrow, at the funeral. But for now I don't want to think about it. I want the car to fill with color and light and youth. I want my Mariana here now. Even though Ninexin called and told me the plane had landed, and I know it is just a matter of time before she is in front of me, one of the ironies of my life is that the older I get, the more impatient I become.

6

Ninexin

I was watching through the glass panel in the door of the VIP lounge. I saw her stride in, rolling her own bag, slowing her gait a little so that poor Joaquin could keep a hold on her elbow, like he was an escort at the debutante balls we used to have at the club. I never had a coming out; by the time I was old enough I was too wrapped up in the Movimiento to consider such a thing. But I remember my sister's, how the boys glowed with pride as they held her elbow to steer her to the dance floor, the bolder ones rubbing their thumb on her bicep where her flesh was visible, just above her long glove. Celia was stunning that night, but she was just as lovely every night of my childhood. She could have stayed that way with a little discipline, but it was as if she gave up after Rigobertito was born and the doctors said there could be no more, as if knowing she would have no more children convinced her she should look like she'd had dozens, like a proper, round matron. Or maybe it was all those years in Miami, all that Cuban food, the neighborhood parties, too-sweet cortaditos and pastelitos for breakfast. Rigobertito is starting to put on weight but he's still handsome, he still looks like Celia did when she was young.

And Mariana, does she look like me? I would like to see something of me in her—whatever is in me that is best, whatever is beautiful, she can have. But all I see as I study her now, without her knowing, is Manuel. His dark hair. His long neck. Her eyes, sometimes I feel they're mine, but that might be wishful thinking, optimism bias, and I can't check now. I don't want her to notice me analyzing my first glimpse of her, watching to see how much of me she carries. So I pull out my phone and try to focus on emails from the office. If I catch her in an unguarded moment I'll see how she's feeling, and I'm not strong enough, not today. If she's tired, I'll think she's already weary of me. If she's annoyed because her feet swelled on the flight and her shoes are pinching, I'll think she's still angry at me, that she'll always be heartsick that I let her go once, my second great mistake.

I remember from a literature class I took at UNAM—one I audited without telling Manuel—that an American poet said the art of losing isn't hard to master. But that woman lied. I lose Mariana again every time I see her and I never seem to get any better at it. Thank God for Joaquin, sweet Joaquin, who will be here to ease the transition from being without her, from the hope of seeing her, to the reality of being with her again and found wanting.

When Mariana was a baby, if she wasn't screaming in pain from the colic, or spitting up from the reflux, there were light-filled moments when I would pick her up and her eyes would widen and she would smile, open-mouthed, toothless, as if gasping in surprise that someone as wonderful as I existed in the world and was lifting her off the floor at this moment. In her face I could see an emotion we don't have a word for, at least not one that I know, not in Spanish, not in English either. It's the combination of shock and joy. "Delight" comes close but it is too soft; this emotion could make her gurgle and squeal, harsh, animal sounds but so beautiful.

At other times, if she was lying quietly and I brought my face too close to hers she would look away, first with her eyes, blinking hard, then turning her head altogether. As if seeing me was too much for her, too much joy and excitement to process. Then she would look back shyly and we could begin whatever task awaited us, the feeding or the rocking or the Weensy Weensy Araña climbing up the water-spout.

She does an imitation of that move when she sees me now, glancing down at her bag before looking at me with the composed, adult face that says, "Hello, Mother, how are you, and how unseasonably cloudy Managua seems today," even though she hasn't spoken a word yet. I grab her and squeeze, wanting to press my memories of her infancy into her. It's so unjust that she has no recollection of the months, the days, the hours upon hours I spent holding her, wondering what she wanted but couldn't express, as well as what she would hunger for in the future, what her life would be like. I never dreamed it would be like this. I've buried a husband and more friends than most fifty-three-year-old women, many of them lost when they were still so young that their lives had barely started. And I buried them all dry-eyed, whether from shock or from the cold comfort of knowing they had been well aware of the risks they'd taken on, going in. But I cried for two weeks after Mariana was born; every day in the afternoon, a wave of sorrow would wash over me like a tropical storm. Sometimes I cried because I was overwhelmed. Sometimes I cried because I was so tired. Sometimes I cried because she cried, and at others I cried because I knew I now had everything I wanted and I feared that someday I could lose her.

Mariana hugged me back; she always does, she's a good girl. But she doesn't linger, she doesn't luxuriate in my arms, nor does she laugh the way she does when we get to the Accord and she disappears into the dark interior, through the door Don Pedro holds open. She enters the car the way Mama taught her to, the way Mama learned at boarding school in New Orleans, where car-entering seems to have been something of a skilled sport: she sits on the edge of the seat first, tilting forward the slightest bit, then, once her backside makes contact with the upholstery, she leans back and swings her bent legs into the car, always keeping her knees together, so that the last thing anyone watching would see is a pair of lovely, slanted ankles appearing to wink at them before they disappear into the interior. As far as Mama is concerned, there's always someone watching. She taught me the move, too, although I pretended I wasn't paying attention. Still, I've found myself using it, at meetings in Paris. The French like that sort of thing and I like showing them that those of us who once fought in the jungle are equally at home sliding into a town car.

But I've never entered a car with the expression I see on Mariana's face before she slides in and collapses against Mama, giggling. It's an expression I don't know if I've ever made, but one that I recognize, because it's the same unnameable emotion that would flash across her face as an infant, delight multiplied. When she was that small, always wet and squalling and covered in pureed banana, I would never have believed that she would grow up to be so beautiful, so vital that it hurts to look at her.

I close the door behind her and walk around to sit next to Don Pedro, to make enough room for her bag in the backseat, and so that we will all be a little more comfortable.

7

Maria

When I see the solid gray Accord I want to break into a run. It seems like I've been traveling for weeks, not a couple of days. And now I've finally made it here, exhausted after the VIP lounge and the flight to Managua, and Beth sweetly getting a baby-sitter last night and helping me find this dress for Abuelo's funeral upstairs on the sales rack at the Banana Republic on Lincoln Road, because there are some shopping trips, she said, that no one should have to make alone. And before that, Beth's house, which smells of macaroni and cheese and, here and there, of poop, thanks to her eighteen-month-old, Olivia, who says "cooka" for cookie and "up" when she means down and "Mawia" when she wants me. And before that, the flight from New York to Miami, and even before that, the fight with Allen— does it count as a fight, if no voices are raised? I guess so, since I stormed out, amping up the drama factor. If a woman storms out of her boyfriend's apartment, and no one runs after her, or even watches her leave, does she make a sound?

He was probably relieved when I first left, happy that he could finish painting in peace. And then, when he was done for the night and he realized I hadn't come back, he probably started feeling a little bit guilty, which he hates, so he began to rationalize: he always tells me not to bring up any serious topics while he's painting, he can't concentrate on anything other than the canvas right now, right at this minute. Ever since we got back from the Berkshires, I've wanted to do nothing but have this talk, make a choice one way or the other, and he's wanted to do nothing but paint. He wouldn't deny that the hazy, happy beginning stage of our relationship is officially over, that we do have to make some decisions. But he would insist, to himself, anyway, that nothing would have changed if I had just waited a day or two to bring up the topic of our future.

The thing is, it's all changing. Everything is different now. That's what he doesn't seem to understand. Months ago, the first time we ever had a fight—because he didn't show up at dinner, didn't even text because he was so absorbed in some painting or other, and I drank two glasses of wine and ate a plate of risotto I didn't want because I felt bad for the waiter and embarrassed that I'd been taking up a table for so long without ordering anything—Allen told me that he figured it was best to let me cool off before apologizing. Which was why, when he finally realized he'd stood me up, at eleven-thirty that night, he didn't call but texted an apology instead, then let the flowers he sent to the gallery the next day do the talking. I explained to him then that I'm not a person who flares up and cools off. That's my mother. And my Bela, too, if I think about it. I'm a fumer, a simmerer, a slow boiler. Every hour without an apology, every minute, is a minute spent with me shoring up my position, convincing myself how right I am, and how wronged I've been. I'm not proud of this aspect of my temperament. But there it is.

I made that clear to him long ago, after that very first argument. So Allen shouldn't have been surprised that, when he called me at six in the morning yesterday as I finished packing my roller bag, I let the call go to voicemail. By the time I got to Miami, the messages had collected on my voicemail, one after another, like layers of paint adding shading and depth. First embarrassed, then conciliatory, then angry, then back to apologetic.

But in none of the messages did he admit that everything had changed for us, and nothing would ever be the same; that the future was here, whether we liked it or not. And I'm tired of being the only person who realizes we're at a turning point. The night before last I sat in his studio, watching him paint, trying to talk to him, waiting for the right moment. He paints so differently than I do, all bold strokes and bright colors. He'd step back now and then and I'd think maybe he was at a stopping point, maybe we could talk now. I'd say something like, "I know it's a lot to consider, but it's important." And he'd mumble, "Of course, very important," and step right back toward the canvas, which is taller than I am and, obviously, more compelling.

At one point his cell phone vibrated on the table next to me. He would have ignored it but I thought it might be an opportunity, an interruption that would be someone else's fault besides mine, and I could take advantage of it so we could finally talk. And when I saw his daughter's name lighting up the screen, I felt grateful to her, maybe for the first time. I knew he'd take her call. When I said, "It's Brianna," he tossed his brush on the drop cloth on the floor and snatched the phone out of my hand. He said thank you as he took it, so maybe "snatched" is the wrong word. But even after saying thank you, he turned his back to me and walked into the bedroom, shutting the door so I couldn't hear him. I could, of course, every word. That's one advantage of dating a man old enough to be your youngest uncle; my hearing is much better than he can imagine. At night when he's in the bathroom, I can hear him brushing and flossing, even opening that jar of moisturizer he hides in his medicine cabinet. So when I stood against the bedroom door, I could make out the sound of him pacing back and forth as he listened to Brianna saying whatever it was on the other line.

"Tell Tad if he takes you where you want to go, I'll pay for his gas. And in a few days, we'll be at Gammy's, and I'll drive you wherever you want," he promised. "Yes, just the three of us this time." I slid down to the floor; this was going to be a long call. "Of course Maria had to get back to work, but that's not the only reason," Allen said. "I would have loved to have stayed, but I also have to finish this painting, for that exhibit we talked about, remember?" His steps came closer to the door, then receded in the other direction. "No, sweetie, that's not it. You're the person I want to spend time with the most, you always will be. No one will ever be more important to me than you are." I heard the bed creak. "So, other than Tad being a jerk about the car, how are things going? What are you up to?"

That's when I walked away from the door. There was no point in me waiting around; I wouldn't be strong enough to force a conversation when he walked back to his painting. Through some weird alchemy, Allen had succeeded in reordering the world so that I was angry, so angry, at myself, not him anymore. Because Brianna and her brother should come first. That's exactly how it should be. I knew all that but I was still so jealous I thought I might pass out from the physical pain, the burning in my throat. I hated that feeling and I hated myself for having it.

Once I stepped away from the door, Allen's voice was just a low rumble. Then it stopped and I heard footsteps and the toilet flush in the adjoining bathroom. And I didn't want to be there to watch him walk out of the bedroom, stride right past me, and head straight over to the painting at the other end of the studio. I was suddenly so tired of being the obstacle that makes it more difficult for a hero to do important work; I felt like I'd been playing that role my whole life. So I pulled on my coat and walked out the door, letting it slam behind me, even though I knew there was little chance Allen would hear it, or, even if he did, notice.

After I stormed out of the apartment, I didn't want to think about Allen or what happened next. Once I got to Miami, I wanted to play horsey with Olivia and cook dinner with Beth, hear how her fertility treatments were going, and shop for mourning clothes, and not think about a world without my grandfather in it.

Abuelo would know what to do about this situation. He always did. When war with the Contras broke out in 1981, he packed a couple of bags and drove all of us across the border to Honduras, where we waited out the worst of the fighting safely. Part of the reason that this situation with Allen is so overwhelming is that Abuelo's not here to help me decide whether we should be building a future or acknowledging the lack of one. My Bela is so emotional, she won't be able to lay things out for me, step by step, help me make a list of pros and cons, advise me on how to proceed. And Madre is the opposite, the stoic of the family; it's not that she won't have strong feelings, she'll just stew about them privately, staring at me like I should know what to do because she's been willing the idea into my head telepathically. But Abuelo, he would have had an opinion, one he could explain calmly but clearly. He seemed to understand that if I listened to his advice and then turned around and did the opposite, that didn't make me stupid or selfish, just opinionated, like all the women around him.

But I don't want to think about what I've lost with Abuelo's death.

I want to pretend, just for a little bit, just for the car ride, maybe, that this is another happy homecoming, a chance for my Bela and Madre and me to catch up on what we still have, not mourn what has been taken from us. I want to lie against my Bela's soft, heavily perfumed shoulder and feel like I'm small enough to be taken care of, and like everything is going to be all right.

8

Isabela

What have you brought me, mi reina?" I ask Mariana. "What do you have to show me?"

"Nothing." She looks startled for a moment, almost guilty, like when she was a little girl, coloring on the walls of the apartment in Key Biscayne, even though I told her that we only draw on paper.

"Nothing?" I take her hand back, holding it in mine. "Haven't you painted anything lately?"

She laughs and I realize how uncommon a sound laughter has been over the past few weeks. Months. Now she's holding her phone in front of me, covering the screen with her hand, hiding something. A photo. Mariana knows how to take pictures with her phone, she's always sending Ninexin an image to show me: an unexpected flower pushing through the pavement on her block, or the foot of a woman whose shoe she particularly admires.

"It's silly," she says. "I should be focusing on discovering new artists for the gallery, not playing at being one." She slides even closer to me on the leather upholstery. "I'm only showing you because you're my muse."

Mariana makes the phone light up, and an image takes over the screen. "There's a bit of a glare from the overhead bulb," she says, but I can see the canvas perfectly, starkly, almost; without a frame it appears as if the painting itself is naked, and I almost feel it's rude to look. In the right corner is a man, in profile or almost, less than that, but you can tell from the sliver of face peeking out under his hat that he's amused. He's wearing a striped suit and in the places where you can see flesh—his neck, his face, his hands—he seems to glow despite the shadow cast by his hat brim.

In the bottom left corner is a woman, a girl, really, in a full-skirted dress the color of a buttercup. Her body is curving downward, almost in half, but in a shape I've never seen in real life, or only at the ballet. She's not folded lazily, like one of Degas's ballerinas lacing up her shoes; there's urgency to her movement, tension in the curve of her pose. She's dropped something and what it is takes up the rest of the canvas. It's a book, splayed facedown on the sidewalk, but it looks as if the letters from the cover have been knocked loose in their fall, they're floating upward in an arc toward the man, spelling out the book's title, getting smaller and smaller as they rise up, so you can barely make out the phrase: *The Elements of Style*. It's the letters that are amusing the man in the hat. The letters or the girl who sent them flying.

The girl is me. Or how Mariana imagines I was then, in 1951, a sixteen-year-old girl at school far from home. She's gotten some things wrong in her painting: the bare hands, I would never have left campus without gloves keeping my hands safe and clean and mysterious. But the feeling is right, the flush visible in the arms that lead to those hands. It was not caused by embarrassment—it wasn't my fault I'd dropped the book. It was a flush of gratitude, of knowing that this was one of those moments when time slowed and that once it righted itself again, the world would be set on a new course.

It was a fall Friday and classes ended at one so that we could take the air now that the weather was cooler, and go out for some shopping or a snoball or to visit relatives who lived in town, and still be back on campus by dark. But the real reason classes ended early every other Friday was that those were the weekends the cadets from St. Michael Military Academy in Pass Christian came down from Mississippi and were allowed to pay court to whichever of the Sacred Heart girls their parents had told them to write and invite for a stroll in the park or tea at Commander's. If the girl had approval from the mistress general and a willing chaperone, a caller might even take her for a ride downtown on the streetcar to see a movie, although permission for the movies was hard to extract, even if the film was on the list of Church-approved pictures, because it was so dark in the theater that only the most eagle-eyed of chaperones could be trusted.

Dolly and I got more mail than most girls, but it was all from Madre, describing the antics of our brothers or her trips to Paris with Papa. No one ever wrote to ask permission to walk out with us, and we didn't expect them to—the only people our parents knew in New Orleans were the parents of other girls. Only girls came to Sacred Heart. Our brothers were younger, and while they might attend Loyola when they were done with high school, until then the Colegio Centro América in Granada was good enough, and would keep them close to home, close to the glove factory my father owned, so they could learn everything they needed to know about its management. It was different for Connie; her father had a cacao plantation in Mexico and did business with several prominent families in New Orleans. He was often invited to dinners at Arnaud's, lunches at Galatoire's, even a few Mardi Gras balls if he was in town during the season. It was only natural for his hosts to invite their other Latin friends, too, so that when the men and the women separated after dinner, his wife could have someone to talk to in Spanish. Connie had been out walking with two or three of the Mexican boys who attended St. Michael Military Academy. But none of them was what she expected, none was like the men she read about in books, men who weren't afraid of passion. Or of fathers.

"He managed to shake off the chaperone," she told me after she'd returned from a stroll in the park with a certain Cristian Hidalgo. She had drawn the white curtains that acted as walls, separating the twenty boarders' beds into would-be "rooms," so that no one passing by would see her, and was waving her hands around, acting out all the parts—the chubby, bumbling chaperone, the straight-backed, strong-armed Señor Hidalgo. I lay on my side on her bed, propped up on my elbow, watching her. A few of the North American girls we took classes with bragged of having television sets at home, but who needed one when I had Connie?

"He said it was so hot, and she'd walked so far, wouldn't madam care to rest and we'd bring her a snoball?" Connie bowed low to demonstrate Señor Hidalgo's elegant bearing, then shrugged up her shoulders, puffed out her abdomen, and nodded, to indicate the chaperone's response. "And I thought, this is it. Now I will finally know what it is to be kissed properly, so that it's a sharing of souls, like it says in that novel. And do you know what happened?"

I hadn't realized that an answer was expected, so I gave none, and she grabbed my hands, pulling me up to sitting. "Nothing! We walked to the snoball stand as he droned on and on about my father and what a wonderful businessman his father said my father is and what a wonderful businessman he himself is going to be someday. And then"—here Connie squeezed my hands so tightly that I pulled them away from her—"we brought the chaperone a snoball!"

So Connie remained an innocent; when it came to the mysteries of what went on between men and women, all her carefully constructed knowledge came from the diligent study of books the Church had banned. She became more than a little miffed at me that, because *Forever Amber* and *Gone with the Wind* were banned, I wouldn't purchase them for her, wouldn't saunter into the bookstore downtown, far from the school, under the pretext of buying composition books to improve my writing, and nonfiction to help me learn about this country, and slip a forbidden novel between a textbook and *Let Us Now Praise Famous Men*. "No one would suspect it of you, Isa," Connie whined. "They check every parcel I walk in with."

But a sin was a sin, even if it wasn't a mortal one. I loved Connie but I wasn't willing to risk my soul for her.

Even though the young Mexicans left Connie unaware of what really happens in a stolen kiss—where do the noses go? And can you taste what he had for lunch?—they gave her valuable intelligence of another sort: her time with them allowed her to survey all the other male specimens who journeyed in from St. Michael Military every other Friday. Most of them came on a bus, arriving sweaty and crumpled. But Cristian Hidalgo, for all his faults, had a car, a navy blue convertible to match his eyes. It may have been the car that had raised Connie's hopes. And he always let his closest friends ride with him. Most of them were older than the North American high school boys, as was Cristian himself, and were doing a post-graduate year that the universities which had accepted them required of foreign students so that they might improve their English before matriculating. These men still arrived mussed, even more so than the ones Connie referred to as "the bus-boys," because the wind had been wreaking havoc with their hair for the entire drive. And what hair! Imagine being so young and lucky that a car with five men packed into it was guaranteed to be filled with lush heads of hair, whipping free of the confines of Brilliantine paste, with bald spots nothing but a rumor of future sorrow, one that could hardly be believed under the circumstances.

So Connie knew, when Silvia Contreras received a letter from a certain Mauricio de los Santos asking her to take a turn around Audubon Park with him the following Friday, that Silvia's parents had somehow managed to pull off a miracle. Silvia was the sort of girl who didn't read any novels at all, just in case one might be the kind the Church would have banned had it made enough of a splash to be noticed. "The pope has more important concerns; he can't possibly read every single book," Silvia told me when I insisted that the novel Connie had lent me wasn't among the thousands of titles on the Index Librorum Prohibitorum, which had just been released a few years earlier; the sisters made sure there were copies for reference in every classroom. "So I like to do what I can to help His Holiness," she explained, smiling at her own piety.

Connie had hated Silvia ever since she had taken a copy of *Madame Bovary* out of her room and turned it into the mistress general, saying she had seen a vision of the Virgen of Guadalupe asking her to clean out Connie's bureau and therefore her soul. It was only because the mistress general also taught French, and Connie's older brother had brought her a copy in the original language from Paris, that she wasn't suspended; the nun believed Connie's protestations that she had asked her brother for novels to help her practice her language skills and build her vocabulary, and had no idea that what he had chosen was forbidden. Still, she had clearly read enough to know what kind of book it was; there was an earmarked page well past the middle. So Connie was required to clean the statue of the Blessed Mother with milk, and, worse, was prohibited from leaving campus for the next four Fridays.

This made the idea of Silvia prancing around Audubon Park with what Connie called "the handsomest man anyone in Louisiana, or Mississippi, or all of this dusty country has ever seen" even more galling. It wasn't that she was jealous. Mauricio de los Santos was beautiful, it was true, like a hero in one of her books. But Connie's parents didn't know him or anything about his people. And furthermore, he was Cuban, and Cubans were, her father said, "a handful."

But just because she wouldn't touch didn't mean we couldn't look, Connie insisted. So she dragged me out of the common room, where I was working on my English assignment, and into the courtyard, where we'd have a good view of the gate the cadets passed through to greet their companions and the chaperones under the appraising eyes of the on-duty sisters. Silvia was there in a dress she'd made Betsy, the maid responsible for the third floor we boarders inhabited, iron twice; the first time the pleats weren't sharp enough. It was navy and I wondered if she'd somehow had it made in time for her date, to match the famous convertible, in the hopes that Cristian would offer joyrides to his best friend's date if Mauricio really liked a girl. But that was jealousy on my part; the truth was she often wore navy, probably to offset the emeralds in the cross she always had on—her father had some mines in Venezuela.

"Mauricio de los Santos for Miss Silvia Contreras, please," I heard a voice say, but I didn't look up. I was shy in those days, and there was no reason to look a man in the face unless he was my father, brother, or driver. Maybe a shopkeeper whose store I was browsing. But as Silvia sauntered past us, her starched pleats making a shuffling noise like the settling of an over-upholstered chair when you sit in it, Connie whispered in my ear: "Those shoes—they're so shiny you can practically see up her skirt. I wonder what the pope has to say about that?"

An image of His Holiness frowning at Silvia's Mary Janes arose before me and I laughed, louder than I should have, because Silvia turned to glare at me and when I looked up in apology, Mauricio had stepped right next to her. He took Silvia's hand, like he was supposed to, but he looked at me and said, "You haven't introduced me to your friends."

"I'm Connie Fonseca, I'm a friend of Cris Hidalgo's, and this is Isabela Enriquez," Connie said when Silvia didn't reply. "But you can call her Isa. Can't he?" She elbowed me in the arm, which I was holding so stiffly that it fell forward at the elbow, sending my textbook flying across the courtyard. I ran toward it, eager to escape all of their eyes: Connie's glittering with glee or mischief, Mauricio's full of curiosity, and Silvia's—it would be years before I could meet Silvia's eyes again, even though alphabetical order decreed that we had to stand next to each other in chapel once Alice Farraday left school. But when I reached the book, Mauricio was already there, holding it up for me, laughing.

"When we get back tonight, I'm talking to the mistress general," he said. "I'm taking you out tomorrow afternoon."

I grabbed the book and held it to my chest like a shield, like it could protect me from Silvia's glares and Connie's questions. But just before I turned around I nodded, quickly, so that he'd know I'd be waiting for him the next day.

9

❧❀❧

Ninexin

We arrive at Monte Olivos funeral home early, which is only right for immediate family of the deceased, and so that after Don Pedro drops us at the door, he'll be able to claim one of the few parking spots. It's a tiny lot, and for someone like Papa, half of Managua will turn up. The streets will be clogged for blocks with chauffeurs idling, napping in their cars or playing cards with each other until their cell phones buzz, telling them it's time to go collect the cars' owners. The chauffeurs are the experts but they're only the stewards of the cars, nannies for automobiles. They clean them and take them to the garage for checkups, coddle them when they're acting up, and they get to play with them, they get the long, slow, sun-filled hours of the afternoon to sing along to the radio or wax the cars until they shine. The cell phone has made life much easier for chauffeurs, Don Pedro told me once. Now they don't have to be mind readers as well as escape artists, sliding through jammed streets, circling the block, hoping to pull up to the door at the exact moment that the señor—and, more important, the señora in her precarious shoes—step over the threshold. But the chauffeurs must occasionally wish the cars were their own, that they could earn them by caring for them so vigilantly, loving them so fiercely. Don Pedro would never admit it, but there still must be a fair amount of discomfort in being a chauffeur, the helplessness when the little señores stretch out their chubby legs and rest their muddy shoes on the leather interior, or a perfectly good car gets given to a teenager who crashes it while driving home from a club early one morning, and walks away secure in the knowledge that his papi will pay off anyone whose home or dog or child was injured in the process.

"Señorita?" Don Pedro says; he's the only person who still calls me that, and only when no one else can hear. He offers me his arm because Mariana is already leading my mother in. They were giggling together in the car, I can't imagine what about. And I'm not meant to; they could have easily spoken up if they'd wanted me to hear but they got used to having jokes just between them all those years they spent together in Miami while I was here. I try to tell myself that I don't mind that, that it's good for them to have their secrets, that I'm happy Mama has some distraction today, some little bit of joy. But I'm not very convincing, so instead I take pleasure where I can, from the empty parking lot. The sight of so many long black cars circling the block still makes me nervous; it's one reason I avoid parties. These days, as foreign minister, meetings, conferences, welcome cocktails, are my natural habitat. If I'm in a hotel ballroom surrounded by thousands, I can focus on work and feel calm and efficient. Or if I'm at Celia's house, with Rigobertito and his kids, his wife's sisters, I can sit on the floor and play Matchbox cars with his boys and enjoy myself. It's the middle ground that I can't handle, the exclusive parties in private homes. I haven't attended one since the night Manuel died, and I don't plan to do so again.

Mariana thinks I'm just being stubborn each time I refuse to go with her to a Christmas cocktail gathering; her eyes get glassy, frosting over like they would when she was in junior high and I'd tell her she had to spend the summer in Managua with me rather than attending art camp in Orlando with her friends. And when she returns from a party here, she complains, "All anyone wanted to talk to me about was you." She was cold to me for weeks after I skipped Beth's wedding at her parents' place, although Beth had always been so kind to me, always invited me and Mariana to join her family during parents' weekends. When Beth was present, the air around me and my daughter softened, life was almost like I hoped it would be, and I could tell myself that now that Mariana was older, I was the one she came to with problems and secrets, not Mama. The truth is that it was Beth she sought out, or at least I hoped so. I hoped she confided in her roommate, that she had a best friend of the kind Mama did back in convent school. Still today Mama has lady friends who will meet her for lunch to hear her troubles or celebrate her birthday. I know people, but friendship was one of the things I gave up in the Revolución. I don't say that to complain or to boast. It was my choice. But I see how much richer Mama's life is because of her friends, and it's something I want for Mariana. Perhaps the talent for friendship is one of the things that skips a generation.

I stop at the door to Monte Olivos funeral home, even though, with only the family and none of the guests here yet, the outer rooms are still empty of people. Right now they're mainly inhabited by flowers, arrangements that stand as tall as a short man, all wearing banners like Miss America would, only printed with the names of the families who sent them and words like "Sympathy" and "Condolences," which sound so much prettier than they should, given their meaning. Soon the rooms will fill with people and those people will be even more cloying than the flowers and the ribbons; they'll smell even stronger and they'll make the added sensory assault of sound, loudly sharing memories and platitudes as they drink their Rojitas and eat their pastelitos and churritos de queso. And soon they'll forget that they're at a funeral home, not a party, and they'll start talking business or about TV and the movies or their children's universities and career plans, summer camps and vacations. And that's fine, that's fair, a reminder that life goes on, the world hasn't stopped just because it feels like it has.

Don Pedro pushes my elbow softly, and before I start walking, I turn and kiss his cheek, because I won't be able to kiss my father's again, not after tonight. It's selfish of me; I've embarrassed Don Pedro. But he indulges me because, under the circumstances, how can he not?

I walk into the inner room, where Papa is lying in his casket. Mama is already sitting in one of the chairs placed next to it, crying, dabbing at her face with a lace-edged handkerchief. That's what I forgot to bring; I knew when I picked up my purse to get into the car that I'd overlooked something, but when I checked my keys were there, and my wallet and cell phone, too, and I couldn't think what else it might be. A handkerchief. Mama is never without one. But this isn't one of her everyday handkerchiefs, machine-embroidered with an *I*, the kind Dolly gives her a box of every Christmas. This one appears to be edged in handmade lace, and she has threaded a black ribbon through it. Or maybe it came that way. Do they make mourning handkerchiefs? Mama would know, but I don't. She's probably told me but I haven't listened. All this knowledge of etiquette and protocol that she has, it always seemed so irrelevant, a useless burden to carry around, but now I find myself wishing I knew about mourning handkerchiefs, wishing, even, that I were the kind of woman who never left home without a handkerchief tucked in her handbag. It seems disrespectful, somehow, not to have one now.

"He looks very handsome," Mama says, and I nod, even though she's lying. He looks like a transvestite except for the navy suit. It's the rouge that offends me; the dead are supposed to be pale. Papa hasn't been ruddy in years, and he never blushed, not that I remember, anyway. Why force him to start now?

It's the rouge that makes hot tears seep out of my eyes. I lean over to kiss Papa good-bye, hoping my mouth or my tears will wash off some of the pink. But when my lips touch his powdery cheek, I realize the rouge doesn't matter. He's not in there. I don't know why I thought that he would be, that it would still feel like I was kissing my father even if he couldn't reach out and put an arm around me, press me to him long enough so that I knew I was special, but not so hard or for so long that it seemed like he was hugging me for more time than he did Celia.

Mama's cook told me that in her neighborhood, they say that the minute a person dies, his soul leaves the body and floats around for forty days, watching those he loved in life, saying good-bye. I wish I believed Papa were hovering around us here, seeing how many silly flowers people sent, how beautiful Mariana looks, how quickly she rushed to be here. And how Mama is crying, wiping her face decorously with a handkerchief that does him credit. It's not that I'm sure he isn't here, it's just that I wish I knew for a fact he was; it's the question of certainty that troubles me, always has.

The one thing I do know is that if he is here, he's not bothered by the rouge on his cheeks or my lack of handkerchief. He never was.

Papa was a rarity for his age and class; he did what was expected of him, but because he felt it was right, not because he cared what others thought or said. I remember so many other times I kissed his cheek while Mama cried, wondering aloud what people would think, what they would say, how she could live with whatever fresh shame I was bringing upon the household. Whatever I did that wasn't to her liking, she could add a variation to that same theme, a situation-specific complaint. When I told her I wouldn't come out at the club, she said I was giving up the best night in a young girl's life, and humiliating her, and hurting Celia's feelings by implying that there was anything wrong with participating in a debutante ball, and that it was all that useless, skinny boy's fault that I had such crazy ideas.

"Ninexin doesn't have to do anything that she feels she shouldn't," Papa said that night, and kissed me on the forehead. "Plus, she'll save me a pile of money."

It was almost the exact same thing he said when I explained that I didn't want a big wedding like Celia's, no tuxedos, no linen table-cloths, just a priest and Manuel and maybe a barbecue in the back-yard. But that time, when I jumped up and kissed his cheek, Papa held me longer than usual and said, "Are you sure you want to do this?"

I realize now that he didn't mean the barbecue wedding. He meant the marriage itself. I was so young. A decade younger than Mariana is now, more. But back then it was normal for twenty-year-old women to marry, and the Revolución gave it all even more of a sense of urgency than the Church did. Neither Manuel nor I wanted to sin. Nor did we want to be separated. And so marriage—a simple, non-bourgeois ceremony—was the answer. It would allow us to be together in every way, physically, spiritually, politically, and to fight for what we believed in. And we believed in so much in those days.

It wasn't what Papa had planned for me, but he was the one who made me feel I could do anything I wanted, even if other people didn't approve. When I got involved in the youth movement, Mama said that our country needed to change, but that it wasn't my responsibility to change it. If she'd had a son who wanted to join the Frente, to fight, even, she would have supported him, she said. "But each time you give birth to a girl," she told me, "after just a hint of disappointment, you feel relief, because a daughter will never leave to fight a war or work far away. A daughter will stay close to you always, even after she marries." She never expected a daughter like me.

I wonder if Papa wished Celia or I had been a boy. He never said so. And when we had vacation after Christmas and at Easter, he taught us how to ride bikes, how to fish in the lagoon. Or taught me, anyway. Celia didn't like to get sweaty or dirty. Still, he didn't exclude her. At the time I assumed that she *chose* not to do those things; she just wasn't interested in them. But now that I've raised a daughter myself, watched her long for things and fear them at the same time, I wonder if perhaps Celia thought she wasn't capable of doing them, or if she worried about inviting ridicule by trying and failing. Mariana would be furious if I ever said it, but that's how she is with her paintings. She says she doesn't show them to gallery owners yet because she's still learning, developing her skills, but it's really because she's terrified someone will tell her they're not any good, even though they're wonderful. Mariana worries too much about what people think; that's another thing that skipped a generation.

Maybe that's what Manuel saw in me when we met in the church youth group—a willingness to try, to walk the muddy streets of the poorer neighborhoods delivering food, and later, ideas. It wasn't so much that I lacked fear. It was more that it never occurred to me to feel it. The world seemed ripe for improvement when I was a teenager, but somehow it felt safe to me, too.

And that was Papa's fault, I guess. He was the reason I turned out this way, even though he steered clear of politics. He made me feel invincible until life taught me otherwise. This was what I had lost now, the person who could still make me feel fearless.

I pressed my cheek against his one more time, just to prove that I didn't fear this either, this powdery skin that didn't warm to my touch. When I rose up, I saw Mariana flinch, then busy herself rummaging through her large leather bag. Had I embarrassed her? She'd asked on the phone if we were going to have an open casket, and the question surprised me; I don't think I've ever seen a closed one, except during the Revolución, if a body wasn't recovered, or was too mangled to display. How can you say a proper good-bye if you don't see a person, or the shell they've left behind, for the last time?

I tried to think of funerals she's gone to, but the only one I know of for certain was Beth's grandfather's in Virginia. They must have closed caskets there. Was today too much for Mariana? Too Latin somehow?

I took my place beside her as she pulled a packet of Kleenex out of her bag. "It's not quite my Bela's handkerchief," she said, and handed it to me with her strange half-smile, which made me accept it although my eyes were dry now.

"He made me feel I could do anything," I told her, because I wanted her to understand. "You know?"

"I know how wonderful Abuelo is. Was," she corrected herself. "But no, I don't really know what it's like to have a father." And just like that the moment was over, and her back was facing me as she leaned over to whisper some words of comfort to Mama.

10

Maria

As soon as I heard myself saying the words, I regretted doing so; talk about hitting a man when he's down! But it infuriates me the way Madre can be so obtuse, so wrapped up in herself. How can she not be aware that every time I see a father holding his daughter's hand on the subway, I wonder what that's like? It's ghoulish, I know, to envy her even this, the pain of losing her father. I'm like a twelve-year-old girl watching *Titanic*, wishing I knew the exquisite pain of having loved and lost because my love would be different than everyone else's, so much grander, more profound.

I told a therapist in college that I had to leave the common room each time Beth spoke to her dad on the phone, to avoid hearing the way she'd say, "Love you!" and hang up, eager to move on to the next activity, already having forgotten what they spoke about, whatever advice he had given her, which she wouldn't remember until his check arrived later in the week. Imagining his unheard responses on the other end of the line, picturing him staring at the phone after she hung up, it made me short of breath. The therapist—he wasn't a psychiatrist, just someone getting a PhD in psychiatry, but he was kind and the mental health services were free if you didn't go over ten hours a semester—he told me that I shouldn't judge my feelings or myself for having them, should just recognize them and let them pass. I laughed, the nervous giggle that was my trademark in college. I couldn't help it. I imagined a scene like something from *The Electric Company*, which my Bela let me watch in Miami; I saw flashing neon words float past me as I waved at them: "Jealousy." "Anger." "Sorrow."

It's a nice thought, the idea that you could remove guilt from a toxic cocktail of emotions by letting the others have free rein. But it's just that—a thought. I know I shouldn't have said what I did to Madre. At worst, it makes me a sadist. Ever since the first time I realized I was the only person with the ability to make my mother blush and stammer, I've reveled in my own power. I'm not proud of this. Well, that's not true. I'm not proud of the reveling, but I am proud of the power. It makes me feel unique, strong in my own right, that I'm the only one who can intimidate this woman who stalks through life, whether in camouflage or in tropical brights, handing down decisions, enacting changes, affecting everyone and everything she touches. I was seventeen and in Managua for spring break the first time I realized I had this talent. I'd been admitted to a summer program at CalArts near San Francisco, but Madre wanted me to spend the summer in Managua with her, interning in her office at the foreign ministry, working on my Spanish, which she said I spoke like an American. "Dude, I am an American," I said, just to annoy her. I knew I would capitulate in the end; I liked being in Managua with my relatives, even, when I didn't let my teen angst get the better of me, enjoyed being with Madre herself. What bothered me was that she seemed to know it, too, and the clearer that became, the angrier I got.

"My Bela says I should go to CalArts," I told her. "And my abuelo, too."

"They're not your parents." She pressed back her shoulders the way she did before she had to give a speech. "They're your grandparents. I'm the one who gets to decide! I'm your mother."

"Okay," I answered. "Then let's just ask my father."

I don't know what possessed me to say that. It had gotten to the point where neither of us ever mentioned Papi much; Madre certainly wasn't going to bring him up and I had moved on from fantasizing about how handsome my heroic papi must have been to noticing how cute the editor of our school's literary magazine was. One point for Sigmund Freud, I guess. But I didn't think it was fair that by her logic, Madre was the only person left on earth who had the right to weigh in on my future. What surprised me wasn't so much that I brought up my papi, but her reaction. She left the room. She didn't storm out or slam the door behind her. It wasn't like anything you'd see on my Bela's TV shows. But she was gone three hours and when she came back she said, "Fine, you can do the program. I made some calls and it comes highly recommended. But after those six weeks, the rest of the summer you're with me in Managua."

Madre said it as if this were her idea, as if she were giving me a command, telling me what we were going to eat for dinner, and where, and with whom. But the truth is, the scenario she was describing was exactly how I would have designed my summer if I thought she'd let me. I wanted to spend time in Managua, to see Rigobertito, whom I grew up with like we were siblings, and whom I only saw on holidays since he'd gone to college. And I also wanted to do the program and live in a dorm with kids who had no idea who I was or who my mother was or why I had no father or even where Nicaragua was. I had gotten exactly what I wanted. And while that fact on its own was mind-boggling, I wasn't so stunned that I failed to notice something else, too—I now knew that when I needed to, I could invoke my father and hurt my mother.

I knew it wouldn't always be the right thing to do. In fact, it usually isn't. And I certainly shouldn't have referred to him, even obliquely, now, at Abuelo's funeral, when I should be supporting Madre and my Bela, or at least keeping track of what's hidden in my pocket, so it doesn't fall into the wrong hands. Instead I had lashed out, and I know what I said reveals me to be stunted emotionally. Beth would say I'm blaming the victim here, but Madre always seems to bring out the worst in me. For so many years, my entire childhood, really, I tried to be my best self around her. On the last day of first grade before Christmas break, our music teacher let us watch a video of "The Nutcracker" in class, and at the end, when she turned the lights on and everyone lined up for recess, Amy Santiago refused to stand. I was the last person in line, and she motioned to me to come over and whispered, "On the way out, tell Miss Thomas that I'm not getting out of my seat until my mom comes to get me." I asked why not, but she just looked down at her desk. And that's when I saw something dripping from the back of her seat. I did what she said, but I couldn't believe it. Not that she'd peed her pants; it had happened to Kimberly Nosewicz in Brownies the week before. But that she wasn't embarrassed to let her mother know she'd had an accident. When Madre came to visit, my Bela dressed me in my cutest clothes and let me stay up late talking to her, singing all the songs I'd learned in school, reading the Spanish picture books she'd brought me. But even though I got all the songs right, Madre never stayed past Three Kings Day.

It wasn't until fifth grade that I realized no matter how good I was, it wouldn't make Madre stay. Plenty of kids were picked up from school by their grandparents, and with Tía Celia around, I still had two people I could give a flower to after the Mother's Day assembly, her and my Bela. I didn't walk around all the time feeling I was different, or missing something because Madre didn't live with us. But this was the first year she was going to be in Miami in time for the Christmas assembly at school, and I was counting the days until everyone got to see how beautiful and cool my mother was. And that she really existed. When I gave my book report on *A Little Princess*, Maribel Guzman asked me if I chose the book because it was about an orphan, like me. I explained that I had a mother, she was just busy "helping Nicaragua." That's what my Bela taught me to say when people asked where my mother was; with so many Nicaraguans in Miami fleeing the conflict, you never knew who hated the Sandinistas or loved them. If I said Madre was helping Nicaragua, my Bela told me, they'd just assume she fought for whatever side they supported. And most of the time, she was right. Still, Maribel Guzman didn't seem convinced that Madre existed. But we were both in choir together and I knew she'd see Madre watching me and clapping after I did my solo. I convinced the teacher to let me sing "I'll Be Home for Christmas" instead of "Silent Night" because I thought Madre would understand it was a personal message to her. When the day came, Madre was there, watching me sing, with tears in her eyes. And she was as beautiful as ever. But Maribel wasn't impressed at all. She was whispering to Dave Gonzalez during my entire solo. And I became convinced that they were talking about me, that they were making fun of me, laughing about what I had just realized: the mother of the little princess, and the blond kid on *Silver Spoons*, and the black boys on *Diff'rent Strokes*—all of those orphans, their mothers died, and they couldn't be with them. But my mother chose to leave me, year after year.

If it didn't matter back then when Madre saw how good I could be, maybe it doesn't matter now when she sees how cruel I can be. Or, more likely, she doesn't care either way; the amount of time she spends thinking about my behavior must take up a total of five minutes on her overfilled calendar. And after the way I behaved tonight, that's probably a good thing. Maybe Madre didn't hear me, or at least didn't notice what I said. She's got plenty of other things on her mind, other people to worry about. Tía Celia has arrived and she and Madre are hugging each other and rocking back and forth a little bit. They're the unlikeliest of sisters, but now they have one more thing in common, they share the same loss. Madre is clinging to Tía Celia's warm, fleshy body as if she has no intention of letting go any time soon. It's not quite a fair trade, this hug; Madre's so thin and fit, all bone and muscle. But Tía Celia doesn't seem to mind. That's what it is to have a sister, I suppose.

And my Bela, I'm almost positive that she didn't hear my exchange with Madre. It seems like she doesn't even really hear the words of condolence well-wishers are offering her, as if they were canapés she could nibble on to slake her hunger. She nods, but then she looks back at her handkerchief and they know they're dismissed. And then, it's strange, but as she holds the handkerchief to her forehead, dabs it at her face, she almost seems to smile a little. Relief, I suppose, at having been left alone until the next sympathetic mourner leans in to offer inadequate comfort.

11

Isabela

Silvia never spoke to me again. I don't blame her. Who knows what hopes she had pinned on the pleated navy dress, what it had cost her father? And she was back at school not one hour after Mauricio picked her up; I heard her heels clicking on the marble of the hallway, and even her shoes sounded angry.

The next night, Mauricio and I were out until the chaperone insisted it was time to leave or I'd miss curfew and she'd lose her position. We'd had coffee at Charlie's Steak House on Dryades, just behind the school; Mauricio told me later he felt it wouldn't be wise to go farther than a few blocks from campus, at least until we'd earned the chaperone's trust. I didn't speak much; it was the first time I'd been out with a man who wasn't a relative. But by the time he dropped us off, Mauricio had learned several important things: first, that if he pressed her, the chaperone could be induced to order a milk punch or a little sherry—"My mother, she does love a glass of sherry in the afternoon, sometimes two. It's quite the fashion in Cuba," he told her.

And second, that once she'd had her drink, she didn't mind if we lapsed into Spanish, which she said she knew, "of course, it's just not my mother tongue." Not ten minutes into the date she'd forbidden us from speaking Spanish, saying it was school rules that I should practice my English, but I think the truth was that she couldn't understand what we were saying, not with the way I swallowed the ends of my words, or how quickly Mauricio nattered on. But by the end of the afternoon, her cheeks were rosy and she was starting to nod off, and Mauricio was bold enough to say, in Spanish, "My mother only drinks at Christmas and Easter," which made me laugh, waking the chaperone. That's when she insisted it was time to go. But on the way back to school we passed a shoe-shine boy and Mauricio whispered to him and handed him something and when we reached the arched gate that spelled out SACRED HEART as if the letters were floating across the sky just like in my Mariana's painting, the little boy ran up with two bunches of flowers, violets for me and sweet peas for the chaperone. "To thank you ladies for the loveliest afternoon I've had in this country," Mauricio said, and the chaperone—we called her Miss Birdie—she actually blushed. She was the one who said she looked forward to seeing him in two weeks, not me.

And so Miss Birdie and I started seeing Mauricio every fortnight, on Friday afternoon, Saturday afternoon, and Sunday after Mass—and by the time I was a junior and given more free time off campus, sometimes Saturday night, too. It wasn't technically allowed, such frequency, not without a girl's parents having given written permission. But Dolly was there and a year older than I, so she counted as an approving relative (although not as a chaperone; that would be taking things entirely too far). Dolly had been significantly harder to win over than Miss Birdie, but Mauricio arranged for Cristian to take Dolly for a spin in his convertible at least once a weekend when they were in town, and she liked having a date, and a reason to walk past Silvia and her emerald cross in her dotted-Swiss afternoon dress. So she wrote to Mama and convinced her to send permission to the headmistress for us to go out in a mixed group when the boys visited, like all the girls from the best families did, so that no one could make fun of our family for being old-fashioned. After that, Dolly waited for the weekend almost as eagerly as I did.

The chaperone was even easier to amuse. Since we couldn't often leave the school's neighborhood, Mauricio brought the city to us. King cake during Lent, Elmer's Heavenly Hash chocolate-and-marshmallow eggs at Easter. And the rest of the year there were beignets from Café du Monde, and almond croissants from Haydel's Bakery, and, once, fried shrimp po'boys from an uptown shack run by some Italians; I never could pronounce the name, but that was Miss Birdie's favorite. She napped sitting upright on a bench for a good forty minutes after having eaten hers, leaving us unobserved in Audubon Park and near a particularly wide oak tree we could step behind but still emerge from quickly when we heard her stir.

Miss Birdie was a lifelong New Orleanian and the way to her heart proved to be through her stomach and her sense of civic pride. As Mauricio and I were finishing our beignets in the school court-yard one Saturday—Miss Birdie had already made short work of hers and was licking powdered sugar off her fingers, glancing right and left to make sure none of the nuns was approaching—she said, "Well, of course they're better warm."

Mauricio leaned forward, pushing his last beignet in front of Miss Birdie. "Why, Miss Birdie, what a wonderful idea!" he said, sounding just like Clark Gable, even though he didn't have a mustache; he said a Cuban with a mustache was asking for trouble when I inquired if he'd ever considered growing one to capitalize on his resemblance to the film star. "We should take Miss Isabela down to the Quarter so she can have them warm, as God intended."

Miss Birdie started to protest through a mouthful of dough and powdered sugar, but Mauricio kept right on talking. "I'll collect you both tomorrow after Mass, and Miss Dolly, too. We'll take the streetcar down for an adventure and Cris will bring us back in his car; we'll have to squeeze a bit in the back, but you ladies are slender enough."

I don't know if it was the idea of warm beignets or the novelty of being called slender, but somehow Miss Birdie agreed and signed out me and Dolly. After that first trip, we enjoyed a culinary excursion at least once a visiting weekend. Mauricio even took Miss Birdie and me to Commander's on my birthday, and she was so delighted to be eating in the Garden Room among the oldest families, some of whom were even Mardi Gras royalty, that she excused herself for not one but three long trips to the powder room, taking her sweet time to ogle the other patrons as she strolled past the tables, and leaving us completely alone for several minutes at a stretch.

In between there were letters. Oh, the letters! The postman knew me by name; I tried to find reasons to pass by the front desk every afternoon when he arrived, to collect my letters myself. It wasn't unusual to find your envelope opened by the time it was left on your desk, whether by a nun acting in your best interest or another girl looking for something to embarrass you with at the right moment.

I thought someone must have been protecting us because our letters were never opened; I imagined it was the Virgen, but maybe that's sacrilegious. In any case, we were careful. Mauricio would write in English describing his progress at his studies and outlining the plans he had for our next visit, and then he would write something like, "I miss you but patience is a virtue and I am strengthened by God's love. It's like it says in the Bible my grandfather left me," and launch into Spanish. The first few lines were always an actual quote or Bible passage, in case someone took the time to try to translate them. But if they did, they'd give up soon enough, he reasoned, and so he would veer from the evangelical and start writing about the warmth of my hand in his, the way he could feel my kisses all the way back to Mississippi, how it made him smile every time he found powdered sugar from our beignets embedded in his jacket. And how next year, when he would be a freshman at Loyola and I would be in my final year at Sacred Heart, we would find a way to be together without the interference of Miss Birdie and assorted baked goods, a way to be together now and always.

For him—I know because it was this way for me, too—a letter a week wasn't enough to cool the fever of needing to communicate with each other. But any more than one envelope weekly would be quickly noticed by the nuns. So we developed a plan. At first he suggested that he send letters to Dolly as well as me, with no return address, and that she just hand them over. I told him he clearly didn't pay much attention to his own sisters if he thought that Dolly would happily pass on letters from her sister's boyfriend while she had none of her own. She loved me, Dolly did, but playing courier for her younger sister—it would be too much. I knew better than to ask.

Connie would have done it in a heartbeat, Connie would have been honored to have been asked, she would have paid for the privilege! But I knew her and she was far too curious to leave what she knew to be a love letter unopened. None of the girls around me could be trusted, really. They would never spy on us out of malice—well, Silvia would. But the others would want to be bit players in our love story, to see what the North American girls would have called "an honest-to-goodness love letter" said.

But I did have one sort of friend who had too much on her mind—

and too much to lose—to meddle in our romance or give it any consequence. "Friend" might be the wrong word, but we were friendly.
And even that was forbidden. The only ugly thing I remember about
New Orleans at the time was the segregation. The colored adults, they
managed. They walked to the back of the bus as if they had intended
to do so anyway. But it was horrible to see the children, the little boys
peering through the gates of parks where they weren't allowed to play,
or staring in at the bakeries where we'd stop for coffee. It was the cus-
tom of the country, and not our place to disrupt it, my father said
when he dropped us off. But when Sister Dunphy, a nun so sour she
reminded me of Silvia, only wearing a habit, said we weren't to speak
to the floor maid, I thought it was some sort of perverse joke. I had
girls to clean my room and wash my clothes at home, they were dark-
skinned, too, and I couldn't imagine not chattering away with them
as they hung up my dresses or pressed my petticoats. How could I tell
them what I wanted otherwise? And, if we never spoke, how could
they tell me that Carolina Santamaria around the corner was having a dress made in the very same material as my favorite skirt, which
I should be sure to wear to Mass before her frock was finished? And
why would they want to tell me that if we didn't get along?

I'm not saying I was close friends with the staff at home—that
would have made everyone uncomfortable. But we enjoyed each
other's company. How could we not? We all worked at the same business: it was our job to bring honor to the family and each of us hoped
to do it well, in her own way. We couldn't begin to achieve that goal
without working together.

So when Dolly and I arrived at Sacred Heart, of course we spoke
to Betsy, who cleaned the third floor where the boarders' lived and
cared for our uniforms and other clothes. She was pretty, with a shy
half-smile that covered a crooked tooth. But beyond that, she had

grown up in New Orleans and we most certainly hadn't. If we didn't speak to her, who was going to tell us where to get our hair set? We knew which salon the other girls went to, but not which hairdresser the best-coiffed among them used. And who would return our hand-kerchiefs and hair ribbons when they'd fallen under our beds or we'd left them in a classroom?

It seemed only natural to us to give Betsy a pair of gloves from papa's factory at Christmas, and she loved them; she wore them to Mass all year. She was one of the bright spots of that lonely first Christmas, before I'd met Mauricio, when Dolly and I were among five boarders who lived too far from home to return for the holidays. On Christmas Eve all five of us homesick girls were crying in the chapel when Mother Dauphinais came in and, instead of scolding us, gave us each a small box of her famous fudge. As we ate the fudge, Dolly and I told her all about Christmas at home—the nacimientos in every house and park, the way the drivers in Granada decorated their horse and carriages. And she invited us to join her in the kitchen the next morning, once the cook had put the turkey in the oven, to help make her equally famous rum balls. Dolly and I had never cooked, and Mama said we were too easily distracted to help her supervise the kitchen, but we didn't want to miss these extra hours luxuriating in the warmth of Mother Dauphinais's presence. I arrived a few minutes before the others, because I had something to confess: I had been reading *Gone with the Wind* to pass the time during the long, lonely vacation. It wasn't my copy, I pointed out, al-though I didn't tell her it was Connie's. But I had been enjoying it. "Oh, you can go ahead and read that, dear," Mother Dauphinais said, patting my shoulder. "That girl just gets what was coming to her."

There wasn't really much for us to do in the kitchen. There was no need for measuring cups, she said, pouring liberally straight from the bottle; she'd been making rum balls since before she'd taken her vows. But we helped stir, and chatted away, and drank tea, and then Betsy stopped by, straight from Mass, wearing her gloves and bringing us each a packet of her mother's famous pralines. And Mother Dauphinais seemed pleased as punch to see her. So we ignored Sister Dunphy's instructions and kept our relationship with Betsy just as we liked it.

To tell the truth, we liked Betsy more than we did some of the students, more than Silvia, definitely, so when Silvia made Betsy iron her skirt twice because the pleats weren't stiff enough, we weren't above making faces behind her back. And when Silvia left the floor, I showed Betsy the trick Gloria at home used to make starch work even better.

So one Saturday when Connie was down the hall in the lavatory and Dolly wasn't in shouting distance, I thought nothing of beckoning Betsy as she passed by the door with a stack of towels, and asking her if she could please button up the back of my dress.

"You going out with your fella, Miss Isabela?" she asked. Then she opined as to how he sure was handsome, and she told me a little bit about her fella, who worked at a restaurant in the Quarter and was saving up for them to marry in a few years. And so I asked her, without even thinking about it, if she wouldn't mind receiving mail for me from Mauricio, if he could send letters to her house, and she could give them to me when I saw her, or leave them in my underwear drawer, hidden under my balled-up stockings. She hesitated for a minute; I can see now that I was asking a lot, too much, maybe. I might have been suspended if we had been found out, but she would have been fired, and I knew her parents counted on her salary to help with her siblings, and needed everyone to do his or her share. But I was young and selfish and in love and I didn't think of this at the time, although I did make sure that the next Christmas I slipped a few bills into the fingers of her gloves to help with her household contribution.

I don't know if it's because she was brave or kind or just didn't know how to refuse me, but Betsy agreed and the letters became even more frequent and still more passionate. I don't know where Mauricio learned to write love letters or how; maybe he copied them from somewhere. I wouldn't have been able to tell, I don't read those kinds of books. Although, years later, when I came across the Song of Solomon, which no priest I had listened to ever read in church, I felt a shock of recognition, not at the words so much but at the style, the ecstasy of belonging to, and possessing, another being.

I wish I still had those letters. I thought I'd remember every word, always, but of course I've forgotten them, as I have so many things I could never have imagined losing. It would be so precious to me, now, to have proof that someone once loved me this way. I'm aware of how people see me, as an excitable old woman, one who is, perhaps, prone to exaggeration. Of course I know how much Mauricio loved me. But how nice it would be, nonetheless, to have physical evidence! Instead of just telling Mariana that revolutionaries make bad husbands, I could show her the kind of men who must make good ones, men who have no higher cause, career, or preoccupation, men whose revolution is you.

But a few years after I married Ignacio, Padre Juan Cristobal urged me to burn those letters; it was a sin to keep them, he said. Burning them would free me, he promised, would lift my depression, and I had my daughters to think about. So I stole away to a quiet corner of the courtyard on Christmas Eve, and when everyone else was shooting guns and watching fireworks, I set fire to my letters and forced myself not to cry while I watched them burn. I drank an entire glass of Ignacio's scotch as I watched the flames, something I've never done before or since. Even at the time I knew I was making a mistake. I don't like to contradict a man of the cloth, but I'm certain it was the burning of the letters that was a sin, not the keeping of them.

I don't know why Padre Juan Cristobal gave me such poor counsel. Maybe he felt loyal to Ignacio, whose family had donated so much to the church in Granada. Or maybe he truly believed he was giving me the right advice, having never been in love himself. Sometimes, now, I pray to forgive him. And to forgive myself. Because the first time I lost Mauricio, I still maintain, was not my fault. But burning the letters meant losing him a second time. And I was the one who lit the match.

12

Ninexin

Celia smells like she did at her debutante ball, sweet and familiar, like the jasmine we used to have in the front yard, and I wish, so strongly that it feels as if I've never wanted anything else before, that we could go back to that night. Not to the country club, of course not, but to a time when everything was ahead of us and Mama glowed with happiness and Papa would always keep us safe. I hold on to Celia for a long time; she makes no move to break our embrace. Finally Rigobertito puts his hand on my shoulder and says, "Tía Ninny."

And even that makes me shaky, that stupid nickname I never forced him to drop. Rigobertito resembles his mother in looks but his grandfather in temperament. He has Papa's way of making sure the machinery of society runs smoothly; if he's breaking up our sisterly hug, it must mean that other people are waiting to speak to us, that they are in need of my sister's embrace, too. So I step back from Celia and immediately feel her absence; I keep feeling the need to reach for something that's not there.

Some colleagues from the ministry are filtering in through the door; they've come not so much to honor Papa but to show respect for my loss. And I wish they hadn't. I don't want to see anyone from work, I don't want to be strong and competent. I appreciate the show of sympathy, of respect, but I wish they had chosen to come to the funeral tomorrow instead; surely I won't be expected to speak to anyone there, and they still would have fulfilled their obligation. But the funeral is an hour away, in Granada, where Papa was born and lived until Mama was pregnant with me. Her father's glove business was starting to falter, and they felt they could escape her family's drama, and expand Papa's law practice, if they made the move to Managua. No one wants to waste a whole morning driving to the funeral of a coworker's relative and back, no matter how much he respects the colleague. I don't blame them; I wouldn't want to either. But did they have to come tonight, when I'm expected to talk to people and smile politely through tears? And now I'll be obligated to take note of who came and lie and tell them how much I appreciate it at work next week, when I know all I'll want to do is hide out at the office and pretend that life is normal and nothing has changed.

The smart thing to do would be to get it over with, to clear Celia out of the way so that my coworkers can march right up and shake my hand, offer their sympathy. But I don't have it in me to face them yet, so I busy myself squatting down to talk to Rigobertito's boys. They're looking a bit shell-shocked themselves; this is probably their first funeral, their first dead body, too, and they loved their great-grandfather in the way that happy, rambunctious five- and seven-year-old boys do a man in his eighties: they climbed on him more than they should have, they laughed with glee at his stories and screamed in delighted terror at the way he'd pop out his dentures to scare them. They'll cry the first few times they notice he's not there at Sunday dinner but soon they'll get used to life without him. He's just one of a vast team of older people who love them. As I am, too, I suppose. They're quiet tonight, but normally they tear around the house opening drawers and upending shelves and it surprises me how much I love it, and them, how eager I am to see them again, to let them rifle through my bag and hug me with cookie-clutching hands that leave crumbs on my suit jackets. I said as much to Mariana last Christmas when she was here, that this must be what it's like to have a grandchild, and she laughed and said, "Well, God bless Rigobertito for letting those two take over his life. Between him and Beth, seeing how they're run ragged, I don't know if I could handle having kids."

"Really?" I asked before I could think better of it. I couldn't articulate why I was surprised. It's not that I view her as particularly maternal, or that I want her to settle down. She's always had boyfriends, so I suppose she's had plenty of chances if she were interested. Even though she's thirty-three, an age at which her grandmother and I both had adolescent children, Mariana doesn't seem in a particular rush to start a family, unlike Rigobertito, who married his college girlfriend before he began business school. Mariana still seems so unsettled, and I want her to make her own life first, a life that matters, before having a family. It just hadn't occurred to me that she might have already decided never to do so, that she wasn't interested in motherhood.

I don't pry into her private life, and she doesn't offer any information unless Mama is around to tease it out of her. Last year, when Mariana was here for Christmas and Rigobertito kept trying to set her up with a friend from business school, she announced that she had recently started dating someone, but she didn't want to discuss details until things got more serious. "That's okay," I told her. "I'm used to dealing with classified information."

I wasn't joking, but she laughed and relaxed. I was grateful for the laughter, the way it eased the conversation. Along with the new boyfriend, she had a new job. She had just switched galleries, taking on a more influential position than she'd had at the last one. And she was happy to talk about that, both what she wore to work (Mama's question) and what the job consisted of (mine). She researched promising new artists, she explained, acquired new works for the gallery, and advised collectors on what pieces were likely to appreciate in value, and would be good investments.

"So impressive!" Mama couldn't stop grinning and I knew she was picturing Mariana waving a manicured hand at some painting, like a model on one of the game shows she used to watch in Miami, as a host of wealthy, single businessmen looked on in awe.

"It's great experience if I want to start my own gallery; I'm making a name, developing a following," Mariana said. "When I get a little more established, I'm going to try and cultivate some Nicaraguan artists, maybe plan a trip to Solentiname." Just the sound of the name made me happy. It's a beautiful word, of course, but also, it may be the one place where Mariana's career and mine could coincide: some of my colleagues had hidden there during the war, and a few still remain today. Inspired by Ernesto Cardenal's liberation theology and cultivation of the arts, they're working toward a better future by creating their paintings and sculptures. I'll admit it's not my idea of nation-building; I like the mental puzzles of political engagement, arguing over new laws, discussing policy with foreign officials. But Mariana is an artist and if love of art and love of politics come together anywhere, it's Solentiname. The area could be common ground for us, I thought. I could introduce her to people, help her in her exploration, and maybe she'd ask for my advice or even invite me to visit the archipelago with her.

The summer she was seventeen, after Marianna returned from

that art school in California, she spent most of her days unsuccessfully trying to find Internet connections to email a boy she'd met while there. But I'd asked her to bring me a new pair of running shoes from Miami, and she brought hers, too, and we did spend one weekend hiking the Canyon of Somoto. We didn't argue once that weekend, but we did talk. I don't think she sulked for the entire forty-eight-hour period. At the time, we agreed to visit one part of Nicaragua that Mariana wasn't familiar with on each of her trips, but since she started working and her visits have become shorter; that hasn't really happened, or it's been relegated to day trips a short hike in El Chocoyero, an overnight in Léon to see the Purísima celebrations. Solentiname would be the perfect place to restart the tradition.

But Mariana didn't invite me, didn't ask my advice. Which hurt me, even though I knew it shouldn't. And so I gave my opinion anyway: "If you want to help Nicaraguan artists, and even the country itself, mi amor, we should work together. With your abilities it doesn't have to just be art for art's sake; you can do things that will have a real impact."

I meant it as a compliment. With her intelligence and warmth, she could do so much good, not just for Nicaragua, but for the world. She's so much easier with people than I am, but she's just as direct, she can get right to the heart of a matter without digging so deep that she wounds anyone. She has so many more gifts than I. Her smile. Her humor. The intimacy she creates with everyone who isn't me, leaning forward, looking right at them, as if she truly wants to know them. Surely those skills could be used to do more than convince rich strivers to buy art they don't care enough about to choose without her help?

I meant it as a compliment, but she didn't take it as such. She didn't yell, or make any retort, she just said she was tired from the flight and went to rest, and Mama asked me if I had always had such a one-track mind or if the war had made me unable to focus on anything but politics. I didn't know the answer. But I knew I was right, that Mariana can do anything she wants exceptionally well, better than I could ever hope to. I just can't tell what it is she truly wants to do. She paints, but she doesn't show her work in any gallery, and doesn't seem to have any plans to do so. I asked her once what her ultimate goal is, and she said, "Really, Madre, not everyone has to change the world. Some of us are happy to just answer the phones, hang the art, and collect a paycheck." But if that were true, why paint at all? If it's just a hobby, why doesn't she hang her efforts in her home or give them to friends instead of being so secretive about them, insisting that they're not ready to be seen "yet"? The only person she even shows her work is Mama.

I know Mariana is good at the art broker aspect of her job, and that it's a source of pride for her. She's never been materialistic, but she called a few months ago, bubbling with news of her latest sale. I heard the energy in her voice, and suddenly I saw her, decades from now, one of those older women in New York still rushing down the street, speed-talking into her cell phone. And I had the same sinking feeling I always do when I realize that Mariana will probably spend her life in that city, she'll never return to the country that her father gave his life for and that I've spent mine trying to improve for her. I've tried to share my love for Nicaragua with her; I don't know how well I've succeeded. She enjoys visiting here, but in twenty years, when my parents are gone, will she have reason to return? Or will she see Rigobertito once a year in Miami, an easier compromise for each of them? I suppose they'd invite me to Miami, too.

"Think of what that money could be used to do if it were donated to an orphanage," I told her. There are several orphanages between Managua and Granada, and I had been harboring a secret fantasy that Mariana might want to move back and put her talents, and her sales experience, to use fund-raising for them; it would be a way for her to build her own relationship with the new Nicaragua. And, although I'd never say this to her, an opportunity for us to spend time together. I never got a chance to tell her that idea. She hung up on me, but not before saying, "Well, I'm sort of an orphan and my commission will pay my rent for four months, so you can feel good about that."

I got her point. She's building her life, and I gave up my right to comment on her choices long ago. So I never shared my fantasy of her moving here, and I will keep my hope that one day she'll have her own child to myself. I thank God for Rigobertito as I lean over to whisper to his boys, the closest thing I have to grandchildren, who are shielding me from all the well-meaning small talk, the sympathetic murmurs that will either upset me or leave me cold, and unable to tell which is worse. Suddenly I hate this funeral home, although everyone who works here has been nothing but kind. A funeral seems like such a ludicrous place, a ridiculous idea, as artificial and constructed as a masked ball or a coronation. Why do we do this? Expose ourselves to so many others in the hour of our grief when it would be more natural, surely, to sit alone with our thoughts and our memories. Society demands calling hours, and I've never been one to worry about what society demanded. But somehow, I must have invited these people into my sorrow. Now, they don't want to be here and I don't want to see them, and we're nervously glancing at each other over the heads of these sweet, disoriented children, like people monitoring the advance of a stray dog on the street; you hope the mutt isn't too badly off, you wish you could help it, but you also don't want it coming too close and licking your hand.

When I glance up from the boys, to steel myself for my colleagues' arrival, I see, behind them, a man, tall, foreign, looking even more lost than I feel. Too young to be a friend of my father's. Too well dressed and too obviously nonlocal to be a chauffeur. And then Mariana is next to him, as if she had teleported to his side. I can't hear what she says, so there is no way she could be described as shouting, but I can tell she's angry, angling herself in toward him, in and up, putting as much force behind her words as she can, and he's backing away from them as if they hurt as they hit their marks. I start to stand to see if she needs my help, but just then, the stranger takes another step backward and collides with a waiter who is walking into the room, carrying a silver tray bearing a glass of Rojita for Mama. As I rise up the tray falls down and hits the floor with a crash and a clang, and the young waiter slips on the red slick of Rojita, falling back into the open door, causing it to slam shut.

When I open my eyes I find myself on the floor again, but all the way down this time, and instead of me crouching over Rigobertito's boys, they're standing over me, and the five-year-old is crying.

13

Maria

I can't decide whom I'm angrier at: Allen, for showing up where he knows he's not wanted, or my mother, for fainting, causing such a commotion, making herself so present in one of the few moments of my life when I didn't want her there. My Bela sat there like a lady, lost in her memories of Abuelo, almost smiling, and Madre—who carries a semiautomatic more naturally than a baby—suddenly became a fragile flower, collapsing at the sight of her daughter speaking to a strange man. I've got a dead grandfather, a bereaved, aged grandmother, and a completely displaced boyfriend—or whatever he is right now—and it's my mother, the soldier, I have to worry about?

The worst part is that, technically, I can't be mad at Madre. It's not allowed. Her father just died, so it's natural for her to be upset. Her fainting is just a sign of her deep-seated goodness and unexpected fragility, and my anger reveals my childish petulance. I could see the shock in her colleagues' expressions when she fell, and then, like a series of kaleidoscope turns, their faces changed, taking on a look of admiration, almost worship. Their fearless leader was vulnerable. The iron lady had her soft spots.

Okay, so Madre's not exactly Margaret Thatcher. But she's just as strong, albeit it with better hair. Stronger, maybe. This is a woman who meets with heads of state on a regular basis, who's drunk shots with Castro, who stalks out of a room whenever the conversation takes a turn she doesn't like, too busy with the business of nation-building to deign to discuss concepts that don't interest her. And now she's got, what, low blood pressure? Anemia? The vapors? And I'm the bitch for feeling pissed off that she once again drained all the force of my emotion, turned my focus from Allen, and our life together— or lack thereof—sharply back to her, when she's already always looming in my mind. And I now feel like a fifth grader singing to her mom again, realizing the woman tearing up in the audience is a total mystery.

I know I'm not supposed to be angry at her. I've always known I'm not allowed to be angry at her. It's not like I was a miserable child because my mother wasn't there. Her absence was just a fact of life, something I accepted, even when other people around me seemed to find it strange. When I was in seventh grade, I broke my arm during a particularly spirited game of volleyball. At the hospital, the doctor said he was going to have to rebreak it before it setting it in the cast, and asked if I wanted to wait for my mother to arrive before he did.

"My mother's very busy, she won't be able to make it," I told him, my good hand clasping my Bela's. And then, because I didn't want him to ask where she was (somewhere in Central America, I wasn't even sure) or what she was doing (fighting injustice, sort of like Wonder Woman), I added, "But don't worry; I'm very brave, and quite mature for my age."

He stared at me for what seemed like a long time, then patted me on the head as if I were a much younger child. But it's not like I was trying to be stoic or anything; I had my Bela there, and I secretly thought it would be cool to have a cast everyone could sign. It didn't seem like an event where my mother was necessary, really, even if the doctor expected a mom to show up; it might have made him more comfortable but I don't know that it would have done much for me.

There were times when I wished she would appear, of course, and on those occasions, I didn't play the strong, silent type. I see now that it probably made her feel unappreciated, or just sad, but I would whine to my Bela when all the other mothers were going to be at the swim meet, or the dance recital, even the pre-prom party where you stand next to your awkward date in your hideous dress and everyone takes pictures and marvels at how much you've grown and it's all "Sunrise, Sunset"; even that late in life I kept hoping Madre would show up to watch me do something. And my Bela, God bless her, never said, "Consider yourself lucky your abuelo and I are here to feed and clothe and adore you." But she would say, "Mariana, you can't be upset at your mother; she's busy helping fix Nicaragua. It's all for you."

I couldn't say I wanted a fixed Nicaragua, but I also wanted a mom like the others, who was always hoping for an excuse to pull out her camcorder and commemorate this recital or first day of school or stupid play. I wanted a mom who was excited to be looking after me, not a whole country. Even as a kid, I knew that desire made me sound like a megalomaniac, even before I was sure how to pronounce the word. "Just always remember your mama in your prayers, and thank God that she isn't in danger," said Bela, who went out of her way to explain that I didn't need to worry about Madre being hurt or killed like my papi was; she wasn't a soldier anymore but a minister in the new government, so she carried press releases, not guns. I knew I should be grateful that Madre wasn't going to disappear completely, that I got to see her as often as I did. I had plenty of people who loved me. It's like my Bela said, "One good thing, maybe the best thing, about your madre working so hard is that your abuelo and I get to spend so much time with you." Maybe it was greedy to want the attention of one more person. But I still kept looking over my shoulder on the important days, to see if Madre might walk in quietly to surprise me. I've been looking over my shoulder my whole life.

And now that I've stopped doing that, whenever I have a big moment, she inserts herself in it somehow. When I made a major sale, she made it seem crass and tacky and small compared to her noble lifetime of public service. Guess what? She was right! And tonight, talk about a moment! It was practically cinematic. I turn around and see that Allen has showed up. All those years I'd been hoping the person I loved would turn up when I needed her, and now someone did, only it's a him and I've spent three days convincing myself that he—and his kids—are better off without me, and that I'll be fine without him, this man who couldn't even find time to talk about a future with me, much less plan one. I was so tempted to run over to him and throw my arms around his neck, but I didn't. I was strong, and kept reminding myself that I wasn't supposed to want him here. In my email, I had asked him to give me time to mourn. And to think. I didn't tell him that I also need this time to keep my promise and deliver that envelope to my Bela. But somehow, even though there's no way he could know about it, I'm angry at him for screwing that up, too. He should have just respected my request, even if he wasn't aware of all the reasons behind it.

More than once he's canceled weekend plans with a text that

said nothing more than, *Caught up in the new painting. Will call when at a stopping point. Thx for understanding.* And I do—I do understand. I am always genuinely excited for him, even though I'm the one who gets stuck making excuses to his friends, or canceling our dinner reservations. So why is it different when I choose to remove myself from the situation for a bit, to go on hiatus? Why can't he honor my request? After thinking about it the entire flight from LaGuardia to Miami, composing and revising the four-line message all through cooking and dinner and our black-dress shopping trip, I'd emailed him from Beth's computer while Olivia slept, saying I was planning to stay in Nicaragua for a bit after the funeral, that I needed a week for myself to think things through. And suddenly he's here? At my grandfather's calling hours?

Still, it's not as simple as that and he knows it. I'm lying when I say he's shown up where he's not wanted. I hate to admit it, even to myself, but of course I want to see him. I want to see him every day, in the morning when he wakes up with an exaggerated growl and bounds off to shower and paint, so eager that sometimes he forgets to get dressed in between and I'll find him naked, dripping on the floor, with a brush in his hand, staring at his canvas. I want to see him at night when he's so tired he can't possibly work anymore so he sits out on his fire escape and looks at the sky as if expecting the universe to entertain him. And it does—that's the thing, it always does! There's always a falling star, or a winking constellation no one has ever heard about, like Delphinus, the little dolphin who found Poseidon his mermaid queen, Amphitrite. Allen says that when the honeymoon period wore off and the couple started squabbling, Poseidon changed Delphinus' name to Mahi Mahi and grilled him for dinner. He always laughs at his own idiotic jokes, like that one. And his laughter becomes the funniest part. He's over a decade older than I am and he's still delighted by everything he sees. He's broken three iPhones because he's always pulling one out of his pocket to film a bird flying across the sky above the park, or two kids in red T-shirts playing basketball, or three nuns in old-school habits billowing down the street. And then the colors or the swooping habits end up in his paintings, and he's immortalized something I would have walked right past without noticing. It makes me want to sit next to him for the rest of my life so that I get to watch what he's seeing, too.

Which is terrible, I know. My mom's made history with her life, she's literally building a nation every day, and my highest ambition is, what—to be a handmaiden to a great artist? His most valuable audience member? I never tell anyone how I feel about Allen. I don't even tell him. But his world is so appealing, it's where I want to live. There's no fear, there's no anxiety, there's just wonder. I used to hide negative reviews of his shows—there was a bit of a backlash after his last painting sold for so much. And then he picked up a pile of take-out menus and other papers from my desk and found a review, read it, shrugged, and said, "You liked the painting, didn't you?" And after I nodded, "How's the new Thai place? Do they give you those ginger candies at the end? I'm always picking them out of my teeth three days later but I just can't get enough of them."

I'm sure it puts some people off, the way he obviously feels so damn at home in the world. It did me, if only for a second. The first day I met him, he walked into the gallery, not bothering to stop at the desk, and strode straight up to one of his paintings, which we'd displayed on a wall of its own. I dutifully walked up next to him and said, "Let me know if I can help you with anything, sir," and he said, "Don't call me 'sir,'" without even looking at me. Which, if I'd known who he was, I might have taken as humble or charming, but since I didn't, and he didn't even bother to take his eyes off the painting to acknowledge the presence of another human being, it just seemed rude. "Then, let me know if I can help you with anything, dude," I said, before I could think better of it. And he laughed so loudly and so hard that I had to shush him. That's when he looked at me and asked what I thought of the painting. I told him the truth, that I found it amazing. That I'd heard people say they didn't know what all the fuss was about, it looked like something their five-year-old could do. But that I felt that's exactly why it was a masterpiece. It was so bold, so bright. It looked like the person who created it had discovered only the beauty of life and not yet encountered the sorrow.

"Wow," he said. And I realized that the man in front of me resembled the photo of the artist on the back of the brochure, only he was much older. "Are you related to the artist?" I asked, and he laughed again. "His brother?"

"I guess it's time to update the photo on my bio." He barely managed to articulate the words, he was laughing so hard. I could feel the heat rising from my neck and knew I needed to get out of there before I blushed noticeably. "If I had that much money to spend on a painting, I'd much rather buy it from you than this guy," I said, shaking the brochure in my hand. "This kid looks like kind of a jerk." I think that between laughing and gasping for air Allen said, "He probably was," but I'm not sure. I was already halfway back to my desk by the time he spoke.

Even tonight, when I first saw him walk into the funeral home, I couldn't help but stand up, and I knew it was joy lifting me out of my chair. It took me a minute to remember how hurt I am that he can't get it together to focus on me, on us, now when we need to find some answers that can't wait any longer. The truth is, there's still part of me that feels that this is all my fault. I shouldn't have said anything before I left. I should have made a decision on my own, or waited until I got back to bring it up again, should have bided my time for the right moment, when his painting was going well, but not so well that he could think of nothing else. But I just couldn't wait. Sometimes you have to think of the future, make a choice one way or the other, and live with the consequences.

Or maybe you don't. Allen's been living in the now for almost half a century. Still, I'm starting to think that existing solely in the moment is a privilege reserved for geniuses, millionaires, and the wildly self-possessed. Men, mainly. Guess what, John Donne? Some men *are* an island.

It's not just men, though. The truth is, my mother is just as self-sustaining as Allen. And here I thought only men had to worry about dating their mothers. Maybe Madre fainted because when Allen showed up she sensed that someone as self-focused as she is had just entered the room, and she's more comfortable with the idea of me living in her long shadow than in his.

The worst part is that Allen knows me better than I do myself. He knew I'd be pleased to see him, at least on some level. That's what finally helped me stoke the anger that had been lying dormant in the pit of my stomach, that smug expression on his face. He walked in, the only gringo in a room full of Nicas, the only person here besides the waiters who never met Abuelo, and he didn't look out of place at all. He looked proud of himself, so sure that his arrival was some romantic, big-screen overture, Rhett Butler buying back Tara, or John Cusack standing outside in the rain, holding up a boom box. He was actually reaching his arms out to embrace me when I whisper-spat, "What are you doing here?"

That's when he looked past me, saw the body of my grandfather lying in state, the eyes of countless relatives staring at him, wondering what his last name was, and his mother's maiden name, and her parents' names and their parents' names and who was he, and what did he want, and should they call for the caretaker? When he must have realized that perhaps he wasn't the director of this movie after all.

"How did you even get here?" I grabbed his wrist and pulled him out of the center of the room, closer to the wall, as if that would some- how make people stop staring at us. And then I added the first idi- otic thought that rose in my head: "You don't take connecting flights."

"I do if it's important," he said, and I softened a little, so that my hand around his wrist was less of a handcuff, more of a handhold. "And it was only an hour layover in Houston. I read *The New Yorker* on your laptop. I thought you might need it."

I had realized that I'd forgotten my laptop on his bedside table the night before last, while packing for my flight to Miami, but I wasn't about to go back and get it after the way I left his apartment, clutching my pride to my chest like it was an insufficient winter coat. I tried to tell myself it was a good thing I didn't bring the computer with me. After all, last time I was in Managua my BlackBerry had been stolen off the table in a restaurant where I'd stupidly left it when I went to the bathroom. I told myself it would be better to be unplugged, so that I would be forced to think, to make plans, with- out the distractions of Twitter or Facebook. But still I felt calmer, somehow, knowing that this link to my life in New York was here with me again. I felt less alone.

"I went to your mother's office first—it was the only Managua address you had in your contacts," he said. "The girl at the desk told me that she'd be here. I mean, that you'd be here. She even got me a cab."

I dropped my hand from his wrist. Allen always got what he wanted from the pretty girl sitting at the reception desk. Thinking of Madre's secretary made me wonder who'd made his plane reservation. I hoped that he'd had to do it himself, that his assistant wasn't back from vacation yet; if he'd asked Katie to book a last-minute flight to Managua, she would have gotten way too excited, thinking that he was planning to propose. Or maybe I was getting ahead of myself, maybe she would find it normal, him coming to comfort me when I needed support. Maybe I was the one misreading the situation, overdramatizing everything.

"We need to talk about this more, Maria," Allen said. Even now when he says my name I hear the *West Side Story* cast recording in the background. *Say it soft and it's almost like praying.* But even though he was saying it soft, his prayer felt like an intrusion. He needed to talk about this more, just when I needed this time not to talk.

"I know how busy you are," I said, trying to sound like my mother when I'd sit in her office over school breaks, listening to her speaking on the phone to some important official in a tone that clearly implied there was no way he—it was usually a he—could be as busy as she was. "But I think it's fair to insist that this can wait until after they bury my grandfather."

It was the perfect thing to say. Elegant. Mature. Concise. But I guess it was too perfect, because when I'd finished speaking in cool, measured tones, making a statement there was no way he could respond to appropriately, even though he's older, smarter, and so much more talented than I am, he stood there for a moment, saying nothing, his mouth slightly open like when he's deep into a painting. Then I leaned toward him, pressing my advantage, adding, "That's not too much to ask, is it?"

And he stepped backward, into a black-vested waiter who tripped and dropped his silver tray, splashing bright red, chemical-smelling soda through the air and onto the floor so that when it met his poignantly shined shoe he slid, falling on his backside, hitting the door with his shoulder, and the clanging tray and shattering glass and slamming door combined into one horrible banging noise. But somehow, after it happened, no one was looking at the poor waiter, as he made his way back to his feet, rubbing his elbow. Everyone but the embarrassed waiter was motionless, staring at the back of the room, and when I looked there, too, I saw my nephews, or the closest thing I have to nephews, standing over the fallen body of my mother. In the next second, an entire phalanx of the foreign ministry moved toward her as if they were executing choreography; even the wounded waiter rushed to her side.

For a split second, I was worried, too. I wasn't yet annoyed or conflicted, wasn't dividing my anger between two worthy targets. I still hadn't thought about what caused her to faint, and how weird it was that she did so, just at that moment, too, as opposed to when she first saw her dead father's body laid out in his casket. I hadn't yet absorbed how strange it was that she'd fainted at all, when I'd never known her to do so. That was more my MO. That time I broke my arm in gym class, I passed out from the pain. Staring at my mother lying on the floor, I hadn't remembered the hospital yet, or the cracking sound when the doctor rebroke my arm, manipulating it back into place. I was just grateful to her for the diversion, for emphasizing the point that I had too much to deal with right at this moment to spend any time straightening out my love life, figuring out my future. Our future.

I turned back to Allen. "Check into the Contempo Hotel. There's hot water and free wifi; you'll like it," I promised. "I'll come see you tomorrow night, once the funeral is over, everyone's gone home, and we're back in Managua."

As I walked toward my fallen mother, I wondered whether or not I was telling the truth.

14

Isabela

I will give Ignacio tomorrow, I promise. From the moment I wake up, during the whole drive to Granada, and throughout the church service and the interment, I will think of no one else. And I will forget about his other women, and how I blamed him for not being one other man, and I will focus on the highlights: Christmas mornings with the girls, waltzing at the country club, cheering at Mariana's soccer games. I should be thinking of him now, as I sit next to his body, reliving the good times, because there *were* good times, moments when I was surprised by his thoughtfulness. After the birth of Celia and, so soon after that, Ninexin, he didn't just buy me a ring or a bracelet, but worked with the jeweler to create a piece that represented each new little person we'd made—my topaz ring is the color Celia's eyes were when she was born, and my diamond brooch swoops to resemble the birthmark on Ninexin's stomach.

After Ninexin's birth, when the doctor told him there could be no more children, Ignacio didn't complain that he'd never have a son, that the de la Torre name would die out within two generations. We could still have relations, the doctor said. And we did, sometimes, after a party where we'd danced together, or on a weekend when the girls had stayed at Celia's for the night, and neither of us had to get up early. But half the excitement came from knowing we might create something together, or at least, that's how I felt. Otherwise, there didn't seem much point, not anymore. Some men might have abandoned me completely then, found a permanent mistress, started another family, even. But Ignacio didn't. We remained a team at home. Not a pair of lovebirds, maybe, but a pair of oxen, doing an honest day's work, tilling the field that was our family.

And there were times when he showed greater strength of character and foresight than most men of our generation. When Ninexin warned us trouble was about to start in 1979, and worse, that her involvement in the Movimiento was putting us in danger, he didn't worry about his practice, he just taped an image of Sandino in his office window, packed us up, and drove all night until he brought us to Honduras, where we waited out the triumph of the fall of Somoza in safety. Two years later, when Ninexin warned us that Rigobertito could be drafted in the not-too-distant future, Ignacio saw it was time to move to Miami, and, more than that, he supported me when I insisted that we take Mariana with us. How happy they were together! Every Saturday morning she would walk him across the street from our apartment to Las Olas café, where he would drink coffee and, if he stayed through lunchtime, rum with the angry old Cubans.

And after she dropped him off, my Mariana would come back with a watermelon juice for me, and we would sit in the kitchen with the fan clicking above our heads and talk about whatever was preoccupying us just then. What to wear to Mass on Christmas. Or her school, and how different her classes were than mine had been at Sacred Heart, where French and Comportment were mandatory. I suppose we talked mostly about what preoccupied me, really, which is how she came to know all about Mauricio, things I had told no one since Padre Juan Cristobal, may God forgive him. And, you know, I would bet everything, all my jewelry, even the gifts from Ignacio after the births of our daughters, that Mariana is still the only person who knows, that she never shared my story with anyone. Not with Ninexin, even in those painful years when I could see them struggling to find things to say to each other, things that mattered, and she could have used the tale as currency, to show that her ultimate allegiance was to her mother. Mariana longed for her mother so much in the beginning; it hurt to watch. But then, before she even became a teenager, she turned a corner. She seemed to appreciate that her mother is a fine woman, a heroine, really, but that I was the one who was there with her every day. Most girls don't love their grandmothers as much as they do their mothers. But we were not most families. If Mariana wasn't loyal to me above everyone else, surely she'd have told Ninexin about Mauricio. And she didn't breathe a word. Not to her mother. And not to Ignacio on their walks to Las Olas or on the Sunday afternoons when he'd take her out fishing and they'd pretend they were on Lake Cocibolca, hoping to catch some guapote for dinner.

Ninexin told me once that she thought Mariana should do more with her life, go into politics or diplomacy, public service of some kind. "Politics has claimed entirely too many members of this family already," I said, which quieted her down for a while. But in a way, she was right. Not that my Mariana should do more, because what greater contribution can there be than bringing beauty into the lives of others? But that she is the one who should have been a diplomat, not Ninexin. In all these decades I've had so much practice letting my thoughts go, left so many things unsaid, that sometimes even my mind is silent and all I can hear is my own breath. But my Mariana is young, she feels everything, thinks about it all. I can see her mind working when she doesn't know anyone is watching her. Her face changes so quickly, mirroring her thoughts; her eyes flicker when she's angry or hurt. And also when she's gathering information, trying to assess her own reaction, waiting until it's the right moment to speak. I see how she can yell in her mind and whisper with her voice, and isn't that what a diplomat should do? Feel things strongly yet speak softly enough to have her message heard?

It's my Mariana's fault, really, that I'm not sitting here thinking of Ignacio, reviewing our life together, blurring the hard edges and magnifying the moments of joy so that the marriage I remember is different from the one I lived, better. That is the job of the spouse who is left, revising.

But ever since my Mariana showed me the painting of the girl with the naked hands dropping the book, and the man in profile beaming at her, I've thought of nothing but Mauricio. People come and go, kissing my cheek, murmuring condolences, and they take my blank expression as shock, and my small smiles as gratitude for their kindness in doing what they can to mitigate my sorrow. When the truth is, I'm not spending every ounce of energy fighting my grief; I'm also, God help me, remembering each letter from Mauricio, each afternoon with him and Miss Birdie, each walk along the banquettes approaching Sacred Heart's gate as dusk fell and my curfew approached. The best I can do is to contain the smiles, keep them from erupting into grins.

By 1953, the end of my junior year, we had been together two years, and I was trying to puzzle out the best way to introduce him to the rest of the family, beyond just Dolly. She had kept our secret, although it bothered her, I know, that I had such a serious relationship and she didn't. At her graduation she would be almost twenty, marriage-able age for that time and our set. She never acknowledged it, though; she said she had no interest in walking out with anyone in New Or-leans, that she wouldn't even consider a suitor until she returned home to Granada. And when she did, she would reacquaint herself with the older brothers of the girls we'd played with as children, and see which one caught her eye. There were only a few families who were at the same level of society as our own, a handful, really, who had homes off the Parque Central, near the papaya-colored catedral, and of those only two, the de la Torres and the Ponces, had grand homes that matched ours. Our houses were lined up in a row along the plaza, and were so vast that the people of Granada called them, together, "the three worlds." It was like that, in a way; our families orbited each other. But that didn't mean that Dolly would have to marry one of the sons of the other two worlds; we weren't that provincial. There were other planets in our solar system, good families who lived a few streets away, or, slightly more mysterious, those who came to town on holidays to see friends but who lived in León or Managua, or out on their fincas. If she didn't like the looks of anyone in Granada, Dolly would start paying attention to our brothers' friends when they came to visit. She wasn't worried. She had a trim waist and a fat dowry; any Granadino—no, any Nicaragüense—would be lucky to marry her.

As for me, I would, of course, marry Mauricio. I never said as much to Dolly, because I didn't want her to think that I disapproved of her plan for a prudent marriage. I didn't; it made perfect sense. But I was one of the lucky ones, chosen to marry for love, to experience the kind of passion we read about in Connie's books. God had given me a gift by sending me Mauricio; I just had to find the best way to make sure His will was done, that no one interfered with His intentions.

I planned to introduce Mauricio to my parents at Dolly's graduation, without letting on how serious our relationship was, how long we had been together. And they would be so charmed by him, by his excellent manners and easy laugh, that they would suggest on their own that perhaps we might spend the occasional afternoon together—with a chaperone, of course—during my senior year, when Dolly would be gone and I'd be lonely. And perhaps that Christmas they might invite him to visit Nicaragua, and we'd announce our engagement on New Year's, to symbolize the start of a new life, a new family. Then we'd return to New Orleans, I would finish school, he'd complete his freshman year at Loyola, and we'd marry in the spring and settle down. After school he'd start working right away, managing his family's sugarcane business but on the import side, opening up an office based in New Orleans. My parents would miss me, but surely they were used to not having me around after three years? And it would give them a bit of prestige, to have a daughter settled in New Orleans, someone they could stop over and visit on their way to Paris each year. It would be Dolly who would feel my absence most of all. But she could visit, too, any time she wanted—we'd have a room just for her. And if she made the kind of marriage she planned on, she might stop in New Orleans en route to shop in Paris each fall, too.

The difficult part would be the initial introduction. It would have to be a carefully calibrated performance. I'd have to show that I held Mauricio in great esteem, that I cared about him, but not too much, because if my parents had known I was seeing anyone so often, or so intensely, they would have put a stop to it long ago. And of course, I wouldn't want to take away from Dolly's day; she'd be the one in a splendid white gown, collecting her diploma and well-deserved accolades. She was a far better student than I could hope to be, she had a drawer full of *Très Bien* ribbons, whereas I more often than not received plain old *Bien*. I could tell she wasn't entirely happy about this part of her life coming to an end. She respected the nuns, loved our friends. And she loved French and music even more—she was quite good at the piano; on weekends she would play for me and Mauricio and Miss Birdie and sometimes even Cristian Hidalgo.

I wanted to warn Dolly of my plan, so that she wouldn't be shocked, wouldn't feel that I had shanghaied her graduation. I needed to be sure that she understood that, in fact, I was doing the opposite: her graduation was such an important occasion that I had chosen it as the perfect time to bring together everyone I loved. And, to be honest, I'd need her help in convincing my parents there was nothing improper in my relationship with Mauricio.

So I sat next to her in the school courtyard, opposite the grotto of Our Lady, on the next Sunday that was an off-weekend, when the boys from St. Michael's didn't come and Mauricio and I had only our letters to sustain us. Dolly was trying to read and I had a notebook out as if I were working on an assignment. There was a piece of stationery on the inside, but I didn't want any of the nuns, or even another student such as Silvia, to notice that I was such an avid letter writer, so I kept it tucked between the ruled pages.

"I have something I have to tell you," I said in Spanish, although we were supposed to speak only English or French on campus. But Sunday afternoon, after Mass, was as relaxed as life got at Sacred Heart. Girls were milling about, gossiping away with each other; no one would be overly interested in our tête–à–tête.

Dolly looked alarmed, so I reassured her right away, "It's nothing bad; it's something wonderful, in fact. I just want you to know." I closed the notebook and looked directly at her. "I'm going to introduce Mauricio to Mama and Papa at your graduation."

She dropped her book, and when I reached to get it for her, she put out her hand to keep me back, picked it up herself, then took her time finding her page and slipping in a prayer card she had been using as a bookmark.

"Why would you go and do that, Isa?" she asked finally, gazing at me as she did at the blind beggar she always gave a nickel to when we crossed his corner on Saturdays to get our sodas at the Walgreens lunch counter. Her expression stung at first. But then I reminded myself that I shouldn't be the object of pity here. If anything, Dolly should be, bless her heart. She just didn't understand what it was like to love someone this way.

"He can meet them the day before or after, we can save the graduation day just for you," I rushed to placate her. "However you want us to do it. I know it's your weekend."

She looked down at her book as if she wished she could be reading it again. "I should never have let you see him that often," she said. "This is my fault."

"No!" I said, too loudly; Connie looked over at us from across the courtyard but she was being tutored by a senior girl and couldn't come and see what the fuss was about.

"You seemed to be so happy with him and we all had such pleasant afternoons together," Dolly continued. "But I thought you knew."

"I knew the minute I saw him," I said. "I knew God had sent me the man I was going to marry."

Dolly put her book down and reached for my hand. I pulled it away but she took it again and twined her fingers through mine the way she would when she was ten and I was nine and we were finally allowed to walk across the plaza to the repostería with our nanny following, instead of standing right between us, holding our arms all too firmly. Walking just the two of us felt like freedom, even though we knew there were watchful eyes immediately behind us. Freedom, but, with my hand in Dolly's, safety as well.

"Who is Mauricio, really?" Dolly asked. "We know nothing about his family or his people. He's Cuban, and Cristian says that the situation there—"

"I don't care what Cristian says." I finally succeeded in pulling my hand away.

"But think, Isa!" Dolly continued. "Where will you live? Here? Where we'll only see each other once a year? You'll lose us, not just me, but Mama and Papa and the whole family. The whole country, too: the Purísimas and Christmas, the Güegüense and Easter. Our whole life. And if you live there . . . what if you hate his family? What if his mother moves in with you, even in New Orleans? It happens. Right now he's a student in a city where he has no ties, but who is he deep down? What will your life be like with him? And without us? And what will I do without you?"

I hadn't considered what Dolly would do without me. The truth is, I hadn't considered any of them at all. It never occurred to me that they wouldn't all be there, in the back of my mind if not in person, on holidays. In Mass on Sundays. When my children were born. But even as I listened to Dolly and knew that what she was saying made sense, I also knew, sure as I did my own name, that it didn't matter. I would always keep Dolly, and the others, close in my thoughts and in my prayers. But I could—and would—start my life over again if that's what I had to do to be with Mauricio. In chapel in the morning, the nuns often spoke of fulfilling the destiny God chose for us, of listening for His call, and not just hearing Him but acting on His desires with a willing heart. Hadn't He brought me and Mauricio together, in this city where neither of us had been born? Hadn't He made me drop my book, made Mauricio notice me despite Silvia's pleats and emeralds? Hadn't He created two people who agreed so harmoniously on everything—the best po'boy, the best psalm, the kind of life a young couple starting out could create? It would be a sin not to follow the path God had shown me.

Dolly and I sat in silence. Somehow our hands had found each other again, our fingers intertwined. Finally she squeezed my palm and said, "You have one more year. Enjoy it if you can. But if you think that extra time will make you sadder when you have to part—or reckless while you're here without me—then say good-bye to Mauricio before we go back to Granada." She put her other hand on the outside of mine. "But just know—and I tell you this because I don't want you to be hurt—that if Mama and Papa so much as see Mauricio's face and suspect anything, there's no way they will even consider sending you back here next year."

She dropped my hands to open her book to the marked page. "I won't tell them, I promise," she said, as if talking to the pages. "I won't ruin things for you. Just be sure you don't ruin things for yourself."

It was starting to get dark and the other girls had left the courtyard. The air was still and heavy, and there was nothing but the noise of Dolly turning her page. But in my mind, that soft swish was the sound of my world crashing down around me.

15

Ninexin

I'm quite sure that I didn't faint at all. I just lost my footing as I went to stand, maybe my heel slipped on the overly polished floor. I believe you have to lose consciousness for it to count as fainting and I don't think I even closed my eyes. It's just that one moment I was trying to stand, keeping my eye on Mariana and that tall gringo, in case she needed me, and the next I was on the floor and poor Ignacito was crying while Rigobertito squeezed my wrist, feeling for my pulse. When I sat up I saw that the group from the office had the good sense to stop a respectful distance away. I was still feeling a little dizzy—I think the last thing I ate was a pasta de pollo sandwich back at the office, and that was probably around noon. So I looked over at Celia and Rigobertito and said, "Help me up, already. I can't sit here all night."

Rigobertito grabbed my right arm and I could feel his strength, he was practically lifting me, not just supporting my elbow. But it was

Celia, jasmine-scented Celia, whom I wanted near, so I clutched her arm with my left hand and listed her way as we stood.

"Gracias a Dios!" she said, as I righted myself.

"I just slipped," I insisted. "I'm fine."

"Well, gracias a Dios for that, too," Celia said. "But also, thank heavens you weren't wearing a skirt."

I looked at her face; she was completely serious. I mean, she was right, of course, it would have been horrible to flash my underwear at my entire staff and offer a free show to my father's surviving friends, perhaps inciting a heart attack or two, adding to the death toll. But it was also such a ridiculous thought, so sweet and silly, so Celia, that I started laughing, softly at first, then way too loud, and soon Celia joined in, too, and we were laughing and crying and hugging again.

I felt a hand on my shoulder and turned to see Mariana, coming to join the embrace. But when I put my arm around her, she patted my shoulder once and slid away from me, in the guise of kissing her tía Celia hello. I shouldn't say it like that. I'm sure she was genuinely excited to see her aunt. Celia had been a big part of her life in Miami; she was there to sign permission slips and help with Mariana's homework after school. I'm sure Mariana would say, if asked, that she had been moving toward her tía Celia, not away from me. Not that I would ever ask, of course.

"Maybe we should start making our good-byes and heading home," Mariana said. "I think we're all a little strung out."

She looked at me hard, a gaze I hadn't seen since she was in high school.

"I'm fine, really, amor," I insisted.

"Well, let's just say this is too much for my Bela, then," Mariana said. "Please, Madre." I shouldn't have felt so glad that Mariana seemed so worried about me. And maybe she wasn't, maybe she was tired from the trip and the drama of the day, or she really felt that Mama had reached her limit. Mama did need her rest. She'd be burying her husband in the morning. My tía Dolores had arrived and was in her wheelchair, sitting opposite Mama, holding her hand. Mama was looking down, as if about to cry, but I couldn't see any tears from where I stood. They seemed like they needed a minute or two more to hold on to each other. I looked at Mariana, clasping her own hands together, perhaps trying to look self-contained, but appearing only forlorn. She didn't have a sister to lean into, and this was another way I had failed her.

"I'll just greet my coworkers and thank them for coming." I gave Celia's arm a final squeeze and turned toward Mariana. "You visit with your tía Celia for a bit, and then we'll take Mama home."

As I walked over to my colleagues I remembered that Mariana had her own good-byes to make. But, scanning the room, I realized the gringo was nowhere in sight.

16

Maria

It shouldn't take Madre too long to say good-bye; she's had lots of practice. On the other hand, she wouldn't rush this; the people she works with are important to her.

Allen often refers to "the spirit of the stairs," except he says it in French, *l'esprit de l'escalier.* Like all great artists, Allen has lived in Paris. Unlike those of us amateurs, who tend to summer in Managua. But in any language, the phrase means the same thing: the act of thinking of the perfect retort once you're walking away from your combatant. I need to come up with a different phrase for the phenomenon I have with Madre; I always have the perfect remark while she's right in front of me, it's just that only half the time, I have the good sense not to make it.

I'm not under any delusion that this restraint makes me a good person. Maybe just a cowardly one. If I were truly a good person, I wouldn't think these things, wouldn't blame Madre for building a life that, when I'm content with my own, I have to admit makes me proud.

But the prouder I am, the more inadequate I feel. My mother has been chosen, again and again, to represent a new nation she's helped build. She's spent afternoons talking to François Mitterand and Fidel Castro. She's a badass! And I'm just an ass. There's a squalling baby inside me whining, "Why do you have to do all these impressive things? Why isn't just being my mother enough?"

I can't begin to fathom how to stop asking that question. I want to, but I can't imagine the therapist skilled enough or the pill blissful enough or the achievement satisfying enough finally to do the trick. And it's getting worse with age, not better. As my own future looms more terrifying, more unknowable than ever, her controlled life seems like more of a reproach.

Tía Celia hugs me, and as I'm drawn into her embrace I realize that my mother was right again. This is what I needed: the comfort of Tía Celia's soft body, of her familiar smell, that jasmine perfume that is way too young for her. There was a time in high school when I tried to get her to change, gave her some vanilla-scented cologne (she likes sweets), and, later, a mélange of different, more sophisticated white flowers for her birthday or Mother's Day. She always used the perfumes I got her dutifully but sparingly, saying she liked to save them for special occasions. And in between, she went around smelling like a Disney princess. Madre told me once that there was a jasmine bush in their yard growing up, that at her debutante ball and, not too much later, her wedding, Tía Celia wore the flowers entwined in her upswept black hair. In high school, I wrote a science paper about how the part of the brain that controls scent and the part that manages memory are located in the same, wrinkled cortex. And I'm starting to suspect that Tía Celia, in her mind, is still stuck at nineteen, that as long as she smells the way she did back then, she thinks she'll still be that girl with the multiple suitors all vying to hold her white-gloved hand.

Right now I'm wearing an essential oil Allen bought me on his last trip to India. But I don't think I'll still be using the scent in twenty-five years. A few feet away, my Bela and my gran-tía Dolores are holding hands, staring at each other, offering each other unspoken comfort, and although I'm yards away, I know from experience that the one smells like Shalimar and the other like Chanel No 5. Both smell strong and complicated and expensive. As they are.

Madre starts walking across the room toward us and I wish I could identify a scent for her, something I could bottle and sniff when I wanted to pretend she was close. But she always smells like herself. Like soap and laundry detergent and coffee and mystery.

17

Isabela

And here I thought that this would be boring—I was tempted to bring a book," Dolly says, and I stare at her, confused.

"Oh, come on, Isabela, it was a joke," she says. "Of course I wanted to be here no matter what, to pay my respects to Ignacio. I'm just trying to make you laugh. And it's true, I never expected so much drama."

"What do you mean?" I finally ask and Dolly wheels her chair a little closer.

"You didn't hear the crash?" she whispers. "See the muchacho fall, Ninexin faint?"

"My Ninexin? That's ridiculous, she's right over there with those other young people." My Ninexin would sooner break into a tap dance routine at her father's calling hours than faint in public. Dolly grabs my hand and sighs as if I'm the one losing my grasp on reality. Need I remind her who's older? It's only natural that she'd start talking nonsense first.

"You're upset," she says, as if she'd know what this feels like, as if her husband isn't sitting in a chair across the room, one elbow propped up on his cane, leaning forward to whisper to his son, probably giving him financial advice. "It's not just the end for Ignacio, it's the end for you, too, of this part of your life."

"The life you chose for me," I say, and she pulls her hand away, then takes out the collectible gold Estée Lauder compact Francisco gets her each year at Christmas and busies herself powdering her nose.

I'm glad the nuns can't see her now. They taught us never to apply makeup in public. If you have to take a quick look in your compact mirror, that is fine, but if that glance shows you have lipstick on your teeth or a shine on your forehead, a lady must always excuse herself to go take care of whatever minor repairs she deems necessary. That is, after all, why they call it a powder room.

But Dolly never did very well in Comportment; it was the one class in which I received *Très Bien* and she plain old *Bien*, and once, when she was caught reading a biography of Eleanor Roosevelt during a lesson on table manners, just *Assez Bien*. Dolly was a bit like Ninexin when she was younger; not as bold or as willful, but just as preoccupied with the few issues that interested her. She thought where you reapplied your makeup didn't matter much. She didn't realize that it is a sign of respect for others that you not perform your toilette in front of them. And of respect for yourself, that you aren't inviting dozens of strangers into your private moments, into your bedroom or dressing area. Sometimes the smallest choices matter the most of all. Dolly always tells me I worry too much about appearances. She doesn't understand that if everything about you appears normal, and polished, you can hide in plain sight. No one will look any deeper.

That's how it was that June in the last week before her graduation.

The weekend after our talk in the garden, Mauricio came up to visit. Dolly had been chosen to play the piano for the hymn we would all sing at the ceremony and had a rehearsal with Sister Harris, and Cristian Hidalgo was giving the senior girls rides up and down Canal Street in his car one last time. Mauricio and Miss Birdie and I were free to be alone together, so we took the streetcar to Audubon Park to enjoy our po'boys in the open air; there was a café in the park then . . . maybe there still is? And after we'd finished eating, Mauricio suggested that Miss Birdie sit and enjoy a glass of wine or a slice of cake—or both—while we took a turn around the park.

"That's a lovely idea, *cher!*" she agreed. "Just stay on this side of the oaks where I can see you."

We walked at an unhurried pace, not touching, me with my gloved hands resting against my own back. I had to force myself not to speed up or gesticulate as I told Mauricio about my talk with Dolly. I had written him right afterward, but all I thought safe to put in the letter was that Dolly seemed upset about graduation and I felt very sad both for her and for me, but I would tell him more in person. That way if anyone intercepted and read the message, they would think I was merely dejected at the thought of missing my sister next year. But he knew that I meant the talk didn't go well—how could he not? We were so enmeshed with each other by then that I often had the strangest feeling throughout the day that I knew what he was thinking, if he was in a good mood or bad, if his economics class had gone well.

"So Dolly thinks it would be a mistake for me to speak to your father at graduation," he said as soon as we were out of earshot of the café. He had led me to a fountain where Miss Birdie could see us, but the sound of rushing water would keep even those close to us, those who weren't currently digging into a brick-size piece of chess pie, from making out our words.

"I didn't even get to that," I said. "I just brought up the idea of you meeting them, both of them, just saying hello, not discussing anything important or specific, just making your presence known."

"And she said it would be a mistake?"

"A disaster; she said it would be a disaster." And then, I added more softly, almost whispering, "She said they wouldn't send me back to finish school alone if they knew."

Mauricio nodded but didn't say anything.

"It's not you." I rushed to fill the silence. "She likes you. It's just she's worried she'll never see me again, and if they don't want me to end up settling down so far from home, she thinks—"

"She hinted as much to Cristian." Mauricio waved his hand as if neither Dolly nor Cristian nor his navy roadster mattered. And then he looked at me. "This doesn't change anything for me, Isa," he said. And I felt his hand on my right elbow, where it was blocked from Miss Birdie's view by my torso.

"Or for me."

"So it's settled then." He gave my elbow a squeeze before taking his hand away. "We'll still get married; it will just have to be much sooner."

"Before I graduate?"

"Before Dolly graduates."

I sat on the edge of the fountain, not caring that my new seersucker sundress from D. H. Holmes was getting wet, the pink stripes darkening into red.

"Things are changing in Cuba, fast," he said. "I had a letter from my brother, and I'm going to have to go home this summer to look after the business, transfer some funds to our accounts here." He took a breath, as if he were about to explain to me the ins and outs of the family corporation, what he had to do with their accounts and why, but then he just smiled. "And you'll have to come with me. It's the only way to make sure they don't bring you back to Granada with them and keep you there."

Right away I thought that Mauricio was crazy. Who would marry us—not the priest at school, that was certain. And what would I wear? I couldn't just throw together a wedding gown in a few weeks. But then, seeing him grinning at me, there was nothing I could do but smile back. "Yes," I said. "Of course! I mean, I do."

Mauricio laughed. "I'd kneel, but under the circumstances . . ." He nodded at Miss Birdie, who was beckoning to us from her seat, the plate in front of her empty.

Now, so many decades later, I can barely believe that I agreed, that I was able to keep it a secret. Not from everyone, of course; I needed to tell Connie I was meeting Mauricio, so she wouldn't be surprised when Betsy came to get me after curfew one night, and snuck me out through the laundry room. But Connie had no idea that we weren't going to the French Quarter to hear music, or to have a late supper, or even to rent a hotel room, but uptown to meet with Father Antony, the priest at Holy Name church at Loyola, who had been advising Mauricio since before he first applied to the university. "It's about time!" Connie said when I told her I was sneaking out to see Mauricio on a Wednesday night, that it was our last chance to be alone together before my parents arrived for the graduation festivities that weekend.

When I returned, Connie woke up briefly to ask, "Do you feel different?"

"So different," I told her. And it was true: after speaking with the priest, I felt like an adult, someone capable of making her own decisions, shaping her future. It turned out that Father Antony wasn't that much older than Mauricio, maybe ten years. And he couldn't refuse when Mauricio told him that whether he liked it or not we were going to be married in the eyes of the law, and we'd like to be married in the eyes of the Church as well.

The priest focused his dark eyes on me and asked, "Is this what you want, too, my child?"

And I looked right back at him and said, "We have to go to Cuba to help Mauricio's family, Father. So we have to be together now. And we don't want to sin."

Over fifty years later, it's still the moment I'm proudest of in my life. By letting him know we'd be leaving the country in each other's company, I made it impossible for him to turn us down. There was no way he could stop us from marrying legally, he could just deprive us of God's blessing. In which case, the real sin would be to turn us away.

Father Antony asked us some questions about my religious education and if we thought my parents would turn their backs on us once they heard we had eloped. I told them the truth, that I knew my family would come to love Mauricio as much as I did one day. Then he gave Mauricio instructions about witnesses and signatures, and we agreed that we would return to the church on Saturday at 4:00 P.M., after the graduation ceremony was over, but before dinner, when everyone else would be resting. My parents regularly took a siesta, especially while traveling. And the girls at school would be so busy packing and writing in each other's yearbooks, no one would notice if I were missing for an hour. It would be just a quick ceremony, not a full Mass; Cristian would be our witness. As soon as it was over he'd speed us back down to school, where I'd melt back into the chaos of the last few days of the year. That night at dinner, Mauricio would show up to take the extra place I'd called Arnaud's and arranged for, and if my parents weren't charmed by him—which I was sure they would be—and they started to issue warnings or threats, we'd tell them it was too late: we were already married. And so happy. And we hoped that, in time, they'd be happy for us, too.

I wanted to wear white on my wedding day, but that color was reserved for the graduating girls. So I settled for an eyelet dress with a white bodice and pale blue skirt, and a matching blue bolero jacket, an ensemble I had found at Maison Blanche when Madre was in town en route to Paris in the fall, and still hadn't had occasion to wear. The dress had puffy little white sleeves, so when I took the jacket off in church, it would be almost like wearing a white dress. And, best of all, it went with a blue hat that had a white birdcage veil. Since the headpiece matched the dress, no one would ever think of it as a bridal veil. Except for me and Mauricio. And Father Antony, if he thought about those things.

Madre and Padre had arrived the previous afternoon, and dinner that evening had been so fun, so full of the stories that made us *us:* about weekends at Abuelo's finca, when we would watch the sweet old horses he pretended belonged to each one of us have races, each cheering on "our" pet, or about our brother Teodoro, who was so in-tent on spending all his money on his girlfriend that he walked across the parque every morning to sit on the wide porch of the club and read *La Prensa* there, saving himself from actually having to buy the newspaper. I felt tears in my eyes at one point at the thought that I wouldn't be there to mock him with Dolly, to sit across from him and say, "Whenever you're done with that paper, caballero." Or to be there for Ana Carolina's last few years at home before she, too, came to Sacred Heart. I missed them all already.

"There's nothing to cry about, silly girl." Madre leaned over and patted me on the shoulder. "I know you'll miss your sister, but it's just for one year!"

Padre added, "We'll make sure Dolly doesn't get married and move away while you're still in New Orleans," and Dolly blushed, then reached for the breadbasket so that the movement would keep us all from noticing. Keep our parents from seeing that she was blushing, rather; I knew her too well for her to be able to hide such a thing from me.

The morning of the graduation, I watched as the senior girls lined up in the courtyard while we all clapped for them from the porch, then I ran upstairs to Dolly's room to leave a graduation present on her bed—a heavy silver frame with a photo Mauricio had taken of her and me in Cristian's car, laughing, her leaning back so hard her hat had almost fallen off. Along with it was a note that said, *I'm sorry if I disappointed you. I will miss you whenever I'm not with you, and I will always love you. Your sister.*

She wouldn't realize what I meant until after dinner, but no matter. I couldn't just leave a present without a note.

During the graduation ceremony, the mistress general talked on, as she liked to do, about honor and how they had tried to inculcate us with it, and, in turn, all they asked was that we act in a way that would further burnish the name of Sacred Heart. I felt a little guilty as she spoke, knowing what I was about to do, but then I told myself that I was acting honorably: getting married in the Catholic Church was exactly what a good Sacred Heart girl should do. I bet some of the North American girls would have just run off to Cuba first and asked questions about marriage certificates later.

The ceremony was lovely; Dolly was even lovelier. When our

parents went back to their hotel to rest, I gave her a hug and told her how proud I was of her, how I couldn't have come here, to school in a foreign country, in a foreign language, without her.

"Some of the seniors are going to the Walgreens counter for malteds," she said. "The mistress general said we've proven how responsible we are, we don't even need a chaperone! Come on, it'll be fun."

"I still have so much packing," I told her. "And you know Connie always spends the last day of school sitting on my bed, watching me pack, talking about the trouble she plans to get in over the summer."

I actually congratulated myself, watching Dolly leave. It had been the perfect thing to say. And when I got back to the room and Connie wasn't there, I was sure it was another good omen. I picked up the notebook on her bedside table and wrote, *Out with my family; join us for dinner tonight at Arnaud's at 8?*

Giving her a place to meet me later would keep her from wondering where I was now. Plus, it might be good to have a buffer. My parents would never speak in anger in front of a well-bred young lady like Connie. I congratulated myself again. And then I picked up my rosary and walked downstairs, humming, until I reached the laundry room door. There I knocked five times quickly and, when I heard Betsy's two knocks back, slipped into the room and out the back door where Cristian Hidalgo's navy car stood waiting. I'd never seen anything more beautiful.

Until we got to Holy Name and there was Mauricio waiting for me. I couldn't believe that I would get to sit across from this person every day at breakfast, and again at dinner. And even more incredible, that he wanted to see me every day, too.

"Shall we begin?" Father Antony asked. Everyone there looked at me—Mauricio, Cristian, Father Antony, and an old woman dressed in black who was sitting in a pew near the front; I didn't know if she was just one of those old women who seem to grow out of the pews in Catholic churches like fruit on a branch, or if Father Antony had asked her there as a second witness, but seeing her made me miss my own abuela, and, at the same time, made me wish I had taken someone into my confidence and asked a friend to stand up with me, to act as my maid of honor. But Dolly would have seen attending as betraying our parents, and Connie couldn't have kept the secret longer than it took for her to comprehend the request. I had asked Betsy to come, assuming that this priest wouldn't mind a Negro girl in his church. At home the morenitos and the chelitos worshiped together; it must have been the same in this city, too. But she had to work that afternoon, laundering the tablecloths from the graduation reception.

I smiled at the funny old woman all in black, then nodded at Mauricio and the priest, and looped my arm through Cristian Hidalgo's, who had just been elected, by me, to walk me down the aisle. We started the slow procession, and then I stopped.

"Isa?" Mauricio said. "Are you okay?"

"There's no music! I always imagined that I would walk down the aisle to music." I laughed, because I knew it was silly. I'd always envisioned myself walking down the aisle on my father's arm, not Cristian Hidalgo's, and assumed that I'd be wearing a custom-made gown, not a cotton sundress. But somehow it was the music that stopped me. "'Ave Maria,'" I clarified.

"Wait!" Father Antony said. "Stay here!" He ran out of the side door of the church; it looked like he was heading behind it, toward Loyola's school buildings. In a few minutes we heard a large crash.

"Maybe we should get this show on the road?" Cristian started toward the door Father Antony had disappeared through, but Mauricio put a hand on his shoulder. "Isa's missing enough other things today. We have a couple of minutes for him to find music."

It wasn't very long before the priest came rushing through the door with a little boy following. At first I thought the boy was going to sing, but then I saw he was holding a record player. Father Antony had him sit cross-legged in the nave, near the only electrical outlet I could see in the church. He placed the record player on the boy's lap, took the album he was carrying out of its sleeve, and put it on the turntable. The boy's eyes followed Father Antony's hand as he slowly lifted the needle and lowered it onto the shiny black surface. There was scratching and static and then a woman's voice filled the church, filled it with a sound that added up the love of God and the love a mother has for her child and the love I had for Mauricio, a sound so big that I could hear each word echo, so big that they must have been able to hear it out on the street.

Now Father Antony was back in front of the altar and he and Mauricio were staring at me. Father Antony looked as if he were holding his breath, wondering was this the right "Ave Maria," or did we have a different version in Nicaragua? But Mauricio was smiling as widely as I was. Hearing the woman singing behind the scratches and the echoes, he must have felt as I did: that now, everything was perfect.

Cristian walked as if he were born to escort a bride down the aisle; his carriage erect, his face pleasant but impassive, as if hundreds of people were watching him instead of just Mauricio, Father Antony, the old widow, and the little boy in the short pants who was really looking more at the record player anyway.

The singer on the record repeated each verse one more time than I was used to, but this was perfect, too. Given Cristian's stately pace, and the way I wanted to absorb every sight and sound of this moment as I walked away from one life and toward another, her version seemed perfectly timed to get me down the aisle. I am sure she would have stopped holding that final, glorious note the moment I stepped into my place next to Mauricio.

But I'll never know. Because before I reached the end, the front doors of the church burst open and there stood my father, Dolly, Connie, and Betsy.

The widow crossed herself but the rest of us near the altar remained still, absorbing the impact of the slamming doors, and stared at the small clump of people massed around my father, who stood in the middle, radiating quiet anger.

"Madre?" I asked, realizing she was missing.

"I wanted to spare her this," my father said in Spanish.

"Señor Enriquez." Mauricio stepped forward. "It's unfortunate that we meet under these circumstances, but I assure you that–"

"Your assurances mean nothing," my father said in a low, controlled voice. "As for this meeting it will be our first and last, so don't waste your regret."

"Nevertheless," Mauricio continued. "Isa and I are in love and—"

"And she is not a citizen of this country and, if I'm not mistaken, you are not either. I have friends in our government and in yours who could make life very difficult for you, and perhaps your family, should you choose to defy me and attempt to continue with this childish scheme."

"Then I suppose it's my turn to say that your words mean nothing to me," Mauricio said, matching Papa's commanding tone with a haughty confidence I had never heard before; for the first time, his voice was entirely without warmth or humor. It softened a bit when he said, "Perhaps we should ask Isa what she thinks."

They all turned toward me. I searched for a sympathetic face to guide me but Mauricio's was so hopeful that it hurt; the force of his determination, willing me what to say, threatened to smother me. Dolly and Padre looked angry, Connie pained, and Betsy, she just looked afraid.

As she had so often in our childhoods, Dolly spoke so that I wouldn't have to. "I thought we agreed, Isabela," she said, "that you wouldn't give up all of us, all our life, for someone we barely know."

"You know me, Dolly!" Mauricio extended his arm as if to reach for me or her, but finally settled his hand on Cristian's shoulder.

"I know you as a boy who is pleasant to talk to on weekend excursions in between exams. I don't know who your family is or what your prospects are or what kind of husband you would be for my sister." She had kept her eyes on the aisle runner as she spoke, but now she glanced up at him and said, more quietly, "I'm sorry, Mauricio. It's my job to protect her."

"How did you know?" I asked, because as terrible as this moment was, if we all stayed focused on it, if it never ended, I wouldn't have to begin a future without anyone in this church.

"Connie walked into the Walgreens." Dolly shrugged. "She assumed you were with me, I thought you were with her. Then I remembered the note you left me this morning, and I got worried. We checked the sign-out at the gate and your name wasn't on it, so I knew there was only one person who could have helped you leave school. The same person Connie said had helped you before."

Betsy looked down at the floor, but before she could speak, Connie stood in front of her. "If you'd trusted me," she said, then stopped, short of breath, and I realized she was crying. "If you'd told me what you were up to, I could have helped you. But you didn't." Cristian stepped over to hand her his handkerchief, but she pressed her wet face into his clean lapel instead, muttering, "I would have trusted you."

"Isa," I heard Mauricio's voice behind me. "Tell your father what you want to do."

"Come with me," Dolly pleaded, grabbing my hand. "We've been together this long and had a swell time so far. I don't want to live the next part of our lives—the best part—without you. Why don't you want to live it with me? Have I been such a bad sister?"

She reached out and swept her hand across my cheek; I must have been crying, too.

"Come back with us and we need never speak of this again," my father said, stepping closer to us, putting his arm around Dolly, the daughter who had yet to disappoint him. "No one in Granada will know what happened here. We'll say you and Dolly chose to return together and that you're finishing your classes by correspondence. That's what we'll tell the mistress general and the Reverend Mother, too; no one at Sacred Heart has to know. If word of this got out, the school's reputation would suffer as much as yours—what parents would send their daughters to a place where this could happen? Come home and you can have your own room, your own life. Come home and the negrita can keep her job."

I felt Mauricio's hand on my shoulder. If he had been standing in front of me instead of behind me, if I had been looking at him, maybe I would have been strong enough to do what I knew was right. What God wanted. What I wanted. But he was behind me and in front of me were Dolly, Papa, Connie, and Betsy, each with eyes wide with anger or pain or fear. I wish I had been looking at him, but I was looking at them. I was looking at them, and when Papa turned his back toward me and started walking out of the church, walking away from me forever, I took a step forward and I followed. With Dolly holding my arm, I walked back up the aisle I had just come down, toward everything I knew and away from everything I wanted.

18

Ninexin

FRIDAY, JANUARY 9, 2009

We have a deal, Celia and I. She tells me what beauty products a woman of our generation should use, and I buy them on my trips to the U.S. The putty-colored lotion I put on my face this morning is supposed to do three things: hydrate my slowly desiccating skin, even my blotchy tone, and smooth my ever-deepening "fine lines." I know all this because if a product costs more than I think it should, she gives me its résumé, telling me how and why it's the most incredible cosmetic invented and the only one we could possibly use. But I think that I might have to start doing my own research. Because when I looked in the mirror by the door as I left the house this morning, I saw an old woman. Not old like mama, a survivor, someone with stories to tell. But tired. Beaten. Someone who had given up. I configured my features into the blank stare I find so useful at conferences but I still didn't look strong, just sour. Maybe this is what happens when a parent dies. Your generation moves up in line, one step closer to death.

I didn't give my appearance much thought at the time, but when I faced death daily, I was beautiful. There's a photo Manuel took of me in Matagalpa, napping against a tree trunk, my gun propped up next to me. Aside from training, I never did much shooting; I was more involved in outreach, talking with the local women, explaining their rights and what we were fighting for, getting them to organize, demonstrate for better conditions for prisoners, and set up safe houses to hide and protect us. I also volunteered at the local grammar school, which served as a great place to spread our message without suspicion. But we were soldiers in the mountain jungle, after all; you needed a gun for protection. I knew how to shoot and I was prepared to use the gun to defend myself.

In the picture, it looks like defending myself is the last thing on my mind. My hair is coming out of its braid, my jacket is slipping off my shoulder, and in my sleep, I almost seem to be smiling. I've never been a very good sleeper. I wake up and can't get back to sleep, and when I do, I somehow twist myself up until the bedding becomes like a winding sheet and I wake up struggling to free my arms. Mama says that as a baby, I had colic that kept me up all night; even then I didn't sleep well. But you would never know it from this photo, in which I look calm and rested and so young, like I had no worries at all. I suppose I only had one—I felt guilty for rushing off so mysteriously, so soon after our wedding, without telling my parents where we were going, or anything other than the fact that we were mobilizing, and it would be safer for them if they had no idea where we were. I doubted the National Guard would show up at their home, looking for us; Manuel and I were still pretty small potatoes in the Frente at that point. But I still felt terrible about putting my parents, and Celia, in any danger by association. In at least two cases I knew about, the parents of our friends in the Movimiento had been arrested and tortured.

Manuel and I suspected—or hoped—that our fathers' status as successful professionals would protect them from that, but for how long?

These were the concerns that normally kept me alert, after I'd snap awake from a bad dream in the late night or early morning, shaking, until Manuel soothed me and told me we were doing the right thing, so that no one would ever have to fear for his or her parents or children again. The only time I really slept well was during the first trimester of my pregnancy, when I wanted to sleep all the time. But if I'm pregnant in this picture it's a question of days. I always thought that Mariana was conceived in Matagalpa. It's my own private theory. I feel that I know the exact moment, although that verges on ludicrous. I'm aware, from the population control seminars I've been to, that sperm lives in the body for up to three days. That shocked me, that you don't actually get pregnant in the throes of passion, in the honeymoon hotel room or by the banks of the River of Dreams, but that the conception can happen up to three days after the act itself; you're writing a speech or talking to a community group, and some slow-swimming sperm is diving into your egg at that very moment. And that's how we all start out. It's so prosaic as to be depressing. But it's also kind of funny. I said as much to Mariana when I got back from the World Population Control conference the year she was fifteen, but she said, "Please, not while I'm eating," and made gagging noises into the phone. It reminded me of the time I tried to explain menstruation to her on a visit to Miami when she was ten, and she told me they'd seen a movie in gym class. She was perfectly civil about it, but she still managed to make it clear that I was not invited to visit the part of her consciousness that considered intimate topics like her body.

I abided by her boundaries. She can say what she wants to about my skills as a mother, but I did always know when to go away. I've always respected her privacy, accepted that there are vast areas of her life that she hopes I'll have nothing to do with. And so she doesn't know that I think she was conceived in Matagalpa, sometime during that same four-month stint when Manuel took my favorite photo of myself. Is it horrible to have a favorite photo that's a portrait of just you? Mariana would think it is. If I were telling her this story, that's what she would come away with, the fact that I have a favorite image of myself. But I hope she has one of herself hidden away somewhere, too. Because what I love about the photo is how unself-conscious I seem in it, how happy. It's the one picture I have of myself in which I truly look blissful.

In any case, I was in Matagalpa winning hearts and minds, and Manuel and his unit were there, too, training and planning various missions he said it was best I didn't know about; this way if either of us was captured we would have little incriminating information to conceal or reveal about the other. Having said the same thing to my parents, I knew he was right. We set off for Matagalpa right after getting married; in a way it was our honeymoon. I know that sounds horrible—a honeymoon in the mountains complete with guns and mud-filled boots and fellow revolutionaries. But the truth is, I felt so happy despite the discomfort, despite my guilt over worrying my parents. Manuel's gift was his ability to feel joy and passion, and I sometimes felt I was a vampire, sucking it out of him, turning his happiness into my own. But his excitement, at just being alive, never seemed to diminish. His passion was why I fell in love with him. He talked about tutoring children in the poor neighborhoods like it was the most enjoyable, most fascinating experience one could have; and he was right, in a way, although being with him was my favorite experience of all, better than family parties or a great book, better even than helping others, making a difference. But when I joined him in visiting those families, speaking to the parents, holding the babies, seeing a slow smile spread across the face of a child as she realized that she understood how to carry the one or read the three-word sentence, it really was a kind of high.

So we were in love with each other and with our cause, and then there was Matagalpa itself. It was so lush it overflowed with leaves and vines and swollen green pods holding coffee beans. It also overflowed with mud the fall we were there but to us, even that was kind of delightful, in a disgusting sort of way. Every night we would sit in front of our tent, blocked from the view of the other soldiers, and Manuel would pull off my boots and we'd laugh, watching the mud slide out of them. Then he would take one of my feet in his hands and rub the feeling back into my toes.

One afternoon when he was done training and I wasn't due in the village until that evening, when a sympathetic local priest had said he would let me speak to the congregation after Mass, I suggested we go to the river and wash our uniforms. It was November and rainy season was coming to an end, so it was a safe bet we'd have several hours of sunshine to dry the most important items. The locals called it the River of Dreams, which sounds poetic, but they used it for everything from bathing their bodies to brushing their teeth. I'd seen some other soldiers rinsing cooking utensils downstream where the river calmed a bit, but Manuel wanted to head upstream, where he said the current would be stronger, and leave the clothes cleaner. "God's washing machine," he said, winking. It seemed less funny after we'd hiked up a cow path for twenty-five minutes; no matter how clean the clothes got, I couldn't see how we'd be able to carry them back through the brush without covering them—and us—in mud and leaves again. But then Manuel grinned and said, "Hear it?" And when I listened, there it was: the sound of rushing water. After several more minutes of hiking, the path ended and the jungle opened onto a cascade rushing into a natural pool.

First Manuel dropped one sock into the churning water. Then the other. Then I threw in the entire bundle of clothes I'd been carrying. He took off his shoes and belt, then his pants, shirt, under-shirt, and shorts, and jumped into the water. I took off my shoes and belt and jumped in after him fully clothed. I was going to wash my uniform anyway, and why should I bother taking it off when he could do that for me?

That night at Mass, I mentioned to one of the women that I'd seen the most beautiful waterfall that day, and she told me that it had first been spotted by a wandering priest who described it as being as strong and pure as the tears of the Virgin Mary, and the villagers still called it Cascada Lágrimas de la Virgen. If Manuel and I had known the name, we might not have acted as we did that afternoon in the pond. But when I found out I was pregnant a few months after leaving Matagalpa, I vowed that if I had a daughter, I would name her Mariana, of Maria, for the Virgen.

Mariana's conception may not have happened that day. It could have happened three days after or two weeks before or a week later; we were in Matagalpa for four months and, although there was a war on, we were newlyweds and the abundance of trees in a jungle made it a prime spot for many things beyond just guerrilla warfare. But if the peaceful look on my face in that photo isn't due to Mariana and the hormonal storms she created, it is still thanks to Manuel, and his in-fectious happiness, the way he could find not just excitement, but also joy, in any setting, the way he could turn a battlefield into a fairyland.

⁂

I dreamed of Matagalpa last night, sleeping in the guest room of my parents' home. I'd slept over because I wanted Mama to have as much company as possible after the calling hours, and Mariana was staying there, too, in what used to be my old room. This way, we could all ride to the funeral together. When Mariana came to get me this morning, I saw her reflection before I saw her. I had been staring in the mirror that's hung by the front door, thinking how Celia's coveted cream wasn't working, and remembering the photo, and I didn't hear Mariana walk into the foyer, down the long hall from my parents' bedroom. My mother's bedroom now.

"The hearse is here," she said as her reflection came into view. "My Bela wants us all to ride behind it, in her car. But she said maybe you want to have a driver bring the office car, too, in case people leave early and someone needs a ride back?"

I realized I was holding my breath. Sometimes, when I see Mariana, I have the same feeling I did when I was sixteen and rushing to meet Manuel: excitement and nerves and disbelief that I'm somehow connected to someone so beautiful. It sounds like bragging to say your daughter is beautiful; okay, it is bragging. But it's also a fact. Mariana is attractive, anyone would agree. But this morning, in the mirror, it was more than that; she seemed imbued with some of Manuel's magic, with the rushing power of the waterfall. She was young and forceful and so unbelievably beautiful.

"Are you okay, Mama?" she asked. I must have been scaring her, standing there, not speaking, because she hasn't called me "mama" since she was six years old.

"I'm fine, mi corazón," I said, finally turning around. "I'll just go splash some water on my face." I patted her on the shoulder as I started to make my way back down the hall.

"Isn't there a bathroom right here?" Mariana said, nodding toward the kitchen door.

"It's for the staff." When she was more mobile, Madre used to barge through the kitchen door to see if she could catch any of the maids or cooks up to some kind of mischief, but now it's just Doña Olga and her daughter keeping the house and I respect their privacy as much as I do Mariana's.

Mariana laughed or snorted, I couldn't tell which, then asked, "Didn't you fight the revolution so that there wouldn't be separate bathrooms for the help?" She shook her head a bit. "Shake" is probably too strong a verb, it was more of a twitch, really, a Morse code telegraphing nerves and annoyance, and with the movement, she somehow shook off the image of her I'd seen reflected in the mirror. The glass had frozen her, giving her a hint of placid calm that she doesn't carry in real life. Even though she's always been a good sleeper, able to rest on planes and nap anywhere, I've never seen Mariana look anywhere nearly as relaxed or blissful as I did in my own, old photo.

I want her to have that serenity. Partly, I'll admit, because if she were happy and calm, my life would be easier. Mariana is so tolerant of my mother. But she is so ready to find fault with whatever I say or do, even which bathroom to use. If she lost the nervous energy she carries around, she might not be so vigilant, so watchful for any reason to be annoyed with me. Maybe the serenity of the photo escapes her because she doesn't know what it is to be loved so completely. And for that, I blame the gringo we saw last night. If he can't make her feel safe and calm, the way Manuel made me feel, even in a war zone, then he isn't the one for my daughter.

That's not fair, I know. It takes two people to be in a relationship. And perhaps I should be sympathetic to him; I know how difficult Mariana makes it to get close to her. But if I don't blame him, then

I have to consider another terrifying possibility. What if the nervous anger comes from something she herself lacks, as opposed to something he has failed to provide? What if no matter how much he loves Mariana, she'll never feel safe, even in a world where the worst thing that can happen is a painting selling for fewer millions than anticipated? And if it's impossible for her to feel beloved or cared for by someone who entered her life fresh just a year or so ago, then what are the odds she will ever love or feel loved by me, after I've spent three decades disappointing her?

19

❦

Maria

Last night Doña Olga had the night off so she could attend the calling hours, so we stopped by Tip Top Chicken on the way home to get some take-out. None of us was really hungry, but there would be no food at home, and, besides, Don Pedro said you should never go straight back to the house from a wake, or death might follow you. When I asked him where we should go for take-out, he suggested Tip Top; it's his favorite place to eat. I sat up front next to him, to give my Bela and Madre more room, and he kept chatting the entire drive, trying to distract me from feeling sad. Or embarrassed; maybe he had noticed the fuss Allen made, the scene I'd caused. I appreciated his efforts because if he kept talking to me, my grandmother couldn't ask the questions that must have been choking her—who was that gringo, and why was I so angry at him? And I would be tempted to tell her the whole, overwhelming story, to describe the situation her grand-daughter had found herself in despite all her years of careful advice-giving and cautionary soap operas starring women who'd been made fools of by more powerful men. Madre would be too proud to ask about the incident, but without Don Pedro's chitchat, she would have made some subtle comment about the unexpected disturbance at the funeral home, or at least some weak joke about having been worried, for a minute there, that she might have to use her combat training. A little reminder that if I would just let her into my life, she might be able to clean up my messes, or at least advise me wisely enough that I wouldn't make messes that needed tidying; even though, in reality, she was never around when I actually wanted her help.

But, gracias a Dios—y a Don Pedro—neither of them said anything. Maybe Madre was embarrassed herself, about fainting. And my Bela also seemed wrapped up in her thoughts. Throughout the wake she had looked glazed, as if there were a sheer curtain hanging in front of her eyes.

"It's a funny thing about chicken," Don Pedro said as we approached Tip Top. "When it's cooked with the skin on, it's the most delicious dish in the world. When it's cooked without the skin, it's tasteless, like eating cardboard."

I had to laugh. He's right of course. But a skinless chicken breast is probably the single food I eat most frequently. What does that say about me? That I'm choosing to live a life of boredom, of self-deprivation?

I ran in to pick up our food, and when I came back, both my Bela and Madre were asleep in the backseat, Madre leaning against my Bela's shoulder. She looked so helpless, cuddled up to her own mother. It made me wonder if she had fainted because she's ill. Madre is the healthiest person I know, never been sick as far as I can remember. Still, she works crazy hours and travels nonstop; she could be wearing herself out. For the first time in my life, I wanted to ask about her health. There'd never really been a reason to before: She doesn't have allergies, had 20/20 vision until her late forties, and has always been able to out-hike me, even when I was sixteen. But I didn't want to wake her, and, under the circumstances, tonight probably wasn't the best time to start a serious conversation. It could wait until after the funeral, when everything had calmed down.

I thought that I could use tonight, the quiet left behind by the tense hum of the calling hours, to give my Bela what had been in my pocket all day; it was the reason I hadn't hung up my jacket at the funeral home, but left it on a chair where I could see it, even though there was no way I'd need it in Managua's heat, now that I was off the plane with its frigid, recycled air.

But once we'd gotten home, as we all sat at the table trying to eat our chicken, I understood that this was not the time to distract my Bela. She was floating in her mind somewhere; maybe looking for Abuelo, whose soul, Doña Olga said, is supposed to be hovering for the next forty days. If I followed her to her room, I might have been able to get her to focus. But it would feel disloyal to distract her if she was with Abuelo in her thoughts. And it would hurt Madre if I got up from the table to go talk to my Bela, leaving her sitting alone. Even though she was the one who left us alone together, Madre is sensitive about how close my Bela and I are. I've learned it's best to give them the exact same Christmas present so that one of them doesn't feel she got the better gift when both decide that the blue scarf is infinitely lovelier than the green, and my choosing it for one and not the other is a coded message revealing whom I love most. Last month, when I had an article in the gallery newsletter, and I mailed one to my Bela, Madre called me just to demand that I send her one, too. I'd emailed her an electronic copy—my Bela doesn't have email— but Madre said she wanted a physical copy of the nice, glossy pamphlet, so she could leave it on her coffee table for guests to see, just like my Bela did.

It's true that if the weather is nice enough for me to walk to work, it's my Bela I call to chat with, not Madre. But isn't it only natural for me to be most comfortable around the woman who actually put in the time to raise me? Besides, my Bela is so much easier to be around; she thinks I'm the greatest thing since control-top panty hose, whereas Madre just keeps judging me, even if it's not out loud.

Still, I didn't want to make Madre feel worse, not after what I said to her at the wake, so I didn't suggest to my Bela that I walk her to her room, and sit in bed for a while, talking, like we used to back in Miami. And I wouldn't bring out the envelope in front of Madre; I pride myself on my discretion. To this day, I haven't told a soul about Amy Santiago peeing herself, not even in the fifth grade when she convinced every girl in the class not to speak to me. She actually apologized for that at our tenth reunion. I remembered that her parents got divorced at some point in middle school, but she told me that was the year her dad moved out. He'd been a Marine, and before he left he'd spent a lot of time watching the Oliver North trials on TV, railing at the screen that North was a hero, and that we should have been sending troops to help the Contras, too. "And you knew my mom was a Sandinista?" I asked Amy. She actually had tears in her eyes; it was as if she was making some sort of formal confession, but she looked about six months pregnant, so it was probably the hormones. "I'd heard rumors," she said. "But I didn't know what was going on. Sandinista, Contra, it was all one big *Saturday Night Live* 'Nightly News' skit to me. I just knew how pissed my dad was at the Nicaraguans. I thought if I was mean to you, I'd be helping him somehow. That he'd be able to tell and it would count."

The other girls forgot about shunning me after a few weeks, but I never really trusted them after that. I had a group of kids I hung out with in high school, but I knew it could happen again, they could turn on me for no reason, or at least none that I knew of. That was the worst part, not knowing why everybody hated me all of a sudden, what horrible aspect of myself I should change, or at least hide. I didn't really have a close friend until I met Beth in college. But at the reunion, I told Amy not to worry about it, that I understood. Because I did. I remember a time when I would have hurt anybody if it would have kept my mom from leaving.

Not giving my Bela the letter meant I'd have to wait until after the funeral, until the next day, probably. It could be days before the right moment came, especially now that I had Allen to deal with on top of the funeral. Just the thought of talking to Allen made me tired. And both my Bela and Madre were glassy-eyed, whether with fatigue or sorrow. But neither of them made a move to get up; it was as if we all thought the longer we stayed awake, the longer we could keep tomorrow, and the funeral, relegated to the future.

I was the one who finally said, "I'm not really hungry; I'm just going to go to bed." I kissed Madre and my Bela both on the tops of their heads before walking across the courtyard to the room that was once the nursery, which is smack in the middle of the place, dividing the wings of the house. Even sleeping, I'd be caught between them.

As I got ready to go to the funeral in the morning, I packed my shoulder bag with my wallet, a notebook, and a camera; it felt a bit sacrilegious to be slipping the camera in with the rest of my things, as if I were going to a party, not a burial. But I want to remember what the city looked like on Abuelo's last day aboveground. Besides, I love taking pictures of Granada. I even felt the tiniest bit guilty for telling Allen he shouldn't come. Granada may be the Nicaraguan town foreigners visit most, with its Spanish colonial churches and brightly painted houses all unfurling toward the banks of Lake Cocibolca; and I love the architecture, the history, the prim-looking homes hiding jungle-green courtyards deep in their interior. But Allen would be more into the topography, would probably make some incredible painting inspired by Lake Cocibolca with blobs representing the islands that float inside it. Volcanoes, parrots, white-faced monkeys—Allen would go crazy for the lush drama of the lake, and scorn the town with its peach and blue churches piped in white gingerbread trim. He wouldn't see that what makes the place work is the balance of the two, that there's something both sweet and brave about such fussy, ornamental structures in the middle of such wildness.

I had told Allen about Granada before, promised that I would take him there if he ever visited Nicaragua. I said Granada looked like a combination of Havana and Walnut Grove, but he had no idea what Walnut Grove is; he seemed sort of proud, actually, of never having read or watched *Little House on the Prairie*. Still, I could tell he had been intrigued; he promised he'd make time for a trip to Nicaragua in the new year. I said that we could come incognito so that I could play tourist, hike volcanoes and swim off the Caribbean coast and not have to visit 101 relatives and coo over their offspring and explain that yes, I really did like New York even though it was expensive and crowded. But Allen put his arm around me and said, "Maybe on the last day we'll blow our cover and go see your grandparents."

He knows how much I love them. Allen gets it. That's the part that makes me wish I hadn't been so proud and so angry, that I had let him see how thrilled I was for that second when I first saw him, that I had let him sit beside me now, in this freezing car bumping its way toward my grandfather's funeral. I think that may be part of why he's here, to support me at this sad and scary time, not just to change my mind or make a grand gesture. Maybe I shouldn't have made him stay behind in Managua. But I'm not ready for these two worlds to crash into each other, to find out if they can coexist or if one would inevitably obliterate the other. I don't want the first time Allen sees Granada to be at my grandfather's funeral. And I don't want to be thinking about him during the service and the burial. I want to be able to remember Abuelo, to wallow in the past for a little bit, and not have to worry about my future.

Once I was ready to go, I checked on my Bela. She was tucking a fresh mourning handkerchief into her purse as I opened her bedroom door, and looking elegant in her black suit with a white camellia pinned to its lapel. She knows how to handle a funeral. And a wedding. And a baptism. She embodies the phrase "rise to the occasion." It's like she lives for these turning points, which unhinge those of us who are less well prepared, because they allow her to exercise all her carefully honed social skills, to say the right thing, do the right thing, wear the right thing. I know it annoys Madre, my Bela's fastidiousness. But it gives my Bela such comfort, knowing how to act in every situation. And I find it soothing, too; my Bela knows so many rules, it makes me feel as if the world is an orderly place governed by them. A false sense of security, but still comforting.

After sitting with her for a bit, I went to get Madre. I didn't mean to creep up on her; I hadn't realized she didn't hear me walk in until it was too late to say something, and I could tell that she was startled to find me suddenly sharing the mirror with her reflection. She had been holding up her right eyelid with the ring finger of her right hand. It does droop, I guess. But not any more than any other woman's her age. Probably less. What was more disturbing than the drooping of Madre's eyelid is the fact that she's aware of it, and bothered enough by it to want to see what it would look like if it didn't hang quite so low. I wouldn't be at all surprised to see my Bela in that position; she's always pulling her face this way and that. Every night she briskly rubs her hands under her chin, one after the other, one hundred times, to prevent jowls from forming. (She's a little late to that party, but who knows, maybe she's less jowly than she would be if she'd never done it? On the theory that it's better to be safe than saggy, if I'm sleeping alone and I remember, I do it myself.)

But Madre is different. She was never concerned with what I wore growing up. She never commented on my weight, like Beth's mom did when she gained a few pounds freshman year, never suggested I put on some lipstick or pluck my eyebrows. I had my Bela for that. Maybe we just weren't close enough for Madre to feel that my appearance reflected on her, especially since most of the time we were in two different countries. But I also never heard her say that she herself was on a diet. She seems to be above worrying about looks in general. If she's preoccupied with aging now, there has to be a reason beyond simple vanity.

I asked her, flat out, "Are you okay, Mama?"

She ignored my question but grabbed my arm as if she were about to stumble on her way to the bathroom. I pointed out there was a bathroom much closer, in the kitchen, and just like that, she switched from a worried middle-aged woman who looked as unhinged as she must feel after losing her father, right back into her brisk, efficient, no-nonsense self, and informed me that it was the staff's bathroom. Which just made me crazy, because, really? This great Sandinista heroine has to use a separate bathroom from the housekeeper? Because social equality is so important to her that she'll risk her life for it, and hand off her daughter to be raised in a different country, but she still considers herself above sharing the liquid hand soap with the employees?

In that moment, I forgot that I'd been worried about her, that she had just lost her father. I forgot it all and I said, "Isn't that why you fought a revolution? So that people wouldn't have to use separate bathrooms?"

She dropped her hand from my arm and looked at me for what seemed like a long time, so long that I started to worry about her again.

"Really, Mariana," she said finally. "The revolution I fought had nothing to do with bathrooms at all."

We've been riding in silence, following the hearse. But just now, half-way through the trip, Madre sighed as we passed the Masaya round-about, curving around the fabulously garish statue of the Güegüense. If it had been my Bela, I might pat her shoulder, or ignore it altogether; my grandmother is one of the world's champion sighers. But it's so uncharacteristic of Madre.

"You're sure you're fine, Mama?" I look out the window so that she won't have to face me with the answer.

"I'm sad."

"I know." Now I turn to her so that she can't avoid facing me, and put my hand on hers. "But you're okay, healthwise?"

She looks at me. "Of course, Mariana."

"Then why did you faint last night? Was it because you saw me fighting–"

"I fainted because I was tired and upset and felt claustrophobic," Madre interrupts. "You know I don't like crowds, social events."

Of course I know that she hates parties. But the calling hours hardly qualified as a celebration. "You were fine all night until Allen showed up," I point out. For the first time, I wish I had told her something about Allen, that she had some idea of who he is or what it could mean that he followed me to Managua. She doesn't even know his name. "You know, until I started talking to that tall guy."

"I was fine until the waiter fell with that huge crash." She pulls her hand out from under mine, then uses it to push her sunglasses up onto her head as she turns to look out the window again. "My fainting had nothing to do with what I saw. It was what I heard that startled me, that horrible burst of noise." She keeps looking out the window, as if she's speaking to someone on the edge of the highway. "You can handle your own discussions; I wasn't worried about you."

20

Isabela

Driving into Granada is like watching my life lived in reverse. Coming from Managua, first we pass the cemetery where we'll bury my husband, where they'll bury me someday, relatively soon, I suppose. If I live twenty more years I'll be celebrated for my longevity and what's twenty years, really? Nothing.

Then we pass Xalteva, the melon-colored church where I married Ignacio. It wasn't the closest church to our house; that was the catedral. But Madre had grown up near Xalteva and she had a fondness for young Padre Juan Cristobal, so we always attended Mass there. It's across the street from a park that's eerily pretty, with vine-covered trellises that whisper as you stroll under them. Dolly and I used to hold our breath as we passed beneath them while walking to Mass when we were home for school vacations, imagining they were haunted.

But once we returned from Sacred Heart, Papa insisted that the chauffeur drive us to the church door on Sundays. Especially in the months after they whisked me back to Granada, and before I married Ignacio, I was never allowed to go anywhere unsupervised. It wasn't a rule, really; no one spoke it out loud. They were all surprisingly kind to me, trying to find reasons to coax me out of bed, to amuse and distract me, transform me back into my old self again. But someone was always with me, Dolly or Mama or little Ana Carolina, and oftentimes the chauffeur or Papa as well, keeping a watchful, masculine eye on us from a distance. I was home four months before I was able to take advantage of the chaos around Dolly's wedding planning to step out alone long enough to post a letter to Mauricio. In it I explained that while it's true I physically walked away from him, it was my body that took the steps; I could never do so in my heart or mind, where it mattered. I would always be with him. It wasn't a choice I had made, to let Dolly lead me back down the aisle, but a lack of a choice, a sin of omission. I wasn't strong enough to disappoint everyone, so I did what was easiest, not what was right. I told him how sorry I was that I had hurt him, and that I wanted him to know how much I had hurt myself, too, by walking away with everyone else.

I can't regret leaving the church with my family that day; if I hadn't, Celia and Ninexin, Rigobertito and Mariana, none of them would exist. But I still regret hurting Mauricio and I'm still embarrassed. No, it's deeper than that. I'm still humiliated by the fact that I buckled, that I chose the coward's way out. It's why I hate that Robert Frost poem about the woods and the snow and the diverging roads. Frost became quite fashionable about the time of Kennedy's inauguration, and when I heard a voice reciting that particular poem on the radio that year, it seemed like a personal reproach.

Granada is punctuated and defined by churches. A few minutes further down the road from Masaya comes Merced, where I wanted my wedding to Ignacio to take place, once I had accepted that it was my fate. After I waited a month to be sure the letter had time to reach Mauricio, and four more months passed without a reply from him, it seemed like the only choice open to me.

Dolly had married just a few months after our return. She met Francisco Castaneda when he came to visit Teodoro for Teo's birthday in July. Usually our brothers were at the factory all day, but Teo took some time off to entertain Francisco, so we all got to see a bit more of him and his guest. Francisco had graduated from Tulane four years prior, and he loved reading as much as Dolly did, although he veered more toward Zane Grey and Mark Twain than Jane Austen. His family business was coffee, and work took him to New Orleans twice a year. As I stood there in my floppy hat, watching their wedding, all I could think was that, if she had let me marry Mauricio, and come home herself and met Francisco, Dolly would still have been able to see me quite often. Everyone thought the tears running down my face during the ceremony were tears of joy that my beloved sister had found someone worthy of her, or maybe of jealousy, envy that she was the one in the embroidered gown, marrying and leaving me behind to move to the coffee farm in Matagalpa. I had a linen handkerchief edged in salmon-colored lace that matched my dress. It was such a pretty handkerchief that when I dabbed it to my face, it was impossible for anyone watching to think that my tears reflected the pain of a loss I still couldn't believe I would survive, a sort of emotional amputation. The object of my love was cut off from me, but I still felt him, a phantom limb. Only Dolly knew why I cried so hard.

"I wish you could be happy for me," she said the next day before she left, first for the Pacific coast, where Francisco's family had a beach house, and then for Matagalpa. "But I know it's too much to ask. I know it's my fault you're here, that you're so despondent." It wasn't all her fault; I was the one who walked away from Mauricio. And I knew Dolly had believed she was doing the right thing. I might have done the same if the situation had been reversed, if I had felt I'd be losing her forever. But I didn't tell her that; let her feel guilty, I thought. Let her feel a fraction of the guilt I suffered every minute.

"Francisco and I, we're not like you and Mauricio, I won't pretend we are," Dolly said. "But now that I know what it's like to plan a life with somebody, to dream up a future together, I can understand, a little, how horrible it must have been to give up all that. I didn't know at the time. I never thought you would still feel so sad." I felt anger, too, of course; it was just buried so deep under the sadness that by the time it rose to the surface, it seemed of little consequence.

"But, even though it's selfish, I'm still glad you didn't stay in New Orleans, Isabela." Dolly clutched my arm, standing at the gate of our house, watching Francisco and the driver pack the car. "I couldn't imagine getting married without you here." I pulled my arm away. "I'm not saying that to make you feel bad." Dolly grabbed me again, my shoulder this time. "It's just that I want us to share this part of our lives. To raise children together." She pulled me to her and I must have been crying because teardrops stained her pink going-away suit. "I know you'll feel better. You'll see this was the right thing. When you meet someone, when you decide to get married, you'll see it's like the old saying: One key replaces another. You'll build a home, and then a family, and you'll be so busy and happy, you'll forget all about New Orleans. It will seem like something that happened a million years ago. I promise." She hugged me even tighter and whispered, "I love you so much, Isabela. Can you still love me? Even just a little bit?"

I had kept my arms at my sides at first, but then I hugged her back. Even though I was hurt, and angry and sad, so many emotions that it all just added up to me feeling numb, I still understood that there was no point in losing another person I cared for deeply. And maybe Dolly was right: there were so many years of life left, something had to fill them, something besides pain.

So when Ignacio proposed—or rather, followed up on his mother's proposal—a few months after Dolly's wedding, I decided to take her advice. I knew I wasn't going to love anyone as much as Mauricio, so what was the point in trying to find pale imitations? Ignacio was familiar; his family were our neighbors. I had come back to Granada, to this life, and he was so much a part of it. It seemed like a good idea to throw my future in with his, instead of some other man's who lived farther away from my family, some man we didn't know as well, and who still wasn't Mauricio. Besides, I had to get out of our house. My sadness seemed to be infecting everyone in it, wafting contagiously from room to room. Every time Papa saw me, he cringed. I thought it was because I had disappointed him so deeply, but after our wedding, as Ignacio and I were leaving for Paris, Papa kissed me on the forehead and said, "It hurts every time I look at you, to think I'm the reason you haven't smiled for almost a year."

I smiled at him then, but he shook his head; he could tell what was real, initiated by joy, and what was cosmetic, born out of politeness. "Ignacio is a good man, from a fine family," he continued. "And so robust, so energetic! I know he'll always provide for you. And I hope he'll make you smile again."

My father was half right. Ignacio gave me our daughters, and they made me smile. And he himself could be charming; all of us young people admired his ability to do imitations, of the priests with their fire-and-brimstone sermons, the ladies gossiping in the back of the church, their husbands leering out the church windows at the young women selling fruit in the square. But halfway through Paris, where he loved the restaurants and the nightclubs and the bookstalls along the river, and I might have, too, if they hadn't reminded me of New Orleans, he turned to me and said, "I've never had to work so hard to make a girl laugh." The next night I told him I wasn't feeling well, and he should use our theater tickets anyway, and I pretended to be sleeping when he stumbled in at 4:00 A.M. and fell asleep with his good shirt still on. I wonder now how our lives would have been different if I'd sat up waiting for him that night, told him that returning at this late hour was unacceptable, screamed at him, showed him that I noticed that he'd been out all night, and I didn't like it—no, more than that, that I wouldn't allow it. That I cared about our marriage and how we were going to treat each other. But it was easier just to lie there.

I had wanted to marry in Merced because it matched my mood. Shortly after the North American adventurer William Walker declared himself president for life of Nicaragua, he burned Granada as punishment for the townspeople's opposition. Almost a hundred years later, Merced still had black marks left by the flames. The church, which had been restored a number of times since Walker's day, was just as grand as the other churches in town, but I felt it had more character. The others were painted the colors of the tropics, the bright blue of the sky or the ripe orange of a melon; Merced was white with black zigzags where the flames had licked it. It had scars, but it was still standing and it had a grace, an elegance all its own. I, too, had been through a crisis that almost destroyed me, and I'd survived. What better place to start the next phase of my life, trying to rise from the ashes of my past? But even though most Granadinos loved Merced for its historical significance, its stately architecture, and its massive bell tower, Mama said she wouldn't hear of me marrying in a church other than the one I'd grown up attending. Dolly teared up when I mentioned the idea. "Are you sure that's how you want to start out?" she said. "It's such a dark church inside. And Xalteva is so bright and happy."

For her, anyway. But the opinion that decided the issue came from Doña Milagro, Ignacio's mother. "If you're not going to marry in your church, then you'll marry in ours," she said, sipping tea in the courtyard during a post-engagement wedding planning visit with me and Mama. Her family went to the catedral, which was right next to their house, and just a short walk from ours. I would have agreed to be married there except that afternoon, after Doña Milagro went home, Madre knocked at my bedroom door. I told her to come in, but she stayed in the doorway; she knew how not to intrude, just to suggest. It's a quality I'm afraid I didn't inherit.

"Regarding the church," she said. "Think about the message you're sending if you marry in the catedral rather than Xalteva. You'll be attending Mass at the catedral, in Ignacio's family pew, from now on. And you have the rest of your life to do Doña Milagro's bidding. Maybe your wedding is a good time to show her that you're a person with her own opinions, and that when you do follow her lead it's out of good breeding and kindness, not inevitability." And so I agreed to Xalteva; this marriage was as much about what my family wanted as it was about my own desires. More so. Years later, when Mariana showed me the photos she took from the bell tower of Merced—it's full of tourists climbing up to the top these days—I told her that I had wanted to get married there, but I had been talked out of it. "I was so easily swayed when I was young," I said. "I had no backbone."

"Don't beat yourself up, Bela," Mariana said. "From what you've told me, sounds like you were suffering from a clinical depression before you got married. Today you'd get therapy or at least happy pills."

Back then, I got a husband. Poor Ignacio. Set up to be my savior. And all everyone expected from me was that I be the mother of his children. It hardly seems like a fair bargain. I fulfilled my end of it, although he never did get a son. And since I'm the one who is still here, I suppose he kept up his end of it, too. I did survive, this long, anyway. Long enough to learn that one of the few advantages of getting older is that, if you live long enough, you start to lose the need to please everyone else all of the time.

We're rounding the Parque Central now, getting closer to the Funeraria Monte Santo, where Ignacio's coffin will be removed from the hearse and placed in one of the funeral carriages Granadinos use. It's one of the reasons he insisted on being buried here. He wanted to be laid to rest near his parents in the family plot, of course, but, also, ever since he was a boy he'd loved the ornate black carriages drawn by a pair of horses draped in white shawls, with solemn drivers in black suits holding their reins. Even as an adult, if he were sitting in a café and one passed by, he would stand out of respect for the dead. As girls, we were told always to look away from the funerary carriages, wishing death far from us, so I found his admiration rather macabre. But he'd shrug when I'd chide him and say, "They just look really sharp." I think he always imagined it would be fun to ride in one. Now he'll get his chance, once we set off toward the burial, first passing my childhood home, then, closer to the catedral, his, then turning and clip-clopping past Merced and Xalteva and finally into the cemetery.

Doña Milagro donated the house Ignacio grew up in to the church when she died—by then it was the seventies and none but the wealthiest families could afford to keep up such large properties. After

Ignacio's brothers ran his father's cotton business into the ground, the de la Torres were no longer among them. Even though there's now a statue of the Virgen in the front courtyard and a religious bookstore in what was once a sitting room, when we pass Ignacio's home I can almost see him on his balcony. Before we left for Sacred Heart, I would sometimes spot a man up there. Ignacio is—was—eight years older than I am, so when I was thirteen he was a man, and I saw him through the eyes of a child. He would stand out on his balcony in an untucked shirt—back then you almost never saw a man less than perfectly put together unless he was a campesino— smoking and looking out over the city. Once I watched him throw a flower down to a woman passing on the street below. It was just one of the jasmine blossoms that twined around the columns of the balcony, it wasn't as if he had gone out and purchased lilies or roses. But still, it was such a cinematic gesture that Dolly and I giggled from our spot on the opposite corner. He noticed us and froze for one frightening instant until he erupted into laughter so loud and deep that I ran into the church to hide. Dolly came in to get me and dragged me home, not speaking to me, she was so mortified by my childish behavior.

The house I grew up in is a museum now, with a café full of gringos on the ground floor. When I was little, it echoed with the noise of my siblings and me running up the stairs two by two until our nannies or Madre stopped us and reminded us to act like ladies and a gentleman; then, after we'd gone to bed, with the sound of grown-up laughter as my parents and their friends sat in rocking chairs on the veranda discussing the events of the day. But when I see the house, I have to force myself to remember those happy times. My first instinct is to look away to fight the heavy sadness that threatens to choke me. I've suffered in my life: I was afraid when we fled to Honduras. I was hurt when Ignacio would go on business trips I knew had nothing to do with business. I'm sad now, and frightened at having to start life all over, alone. But I've never been as profoundly sorrowful as I was in that house after I returned from Sacred Heart.

I was happy only in my sleep; I went to bed speaking to Mauricio in my mind, composing letters I was too nervous to put down on paper, but when that got too frustrating I would concentrate instead on reliving one of our dates, trying to remember what I wore, what he said, what Miss Birdie ate. That way the hollow feeling in my stomach would disappear, and my headache would ease up, too, until I was blissfully unconscious. I'd sleep as long as I could in the mornings, but my family were early risers, as were most Granadinos, what with the sun coming up over the lake by five-thirty in the morning. By seven-thirty the maid couldn't wait any longer and she'd enter my room to start tidying up. I'd feel too embarrassed to lie around while she was working, so I'd dress myself, which was a kind of respite, too, if I focused hard enough on which blouse looked best with my skirt, and maybe used a new ribbon to update the trim on my hat.

But then there were still at least four hours to go before lunch, and no one else wanted to spend them wandering around the city with me. Before Dolly moved she would pull me into some wedding-related task, looking at fabrics for her dress or shoes or linens for the reception. But that only took up an hour or two and then I'd find myself sitting on our balcony, or in a shady corner of the courtyard, holding a book and trying to read but going over the same sentence again and again. The interesting books, even the ones that had been forbidden at school, were too complex for me to follow with my mind as muddled as it was. And the religious ones I had read too many times. I could scan the lines and turn the pages and even be mouthing the words to the prayers, but as much as I tried to fill my brain with saints and storylines, my thoughts would end up back in Father Antony's church, taunting me with the horrible image of what Mauricio's face must have looked like staring at my back as I walked away from him.

In New Orleans I had admired a local author, Frances Parkinson Keyes, had even passed by her grand yellow house in the French Quarter. Miss Birdie told us it had been owned by the Confederate general Beauregard and I made myself look impressed although I had no idea who he was; it was hard enough to remember the American generals who had won their wars. But back home in Granada, I would start reading *Crescent Carnival* or *Dinner at Antoine's* and the sounds and smells of the city I loved would overtake me; I wouldn't realize I was crying until my tears stained the flimsy pages. This display of emotion disturbed whoever found me weeping into the book, and exhausted me so that I'd have to return to my room, get under the covers of my freshly made bed, and stay there until it was time to go down to the table again. Ana Carolina would sometimes come in and do dances or sing songs for me, but I often couldn't stop crying and this scared her so much that she would start sobbing, too. Dolly finally took the books away, promising she'd save them for me in case I ever felt I could read them without hurting. I wonder if she still has them? Maybe in the end she gave them to Ana Carolina, who was always so curious about them, and the books are moldering in her grand apartment in Panama City, where she moved with her husband decades ago. Because even little Ana Carolina is a great-grandmother now, although the days of her childhood remain so vivid in my mind.

The afternoons were better, because I could always talk someone into going with me to the cinema, whether it was Dolly or Ana Carolina, who managed to cheer up from our crying sessions with a swiftness that can belong only to a ten-year-old. But Granada had just one cinema, and it showed only one movie at a time, usually a Hollywood film that had been a big hit in the States months prior. And even though I was no longer at Sacred Heart, I was still a Sacred Heart girl; I was mindful of needing to behave appropriately enough not to dishonor the school, or expose my younger sister to immoral behavior. When the cinema had opened a few years before, Padre Juan Cristobal gave us a phone number we could call to find out if the movie being shown had been approved by the Legion of Decency or if it was on the list of condemned, immoral films, which would make watching it a mortal sin.

It was important to call only during daytime hours, but not during the siesta, because the number belonged to one of the few homes in town that had reliable phone service, and calls were answered, Padre Juan Cristobal told us, by a noble lady who had volunteered to provide this service for the Church. Dutifully, I called at 11:00 A.M. each week when the new movie was announced. I thought I recognized the voice, but I couldn't be sure. Until one day, the voice on the other end said to me, "Isabela—this is Isabela Enriquez, isn't it?"

Shocked that this Church-approved voice knew my name, I nodded, bobbing my head respectfully although I was alone in the room with no one to see me.

"Can you hear me, girl? Is this Isabela?" the voice said again.

"Yes, ma'am."

"Well, Isabela, you're the only girl in town who uses this number," Doña Milagro said. "I think you're the one for my Ignacio Sebastian."

That week, the film was *Salome*. And when I arrived at the cinema with Ana Carolina, Ignacio was standing there with a look of resignation on his face, and three tickets in his hand.

21

◦৯৯৹◦

Ninexin

We used to come to Granada every other weekend when I was little, to visit Abuela Milagro before she passed. Abuela Milagro was the first—and maybe the only—person whom I both admired and feared. Partly because she made Mama so anxious; in the car on the way to Granada, Mama would endlessly straighten our dresses so that the smocking on our chests lay in straight, geometric patterns, and make sure that our lace-edged socks were folded properly. But it was also Abuela Milagro herself, the way she sat, that intimidated me. I remember reading a biography of a politician on the beach in Key Biscayne during a visit to see Mariana in Miami, in which some diplomat was described as having "erect carriage." My English wasn't as good then as it is now, and I can't recall who was being described or even who the subject of the biography was, but right away an image of Abuela Milagro popped into my head and I had to put the book down and dive into the ocean to celebrate, both my triumph in understanding what the author meant, and also my glee that there was a phrase that so perfectly described this characteristic. It was like learning the word "watermelon" for sandía; the name explains just what it is, a melon, but one so juicy and light that when you take a bite it's as if your mouth fills with the most refreshing water. So descriptive, this name. So perfect.

I sound like a crazy person. But the older I get, the more I find myself having these moments where an apt phrase or a smooth pillow or an unexpected sight causes me to feel joy that even I know is wildly out of proportion to the catalyst itself. Maybe it's that part of my nervous system coming alive again after having felt so little joy for so long. Or maybe I'm going crazy with middle age. Mama says she became unhinged herself for a few years before and after undergoing the change, but with her it was crying spells and headaches, and Tía Dolores says that Mama has always been depression-prone, ever since they were teenagers and returned from New Orleans.

Whatever the reason, it doesn't happen very often. But once every few weeks I see or hear something that makes me feel almost giddy, the way I used to at the end of our long visits with Abuela Milagro, when Papa would return to collect us. He always made some excuse as to why he couldn't sit with us drinking ice water in glasses wrapped in cloth napkins and staring at our shoes; he had to go discuss an important matter with his brother-in-law, Tío Teo, who would be reading his newspaper at the club, or to make an urgent deposit at the bank. As soon as Papa strolled in, back from his errand, Abuela Milagro's quizzes—of course we could say the Lord's Prayer in Spanish, very good, but now could we say it in French?—came to an end. Then we would walk in a straight line, with Abuela Milagro leaning on Papa's arm, over to the social club, to enjoy our guapote in peace, Abuela Milagro always said, without having to watch all the pobrecitos splashing away in the lake.

The flickering of freedom I felt when Papa showed up and ended those airless encounters thrilled but also worried me; I always teetered on the verge of bursting out into uncontrollable giggles. If I felt these brief moments of almost hysterical joy even as a child, that means that the tendency has always been in me, I suppose. But, after so many years of being a self-contained, serious adult, I like to think that the fact that they're coming back shows a kind of progress, too. Maybe I'm rediscovering the thing I loved about Manuel, only in myself. And if that's true, that has to mean that, on some level, I've forgiven him. And that, if he still exists in some form, a soul, or just echoes of electricity left behind by the firing synapses of his youth, he's forgiven me, too.

Mariana also must have forgiven me for whatever her most recent grievance was, because, now, as we arrive at the Funeraria Monte Santo, she's putting her hand on my shoulder and pointing at the shingle they have hanging in front of their door, a naive drawing, almost a cartoon, of a smiling man in a black suit rising up out of his ornate coffin, his arms upraised as if he's praising Jesus or the American football player who just scored the winning touchdown.

"I love that sign," she says. "The corpse is just so happy with the customer service here that he's jumping out of his coffin!"

I've seen this image hundreds of times since I was a little girl, but I never noticed how simultaneously glorious and ludicrous it is. I've always just been impressed that this small family business keeps thriving; customers are dying to get in, ha ha. It's the artist in Mariana that noticed it.

And then it happens. I do start giggling uncontrollably, my shoulders shaking with laughter. Heads turn to look at me in confusion, even Mama snaps out of her reverie to glare at me, at this outrageous display, violent laughter on the morning of my father's funeral. But there we are, Mariana and I laughing as the horses stamp their feet, waiting for the transfer of the coffin from the hearse to the carriage. The sound of their hooves on the pavement reminds me of walking across the Parque Central with my papa as a little girl, the one time I slipped out of an audience with Abuela Milagro. That hot afternoon my socks were especially itchy around my ankles and, as he turned to leave, I couldn't help myself from rising out of my seat, too. And Papa saved me, saying that he'd noticed the quarter-inch heel on my white patent leather shoe was loose, and he was just going to bring me to the cobbler to fix it, so I didn't slip and fall and dirty my pretty dress. It was an excuse Mama and Abuela Milagro couldn't find fault with. And so, without so much as a backward glance at Celia, still a prisoner in her chair, I skipped off, holding my father's hand. We didn't go anywhere near the cobbler, just petted the horses and ate some vigorón from one of the kiosks in the park, and bought leche de burra candy in paper bags from a boy about my age. Feeling a little guilty, I chose an extralarge packet for Celia to eat on the way home.

Now I am no longer shaking with laughter, but crying into Mariana's shoulder, because I will never again walk through the Parque Central holding my papa's hand. And the sound of the horses' hooves on the cobblestones have brought him back through some unknowable alchemy, and he isn't the corpse in the coffin, but I can feel him all around me, in the clouds above and the grass below and the smell of some nearby bonfire. He is everywhere, surrounding me the way that, if I tried very hard, I felt God was everywhere when I was a little girl listening to old Padre Juan Cristobal mutter indistinctly from his pulpit when we'd visit Granada. By the time I was old enough to pay attention to his sermons, the priest wore false teeth and was hard to understand. But on certain occasions, when the light streamed through the stained glass window, staining his bald spot blue, his voice would deepen and his words turned into a song even though they didn't rhyme, and on those occasions I could see the priest my mother remembered with so much reverence, and I could feel the God he spoke of, tangible in the very air I was breathing.

It is a day for miracles because, through my tears, I realize that Mariana is crying, too, and we're holding on to each other as the employees of Funeraria Monte Santo walk around us, going about their business. I want to stop and thank them for their kindness to us, and to my father on his last day. Only moments ago Mariana was laughing about the sign with the dark humor I always admire in her because I know it will help her withstand whatever heavy moments await her, that she has the power to lighten them herself, and doesn't need anyone to do it for her. And even though I know she'll be all right, it still hurts me to see her in pain. Hearing her cry this hard reminds me of all the times I left Miami when she was a little girl, when I'd tell her, so that I could hear it myself, too, that she'd be fine, that I'd be back soon, that once they dropped me off at the airport, Abuelo would take her to Swenson's for ice cream and that her abuela had so many fun excursions planned for her next week. Now I tell her what I think so often but seldom let myself say anymore, that I love her. And Mariana makes a strange sobbing, choking sound that I think is her crying and laughing at the same time.

I was laughing a moment ago, too. But the sound of the horses' hooves brought him back, and therefore took him away again, reminding me that I'm preparing to bury my father, I'm not just strolling in front of Funeraria Monte Santo on another sunlit Granada day. And it feels like losing him one more time.

Once when I was visiting Mariana in Miami, I read a science paper she wrote about the connection between smell and memory. I know I said I always respected her boundaries, her privacy, and it's true, I have never so much as opened a desk drawer of hers to find a pen, as I didn't want to come across a diary or a folded letter and be tempted to read it like so many mothers do, like I know my own mother did. But she had left the paper on the hall table, and the red A on the front was as bright as a neon sign. The pages described how the same area of the brain that regulates our sense of smell controls our memory. Supplementing the scientific studies she cited, Mariana drew on the writing of artists and authors, as well as the words of some people she'd interviewed, including one man who had lost his sense of smell in a car accident, to demonstrate the connection.

I'm sure Mariana's right about the link between scents and memory. She got an A on her paper, after all, raising her overall average in that class to a B+ and keeping her on the high honor roll. (She thinks I never noticed that kind of thing, but I am her mother. A mother remembers, even if she's not the type to crow about her child's brilliance.)

Smells have always left me unaffected, except when I was pregnant, and our latrines and the local cheeses, and the smells of the cows and the coffee beans in Matagalpa, had me retching in embarrassed disgust. What brings the past back so sharply for me, what makes it more real than the present, is sound. Like today, when I heard the horses on the pavement, I could hear the voice of my father in his prime, sing-songing, "paca paca, paca paca," our baby-talk name for a horse, the sound they made trotting by. And last night, when I heard the crash of the tray above the brittle chitchat of the calling hours, I suddenly saw Manuel's surprised eyes, which reacted before the smile had a chance to fade from his face, as the bullet pierced his stomach and I stood across the hall, watching while he died.

22

❧

Maria

I've never been to the graveyard in Granada before; I've never had occasion to come. And now I wonder why I never thought to take a horse and carriage out to see it. It's just as beautiful as the cemeteries I've toured in New Orleans and Paris, albeit a little shabbier. There are angels everywhere, tall marble ones with outstretched wings rising from gravestones, and little plaster ones sitting cross-legged at the foot of a mausoleum. And all over there are practical signs of people's devotion: flowers left for loved ones, or here and there a bottle of Flor de Caña placed inside a glass-fronted grave marker. I want to return alone, to take pictures and to bring Abuelo his Halls Mentho-Lyptus cough drops, scatter them on his grave. If the scent of his beloved fumey candies can't get through to him, nothing can.

Right now, though, I wish I were anywhere but here. The sun is too bright and the air too smoky with the odor of someone burning trash nearby, my eyes are watering and my stomach feels both hollow and agitated, as if a fan had turned on somewhere deep in my intestines. But beyond that, the day seems unreal and I feel as if I might be invisible, as if, if I didn't hold on to Madre's arm or my Bela's shoulder, I could rise up and float away. Everything made sense last night, during the calling hours. I was sad Abuelo was gone, but he had lived his life, updated his will, given away much of his minimalist's stash of possessions. His death wasn't a surprise to any of us, least of all him. But somehow, I'm shocked to be here, burying my grandfather in this baroque cemetery.

Partly it's the loss of Abuelo sinking in, I guess. Although I've missed having a father almost every day since I was old enough to notice that most people had one, Papi died when I was less than a year old. Abuelo is the first loved one I actually remember losing. Maybe other people, who've suffered more losses than I, know this, know that no matter how you've prepared, how many doctor's visits you've attended during which a lowered voice tells you it's time to get his affairs in order, it's always a surprise when you realize the deceased is really, truly gone, that he won't be coming back.

From the middle of the cemetery you can see the volcano Mombacho, majestic but somehow a bit coy, with its top usually hidden by a cloud, leaving a little something to the imagination. It hasn't acted up in over four hundred years; to me there's something reassuring about the sight of that massive, volatile mountain, which has the power to bury us all, just sitting there, lazily, with its head quite literally in the clouds. I used to feel that the volcano was watching over Granada.

But the volcano hasn't protected the town from invasion, destruction, civil war. When William Walker torched the place, he left behind a lance inscribed with the words, HERE WAS GRANADA. I carry an image of Walker in my mind, ever since last year, a few days after Christmas, when we all drove up here for the day to have lunch at La Gran Francia, because Abuelo was in a nostalgic mood. Everyone bickering in the car was making my brain hurt—first the air-conditioning was too cold, now it wasn't strong enough—so as soon as we arrived I said I needed to hit up an ATM and fled, leaving them looking over their heavy, embossed menus. I was wandering around, decompressing, when I saw a placard that said, ENJOY THE SILENCE!—an ad for Café Sonrisa, which, the sign explained, was run entirely by deaf-mutes. After an hour-long drive with my family, silence was a major selling point. So I veered right, passing a workshop of guys making hammocks, and walked into the café. There on the wall was a mural showing the history of Granada, from the Nicarao Indians to Walker, to present-day smiling schoolchildren. I didn't think it was quite an accurate representation; in the mural, Walker was wearing a Spanish conquistador's hat, although he was a mid-nineteenth-century American filibusterer. But there was no mistaking him, because HERE WAS GRANADA was emblazoned above his head, in English, just as he would have written it.

By the time I had finished my jugo de sandía, the wall painting seemed both absurd and amusing, and I felt I could face Madre and my Bela and Abuelo again. After lunch, Madre took my Bela to her favorite panadería to buy pastelitos to bring back to Managua, and I volunteered to go with Abuelo to visit his childhood home. "I just need to run to the market to get a little dress for Olivia first," I told him. "Beth loved the one I brought last time. Why don't you sit here and have another lemonade and then we'll walk over to the house together?"

Abuelo surprised me by saying he knew the shop with the best embroidered children's clothes in town and that he'd take me. "But it's so hot," I protested.

"It's right on the Calzada, just behind my home, niña," he said.

"Besides, I want to send something to Beth, too; she's such a nice girl, such a fine lady."

Abuelo's highest compliment was to call someone a "fine lady," and he meant something different by it than did the writers of the social pages in my Bela's *Vanidades*; it wasn't crowned heads, but a certain inner calm that he admired. His mother was a fine lady, he said, and Don Pedro's wife. So I gave Abuelo my arm, or he gave me his, and we strolled to the pedestrian street where we ducked into a dark shop I'd never noticed before called Bordados Tres Hermanas; "Three Sisters' Embroidery."

The old woman who ran the place flipped on a light switch as I entered and asked how she could help me. But when Abuelo came in, she lit up herself. "Ignacio!" She patted her jet-black hair; I would have bet money that it was darker than the shade she was born with, it looked so artificial next to her pale skin and wrinkled face. But when she smiled, the raven hair somehow had the effect of making her look a little like a geriatric Snow White. "I haven't seen you since you came in with those strapping grandsons of yours!"

One look at the glass display case told me that this was where Rigobertito's sons' onesies came from, although Beth taught me they're not called onesies—those are the undershirts with the snaps at the crotch—they're called John Johns because Jackie Kennedy favored them, too. That's the kind of thing Beth knows. Fine ladies have to stick together, I guess.

"The store is such a mess today, and I am, too!" Snow White continued, although her shop was spotless as far as I could see.

"Flor, you're as lovely as ever," Abuelo said before turning to me. "Mariana, do you know you're standing in the shop of Granada's celebrated roller-skating champ?"

"Ah, the famous Mariana!" Flor gushed.

"It sounds like I'm not the famous one," I said, although my Bela had never mentioned Flor, so she couldn't be that much of a legend in Granada; my Bela knows everybody in that town, going back several generations. "Is there a rink here?"

Flor blushed so bright it showed through her face powder. "There used to be, a beautiful outdoor rink at the edge of town. They built over it to expand the train station."

"And you know what that means?" Abuelo said. "Flor remains undefeated. No one will ever break her record. Sixty-six spins in a row!"

"Oh, go on." Flor flapped a hand at Abuelo. "It was sixteen," she said, speaking to me now. "Sixty-six would be impossible. Such a joker, your abuelo! Now, how can I help you?"

We had strolled slowly over the Calzada, with Abuelo almost leaning on me for support. But after we bought a miniature wardrobe of smocked and stitched frocks for Olivia, he walked so fast back toward the square that I was practically trotting to keep up as we passed the fake Christmas tree, festooned with red ornaments and twining ribbons all bearing the name Claro, one of several competing cell phone providers. We stopped with our back to the tree, not out of any disgust at the commercialization of Christmas or the invasive nature of advertising—I actually thought the tree looked quite nice, with its unified color scheme—but because it was located smack opposite Abuelo's childhood home.

"Does it make you sad, that the house doesn't belong to you anymore?" I asked.

"Mi corazón, I learned a long time ago that nothing really belongs to us; not houses, not businesses, and definitely not people," he said. "They're all on loan, and you have to enjoy them while you have them."

"Way to bring down the room, Abuelo."

"When you're my age, niña, seeing things you lost doesn't make you sad. It all seems so far away, like a dream. And this place, it makes me happy. I was so full of energy when I lived here, ready to see where my life would take me, what I would make of it."

"You did good, Abuelo," I told him. "None of us would be here if it weren't for you."

He smiled, so I thought I'd milk it a little. "Seriously, I bet if you and Bela hadn't brought me to Miami, Madre would have married some revolutionary she met on a trip to Cuba and they would have raised me in a Siberian commune or something. I'd be working in a factory making Che Guevara T-shirts."

Now Abuelo was full-on laughing. "I didn't do anything, hija," he said. "But there is satisfaction at approaching the end of your life, and seeing what you're leaving behind; for me that's your mother and Celia, you and Rigobertito, his boys. I can't take credit for all of you, Isabela did most of the work there. But I'm proud of the small role I played in your existence. There is comfort in that, certainly." He looked at the building again. "When I lived here, there was so much hope. That's the gift a young man has, and the burden, too. Everywhere he goes, a cloud of possibility surrounds him."

I don't feel like that, crushed by my own potential. Maybe it's a male thing, to be convinced that you owe it to the world to be a star instead of just a productive citizen who pays her taxes on time and doesn't cut in line at the post office. Or maybe it's that I'm not really young anymore. At my age, Abuelo was already a father of two school-age children, running his own law practice in Managua. When he lived in this building, he was in his teens, his twenties.

"That was my bedroom," Abuelo said, breaking the silence. He pointed to the corner balcony on the second floor. "I used to stand up there and throw flowers down to pretty girls."

I thought that might make a nice painting, a man on a balcony in the upper left corner of the canvas, a woman with an upturned face in the bottom right, and in the middle, an oversize rose or calla lily. No, something brighter. Maybe a single, ridiculously enlarged bougainvillea bloom. But I didn't say as much to Abuelo, who, supportive as he tried to be, did once ask me why nothing in my paintings is the same size as in real life. Instead, I said, "You and my Bela must have had quite a courtship."

Abuelo laughed. "Mariana, Mariana." He patted my arm. "You don't throw flowers at the kind of girl you're going to marry. Flirting is about possibility, imagining all the wonderful things you could be. Marriage is about reality, accepting that it turns out you're not so wonderful after all."

"Maybe I'll never marry then." I shrugged. "I prefer the flowers to the ring."

Abuelo laughed so hard he started coughing and had to sit on a bench on the pedestrian walkway that now borders the house, staring up at his old bedroom. I wonder what he would think of my predicament now; if he would still find my words quite so amusing.

The Funeraria Monte Santo is just a few blocks down from Abuelo's old house. Years ago I took a picture of the sign in front, I thought it was so funny, the dead man jumping out of his coffin. It reminded me of a song, "Zombie Jamboree," that Beth's a cappella group used to sing in college. When I showed my Bela the photo, she shuddered and covered her eyes, not wanting to acknowledge that funeral parlors, even ones with surprisingly chipper corpses, exist.

Still, I'm pretty sure that my Bela is the exception to the rule; the sign is, empirically, funny. Even Beth cracked up at the photo—she had me tape it to our dorm room door in college—and she's not ex-actly one for dark humor, as the a cappella group membership indi-cates. I wanted to cheer Madre up, to let her know that I felt guilty about the separate-bathrooms comment, so I pointed out the sign to her this morning, when we arrived at the funeral home. She got it, right away; she erupted in uncontrolled laughter. And then she grabbed me and started crying.

And soon, I was crying, too. Because I'm not used to seeing my mother, the comandante, in tears, and because as terrible as I feel the loss of Abuelo is, she loved and relied on him for two decades more than I did. I know what it is to miss a father you never had. But I'm realizing it just might be worse to lose one you adored. I've spent so much of my life obsessing about how my mother felt about me, try-ing to calculate exactly how much she loved me, or if she, who has spent my whole life walking away from me, was capable of loving me at all, if I even crossed her mind on the days that she was in Mana-gua, meeting with world leaders, and I was in Miami, learning how to divide fractions. It never occurred to me to think for a minute about how much she loved anyone else. Her father. My father. Anyone.

I had been trying to comfort her, pointing out the amusing sign. But somehow we ended up with Madre, who had stopped crying, rub-bing my back, still holding me and whispering terms of endearment. "We'll all miss him," she said more clearly.

I took a long, shuddering breath through my nose and wiped my face with the back of my hand. After weeks of worrying almost single-mindedly about Allen, our future, and what I should do, my thoughts had been all over the place all morning. But now, having cried, I felt cleaner, lighter. I could concentrate on Abuelo.

❧

"In a place of light, in a place of green pastures," the priest intones, as the coffin is lowered into the ground. I like the phrase, love imagining Abuelo in a place of light, in a place of green pastures. It makes me think of the time he took me to Bill Baggs State Park to teach me how to ride a bike; I can hear the sound of my laughter as I finally rode off, wobbling, and the look of triumph on his face when I closed the small loop around the very tip of the park and rode back toward him, pumping his fists up and down with the palm trees and sea grass behind him, the sun sending shafts of light bouncing off the ocean.

People are stepping forward to drop their flowers on the casket. I take two, an imported rose and a local hibiscus, one to thank him for being the only father figure I had growing up in a city where I didn't quite belong, and one for being my grandfather, a man so tied to Nicaragua that his love of the country fueled mine. I step forward and lean toward the casket, dropping in the hibiscus, then the rose. I want to throw in all my other concerns to be buried as well, so that I will be left with nothing but the hollow sense of loss, and the love I had for Abuelo, which remains to fill the void.

But I don't believe Abuelo is in that coffin. I feel him around me, around all of us, but I know he's not confined to that fancy box. So I straighten up to make my way back to my Bela. And as I look into the crowd I see him, standing in the back behind relatives and friends and old Granadinos I swear I've never met but who, any minute now, will come up to me and ask, "Do you know who I am?"

Allen. I see him and, at first, I feel so much lighter, and brighter, as if a cloud shifted from its place blocking the sun, and I have to shade my eyes. Here he is, a promise that losing Abuelo's love and protection doesn't mean that my life will be without joy or affection. But then I remember that he hasn't made any promises, that I'm reading into what his appearance here means. And the cloud has shifted back again, and my world darkens.

If Allen is here it's because it's finally a good time for him. He's in Granada on his terms, not mine. He hasn't honored, maybe never even considered, my request to stay in Managua. He couldn't even give me this day. Give Abuelo this day. And if his presence here isn't a promise, then it's just the precursor to another loss. He's just as likely to be here to end something as to begin it. And I'm not going to let him touch today. He doesn't get to muddy my feelings with a new swirl of emotions. Today is Abuelo's. And mine.

Allen is standing just far enough away that I can try to convince myself that my mind is conjuring him, that he's just another gringo drawn to this scene of natives participating in a sacred ritual. But he sees me notice him and smiles apologetically, ducking his head the way he does when he shows up three hours later than agreed upon, having lost his sense of time in a canvas.

There's no way he can be sure that I've actually seen him; the sun is out, we're all wearing sunglasses. I turn to my Bela, who has taken up one of the graveside chairs and is sitting with her eyes closed. I lean over to hug her for a long while, feeling her chest rise and fall with a series of deep sighs. "You gave him so much joy," she says into my ear. "More than I ever could."

"That's not true." I rub her back. "You had a marriage lots of people would hope for." I mean it; they get points for longevity if nothing else. They had each other's company all these years. For some people, that would be more than enough. It's sad that Abuelo and my Bela were too hungry, and too shrewd, to be those people. Or maybe just too damaged by the time they found each other. My Bela had already lost Mauricio, through her own actions, really, if we're being honest. And she told me once that Abuelo had wanted to marry another girl, one his mother thought was too wild, from a family not quite as respectable as his own. He never spoke of her to me and he was always so private that I was too shy to inquire, although I dropped hints. I asked him, after we watched *Casablanca* together, if my Bela was his great love. The right answer was yes, of course; I wanted to think that there were times when they didn't just coexist but delighted in each other, not just in their shared joy when I won a prize or made a painting or learned a Spanish song. But he said, "Great loves are for movies and books, niña. In real life, we love our families and God, and that's enough." Maybe that was true for him. But even at eleven, I knew it wasn't true for everyone. Not for my Bela or Madre. And I hope not for me.

As I rise, my elbow gets caught on the strap of my Bela's purse, and suddenly I know that God, or Abuelo, somebody is helping me, showing me what to do. I lift the crocodile bag out of her lap and say, "Bela, I'm going to go put this in the car so you don't have to worry about it."

People are already starting to inch their way over to shake her hand, complete their obligation, then go home to continue with the rest of their lives. "Thank you, mi hija," she says.

"No problem." I kiss her quickly, casually, one more time, as I pick up the bag. "I need a minute to myself anyway; it's a good excuse to escape."

I sit in the backseat of the car, staring at the envelope with "Isa" written on the front in shaky script. There's so much to explain, so much that I thought I'd be able to say when I handed this to her at some imaginary, perfect moment in the future. Now I don't even have a good pen with me, just a cheap ballpoint I borrowed from a flight attendant in order to fill out the immigration form. I turn over the envelope to scrawl something across it; there isn't time to think this note through, but if I don't make this delivery now, I don't know when I'll have another chance.

I met Cristian Hidalgo at Mt. Sinai when Abuelo was there for tests the last time, I scrawl across the sealed flap. *A couple weeks later, this came to my gallery by DHL.* I'm not sure my Bela will know what DHL is. *There was a note saying I could deliver it or not, as I saw fit, and thanking me for my help. I decided to wait for the right time. I hope that's now, and that I'm not making things worse. I don't know what's inside—damn sealed envelope!—but I hope the contents will make you happier than they will sad. Either way, it didn't seem right to keep it from you any longer.*

Before signing my name, I add, *Be kind to yourself and don't worry about me for a little while. I love you always, your Maria.* And then, because I know that at this moment what matters is not independence but kindness, I add the *na*, signing not with the name I use for myself but with the name she calls me, the name that belongs to her and to Nicaragua, and, I suppose, to Madre, too.

I leave the envelope sticking out of her purse so that she'll notice it, with my ugly handwriting sprawling across the back. And then I get out of the backseat using the door that opens to the street, not the cemetery, narrowly missing being mowed down by a speeding (and now, swearing) motorcyclist. I run across the highway so I'll be less noticeable to any early birds eager to exit the funeral as fast as possible. And then I see further proof that God or Abuelo or luck is with me, because an empty caponera passes and I'm able to flag him down and hop in, and although the autorickshaws drive far slower than regular taxis, it's perfect because no one would ever expect me to be riding in this contraption.

As we chug toward town and the cemetery begins to recede behind us, I start to feel guilty about abandoning my surprisingly stoic Bela and an obviously heartbroken Madre when they most need me. I should have at least left a note for Madre, too, and thought up some sort of explanation for both of them. I'm tempted to turn back. But I can't stick around; I have to figure out this situation, and my future, on my own, without Allen's voice-of-God exhortations, without my Bela's chatter or Madre's pursed lips as she struggles not to be the kind of mother who tells her daughter what to do, even though she always has an opinion about everything. There is no other way— at least, that's what I want to believe, so I'll feel less horrible for running off. In an effort to convince myself I'm doing the right thing, I twist at the waist and peer out the dirty, plastic-covered back window, trying to pick out Allen's salt-and-pepper head rising above the crowd.

When I spot him, or at least some tall, middle-aged man with good posture I assume is him, the whirring fan in my guts gets worse. So I force myself to remember that, although he knew full well how serious this situation is, how unfathomable, every time I'd wanted to talk, he was too engrossed in a painting to stop and concentrate. And now, when I want some space to work through my alternatives, my thoughts, to formulate some sort of plan or survival strategy, he shows up, demanding to be heard. Hijacking my grandfather's funeral. Invading Granada, and my psyche, as sure as if he were some nineteenth-century megalomaniac in a conquistador's hat. And with that image, I've done it. I've worked myself up into such a flurry of righteous indignation that a calm settles over me, and I feel like the lake after a downpour.

23

Isabela

They pass in front of me, shaking my hand, a blur of black and gray, circles of perspiration just beginning to show under their arms. Do people perspire more these days, or is it me, has my eye become more critical than it used to be, seeking out the flaw instead of the beauty in each person? They are trying to be kind, I know. It's stamped all over their puppyish faces—smiling lips, sad eyes. At least they have the respect to remove their sunglasses before coming over to offer their condolences. But it might be better if they kept them on, because in their eyes I can see what has them all looking a bit ashamed, along with bereft. It's relief. Relief that it isn't their husband or father or grandfather who has brought us here. Relief that they aren't the ones in the coffin, now drowning in flowers.

I know because I've felt it, too, at every funeral I've attended, and there are more and more each year. I've even tried to bargain away the lives of those I love, just not quite as much as I love Ignacio, to offer them up as sacrificial lambs. At my age, you know death is going to be a frequent visitor and you start to hope, pray, and even make divine bargains to ensure that, when he comes to knock on your door, he'll get confused and end up stopping by your neighbor's instead.

Six months ago, when we needed a new rocking chair, I asked Don Pedro to drive me through Los Pueblos Blancos, and, when I found the perfect rocker in Masatepe early, and at a good price, I had him load it in the trunk and continue on to Diriomo, where my girlfriends and I used to go when we were younger to have the brujas read our fortunes. There was so much still unknown back then: would we get pregnant again, would our husbands ever stray for good, and, later, would our children marry happily, would they return from the front? While our children fought to change the future, we suffered worrying whether they would even have one. Padre Juan Cristobal said it was a sin to seek out divination, but even when we went seeking relief for serious concerns, the ladies treated it like harmless fun. I couldn't just listen to their fortunes and not take part myself, like a voyeur, could I? Sins are sins, but no priest will ever convince me that Jesus wants us to be rude.

And besides, the brujas had rosaries in their pockets, and statues of the Virgen in their windows. "Who was it who gave me my gift, if not God?" one demanded when I mentioned that my priest had warned me not to have my fortune told. That bruja explained that they had their own code to protect their God-given gift; it's what keeps them brutally honest, instead of just continuing to collect money from ladies to whom they feed nothing but happy stories, telling them what they want to hear. The brujas feel it's a sin to hide what they've been shown. One even told me, when the girls were teenagers, that Ninexin would marry for love, but it would end in blood. That terrified me. Later, when she assured me that Ninexin would live a long life, I relaxed. I didn't mind losing Manuel. Better that my daughter should be a widow than that I should have to live without her; I wasn't sure that I could.

Last summer, after I bought the chair, part of me said I shouldn't go to Diriomo, but I wanted to know what was going on with my Mariana. She was so busy at her new job, she couldn't always talk to me when I called, and last year, when she was at home for Christmas, she'd mentioned there was a new man, an older man, but didn't offer any more details. I knew I would never hear the full story until she was standing in front of me again and I could glean information in her eyes that her voice wouldn't reveal.

I wasn't sure if the yearning to understand Mariana was enough to warrant even a small sin; it wasn't serious worry that would be driving me to see the bruja, just petty curiosity. So I thought I'd wait twenty minutes and see if I still had the craving for divination; it's what Celia tells me she does with sweets. Thinking of sweets gave me an idea. I told Don Pedro that I wanted to buy cajetas, so he took me to a candy shop. Diriomo is also famous for its cajetas, for dulces and divination, as Mariana likes to say. But then my mind was made up for me, because sure enough there was a bruja in the shop, biting into a bright pink cajeta. Who knows, maybe God had sent her there? In any case, when she invited me to have my palm read while the muchachita packed up my sweets, I agreed. Everybody has to earn their pennies somehow, I told the voice of Padre Juan Cristobal echoing in my head. Besides, the requisite twenty minutes had passed and still I wondered, would I live to see my Mariana as a bride?

The bruja saw Mariana right away, and assured me that I'd one day bounce great-grandchildren on my knee. But then she leaned forward, out of the ray of sunlight coming in through the window, and her face darkened, or maybe the whole shop did. "I am sorry to say this, señora," she told me. "But you will soon suffer the loss of a family member, a man a bit older than yourself." I grabbed my hand away and threw a few córdobas across the table at the dirty, skinny woman. But not before praying, before I could stop myself, "Dios mío, let it be Francisco." Francisco, whom I've known since I was a girl of nineteen. Francisco, who has always been so kind, even lending us money that first year in Miami when we couldn't access our bank accounts here. Despite all of that, in my heart, I tried to lead death to Dolly's husband so I could spare my own. I hadn't exactly dreamed of spending my life with Ignacio, but I did live it with him. He was a part of me, of my everyday. For so many years I resented Ignacio for being just my reality, while Mauricio was my fantasy. But when the bruja forecast a death in our home, I saw that losing Ignacio would mean losing a large part—maybe the largest part—of my reality. And the older you get, the closer to the inevitable loss of everyday life, of the smells and shouts of the market, the rumble of hunger in your belly when it's still too early for lunch, the petty remarks of your sister or husband, the less irritating all those things seem. They become almost precious in your mind. Not almost. They become quite valuable. Because even mundane reality is irreplaceable once it's gone.

Nobody knows about the bruja's prediction; I couldn't even bring myself to tell the new young priest in confession, I know he recognizes my voice, and they're so soggy, priests today, what Mariana would call wishy-washy, always saying things like, "It's human nature to have such thoughts, just try to act with loving-kindness." I know a sin when I commit one, whether I meant to or not; just give me the right penance and let me be done with it.

When I heard the housekeeper screaming that Ignacio had died, the sharp stab of pain I felt seemed like a just punishment for my eagerness to dispatch with Francisco, to send grief to ring Dolly's doorbell instead of my own. But when I saw Ignacio's face, finally at rest,

I realized that it was simply his time. Ignacio's death had very little to do with me. Thinking that I caused it only inflated the importance of any role I actually had in his death. And in his life.

As they lean over to hug me, wishing me farewell, the mourners avert their eyes. But I don't begrudge them their relief; in fact I pity them their shame over it. I wish I had the power to absolve them, to place my hand on their heads and offer a blessing. I want this part of the day to be over.

And just when I'm thinking it's not possible to feel any more exhausted and empty, I see her. Flor. She was Ignacio's girlfriend, his last real girlfriend before me. He always had lots of women hovering around him; he was handsome and well-born and had a way about him that always made him seem significant, like a man, even when he had barely grown out of being a boy. Maybe it's because he was so young when his father died, and his brothers were already grown and married, leaving him the only man in Doña Milagro's home. His mother knew he went dancing with lots of girls, and probably suspected he did more with them than that. I'm sure it bothered her. Still, it wasn't the idea of her son having many girls that made her decide he needed to marry, but the fear that he'd end up with the wrong one. Flor.

Years after we were married, when the girls and I had come to stay in Granada because we were having some work done at the house, as my mother-in-law and I waited at the train station for Ignacio to join us for the weekend, she turned to me and said, "It was this place."

"Pardon, Madre?"

"It was this place that made me decide I needed to find the right wife for my Ignacio," she said, and although she was talking about me, she didn't seem to be talking to me; she looked straight ahead at the tracks. "Remember how it used to be a park, with a big cement circle that the young people used as a roller-skating rink?" she said. "I was bringing a donation to the nuns one afternoon and I finished my visit with the sisters early, so I thought I'd pick up some vigorón to bring back to Ignacio for a snack. And when I came to the vigorón stand in the park, I saw her: Flor Zaragoza, skating away as bold as you please, dropping to the ground with one knee up and her leg outstretched in front of her."

"Shoot the duck." I thought if I spoke she might stop talking, and part of me wanted that, I could tell I wouldn't like where this was going. But the curious, and also the self-righteous, part of me wanted to hear the story unfurl, to have one more piece of proof that I was more moral than Ignacio, that I was the wronged party in our marriage. "The girls roller-skate on the patio sometimes. I think that move is called shoot the duck."

"Well, it couldn't be more vulgar; really, you must make them stop it, Isabela. No granddaughter of mine is meant to roll around on little wheels, flashing her undergarments to passersby. It encourages immoral behavior! Both in the girl roller-skating, and in the men watching." My mother-in-law had been looking at me when she admonished me not to let the girls skate, but now she turned back to the station, where the train had yet to arrive. "The last time Flor dropped down like that, Ignacio skated over, grabbed her hands, and lifted her up to standing. She giggled and fell into his arms. In front of everyone! And that's when I saw how stupid I'd been; Ignacio must have been walking out with her for who knows how long, and everyone in town seemed to be aware of it but me. Her parents were nice enough, and one of her sisters has a beautiful voice, but the Zaragozas are common shopkeepers. And Flor was wild. Ignacio had that side to him, too. He needed to settle down, and with a girl who would bring out his steadier qualities, the aspect he gets from me, not from his father."

She looked back at me now. "I chose you. You were religious. You were respectful. And even at a young age you seemed to know that life has its disappointments. Marriage is hard work. I could tell you'd be good at it. And I was right."

I have to admit, I felt flattered. It was as if Sister Dunphy, the strictest nun at Sacred Heart, had given me a *Très Bien* ribbon. But that night, I made Ignacio take me for a walk and I told him I knew all about Flor. I demanded to know if he'd seen her, been with her, since we were married. "Isabela, you're being silly," he told me. "A man doesn't want two wives. It's twice the headache, not twice the fun. If a man seeks a little excitement outside the home, that's exactly what he wants: excitement. Mystery. Youth. Flor and I had fun together when we were kids. We might have gone on having fun with each other, under other, different circumstances. But then I wouldn't have had the girls. Or you." He pulled my arm through his and started guiding us home.

"A good man wouldn't go looking for excitement," I said. Because even though I knew everything was going to be fine, and that's what I wanted, I was worn out from the emotions of the day. I wanted him to suffer a little, too.

"I can say this." Ignacio didn't slow down, he kept walking, with my arm in his, so I did, too. "I've never wished I was married to someone else. I don't think you can say the same to me."

In the darkness, I couldn't see his face. And I didn't need Padre Juan Cristobal to tell me that lies are a sin. So I didn't answer.

⚖

"Isabela, after all this time!" Flor takes my hand, and I won't give her the satisfaction of pulling it away. That would make me the rude one. "I haven't seen you since you moved."

"The girls were already in school by then," I say. "We had no need for baby clothes."

"My deepest sympathies to them, and to you." Flor looked right at me, bold as brass. "Ignacio was a good man. Now he's in a happier place."

"Don't worry, Flor. Ignacio was perfectly happy in this place, too," I say as I pass her hand over to Ninexin and turn to the next mourner.

The confrontation with Flor gives me a little burst of energy. But then she's gone, almost everyone is, and I'm still here, sitting in a chair at my husband's funeral, a widow. And so very tired again. I want to ask Ninexin if she sees anyone in the distance, or if this interminable receiving line is finally truly over and we can join the relatives for a simple, subdued, but elegant meal at La Gran Francia, and then return home to our beds. I feel I could sleep for days. She's standing behind and to the left of me; she'll be able to see far enough to spot any stragglers. As far as I can tell, the graveyard has emptied out, at least as far as the people aboveground are concerned. But I can't get Ninexin to catch my eye; she's focused on something or someone a short distance in front of me, and as I turn to see what dog or bird or person has her attention, I hear a man clearing his throat and I feel a hand on my arm. The hand looks vaguely dirty, as if its owner hasn't washed well enough, and it's at odds with his expensive white shirt, the kind that requires cuff links, which Ignacio was always leaving in hotel rooms. I had him buried wearing the pair I gave him for our tenth anniversary; silver X's, the Roman numeral for ten. It's a little joke between us, our last little joke. He asked me about a year ago why, whenever Mariana e-mailed letters for him, and Ninexin printed them out, "XOXO" was typed at the bottom? Was this a Basque word he didn't know? I told him it stood for hugs and kisses, and he was as delighted as if he'd learned a whole new language instead of just a silly shorthand used by busy young people when they're too grown-up and far away to offer real hugs and kisses. After that, every time he spoke to Mariana on the phone he would say, "XO, mi corazón. XO." So I sent him to his rest with two kisses on his wrist: one can be from Mariana, and one from me. Ninexin gave him the tie he is wearing and Celia the tie pin. Since we raised Mariana like a third daughter, all those years we were living in Miami together, the cuff links can be a reminder of all the things the three of us learned together, all the little delights we shared.

"Mama," Ninexin says from beside me, louder than I think she really needs to, given the setting. But of course, she means to point out that I'm ignoring the silent owner of the hand on my arm. So I look up into two caramel-colored eyes that immediately wrinkle at the edges. "You must be Bela," he says. And I know this man has to belong to Mariana, because nobody else calls me that.

"I wish we were meeting under happier circumstances," he continues. I'm just glad to be meeting him at all. Even in death, Ignacio is full of surprises. Because the reason this man is here, that I finally get to see him, is thanks to my husband. "I'm Allen Knox, Mariana's friend."

"Charmed, I'm sure," I say, proud of myself for remembering the American phrase.

"Wow." The man laughs. It's a nice sound. "I knew you lived in the U.S. with Mariana, but I didn't realize your English would be better than mine!"

"My mother was also educated in the States, long before my parents moved to Miami," Ninexin says, inserting herself into our conversation. "She went to high school in New Orleans."

"I know all about Sacred Heart." The man smiles. Like all Americans, he has nice teeth. "I've seen the painting." When I don't respond, he elaborates, "Of the grammar textbook flying through the air."

"I don't know that one," Ninexin says, and of course she doesn't; Mariana is so private about her art. She shows only me, really. Me and this stranger, I suppose.

"She's so talented." Allen had been leaning forward a bit to talk to me seated in this wooden folding chair but now he straightens up so that he's face-to-face with Ninexin.

"Zach's wrong about them being too whimsical. There's a market for humor in contemporary art; look at Roy Lichtenstein, or Jeff Koons. Maybe Maria's paintings aren't right for his gallery in terms of subject matter, but the quality is there, definitely. I really think he was prejudiced, that he expected them to be more forceful and conceptual, more abstract." Allen shrugs. "More like my work, I guess. Which isn't fair. The joy in Maria's paintings is what art needs more of, what we all need more of." He's been talking so fast he seems almost out of breath. I look at Ninexin; the truth is, I understood only about half of what the gringo said. Maybe less. That he thinks Mariana's paintings have joy in them—of course they do. As well they should. So why is he so agitated?

"Listen to me, rattling on about the art world, when I know you all have somewhere to be." He runs a hand through his hair so that it now stands up in ridiculous tufts. "I just wanted to pay my respects." He grins, a smile that all three of us can tell most women he meets find irresistible. But the spiky hair is ruining the effect. I pat my own hair to my scalp, although I had taken great care to spray it before leaving, and smoothing it now is undoubtedly doing more harm than good. But he doesn't notice my subtle hint, or if he does, he doesn't care. He's busy looking around. "I was hoping to give Mariana my sympathies, too, but I don't see her."

Ninexin grabs the scarf at her neck and scans the cemetery a little too frantically. They're both like that, Ninexin and Mariana: anxious when the other one of them isn't around, but arguing half the time when they are in the same place.

"Mariana is in the car," I say in English.

"She is?" Ninexin asks.

"She is." The gringo nods as if I have just said something very wise. "My purse was heavy and in the way and she brought it there," I say, switching to Spanish. "She said she needed to escape for a while."

Ninexin's hand falls from her neck and she reaches out and takes the gringo's hand. "Allen," she says, infusing the word with wonder as if he is a long-lost relative or a celebrity she has read about for years but is only just now meeting in person, someone both familiar and longed for. "Why don't you give my mother your arm and we can help her out of her chair? Then we can all go to the car and find Mariana."

I know what Ninexin is up to: she wants to see how Mariana will react to seeing Allen. Will she melt into his arms, thrilled that he is here for her to lean on? Maybe they're secretly engaged, and she'll tell us that they have an announcement they wanted to make, but had agreed to wait to do so until the funeral was over. Or maybe she won't be as excited to see him as he is to be near her.

Whatever Mariana's reaction, now I desperately want to see it, too. Not out of curiosity or boredom; I'm not turning my granddaughter's life into a telenovela for my own amusement, of course not. But because when I see them together I will be able to feel it, I will know. Is he her Mauricio, or is he Mariana's Ignacio? Because he's definitely a person of some importance, at least in his own mind.

I turn to the gringo and speak to him in my best Sacred Heart voice. "Allen," I say. "You simply must join us for luncheon."

24

Ninexin

He's handsome, I think, shaking Allen's hand. And he looks to be somewhere in his mid-to-late-forties, halfway between Mariana's age and mine. I open my eyes a little wider, to mitigate the sagging of my eyelids. And then I drop his hand and look down at my shoes to keep from laughing at my own idiocy. He's not a reporter, here to venerate the great lady warrior, to ask respectful questions, and then, like the guy in San Francisco, mutter to a colleague as I walk away, "Hillary Clinton wishes she could rock a pantsuit like that."

As if Hillary Clinton and I have anything in common besides being female politicians. Although I suppose we did both marry men who struggle with impulse control. Maybe that's an unfair comparison; Manuel was only twenty-four when he was killed, still a child, really. I was in Washington at the time of the Virginia Tech shooting, and I saw a psychiatrist on a morning television show explaining that the emotional center of the brain isn't fully formed until the age of twenty-five, which is why young adults are so much more volatile: they lack emotional maturity. I was shocked when I heard that comment. I thought of myself as completely grown-up at twenty-five; I was already a widow, a mother, and a comandante. But now that I'm more than twice that age, I see how much evolving I still had to do. The girl I was in my twenties—so lonely and confused, so guilt-ridden about my child, and, at times, so exhilarated by my cause and my work—she barely resembles the woman I am now. At least I hope she doesn't. I wouldn't go back to my twenties. Except for the nice firm eyelids.

Mama's turning on her Southern belle charm for Mariana's beau, although I'm not sure Mariana would want us to charm him, or talk to him at all; she seemed rather angry at him last night. I'm trying to come up with a way to ask him, in not so many words, what exactly he's doing here, but perhaps the best thing to do is to keep quiet. It's a technique I use in meetings and negotiations sometimes: keep my mouth shut and a smile on my face and the other party is forced to ramble on to fill the silence, which makes so many people uncomfortable. It's amazing how even the most stoic politician will end up revealing something about himself or his position that he'd be better off keeping hidden. My strategy seems to be working; showing surprising restraint, Mama didn't rush in with reminiscences after he mentioned Sacred Heart. And now Allen has up and started talking about Mariana, about her art.

Whimsical? Her paintings aren't whimsical, not the ones I've seen. They're light-filled and warm, and gentle, but not in a silly, girlish way. I don't have such a large sample size to choose from; she doesn't really show me her work that much. But she does send photos of her paintings to Mama, who always shares them with me. Each time I see them, I am reminded of the words carved on the wall inside the Natural History Museum in New York, where I took

Mariana once when she was little and I had meetings at the UN. It's a quote from Teddy Roosevelt speaking to the Boy Scouts. And while I have lots of thoughts about his invasion of Cuba and manifest destiny and even his hunting of large game (weren't there enough human beasts and social ills in his own country to hunt and tame, did he have to go abroad to find animals to annihilate?), I couldn't help but tear up when I read it. Boys, it says, BE BRAVE BUT TENDER. It made me cry because Mariana was standing next to me, and I knew she was both those things, both brave and tender, and that it's not an easy way to be.

Her paintings reveal the part of Mariana that she shields from me. The softer side. That may be why she doesn't show them to me very often, or to anyone. She did have to exhibit a series of paintings in the campus gallery to get her master's degree from the School of Visual Arts, but she said that I shouldn't miss any of the World Health Conference in Geneva to go to it, that it wasn't a big deal, like graduating from high school or college. Papa's health was already starting to fail, he spent most days sleeping, and it was too far a trip for Mama to make alone, even if she had been willing to leave him in the care of the housekeeper, which she wasn't. But when Mariana sent us the graduation program, as she promised she would, all the other students were photographed in front of their work, surrounded by their relatives. She stood alone in front of a series of paintings of everyday scenes—a couple in love, a mother and child, a girl learning to ride a bike—all set against backdrops of volcanoes. Geneva was a good conference. But when I saw Mariana by herself in front of her paintings of lovers and families, I regretted attending it, even though she told me to go, and never said a word about the exhibit other than, "I passed and I didn't spill wine on anyone's paintings, so it was a huge success!"

I asked Mariana once why her grandmother got to see her artwork and I didn't, and she said, "I don't show anyone but my Bela my paintings. Working with real artists, I can tell how far I have to go before they're good enough to be seen."

"But why Mama, then?" I asked.

Mariana laughed. "Because it makes her happy, like when she used to stick my fingerpaintings to the fridge with a magnet."

"I had your drawings up in my office, you know," I said in the hopes of convincing her to e-mail me the occasional snapshot. But she just looked at me as if I'd confused her and said, "Yeah, I guess you did. On the side of the filing cabinet. I'd forgotten."

She still didn't email me images of her work. But when I've looked at the pictures she's sent to Mama, I have felt the same warmth I did this morning when her arms were around me as we cried. She makes me feel less alone. I'm half an orphan now, something she's been virtually her entire life. That's what makes her paintings the opposite of whimsical; they're profound in that they show moments of hope, of beginnings. The people in Mariana's paintings are leaping into something they believe in, even if it's against their better judgment.

Allen refers to his own work as if we should know it, and, by the overly humble shrug of his shoulders when he describes it, he seems to think we would have seen his paintings whether he was dating our Mariana or not. As if I have time to sit around Googling contemporary artists. If he'd started an NGO or proposed an international treaty, maybe then I'd be familiar with his work. And now I'm worried again, for my daughter. Because no matter how emotionally stable this older man is, he's had a good decade or more head start to make his name in the art world. And if he's as important as he thinks he is, no matter how profound her work is—and it is, and I just realized how much I hate the word "whimsical"—it will always be an afterthought.

I have no idea how Mariana really feels about this man. She mentioned him last Christmas, so they've been together over a year, but a year can be lived in countless different ways. Their relationship has to be serious; he came here today, didn't he? But she wasn't happy to see him at the calling hours. Mariana has never been forthcoming about her romantic life with me, or her feelings in general. Even her anger tends to come out as biting comments, not shouts and tears. But I have never been under the impression that because Mariana does not discuss her emotions, she doesn't feel things strongly. Everything she says, even the sarcastic remarks, or maybe especially those, is backed by a force of emotion so strong that it sometimes seems the words have been detonated more than spoken. Mariana's psychology resembles Granada, with its brightly painted, windowless houses that flow one right into the other, snug under their sloping, tiled roofs. They look so prim, like they're hiding something. But once the lacy ironwork that bars the door has been laboriously opened and you pass through into the home, you're steps away from a sun-filled courtyard overgrown with vegetation. The rooms are built around the interior garden, and their windowless outer walls keep the dust and heat of the street from violating the cool interior of the house. But on the other side they open into this secret, lambent Eden.

Allen asks where Mariana is and I realize that I don't know. She was here, on the other side of Mama, throughout the entire burial, up until a minute ago, it seems. I watched her leaning over Papa's coffin, dropping two flowers into it, and just when I thought I couldn't feel anything more, I was so tired and so numb with grief, I felt joy enter my body as if I'd inhaled it. Papa was already gone, the coffin closed, flowers starting to pile up on top and slip off its sides into the waiting, open earth. But as she released the stems, Mariana was a worthy subject for one of her own paintings. She was so beautiful it hurt to see her, and yet the joy I felt was so tangible I could breathe it in great gulps. It was the same feeling I had when she was a baby and I felt scared and overjoyed and weepy and amazed that it was possible to love someone this much. And determined not to let anything, or anyone, ever hurt her.

Mama says she's only gone to the car, but I can't shake the feeling that I have just lost Mariana, as well as Papa. I adjust my scarf to steady myself, and try to move events along so that we can go find Mariana, asking Allen to take Mama's arm and help me lead her up out of her chair and over to the car. She's delighted by his offering her his arm, of course. Almost eighty years old and still a sucker for male attention.

I'm tempted to laugh at mama's Scarlett O'Hara routine, but I cover my mouth and pretend it's a cough. Wasn't I the one wishing I had tauter eyelids while trying to put this handsome stranger at ease just a few minutes ago? I suppose I'm just as susceptible to a good-looking man as Mama is. Anyway, I can afford to be generous with my thoughts because Mama is now patting the back of the last, straggling well-wisher, who has found us at the entrance to the cemetery, a sweet, weathered man almost bent in two who was at the Colegio Centro América with Papa when they were young. He seems to have popped out of nowhere, but here he is telling a long-winded story about a prank they played on the student who was named príncipe of their year. He shakes a little, with laughter or tears or Parkinson's. I feel badly that I don't ask what his name is, but instead just shake his hand and thank him for coming and then watch him precariously make his way to his car with the help of his chauffeur.

Now our time is our own. Allen says something that makes Mama laugh and I start to think I might actually like him. It's exhausting, all this assessing and reacting, scrutinizing his every word and action.

I just want to see how Mariana treats him, to follow her lead. But when Don Pedro opens the car door, there's no one there, just Mama's purse sitting on the backseat as if it's a very patient passenger who has been waiting on us all this time.

"Where's Mariana?" Mama asks Don Pedro, then translates his response for Allen: "She went ahead to see that all was in order for the luncheon." Turning to me, she adds in Spanish, "She could have thought to tell him who she was going with so we didn't worry—the Ferreras, do you think? Or the de Santiagos, they left rather early."

I nod, not wanting to worry Mama, and I ask Allen to please take a seat up front. Once he does, and is looking in front of him, distracted by the horses and the motorcycles and the extravagantly colored churches all sliding past him, I pull out the envelope that is sticking out of Mama's purse. It has Mariana's spiky handwriting climbing across the back, and I breathe deeply to try to slow my heartbeat as I read the note.

I hope that I'm wrong. I hope that I don't know my daughter as well as I think I do, and that I'm misinterpreting this message as I have so many others in word or deed throughout her life. Because the first part of the note is just one of the many private conversations Mariana and Mama always seem to be continuing. But when I see the postscript, the words "don't worry about me for a little while," and the fact that she signed her whole name, I have the sickening feeling that Mariana won't be at La Gran Francia when we get there, that she, too, is gone from me.

25

Maria

I had the caponera drop me off in front of the ATM so I could take out some córdobas to pay the driver; I had gotten cash at the airport in Miami, but it was all American dollars and while most people here accept those, it didn't seem fair to make the driver pay change fees for what amounts to just over two dollars. Plus, I need more cash for my trip; I'm still not sure how far away I can get, or for how long I'm going, but I need to flee, to be able to avoid the questions in Allen's eyes and concentrate on the ones in my head.

I had come to Nicaragua to say good-bye to Abuelo, to bury him, and now I had done that. As soon as I'm back at an easel, I will paint him throwing a flower down to a lovely young woman. Only in my version, the girl with the upturned hand will be my Bela. That's the point, or one point, of art, isn't it? That it can depict life as it should be rather than as it is.

The painting will be an apology to Abuelo for delivering the letter. It felt like a betrayal, slipping it into my Bela's purse today of all days, but I had been carrying it around for so long. And when Allen showed up there wasn't time to wait for the perfect moment to interfere in my Bela's quiet life. I have to focus on my own life instead, or I'll end up like my Bela, letting others make all the most important decisions for me. If Abuelo were here, we could talk about everything calmly; he'd help me clear away the clutter and decide what it is I want. But he's gone, and I have to do this myself, just like when he let go of the back of my two-wheeler on Key Biscayne.

I should have come home for Christmas, spent one last holiday with Abuelo. Every year in Miami, he was the one who softened the edges of the triangle my Bela, Madre, and I form. When it was just the three of us, one of us was always getting hurt; Madre felt left out that my Bela knew the names of the other girls who were in the choir with me, or the boys who took me to dances, but she didn't. My Bela got anxious, trying to make sure we all got along, that Madre didn't make any comments about my choice of reading material (*Sweet Valley High* not being her idea of intellectual stimulation, although I found it very educational) and I didn't make any snide remarks about Madre not being around enough to notice when I was actually reading literature—or ever, really. Even when we were having fun, laughing, catching each other up on the news of Doña Olga's family, and life in Managua, and the antics of the neighbors in our condo in Miami, I'd always get quiet, wondering what was wrong with me that my mother didn't want us to be like this, together, always. And my Bela would notice I was subdued and try to cheer me up with one of our favorite treats, a walk to the Cuban coffee shop or a visit to Bal Harbour to watch the koi swim in their ponds and the rich people shop. None of which Madre particularly enjoyed, so she'd end up feeling left out all over again.

But when Abuelo was around, we were balanced, a square. He didn't expect every holiday to be the best Christmas ever like my Bela does, or a prelude to rejection like I did, or a disappointingly bourgeois ritual the way I imagine Madre saw all of our little celebrations. He just wanted to sit there together watching *It's a Wonderful Life* or *Qué Pasa, USA?*, sharing the jokes the Cubans at the coffee shop told him, and staring at the three of us like we were something special.

But I didn't come to Managua for Christmas this year because I wasn't ready to see everyone, and I thought it would be easier to hide within the dramas and celebrations of someone else's family than to negotiate my own. Our family dynamic is difficult even at the best of times. And these are not the best of times; I didn't think any of them, even Abuelo, could ease the confusion that is overtaking my life right now. So I thought I'd protect them from the chaos. Even, I'll admit, from the shame. My cowardice, or at least, my inability to figure out how to move forward, cost me my last Christmas with Abuelo. Now I don't have him to soften the edges of my life anymore. I have to figure out what happens next. And I need to do that alone before Allen and I—or Madre, my Bela, and I—can begin doing so together.

After stopping at the ATM I cross the park to sit under Abuelo's balcony one more time, to spend a few surprisingly happy moments staring up at the railing, imagining Abuelo there, as a boy in short pants like in the black-and-white photo at my Bela's house; as a young man in his wedding portrait; as a middle-aged man in a short-sleeved button-down shirt, sending my bicycle flying down the path with me on it, laughing away; and as an old man looking out the exam room's window down onto Biscayne Bay, saying he was ready to go. It feels as if Abuelo is sitting next to me, as if he could see the figures on the balcony, too. But I know that is just wishful thinking, me being a little maudlin, what with the heat and the fatigue and the emotion of the day. So I blink hard and stand up, telling myself that it is time to get moving.

I consider walking down the pedestrian street to the lakefront, but it's too risky; I'm bound to see someone I know, or who knows my family, shopping for chocolate croissants at the French bakery or embroidered children's clothes at Bordados Tres Hermanas. So I backtrack to the horse and carriages and climb up into one, refusing offers of sight-seeing tours, and ask the driver to take me straight to the port. Anyone noticing the carriage *clip-clop* past him on the street will be more interested in the horse than in the gringo tourist he'll assume is inside.

I thought I'd calm down as the town recedes and it becomes more and more unlikely that anyone will spot me. But instead I feel my heart beating in time to the horse's trotting hooves. When we reach the banks of the lake, which is so vast that it looks like the shore of an ocean, children are wading in their clothes, their backs to us, and their brown limbs flailing in the still, muddy water.

We pass the first dock, where pleasure boats and canoes vie for the opportunity to lead locals and gringos on tours of the isletas; it is too crowded and my purpose too unusual. My request would undoubtedly provoke discussion and commentary, necessitating an impromptu committee of seamen to settle on a fair price. It isn't until we reach the end of the peninsula, beyond all the lakefront restaurants and the grazing cows, where a few sailboats and speedboats idle, that I ask the driver to stop. Lake Cocibolca has several hundred islands, many of the isletas uninhabited, except by cranes or spider monkeys. But a number of the larger ones have schools, and villages of little shacks inhabited by some of Nicaragua's poorest citizens, whose families have lived on these island for generations. On one is a church where, each Holy Week, pilgrims row out in canoes, carrying a statue of the Virgin Mary in a floating procession. I watched the faithful water parade the spring break I was fourteen, from the lake house of a coworker of Madre's, some important Sandinista whose name I don't remember although his handsome bodyguard was called Elvis. Because that's what rests atop many of the other isletas, the stunning lake houses of wealthy Granadinos, and the weekend places of Managua's glitterati.

I'm remembering that spring break now, while assessing the speedboats at the dock we've finally trotted up to. Most of them must belong to the men who own their own islands, driven by caretakers who drop off and pick up their patrons and invited guests. When I ask who can take me to Solentiname, the guys idling by the boats laugh at me as if I'm an adorable but not very bright child.

"Solentiname . . . let me guess. Do you paint?" asks a man with a mustache that looks drawn on, as if he had gone to a costume party dressed as a French chef and forgotten to wash his face when he changed his clothes. I nod.

"But I'm betting you don't sail?" The laughter the men had been suppressing momentarily explodes around me again.

"Sadly, no."

Finally a guy who appears to be about my age steps forward. He has a mustache, too, but it looks more genuine, or maybe it's just overshadowed by his eyes, which remind me of the close-up of the Charioteer of Delphi in the textbook of the first art history class I ever took, bright and open almost too wide to be believable.

"A ferry leaves here at two on Mondays and Thursdays, but it doesn't get to the archipelago until six the next morning," he says.

"I guess it's farther than I thought." I'm feeling a little light-headed, so I look around for a place to sit down while I rethink my plans, but

I don't see one. I close my eyes for a minute instead, reverting to my childhood logic that if I can't see these men staring at me, waiting for me to make my next, hilarious move, they can't see me either. I could turn back before anyone even notices I've left, hail another carriage, find my family all at La Gran Francia and say I'd just needed air and gone for a walk. But the city is so crowded with memories of Abuelo, and Allen's force of will is so great, and my own uncertainty is so vast that it would swallow me whole before I had time to decide what I needed, and I'd end up doing what's best for Allen simply because Allen always knows what he wants.

"It is far; the islands are in the south of the lake, near the mouth of the river," a voice says, and when I open my eyes I see it was the Charioteer who spoke. "But also, the ferry stops on Ometepe first."

"Maria." I extend my hand.

"Marlon," the Charioteer says, and as he shakes it, the crowd around us slackens a bit, some of the men going back to their boats. Now that I'm a person with a name—the name of the Virgen, after all—my stupidity is less likely to be a source of amusement. If they stick around long enough, they might even have to help me.

"Pleasure, Marlon." The first thing the woman who trained me at the gallery told me was to repeat a potential buyer's name often, to roll it around in your mouth as if it is the most delicious treat in the world. Each time you say a buyer's name, she swore, the likelihood of your making a sale increases by 17 percent. (She also told me always to give a price in odd numbers, so the buyer thinks you're shaving a bit off and giving him a deal. Otherwise, I suspect, she would have sworn the name trick worked in increments of 20 percent.)

"Tell me, Marlon, how long does the ferry to Ometepe take?"

He shrugs. "Four hours, more or less."

"So you could take me there in your boat?"

He turns to study the shiny speedboat behind him and he puckers his lips slightly, which makes me think he's doing math, figuring out how much gas he has, trying to remember if he has an extra container on board, and to calculate how long it will take to get to Ometepe and back.

"I could," he says. "But it would be expensive."

"How expensive?" I have to keep enough money on me to stay on Ometepe three nights, waiting for Monday's ferry, then to support myself on Solentiname for however long it takes to figure things out, wait for the next ferry back, and maybe even scout some new artists while I'm at it, so I can charge this folly to the gallery. But after some more lip-puckering on Marlon's part, and negotiating down to an odd-numbered sum on mine, we agree on a price.

I jump onto the boat quickly; all I have with me is my purse, and I don't want Marlon to overthink this, change his mind. It isn't until we're already motoring out of the dock that I realize Marlon is wearing a polo shirt with the words EL MIRADOR stitched above his left nipple. This isn't his boat, then; he's not an independent contractor offering speedboat tours to day-trippers or water-skiers, but an employee from one of the grand homes. El Mirador is probably the name of the property he tends. Of course, the shirt is just as likely to be a hand-me-down, or something he picked up in one of the many stores selling secondhand goods. It doesn't really matter. I don't care if he's bending any rules by picking up a side project; I'm just glad he's agreed to let me aboard, and to take me so far. Lake Cocibolca is bigger than Puerto Rico, I remember Elvis's boss, the nameless Sandinista, telling me when I was fourteen, "You could fit Puerto Rico inside it, it could be an island in the lake."

"But then where would all the other isletas go?" I asked in all seriousness, and the important man laughed and chucked me under the chin, saying, "You're just like your mother." Which, if he knew anything about my mother, would mean that I abhor the kind of man who chucks people under the chin.

In minutes the speedboat has left the shore behind and I feel as if I'm in a Japanese painting, what with the volcano in the distance and the massive water lilies floating past. The plants are even more stunning than I remember, big as dinner plates, and open wide as if they're waiting for blessings from the sky to drop into their centers. But the smell of the diesel from the motor is spoiling the view for me, so I move to the next seat up, diagonally behind the driver.

"If I'm going too fast, let me know and I'll slow down a little," Marlon says. I nod. "But not too much," he adds. "I need to get back tonight; my son's birthday is tomorrow and my wife will murder me if I'm not there, or if I'm too tired to oversee the piñata." He's smiling already, whether at the thought of his boy or his quick-tempered wife, I'm not sure.

"How old is he turning, your son?" I ask.

"Five." The grin again. So it was for the birthday boy after all.

"What's his name?"

"Marlon." I should have guessed. Marlon-papa looks even more like the Charioteer now, gazing ahead at the distance he has to cover, the remains of a smile on his face as he thinks of his son. No matter how often I hear them, I'm amused by the way so many people around here have names that haven't been popular in the U.S. since the middle of the last century. Just in the course of Abuelo's calling hours I met chauffeurs younger than I am named Oswald, Norbert, and Wilfred. The roll call at Granada's kindergartens must be identical to the list of residents at the assisted living facility where Beth works in North Miami Beach.

"Marlon- hijo," he clarifies, because I haven't asked another question and he's still eager to talk about his son. Palm trees lean off of isletas as we zoom past, threatening to topple into the lake, and cranes practice yoga poses, balancing on rocks that pierce the surface, but Marlon-papa seems oblivious to all of it, as if he's thinking not of the scenery but of his boy.

I wonder what it's like, to have someone be your first and last thought each day, but without the electric uncertainty that underscores my thoughts of Allen. To love someone more than you thought possible but with the calm of knowing that you belong to each other and have from the beginning. The devotion Marlon-papa has for his child is as visible as the name on his shirt, and it overwhelms me. I wonder if I'll ever be capable of loving someone that much, that single-mindedly, and if Marlon-papa was always so openhearted, or if he learned to love this way with the birth of his son. How does it feel for him: Does the weight of that love drag him down or buoy him up, carrying him along like this boat? Or both?

I consider asking him; he's smart and friendly, and doing me a favor, really, even if he's being well paid for it. And a little conversation would take my mind off the bumping of the boat, which makes me feel like throwing up, although I can't remember the last thing I've eaten. But I don't say anything because if I ask Marlon-papa to describe what he feels for his son, the answer could be so large it would knock me out of this boat and send me sinking past the water lilies down to the bottom of the lake.

Or maybe it would be my own jealousy that would drag me down. Because, I have to admit, part of me envies Marlon-hijo for having a dad who sees his son's face before him even as he speeds past cranes and monkeys and canoes. If the love of a father is as pronounced as the yearning for one, hearing Marlon-papa describe it would crush me.

I'm being melodramatic. Abuelo would say he raised me so that nothing could crush me. It's the hunger, or the emotions of the day, that have me thinking like this. I know better. Not having a father, I've learned to fill my life with other things, to do without. And besides, who's to say that my dad would have been the must-get-back-before-the-piñata kind? Maybe he would have been so busy creating the new Nicaragua that he wouldn't have noticed my birthdays, and I would have spent my childhood longing for him even when he was there. As I did Madre.

"He's adorable," Marlon-papa is saying about his son, even though I still haven't managed to come up with any follow-up questions. "He's chele, like you. Like his mother. I'm the dark one." Marlon laughs at the whims of fate and genetics.

I laugh, too, because I've lived in America long enough that it always surprises me how openly people here talk about race and weight and age and all the things I've trained myself to pretend I don't notice.

"I'm the dark one in my family," I tell Marlon. "I mean, we all have light eyes but my mother has much lighter hair, chestnut colored."

By now several hours have passed since I left the graveyard. Everyone will have noticed my absence at lunch. My Bela will have found the note. And even if she focuses on the luncheon and follows my instructions and doesn't worry, she's bound to wonder where I am or what I'm doing. And Madre, too. Maybe I should have left a note for her as well, or at least jotted another line to my Bela, saying, *Tell Madre I'll call her when I get a chance.*

For most of my life, I could have sworn that my whereabouts were below literacy campaigns and free immunizations and party-appropriate neckwear on Madre's list of concerns. But of course she was upset today at the funeral home, and she seems to be missing Abuelo sharply now that he's gone. Maybe she's more susceptible to the absences of her loved ones than I would have guessed. She told me she loved me this morning, in front of the Funeraria Monte Santo. I believe that she meant it when she said it. I'm just not sure that I believe she knows how to express that love. Or maybe it's that she's good at being a loving daughter, a thoughtful person, a philantrophist, but something limits her ability to show her love as a mother, or to let it drive her in the overarching way other moms seemed to do. Is it her independence? Her selfishness? Or maybe it's the opposite, her altruism; it would be more selfish to love one child rather than all the children of Nicaragua. That's what my Bela would have me believe, that my mother always loved me so much from afar, but that so many other people besides me needed her, too. With Madre gone, my Bela's love for me had so much room to grow. Maybe it became so powerful that it blocked Madre's love from reaching me.

It doesn't seem fair, how people can be so skilled at one kind of love and stumble so badly at another. I know I'm a standout granddaughter. And I haven't been a bad daughter, I don't think. I see Madre more than many of my friends in New York do their parents who live a few states away, and who were with them every day until they turned eighteen, give or take a few weeks of summer camp. But I'm not delusional enough to believe that I've been a loving daughter. I don't seem to be that skilled at loving Allen either; I'm either adoring him to the point of erasing myself, or convincing myself that he's so insufferable I never want to see him again.

It's time for me to stop thinking about what I want Allen to do and determine what it is I want to do about loving him, and if I'm strong enough to expand my capacity to love, or shrewd enough to realize that it's a hopeless case and I should walk away and save myself, and everyone else, more disappointment. And I suppose that's even truer for Madre.

I don't want to talk to Allen until I know what I have to say. But it seems right to let Madre know that I'm fine and will be in touch soon, so that I'm not adding to the pain of the day for her. I pull out my phone to send her a text message; she'd never hear me in all this wind and I don't want to be interrogated into letting her know where I am or what my plans are. I type, *I'm taking a little trip for R+R. Will call soon. Don't worry.* But when I hit "send," the words stay on the screen, and I see how empty they are. I start deleting them, to try again, but Marlon-papa leans forward to let me know, "That won't work here."

"We're out of range?"

Marlon-papa shrugs in sympathy, but he's smiling like a man who can sail to the middle of Lake Cocibolca, halfway across the imaginary island of Puerto Rico, miles away from everyone he knows, and still not be out of touch.

26

Isabela

Mariana's tall beau sat in the front, next to Don Pedro, which made me pity Don Pedro—gringos always feel compelled to make conversation with drivers; they don't understand that part of what attracts a man to this job is the opportunity to spend hours alone with his thoughts, even if the car he's maneuvering is full of chattering people. But it's a good thing Mariana's giant sat up front, where he's using a very odd, very loud, very slow brand of English to point out to Don Pedro that it is a nice day, sunny, and the sky, it is blue, and the houses of this town, they are so pretty, because from up there he can't see Ninexin frantically waving the envelope at me, stabbing at the note Mariana left across the sealed back in her abominable penmanship.

"She did look a bit suffocated, surrounded by all those people," I say to Ninexin, once I finally make out the words Mariana had written. "She'll probably sit at that café she loves so much, the one with the deaf people, pobrecitos, until the lunch is over, and then she'll come find us before we're ready to drive back to Managua."

The real mystery isn't where Mariana has gone; my granddaughter is a wanderer, she loves to set out for someplace unexpected, but she always comes back to me. The question that interests me is what is this letter she's being so mysterious about, what could Cristian Hidalgo have to say to me after all these years? Perhaps he's been going through his things and has sent me a note, maybe even including a few photos of when we were young: scallop-edged black-and-white images of such a vibrantly colored time. I would love that so! It would be a gift from God to have some unexpected happiness come to me on this day. I don't want to delay opening the letter any longer, but Ninexin is gripping it as if it were her ticket to Paradise, even though Mariana clearly left it for me.

"What about this?" she whispers, but it's such a loud whisper that it's a hiss, and she's poking at the envelope so viciously that I'm sure she's going to tear it.

"Calm yourself!" I insist. "And speak up! If this one knew Spanish, do you think he'd be talking to Don Pedro like we're living in slow motion?" I grab the envelope and study the line she was attacking with her nail; writing across the flap of the sealed envelope has made Mariana's penmanship even more uneven and difficult to decipher. "*Be kind to yourself and don't worry about me for a little while*," I read out loud. "So maybe she's gone for a long walk, or is going to check into one of the hotelcitos and relax for a few days. Some of them have spas, you know. Doña Chelita has a massage twice a month, the doctor says it's good for her back."

Ninexin nods but her lips have grown small and her eyes wide, just like when she was a little girl fighting with Celia and trying not to let her big sister see her cry. I clasp her hand, which is still extended in front of her, empty now that I've taken the letter away. "She's a smart girl, a grown woman, and she speaks the language," I say. "I promise she'll be perfectly fine. Better than that. She'll manage to squeeze some happiness out of this sorrow-filled trip! Let's just get through the lunch and if she hasn't arrived by the end, we can call her without this giant sitting right in front of us, listening to her voice come through the phone, and ask her how much more time she needs, what she wants us to tell him."

Ninexin nods and looks out the window, but her hand squeezes mine. "You're right, this is probably something between them," she admits. "It's not any of our business. But still—"

"You know how young people in love are, they have no concern for their families' feelings," I say, just a little pleased that Mariana is finally giving Ninexin a taste of the suffering I went through when Ninexin was running around the poor parts of town and then clambering around the jungle with that Manuel; Mariana's always been such an easy girl, nothing like her headstrong mother. "It's not a bad idea to make a man chase you a little bit."

"But she could have told *us* where she was going." Ninexin turns to me. A tear escapes her left eye, but she wipes it away so quickly that I'm unsure it was there in the first place.

"And put us in the position of deciding to tell him where she went or not? And of explaining why? No, thank you," I say. "My granddaughter knows what she's doing."

Ninexin looks out the window again. "You mean my daughter knows what she's doing."

We're creeping along, keeping pace behind the few mourners who are so young, so respectful, or so poor that they're walking from the cemetery to the center of town. Mariana's giant has given up trying to chitchat with Don Pedro and taken up humming instead. I think it's "The Rain in Spain." That's probably as close to a Nicaraguan song as he can call up. Poor, lost gringo.

Ninexin and the gringo are each looking out their own window, so I take a pen from my handbag and use it to slice open the envelope without ripping apart the note Mariana has scrawled across the front flap. But despite my efforts, the pen gets stuck on the corner of the envelope, and when I pull it back, I force a corner of paper out as well.

I drop the pen and shove the folded paper back into the envelope, finally turning it over so that I can see the front of it for the first time. There's no address, just a single word: my name. And then I put it right back in my purse, only deeper than Mariana had, under my glasses' case and my handkerchief and my cough drops, so that it can't possibly creep to the top and peek out. Because the handwriting on the front confirms what I suspected—no, what I knew—the minute I saw the words on the stationery slipping out of the corner of the envelope after I tore it open. The script is shakier, the words slope more sharply upward, but even in the three letters on the front of the envelope, in the nickname that no one but Dolly has called me in decades, I can tell it's the same handwriting I once knew so well that I could describe the shape of every letter, exactly where the bar of the *t* crosses the stem, how the loops of the *g*'s never quite close at the bottom. This letter has nothing, or at least, very little, to do with Cristian Hidalgo. This letter is from Mauricio, and it's the first I've had from him in over half a century. There's no way I can read it in the backseat of this car, with my daughter, mine and Ignacio's, sitting to my right, this too-tall stranger humming show tunes in front of me, and Don Pedro rolling his eyes in the rearview mirror.

"What does this Hidalgo say?" Ninexin asks.

"Trying to scan it in the car made me feel sick," I say. "I'll read it after lunch."

We arrive, finally, and Allen helps me out of the car before Don Pedro can make his way around, depriving the poor man of his ability to do his job. When I suggest to him, "Perhaps you'd like to refreshen up before luncheon," my English hardly has an accent at all, and he strides obediently toward the bathroom, undoubtedly wondering what is caught in his teeth that I'm too polite to mention. I take Ninexin's arm and lead her to the hostess desk.

"Right this way, Doña Isabela," says a pretty young Indian-looking girl with a forehead so smooth I can almost see my reflection in it. "May we offer our condolences?"

"Thank you, dear." I focus on the Moorish tiled floor in front of me, as if human interaction is too painful today, then lower my voice a bit to add, "Would you be kind enough to book us a room for tonight? Two beds, for my daughter and myself. I just don't have it in me to drive back to Managua after lunch."

The sweet girl is sure there won't be a problem, but asks for a moment to confer with the manager, whose office is across the courtyard.

"Are you feeling all right, Mama?" Ninexin asks, tightening her grip on my arm as the girl walks away.

"Perfectly fine!" I shake off her hand. "I'm tired, that's all, and there's no reason to rush back to Managua if Mariana's not coming home with us right away. If she needs a few days to herself to unwind, we might as well wait for her here until she's ready to see us, relax a little bit ourselves."

Ninexin kisses my forehead and the hostess smiles as she walks towards us, pleased that the poor old widow has such a loving daughter to support her. Mariana's giant is crossing the courtyard at the same time, carrying his hands before him as if he's a surgeon heading into the operating room. If he's one of those who never dries his hands after washing, I don't know how Mariana can stand it. He's smiling at me, too, so I feel a bit guilty, but also rather pleased with myself that neither of these fine, strong, relatively young people can tell that I'm lying. Because while I do think we should get out of Mariana's way and let her have a few days to herself if that's what she wants, I have no doubt that she'll come back to me when she's ready. And I am exhausted, but I'd be just as bone-tired in Managua, in the home I shared with Ignacio. It's a fine place to rest, but it's no place to bring another man's letter. Here, in Granada, there will be moments when Ninexin steps out to make a phone call or grab some dinner, and I will be left alone to sit in one of the inn's cool, high-roofed, tile-floored rooms, under a painting of a saint or an angel or some crusading general, and free to read this letter I've been waiting on for over half a century.

"We've reserved one of our nicest suites," says the hostess with the smooth forehead. I nod my creased one at her in return, thread my right hand under Ninexin's forearm, and lead her to the doorway of the dining room, stepping in front of the gringo. With my daughter by my side and Mauricio's letter in my handbag, I walk into the dining room, smiling sadly at the faces of my late husband's relatives.

27

Ninexin

There was not one moment during the entire luncheon that I didn't spend worrying about Mariana, wondering where she's gone and with whom. I sat pretending to listen to people's remembrances, their toasts to Papa's memory, and I'm sure everyone thought that my pale cheeks and chewed lip were the result of grief for my father, not fear for my daughter.

It's silly, I know. Mariana dutifully calls me every other Sunday or so, and if something important happens or we need to coordinate travel plans, we'll email in between. But there are days, sometimes even weeks, in a row when I don't hear from her, when I'm not sure if she's in New York or in Miami visiting Beth or even in Paris attending an art show. And while I think of her, of course, all the time, I seldom worry about where she is or what she's doing. But now that we're in the same country, in our country, or mine, anyway, and I don't know her whereabouts, all I can imagine are the ways she could be suffering somewhere out there. Was she mugged trying to take money out of an ATM? (It feels disloyal even to think that, given all the press releases I've sent touting Nicaragua as the safest country in Central America.) Is she drowning in her own grief over Papa? Or, less scary but more hurtful, is she doing the best she can to disappear, renting a hammock in some dirt-road barrio off the side of the highway just so she can avoid spending more time with me? When Mariana was a little girl, those first three or so years in Miami, each time I left she would beg me to stay longer, to stay with her for good. She'd get very quiet, watching me as I packed my suitcase, and then when it came time to hug and kiss good-bye she would start crying and cling to me, wailing into my ear, "But I really want you to stay." I always managed not to cry myself until I got into the cab, but it was awful. Until the year she was ten and she hugged me and said, "Bye-bye, Mama. Have a safe trip." And that was even worse. I tried to tell myself that she finally understood what Mama and I always said, that I had to leave because I had important work to do, to help all the little girls in Nicaragua. But when she waved at me, dry-eyed, it felt less like she knew I couldn't stay and more like she no longer cared if I did. As Mariana grew older, she became the one to leave early, shortening her high school summers in Managua, spending no more than a week here at Christmas. This time, now that she's gone, it feels like she might be choosing to leave for good. And I want to cling to her and say, "But I really want you to stay."

I was running so many scenarios about what Mariana might be doing through my mind that I didn't hear what Celia said about Papa, although she was looking right at me, knowing it was a memory we must share. I smiled back at her sadly, benignly, a front to hide the emotion swirling behind it. Celia stopped speaking and everyone in the room turned to me, as she prompted, "Ninexin, whenever you're ready to share what you'd like to about Papa."

I hadn't written a prepared speech; this wasn't another conference. But I did jot down some notes this morning to help me work through my thoughts, writing out a few anecdotes to show how Papa loved his family, and his country; how, though he had left Nicaragua for several years in body, in spirit he was always here. I wanted to say something to demonstrate how he had acted as a father to so many of us, not just to his daughters but to my daughter and to so many young people who looked up to him, both among our extended family and among the young lawyers he worked with in his practice. I had worried over that; whether I should allude to the absence of Mariana's own father even obliquely, whether it would upset her. With Mariana gone, my concern was irrelevant. But I didn't want to say any of that anymore. I didn't want to call attention to her absence. And I was no longer willing to share my father with anyone, not the lawyers, not Nicaragua, not even Celia or Rigobertito. With Papa gone, and now Mariana, too, I felt like the last kid left on the playground after everyone else has been picked up from school. Abandoned. And I couldn't help but think that if Papa were here, Mariana wouldn't have run off. He would have held us together. None of the anecdotes I had prepared seemed right anymore. So I stood and up spoke the truth. "My father is the only person who told me that I could be anything I wanted to be," I said. "And I believed him. I will always be grateful."

I sat down, but still no one spoke; I couldn't hear a sound, not even ice clinking in people's glasses. Then Celia jumped up and said, "Thank you all for coming?" as if it were a question, not a statement. She wouldn't mention anything, she wouldn't want to criticize, especially not today, but she clearly expected more from me; I'm the maker of speeches in this family. And Mama would undoubtedly think what I said made her sound unsupportive. It's not that she was. Well, she was, actually. She wanted another debutante for a daughter, not a soldier. And I knew my choices were putting my family in danger, causing her worry. Even before I joined the Movimiento, though, Mama was the guard who made sure society's rules were followed, or tried to; I learned early on that if I just nodded when Mama spoke, then went on and did exactly what I wanted, there would be no consequences besides her loud sighs, complaints, and tearful prayers to the Virgen, asking what she had done to deserve such a headstrong daughter. Maybe I would have been more moved by those if I hadn't recognized the same gestures and heard the same expressions in the telenovelas Mama watched in the afternoons. As I grew older, I developed the conviction that if Mama disapproved of a course of action, it was guaranteed to be the most exciting thing I could do. And I was right every time, whether it was joining the Frente or marrying Manuel, or even just cutting my long hair.

Mama always clung to the status quo; she still does. Papa, in his own, quiet way, was the revolutionary. Or the reason I had it in me to become one. Actually, it wasn't just Papa. It was him and the nuns who taught me at La Asuncion. They took us, the daughters of Managua's elite, to do charity work in the poorer neighborhoods and taught us always to think of the less fortunate, to follow Christ's example of service. A number of us girls ended up joining the Sandinista movement, and I don't think it was a coincidence; those nuns had radicalized us without knowing it. And the irony is that Mama was the one who insisted that Celia and I go there, because it was the one place in Nicaragua that reminded her of own beloved convent school, Sacred Heart. So I suppose, in her way, Mama made me a rebel, too.

But in her own life, she has always followed the rules of polite society. Whereas Papa, even as he moved the family to Miami, he gave money to the aspects of the Revolución he believed in: the literacy programs, the medical outreach. When I took an English literature class at UNAM—the last one the university offered before it was deemed unpatriotic—he was the one who bought me Fitzgerald's books, stopping at the English-language bookstore on the way home from the office after I said I didn't want to be seen shopping there. And he told me that while he understood why I might want to regulate my behavior to fit in with my peers, I should never let anyone control my mind.

Maybe it was because he secretly wanted a son that Papa was willing to have a daughter who read unfashionable books and volunteered in dangerous neighborhoods—always chaperoned by a liberal priest, of course, but still, most of my girlfriends weren't allowed to work with the poor even if their brothers did. And when Manuel asked him for my hand, which I insisted on because Rigoberto had done so with Celia and because I thought Papa would expect it, he told Manuel that any marriage I entered into of my own volition would have his blessing, and that no one should get to choose the path of a woman's life except the woman herself. Manuel was so embarrassed! "See what you got me into with your bourgeois leanings," he joked, throwing an arm around me as we walked down the street, now that we were official. "Imagine, Don Ignacio lecturing me on women's rights!"

Everyone at the funeral luncheon knew me, knew my history. They would assume that what I said about Papa was a political statement, that I was hinting that my father had supported the Movimiento, and they would think, understandably, that I was rewriting history. But what I said wasn't political at all. All I meant was that Papa was the person who made me imagine a life for myself that didn't resemble Mama's and her mother's and her grandmother's.

And look where that life got me, shaking my ankle under the

table waiting for my relatives to get the hell out of town already so I that could begin searching for my daughter, who was, apparently, busy pursuing alternate futures of her own. I knew Mama must see Mariana's little rebellion as my karmic retribution, not that she'd put it that way. "You, my girl, simply got what was coming to you," she'd say, one of her favorite pronouncements. It's what she said after I insisted on racing the neighborhood boys on my bike and fell and skinned my knee, after she rubbed salve on it and settled me in my bed surrounded by pillows and the radio. Mama was always so high-strung and nervous, warning us not to ride our bikes on the street, not to chew ice in case we choked, not to eat mamón so we didn't accidentally swallow the pit and get it lodged in our throats, causing us to suffocate. And now Mariana had disappeared and was wandering the world without a plan or a purpose or a companion, as far as we knew, and Mama was sitting at the table with a far-off look in her eye, sipping fruit punch and nodding at each tribute to her deceased husband.

But once everyone left, including, finally, Celia, who first had to be convinced that I could manage both Mama and Mariana—whom we said was lying down upstairs, undone by the trip from the U.S. and the emotions of the day—I realized that I was being uncharitable. Maybe Mama hadn't been listening to the speeches, but had simply been thinking of Papa, comforting herself with her memories. Because she didn't gloat about Mariana running off and how it serves me right. And she didn't even complain about what I said in tribute to Papa. She just asked me and Allen to lead her to the room so she could rest.

For a minute I thought she'd forgotten about Mariana altogether. But as we left her there alone, with her big black bag on her lap, she grabbed my arm and said, "Don't worry too much about Mariana.

She'll be back soon. We raised her well." And I had to step into the hall and make a big show of going to the front desk to ask for an extra pillow so that neither she nor Allen could see how grateful I was for that "we."

"I need a room, too," Allen says and I realize that he's standing behind me, although I hadn't noticed him following me until now. The girl at the front desk goes to confer with her manager, and now that it's just the two of us, I will have to speak to this man, although I don't know what Mariana would want me to say.

"Ninexin," he says, and I turn around. "Mariana's not resting upstairs, is she? I didn't want to say anything while your relatives were around but—what aren't you telling me?"

"She left a note saying she needed some time to herself and not to worry," I admit, speaking quickly because I see the receptionist heading back toward us with a key. "And now I must ask, what is it that you are not telling me?"

He looks down at his hands, as if he's just noticed they're covered in stains. I've seen guilty men before, I can tell that he knows something.

"Señor," the girl says, putting a key on the desk in front of him. "We do have one room. Will you be wanting breakfast inclusive?"

"I'll let you check in," I tell Allen. "I'll be upstairs in the bar when you're ready to talk." I walk up the stairs slowly, so that my rising panic won't be obvious to him or anyone, and I settle in at a table on the balcony, overlooking the street below, where a stray dog is sleeping and the Eskimo Ice Cream man has stopped to sell Popsicles to three boys. If I focus on them I'll be able to stay put, calm down, and think rationally, because the cooler I am, the more likely this gringo is to reveal everything he knows that could be of use to me, everything about this situation he'd rather keep hidden.

He's taking longer than I think he should, and I want to run down the stairs and ask what the hell is going on here, but instead I tell the waitress—the same nice girl who helped arrange for the room where Mama, lucky Mama, is napping right now—that I'd like two whiskeys, please, one for me and one for my friend who is going to join me. What I'd really like is a cup of coffee but I want him to feel obligated to drink what's in front of him, and if it's whiskey, he's more likely to tell me everything he knows. Finally, I hear footsteps.

He sits down, picks up the whiskey, drinks it, and signals for another. "Thanks," he says. "I just called the hotel where Mariana told me to stay in Managua—she's not there. I said she'd left her wallet here and I need to find her to return it, and they promised they'll have her get in touch with me if she shows up. I'll call back in a couple hours, just to be sure."

It was smart of him to contact the Contempo. But I don't tell him that. "Do you have any idea why Mariana would run off like this?" I ask.

"She was really upset, about her grandfather." He looks down at my whiskey as if he would like to drink it.

"We're all upset, Allen," I say. "My mother, my sister, me. But none of us ran away. Just Mariana did. And none of us know why. Or why you're here."

He doesn't speak, and I don't either. Instead, I take a sip of my whiskey, my first sip, and watch as he runs his grubby hands through his hair so that it stands up on end. Mama would hate that.

"I'm here because there were things Mariana wanted us to talk about before she left, but I've been really busy with this painting." He glances up at me in a look I recognize from the stray dog below; he's hoping I'll throw him a scrap or at least not kick him. I just shake my head. "You know, she wanted to talk about our future, what's next for us."

"And you did not want to talk about this?"

"Not right then. But I do now." The waitress brings his second whiskey and Allen settles back in his chair, as if remembering he's a man, not a dog, after all. "That's why I'm here."

"Perhaps she is no longer ready to talk."

He sighs. He clearly thinks I'm criticizing him although I'm not. I'm just stating a fact. Sympathizing, almost. Because I know what it is finally to have time for Mariana and to find that she no longer has time for you.

"A day late and a dollar short," Allen says.

"What?"

"It's an expression. When you haven't put enough effort into something and now that you're ready to fight for it, it might be too late."

"A day late and a dollar short."

Allen smiles at me, which, I think, is a day early and five dollars too much. He still hasn't told me anything about where Mariana might be.

"So she is maybe not wanting to speak with you, okay," I say. "But to run off?"

"I know!" Allen tugs at his hair again. "It's the kind of stunt my kids would pull."

The whiskey burns my throat. "You have children?"

"A seventeen-year-old son and a fourteen-year-old daughter who isn't as nice to Maria as she should be," he says, finishing his second glass. "And an ex-wife who's pretty pissed off that I canceled the kids' visit to my mother's cabin to rush down here for the funeral of the grandfather of the younger woman I'm dating."

Mariana has told me none of this. And my throat is still burning, not just with the whiskey but with anger that this man has made such a mess of his own life that his almost-grown children are making my poor daughter's life difficult. Difficult enough that she might want to run from him, and therefore from me.

"Maybe if you'd stayed at the cabin where you should be, my daughter would not be missing."

"That thought has crossed my mind." He looks down at his hands again and for a minute I think this large man is going to cry. But then he looks back at me and says, "But the important thing now is how are we going to find her?"

I don't correct him, don't point out that I am the one who will find her, that she will come back to me, not to him. Because he's right, finding her is the important thing. And he might be useful; it was quick thinking to call the hotel.

I ask the waitress to borrow her pen, pull out the notebook I have in my purse, and turn the page on which I'd written the notes about Papa that I never used. On the new, clean, white page, I start making a list. "First, I will call my contacts at the Ministry of Transportation and ask that they have people at the airport watch for someone traveling under her name, or who matches her description. Watch discreetly, of course, so Mariana does not notice, and then notify me if she passes through."

Allen nods.

"The ports also. Anyplace that sells tickets and keeps a record."

"What can I do?"

"E-mail Beth, and anyone else she is close to, and see if Mariana has made contact."

He nods again.

"We also can split up, go around town asking people if they have seen Mariana; you can learn very much from on-the-ground intelligence."

Allen taps his hand against his head and says, "Aye, aye, Captain!"

"I prefer 'comandante,'" I say, without smiling. While it's nice to have someone else who is ready to work to find Mariana, unlike Mama, who seems to think she will turn up at any minute with a camera full of photos and a travel journal scribbled with adventures, it's a little too soon for him to be making jokes.

"Comandante," he repeats, but when he says it, it sounds like he's talking about Moses' tablets. "I'll do whatever I can to help. Although, I should tell you, I don't speak Spanish. Despite the best efforts of Señor Weisberg at Larchmont Prep."

"Many people here speak English; you can interview the other tourists," I say, although what I'm thinking is that he's lucky that Mariana was willing to spend any amount of time with someone so provincial. The dog below barks and the man selling Eskimo pops pushes his cart down the street. Mariana's favorite is the watermelon.

"I heard what you said about your father during lunch," Allen tells me. "It was really moving. I'd like to be able to do that for my children."

"Mariana never mentioned that you had children."

"She's full of secrets these days, I guess. I thought Maria was happy, overall. I thought I knew what she wanted but . . ."

He doesn't finish his sentence, but I know he'll get around to completing the thought if I'm not careful. I can tell from his rough, deep voice, the way he's leaning forward and looking at me over the whiskey, his golden eyes darting back and forth from my face to the glass: he clearly has no idea where Mariana has gone, he doesn't even seem to be sure why she left. And that's all I care about. I don't want him to confide in me about their life together, to tell me things that will make me see the situation from his point of view. I don't want to feel sorry for him. I don't want to have an opinion as to what Mariana should do. I just want my daughter back, and then she can do whatever she wants, live with or run from anyone she likes. I reach for my bag and say, "Excuse me. I must now check on my mother."

28

María

Marlon waited for a taxi to come pick me up at the dock, but he was speeding back across the lake by the time I closed the cab door. I didn't blame him; he had Marlon-hijo's party to get to. He had dropped me off at San José del Sur, the smaller port closer to the hotel where I wanted to stay. I had picked out Villas Paraíso when I Googled Ometepe a few months ago, planning an itinerary for Allen's promised trip to Nicaragua in the new year.

Maybe that's what had me feeling so alone as I watched Marlon motor away, that I had planned to come here with someone I love. Instead here I was, far from New York, on a vast lake in the middle of a tiny country, in the same predicament I had found myself in back in Manhattan: facing all of this alone. Or maybe it was the island itself, made up of two volcanoes, connected by a land bridge formed by a long-ago lava flow. As we had approached them, the volcanoes looked eternal, joined together forever. One of them, Maderas, is dormant, and the other, Concepción, is active. Allen would have to be the active one, bubbling with artistic energy. And that left me dormant, which seems about right, attached to the active volcano by its creative overflow, but perhaps never to erupt in an explosion of talent that is both beautiful and terrifying.

At Villas Paraíso, I spring for a cabin with hot water. I want to be the girl who can relish a cold shower; I know my mother could at my age, although lately she stays in four-star hotels, so all of her showers have side jets and come equipped with aromatherapeutic bath gel. But even the tepid water at my Bela's house felt like it was piercing my skin last night; ever since I arrived in Nicaragua, I've been much more sensitive to temperature. Besides, the cabin is slightly cheaper because I'm alone.

Sitting in a rocking chair on my porch, overlooking the lake, I remember the afternoon Abuelo, my Bela, and Madre dropped me off at college. After they had helped set up my room and driven away, I ventured into town to set up a checking account. I sat on a bench opposite the bank for twenty minutes, awed and proud and scared that, for the first time in my life, no one had any idea where I was. I'm embarrassed to admit it now, how sheltered my childhood was. Abuelo and my Bela always knew if I was at school or a friend's home, or at art class. Once or twice I told them I was staying at a friend's and we snuck out instead to a party at some boy's house. But even then, they knew I was with Lorena or Jennifer or Melissa; if something horrible had happened, they could have tracked me down through her.

Part of being an adult, or a single one, anyway, is that most people have no idea where you are at any given moment. They know you're at work during the week, but that could mean sitting at your desk, or lunching with a client, or maybe you ducked out in the middle of the day to get your hair cut. It's one of the things I like most about living in New York, that no one comments on my comings and goings.

I should feel that way now—exhilarated by my freedom, sitting alone in front of a Paradise Villa, knowing that I could go down into the lake and swim to the next volcano or let myself float away, never to be heard from again. But instead I'm feeling sorry for myself, wishing I had a reason to stay firmly rooted, someone inextricably linked to me as if by an isthmus of hardened lava. If I really were attached to another person forever, though, would that link begin to feel less like a miracle of nature and more like a chain? That's my biggest fear, that if I make the wrong decision now, I'll do something that can't be undone, at least not without the suffering of several people, should I decide, Oops, this isn't for me. There are so many ways I'd be a better person if I were like my mother: braver, bolder, more energetic. But what if the thing I've inherited from Madre is the quality I hate about her: her ability to walk away from the person who loves her most, again and again. I wouldn't be able to live with myself if I ever hurt someone that way. I'd rather not have that kind of love in the first place.

"What are you drinking?" a voice says, and when I look up it belongs to what my Bela would call a typical backpacking gringo. I tell him it's hibiscus tea, and he smiles in that intrusively friendly way Americans do when they're traveling and meet a fellow countryman. It's a hopeful, overly familiar grin that resembles the smiles of the street children who make flowers made out of palm reeds in Granada, only this guy is begging for attention instead of coins. He's cute, the backpacking gringo; I bet most people find such puppyish small talk charming, especially if they're traveling alone. And suddenly I don't want anyone, not even this stranger, not even myself, to notice that I'm not as open as most people. So I do what I imagine Beth would if she were ever to find herself on an island with another roaming American: I ask him who he is and what he's doing on Ometepe.

His name is Dylan, "for Thomas, not Bob," he points out, and he's traveling with a friend from architecture school. It's their last fling before they start at different firms, and they're determined to do everything they won't be able to when they're sitting behind desks in San Francisco and Portland, respectively: kite surfing, ziplining, surfing on volcanic ash, watching sea turtles hatch in nature preserves. I nod and say, "That's cool," because it is. But I don't tell him I'm Nicaraguan because then he'll want all sorts of advice I haven't lived here recently enough to be able to give. We're both quiet for a minute, because I'm not giving him any leads to follow up on, and also because we're watching the sky and the lake turn pink as the sun sets.

When he says, "Sienna," I know he's referring to the color of the sky.

"Like the crayon?"

Dylan nods. "But the crayon's a little more orange." He's right. You can never exactly match the colors of nature, not with a crayon. With paints you can, if you mix them, but it takes time and if you go too far, you can ruin it. Except if you're painting bougainvillea. That's the exact color of a pigment called "Opera." I tell Dylan this because I like the paint's name, and the fact of its perfection.

"I don't really paint," he says.

"I guess you're not into hobbies that have no risk of breaking your neck. Besides coloring, I mean."

He smiles and looks back at the lake. "I'm meeting Ryan in the restaurant if you want to join us for something a little stronger than hibiscus tea."

I watch as the sun disappears into the ocean, and imagine painting over a canvas covered in Opera with blues and grays so that just the tiniest hint of the pink shows through.

"Thanks," I say. "But I can't." Because even though I'm alone and feeling melancholy, it's true. I just can't.

29

Isabela

There's a painting of an angel on the wall above the bed in what the elegant Indian hostess called my "Grand Suite." I tucked one of the brochures from her desk into my purse after the luncheon, because it had a yellow slip of paper sticking out of it that I knew would be a price list; Ninexin just signs any check that's put in front of her, so it's left to me to make sure we're being charged the proper amount. Even when she's in her seventies, a mother still has to take care of everything herself, especially when her daughter is a dreamer, with her mind always on bigger and better things rather than the mundane details of life.

In the brochure this room is described as the honeymoon suite; they've rolled in a cot for Ninexin. I suppose the pretty receptionist didn't tell me the name of the suite out of courtesy, misplaced kindness, thinking it would be rude to let an old woman at the end of her life, a widow who has just lost her husband, know she's staying in a room where young couples come to begin their life together.

I know what people see when I pass them leaving Mass; I know because I thought it myself when I was a young girl tripping through the streets of Granada, practically galloping past slow-moving older ladies. I was aware that those women weren't born old, I knew intellectually that they'd been babies and girls and young women. But when I'd see a heavyset older woman picking her way along the sidewalk, leaning on the arm of a child or a grandchild or a servant for support, it seemed as if she'd entered the world in that state, fragile yet imposing, here to judge the young people swirling all around her. Somehow it happened that now, I'm the fragile yet solid older woman; my waist measurement is half again the size my hip measurement was in the days I attended Sacred Heart, but that's a secret. And I've learned that I carry all those other selves inside me. I'm still the little girl, wide-eyed with wonder, thrilled and also a bit nervous to go with my papa when he takes me to see the pony he says will belong to me even though it will live at my abuelo's farm. And I'm still the young woman who looks so calm, so proper, but who is convinced she must be dying, bleeding internally from the jagged edges of her broken heart.

It was the old woman in me who settled into the easy chair opposite the honeymoon bed with the help of her daughter. I was sitting here in this easy chair, like a lady, when Ninexin fluttered out of the room, trying to hide how nervous she is. The gringo looked increasingly anxious throughout lunch, too; he kept his lips pressed together into a tight line, which makes him look even more North American. I'm not sure how much he knows but at the very least, he has to suspect that Mariana isn't just in another room, taking a well-deserved nap. I'm the only one who is not nervous, who is sure that Mariana will be fine. If I had been half as bold as she is, half as capable, when I was her age, my life would have been very different.

But then, if my life had been different, Ninexin and Mariana wouldn't be here. So I suppose it all worked out for the best, as it was supposed to, as God intended. I look to the angel in the painting for a sign, to confirm that I'm right and not just heaping platitudes on myself in order to feel better about a life that may have been lived properly, but wasn't lived the right way, the way it should have been. The angel is smiling a sweet smile, but a bit sly, too; it reminds me of Mother Dauphinais's face when she told me that Scarlett O'Hara was a girl who just got what was coming to her. Am I that now? A girl who just got what was coming to her, only it wasn't scandal and penury and dresses made out of curtains, but sitting quietly in an overstuffed chair?

When our relatives finally left, and I saw the worry on my daughter's face, I felt every one of my seventy-five years. But even though a spotted, bumpy hand, swollen at the knuckles, pulled out Mauricio's envelope, it is the heartbroken young woman in me who reads the words.

My Dearest Isa,

Many times I've told Cristian Hidalgo that he's the best friend any man could have, and I meant it each time. But it was never more true than the first and the last times I said it. The first was when he offered to drive us to Loyola for our wedding, although he knew that if things went wrong, he could be reported to school officials, and his admission to the college for the fall might be put in jeopardy.

And the last was when he returned from Miami where he'd gone for a follow-up to his heart surgery last year, and told me he'd met your granddaughter in the hospital. He said that when he saw her, he felt as if he knew her somehow, and that it was more than just the nostalgia of an old man seeing a beautiful young woman and recalling how girls looked when he was young. Then he noticed that she had crossed her legs at the ankles, the way you girls were taught to at Sacred Heart long ago, and he started talking to her, which is one of the benefits of becoming a truly old man; young girls are no longer nervous when you make conversation with them. She explained she was waiting for her grandfather, who was in town from Nicaragua having some tests. Cristian told her he'd had a friend from Nicaragua when he studied in New Orleans, a young woman from Granada. And so the secret came out. Cristian told me that your granddaughter knew about me—Isa, I think that is what gives me the courage to write now—and when he asked for her information, she hesitated for a moment but gave it to him.

When he put the piece of cardboard with her address in my hand— she wrote it on one of those rings they slide around paper coffee cups so that you don't burn your hand—I sat down to write this letter. Cristian told me I should have one of my children send it through the computer, that it would get there faster. But I didn't want anyone else—not my children, not your beautiful granddaughter—to read what I have to say. And besides, I want to imagine the letter making its way to you like the love notes we exchanged long ago. I still have all of yours. Have you kept mine?

In those days I would sit down to write to you and in what seemed like minutes ten sheets of paper would be filled, and my hand would be covered in ink, one of the drawbacks of being left-handed, and perhaps a reason I should have let the Jesuits cure me of it when they had the chance. This time I will try to keep it brief. So much has happened in the past—is it over fifty?—years, I could never explain it all. But wherever I went, whatever I did, I carried your letters with me.

I even had them tucked in the lining of my suitcase when I left for Cuba the day after you walked out of the church. I almost threw them into the river, but I couldn't do it. So I tucked them away where no one else would find them, where they would require effort even for me to reach, so that I wouldn't be tempted to read them too often. I secured passage on the first ship I could find; I couldn't leave New Orleans fast enough. I swore I would forget you, or at least hide my memories of you, like your letters, where they would be less noticeable. But when Castro took over in July, we lost our business and I lost my home, and none of it mattered compared to losing you.

I came to Nicaragua then . . . did you know that? I suppose not; how would you have found out? I came to Granada and asked a woman selling vigorón in one of the stands in the park if she could tell me how to find the Enriquez home. She said it was right on the Parque, but that no one would be there—they were all in the church at Xalteva where the Enriquez girl was getting married. Which one? I asked. The woman didn't know the family personally, she said, but she'd heard it was the beautiful sister who had just returned from New Orleans.

I left town that afternoon and headed to Costa Rica, then Honduras, traveling until my money ran out and Cristian came to find me. He asked me to join his family business; I had experience with my own family's import operations, and that knowledge would transfer, he said. I needed the money. So did my parents. And I appreciated Cristian's kindness. So I moved here to Mexico. It's where I met my wife, where I raised my family. We had a son, two daughters, and another son, all of whom were already grown and out of the house by the time my wife left. She is a painter now, in New Orleans of all places. It wasn't until after our oldest son was born that Cristian handed me your letter; one of the brothers at St. Michael's had given it to him when he last passed through New Orleans. He had it with him when he came to find me in Honduras. He hadn't read it, but when he saw how bitter I was, how

drained, he decided to hold on to it until I was stronger; he worried it
would only cause me more suffering.

I never told him how right he was. By the time I read it and realized
it was Dolly's wedding I had almost ruined, not yours, by the time I
realized that you had wanted me, too, I was already a husband and a
father. Perhaps you were already married, too, and everything that led
up to the beautiful girl crossing her ankles in the waiting room at Mt.
Sinai had already been put in motion. If he'd given me the envelope
sooner, maybe I would have come back to Nicaragua, tried one more
time. But I had already lost more than a year of my life trying to find
you and then to forget you; I could understand why Cristian wanted
me to be firmly on a new path before he gave me the letter.

"Why show it to me now?" I asked at the time. And Cristian said
he didn't do it for me, but for himself. He couldn't bear the burden of
holding on to your thoughts, to thoughts that belonged to me, any
longer, regardless of what the letter said. I had never seen him look so
wretched, so afraid. So I told him he'd done the right thing. Because I
knew, in the end, that I was at fault for all that had happened. When I
fled Granada, I did so in anger. I should have looked for you. I should
have fought for you. I should have come to the church where I thought
you were being married and demanded the wedding be stopped. But I
didn't, because I didn't want to be humiliated again. And because I
didn't know if you would turn and walk down the aisle away from me
once more—only this time, toward another young man you loved, a
groom instead of a father.

Forgive me, Isa. Forgive me my pride and my cowardice. I hope
you've lived a wonderful life and thought of me only occasionally, but
with great fondness. And if that's the case, then forgive me for what
I am about to write, and pray that God forgives me, too. But when

Cristian saw your granddaughter in the hospital, I knew this was my second chance. I cannot stay silent any longer.

Isa, you are my one true love. It sounds like one of the books you girls used to hide from the nuns, but I can't think of another way to say it. I don't know what your life is like now, or what your feelings for me are, if any. But I want you to know that I love you and always have.

My health is not perfect; whose is at our age? My grandson attends the American school in the capital and he asked me to answer some questions for him, about what life was like when I was young, and one, the last one, about how I would like to spend the rest of my days. I lied to my grandson, Isa. I told him I wanted to live and die peacefully, surrounded by my children and grandchildren, on our farm in Cuernavaca. But that's not what I want at all.

I want us to be together again. When Castro dies, I want you to return with me to my hometown, Camagüey. I know this is a ridiculous thing to tell a married woman whom I haven't spoken to in over half a century. But I am old enough to have learned from my mistakes and to know that if I have a desire, and I never tell it to anyone, there is no one else to blame for it not coming true. Not Cristian. Not you. Not your father. Just myself.

I said I would keep this brief, and, once again, I've failed. Who knows? It may not even matter how long I carry on, or what I write; I don't know if you'll ever read this. Mariana was very clear with Cristian when he emailed her; she told him that she'd be happy to receive the letter he wanted to send, but couldn't promise when she'd pass it on—there was a great deal happening in your life, and this wasn't the right time to add to your concerns. I accept that.

But I want you to know that I feel better already, just having written this down. I feel understood, as I always did by you. Perhaps I *should feel ashamed, immoral. But I feel proud. And relieved. As if I may finally be acting like the man I should have been all along.*

A better man might accept this peace as its own reward and put this letter in his desk drawer, to be discovered after his death by curious grandchildren with indulgent eyes. But I am not a better man. I am just the man who loved you once, and who loves you now, and who always will.

I remain your,
Mauricio

30

❧

Ninexin

We were at breakfast in the courtyard of La Gran Francia this morning when we found out where Mariana is. The answer arrived having nothing to do with my connections at the Ministry of Transportation. It was Mama who got the news.

I was pushing pineapple and papaya around on my plate and Allen, Dios mío, he was on his third dish of gallo pinto—I know some people eat when they're worried, but what is it with gringos and gallo pinto? Mama was sipping her manzanilla tea when the phone rang, as it had every morning when Don Pedro called to ask if she needed him to pick her up, if she'd be coming back to Managua today, or if there were any errands she required him for. I heard her telling Don Pedro that no, we were going to hide out in Granada a bit more, we weren't ready to face the empty house, and then she paused and I knew he must have said something surprising because tea sloshed over the side of her cup. It wouldn't have meant anything if I had been the one slopping the tea, but for Mama it was unusual. She placed the teacup very carefully in its saucer and said, "Yes, it is her way, our Mariana. She wanted to see more of Nicaragua, to bring some happiness to such a sad trip."

I was so desperate to hear what was being said on the other end of the line that I actually stood and leaned over the table toward Mama's phone, but she waved me off as if I were a housefly, slapping her napkin at me, then asked, "And how did you know she was traveling, Don Pedro?"

"He found her," I whispered to Allen. He opened his mouth but I raised my hand in front of it so he'd know not to speak while I listened in on Mama's conversation, trying to decipher what was being said on the other line. It seemed like Mama was silent forever but I finally heard her say, "Gracias, Don Pedro," and that she'd call and let him know what time to arrive tomorrow or the next day, she felt she was almost ready to return to Managua. She made a great show of placing the phone in the interior pouch of her Chanel bag. But I wouldn't give her the satisfaction of asking what he'd said; I knew she was dying to tell me and wouldn't be able to hold out more than a few seconds.

"For the love of God, Bela, where is she?" Allen shouted, and the tourists in the courtyard turned to stare at us as if they hadn't been just as loud while debating the merits of an isleta tour or a hike up Mombacho.

"I do not know about God," Mama said in English, "but Don Pedro's granddaughter, Fatima, he just got married–"

"Yes, to the neighbor's son who works for the phone company," I broke in. "Mama, where's Mariana?"

"That's what I'm telling you!" She switched into Spanish, becoming impatient with her woman-of-mystery act. "Fatima and Jackson went to Ometepe on their honeymoon; she called Don

Pedro today to say what a wonderful time they're having. And she said that on Sunday morning when they arrived, they saw a woman who looked familiar checking out of their hotel. But it wasn't until the lady paid and headed down to the dock and a man in a boat yelled up, 'Señora Vazquez?' that Fatima was sure it was Mariana; the last time she'd seen her they were kids playing Legos in the courtyard with Rigobertito. Don Pedro only mentioned it to say how nice it is that Mariana was able to stay on and travel a bit, how he hoped the trip is helping ease the loss of her abuelo, whom she loved so much; he'd never seen her looking so pale as she did at the funeral."

I turned to Allen to translate; it was almost difficult to speak, I was smiling so hard. Mariana was fine, gracias a Dios.

"But where was she going on that boat?" Allen shook his head. "Was she coming back here?"

"I forget to say," Mama said in English. "The boat driver, he yell, 'Señora Vazquez? For Solentiname?' Don Pedro's granddaughter, he think maybe that's a nice place for a honeymoon, too."

"*She*, Mama, Don Pedro's granddaughter is a she," I said automatically. Mama shrugged off the inadvertent sex change, the way she always does; Allen understood what she meant, after all. And she was right, she's not the stupid one here. Mariana has been asking me about Solentiname for years; I should have guessed that's where she went when she took flight. Anyone could have guessed. She's a painter, and an art dealer, and the archipelago has been an artists' cooperative since the sixties. It's the kind of suggestion I make all the time at conferences when some minister or other official leans over and says, "My daughter's studying Spanish in Costa Rica and she's going to pass through Nicaragua on the way back. Where should she go?" I don't say, "Let me lend you a *Lonely Planet* guide," but I smile and ask, "What's your daughter like? Oh, she's creative? Well, she should time her trip to coincide with the poetry festival in Granada, and take in a performance at the Teatro Nacional Rubén Darío, and if she likes primitivist art, she'll love Solentiname."

How many trips have I planned in thirty seconds or less for the children of other diplomats looking for a little culture, a bit of adventure, and I couldn't extend the same amount of consideration to my own daughter? Why is it so impossible for me to imagine Mariana's thoughts? Not thinking of Solentiname was starting to feel worse than an oversight. It was beginning to feel like a sin.

"Finally! After three days of calling and searching and waiting!" Allen tipped back and forth in his chair the way children do before a concerned adult tells them to stop or they'll fall over.

I nodded. "And they heard on the third day, according to the Scripture."

Allen shrugged.

"I'm not great on Bible verses; my parents aren't religious." He grinned. "Mariana always says I'm a man with no archetypes—Jung would have no idea what to do with me."

It sounded like something she would say. But I'm not sure it's a compliment. A man with no context is a man with no past, someone who's created himself out of nothing. A person with no beginning, and, maybe, no end. But Allen, with his children and his ex-wife, is hardly free or unencumbered. Certainly not compared to Mariana.

"How do you get to Solentiname from here?" Allen asked.

"Drive to San Carlos, hire a boat. We'll be there in time for a late lunch," I told him. "Only a few of the islands are inhabited, there's just a handful of hotels. Mariana won't be hard to find. We've got her." I smiled to make the words sound less like an old Western, but Allen was laughing anyway.

"I guess you can call off your dogs, huh?" He seemed to have caught the imbecilic grin I'd been afflicted with a few minutes ago. "Tell the Sandinistas thanks for the help, but if I ever start a government, I'm making Bela my chief intelligence officer."

Mama was drinking her tea but I could tell she was smiling, although it seemed to be more at Allen's collar than at his face; she was casting her eyes down as if she were playing Madame Butterfly. "You catch more flies with honey, no, Mr. Allen?"

I stood and my chair ended up on the floor behind me, although I wasn't aware of rising with any particular force. "Mama, call Don Pedro and tell him you've decided to go home today," I said in Spanish, and it was a command, not a suggestion. Then I switched to English. "Allen, Scarlett O'Mama can go back to Managua today. I'll have the office driver bring us to San Carlos. Can you be ready in an hour?"

Allen stopped rocking his chair. "I'm not coming." When I didn't respond, he added, "I'll stay here with Bela. She doesn't have to rush back tonight. She already told Don Pedro that he has the day off; who knows what he wants to get up to? We'll set up a nice homecoming lunch in the restaurant for when you return tomorrow."

"But, Allen," I started, so surprised by what he said that English was coming to me more slowly than usual. He stood, and I assumed it meant he'd changed his mind. But then he leaned over, so close to my face that I could smell the gallo pinto.

"I came to the funeral and she ran away," he said, soft enough that Bela wouldn't be able to hear him. "From me," Allen continued. "She ran away from me. I know she and I need to talk, but if Maria's willing to go to such great lengths to avoid me, it's going to have to be when she wants to, not when I decide to show up."

All this time when he had been drinking whiskey and playing games on his phone, or doodling on the paper napkin his silverware came wrapped in, I thought he was fidgeting, wishing he were in a cabin in the woods with his horrible kids, maybe even wondering how he could make a final clean break from this wild girl and her even crazier family. But no. He must have spent the last three days doing the exact same thing I had: thinking about Mariana. Wondering what she's feeling, and fearing that when she finally decides what it is she wants, it will have nothing to do with him.

He sat back down and crossed his ankle over his knee. Neither Mariana nor I would ever sit like that; Mama raised us better than to show people the soles of our shoes. I haven't decided yet how much I like this man or not. But he's definitely smarter than I thought.

"So you're just going to wait?"

"I don't have a choice." He finally looked up. "If I come, what if she runs again? What if she won't return with me?"

I didn't want to look in his eyes, to see how anxious he was. Anxiety is contagious and I needed to stay calm so that I could find Mariana and bring her back to the people who love her. If I had to face Allen's fear that she had no interest in seeing him, then it would become harder to ignore the fact that she hadn't called me either, that she hadn't left me a note saying not to worry, that we had no reason to think that she had any desire to see me. That I might be the person she ran away from. So I started collecting my cell phone, the water bottle, a packet of Splenda from the table, although the only person I know who hoards Splenda is my mother and she'd be here with Allen and all manner of artificial sweeteners while I was trying to bring our girl back. "All right, then," I said. "I'll call you as soon as I find her."

Now that I'm in the backseat of the car, alone, racing to San Carlos, trying to imagine what he and Bela could possibly have to say to each other and how, I wonder if I should have said more, should have left Allen with some words of hope or comfort. I didn't say, "You're right to stay." I didn't say, "I'm sure she'll come back." I didn't offer him any reassurances at all. I'm not sure she'll come back. Under the relief of knowing where Mariana is, I feel anger percolating. And fear.

I can still see Mama sitting there holding her teacup, smug and smiling. But it's not her I'm angry at; I don't care how we find Mariana, whether it's through my government contacts or Mama's old friends, confidantes, and lackeys. It's Allen who makes me mad. Because even though he may be right to give Mariana space and time and distance and all the things people say they want when they really want comfort and safety and affection, and even though it may be slowly suffocating him to stay behind, his doing so means that I have to go retrieve her alone. And that if she blames anyone, or rejects anyone, if she runs farther away and never returns, the person she'll be running from—again—is me.

31

Maria

Dylan and Ryan wanted me to join them on their hike, on their swim, for their pitcher of Macuás. Which would have been nice, under any other circumstances. Now it was just sort of maddening that I could be sitting on these floating volcanoes in the center of a sea-size lake, in the heart of an obscure country, in the middle of Central America, and I still couldn't escape Americans. Friendly, honest Americans who were eager to find themselves and everyone else, who wanted to tell me all their plans and hopes and fears and dreams, and wanted to hear mine, too. So I told the girl at the desk that I didn't want to have to wait for the ferry, and she said she could get me on a private boat with some German tourists who were going to Solentiname on Sunday morning. Germans. It was perfect. If I nodded hello and immediately pulled out a book, the Germans would know what that meant, and how to act accordingly.

I didn't tell Dylan and Ryan I was leaving; I was hoping to sneak out without them noticing. The boatman almost ruined it, yelling my name so everyone sitting at breakfast could hear it, but I dashed out of my cabin, waved at the boys and mouthed, "I got a ride!" while speed-walking toward the boat. I felt a little guilty.

That's a lie. I knew I *should* feel guilty. I told myself that I would look them up on Facebook someday, message them hello, inquire about the rest of their trip. But the truth is, I didn't feel bad about leaving at all. Hopping on a boat right under their noses made my stomach writhe, but in a good way. Running off suddenly added to the excitement of making a clean getaway.

And when the boat dropped us off on Mancarron, and I walked up the long dock into the woods, to the whitewashed hotel that looks like a monastery—I guess a convent would be more appropriate, under the circumstances—I knew I'd made the right decision. It's perfect here. There are no cars, just a wooden boardwalk that winds through town past houses with folding tables in the yards covered in brightly painted balsa-wood animals, which, it seems, everyone here makes and sells. Sometimes the bushes in front of the cottages are covered in drying laundry, so it looks as if the branches grow vividly colored shorts and T-shirts and bras instead of flowers. That seems possible here. Anything seems possible. There's a bibliobote, a floating library that sails up to the island regularly so the dozen or so schoolkids can rush out to see what's new. The white church where Ernesto Cardenal preached liberation theology is still here, and every time an older man passes by I look to see if it might be him with his white beard, white hair, and trademark beret, his jolly belly making him look like a Sandinista Santa.

When I sit on my veranda before the sun sets, watching what I think are South American guinea pigs hop past and bats swoop in histrionic arcs, I have this little daydream that I'll bump into Ernesto Cardenal and he'll invite me in for jamaica tea. I'll tell him everything and he'll know exactly what I should do, and guarantee that if I do it, everyone concerned will be happy and satisfied for generations to come. In my fantasy, he takes on the role of über-grandpa because he sees how much my painting owes to the primitivist art the islanders on the archipelago make, how I try to show everything not as a photograph would represent the scene but as I see it, just as vivid and shaky and off-center as in real life. The locals here must have always been artistic; the petroglyphs I saw on my hike into the jungle, covered in swirls and faces and symbols, prove that. But Cardenal is the one who organized them into a collective, bought them materials, showed them they could sell their paintings. He's my vision of an art dealer hero: spotting talent, shaping it, and spreading it to the world. In my daydream, he recognizes me as a fellow artist and appreciator of the arts, and that's what makes him take an interest in my predicament, in my future. In my soul.

But he's off-island now, probably collecting a peace prize or poetry award. And I'm going to have to figure out my future, and, as a result, shape everyone else's, myself. Somehow that's not as frightening here as it was in New York or Managua or Granada, or the no-man's-land of the plane ride from Miami. Part of me thinks I could stay here forever, try to blend in, focus on my painting, sell a few to passing tourists or in the exhibitions in which local artists like the Posada family show their work. But the rest of me recognizes that this would be running away. Still, it's nice to roll the idea of doing so around in my head like a marble, colors flashing.

I've spent the past two afternoons at the Posadas' house on La Venada. They're fairly well known in primitivist art circles, and I knew that if and when I made it to Solentiname, I'd want to look them up. The Germans have their captain and boat on retainer, and whenever he picks them up to take them out on the lake, he drops me off on the islet, at the foot of the concrete stairs that lead up into the Posadas' home; I've been talking to them about bringing some of their work back to the gallery to sell on commission. I've met three generations of artists already: Don Alejandro and Doña Clara, their daughters, and their granddaughters. Each member of the family has a different style, but it's the older couple whose work interests me the most. Don Alejandro mostly paints community scenes, long-ago festivals when everyone would row out in their dugout canoes to venerate a statue of the Virgen and celebrate her Immaculate Conception during the Purísimas, for example. His paintings immortalize the lush beauty of the islands, but he focuses on the people, too; they're not faceless stand-ins but individuals in different clothes, with distinct expressions on their faces and varying skin color, even their own hairstyles. The first time I knocked on the door, I was tripping all over myself apologizing for intruding, but he just stood up from his hammock, pulled on an ancient short-sleeved button-down over his undershirt, and ushered me in, welcoming the company. His paintings are amazing, but they're exactly what you'd expect him to paint. He lives for community, for celebration, for interaction.

It's Doña Clara whose art is such a surprise. Each afternoon when I showed up she was wearing a blouse in an imitation silk fabric, a tailored skirt, and Ben Franklin eyeglasses, her hair pulled back into a strict bun. But her paintings! The canvases erupt in swirling greenery and animals that look so alive, so alert, that I found myself tensing to listen for the sound they had clearly just heard. There's no way to describe her paintings except to say that they're full of passion, they betray a side of her that I never would have imagined existed. I told her how much I loved her style and she sat with me and described each of the animals—the tapir, the yellow-tailed birds, the jaguar—all of which are native to the archipelago. The way she spoke about the animals made me feel they had more interesting thoughts and experiences, richer interior lives, than most people.

The second time I went to see the Posadas, yesterday, I went less for the art and more for the company. I bought some bags of rosquillas from the manager of the hotel and Doña Clara made some instant coffee to go with the cookies. We sat and looked at their work and I showed them the photo of the painting of my Bela and her flying textbook that I carry on my phone. "It's nice," Don Alejandro said. "But there's so much empty space in the middle; such a big canvas for those words to cover."

I see his point; his paintings are action-packed, each inch is dense with flowers, even the water of the lake is created with several pigments and minute strokes. But Doña Clara took one look and told him, "She left the space for the people looking at the painting to fill with their minds."

I hadn't thought of it that way; I just couldn't imagine any other way to depict the scene. But I've been considering the remark since she made it yesterday and I realize that Doña Clara is right: most of my work exists on the fringes of the canvas.

The Germans have gone kayaking this afternoon, so I'm alone in the boat to La Venada and I feel bad about the captain using up his gasoline on me. I'll have to remember to tip him when we leave tomorrow. Or maybe I'll tip him and wave from the shore as the Germans leave and I stay behind. I have enough money to hide out at the hotel through Friday; by then I'll have come up with some kind of plan. I hope.

The boat bumps on the surface of the lake and I can feel my stomach rolling and clanging like a metal bowl dropped on a countertop. Maybe it's not the choppy water that has me unsettled, but knowing that I have to make a decision tomorrow, about whether to leave with the Germans or not. Or maybe I'm anxious about today's visit; I plan to show the Posadas the sketch I made for the painting of Abuelo tossing bougainvilleas off of his balcony into my Bela's upturned hand. I did it on a sheet from my sketchbook, which I've rolled up and dropped into my shoulder bag, and even though it weighs nothing I can feel it bumping against my thigh each time the boat rises and falls.

The captain kills the motor and as I step onto the dock, I can hear Don Alejandro talking. "Now with the mobile phone, it's so much easier to sell paintings. I get calls every month with commissions, from Managua, Granada, León. Things have changed in the last thirty years, compañera, haven't they?"

They have visitors, or a visitor, anyway, and it sounds like someone they've known a long time. Now I'm even more nervous; I don't want to get in the way if they're making a sale or catching up with old friends. And I'm not going to show them my sketch in front of a stranger.

"More than any of us could have imagined," says a woman's voice. Maybe I'm not nervous. I must be sick, because I seem to be hallucinating: the stranger sounds just like my mother. I turn back toward the boat but the captain has already pushed off from the dock, with the help of the captain of the boat next to his, the one that must have brought the woman with the doppelganger voice. I tell myself to stop being an idiot, there's no way Madre could have found me here, in Solentiname; aside from showing the Posadas my painting, I haven't even turned on my cell phone for three days, out of paranoia that somehow she might have the power to track me.

"Mariana!" Doña Clara calls, spotting me through the open window. "Come on up!" I have no alternative, so I climb the steps and there's Don Alejandro, shirt already on, flip-flops on feet I've only ever seen bare, and next to him is my mother, her arm resting on his shoulder as if they're old pals posing for a photo.

"Mariana!" Doña Clara says as I walk through the door. "All this time you didn't tell us who you were! Don Alejandro knew your mother in the Revolución."

Doña Clara is smiling, Don Alejandro is grinning, and my mother has an expression that reminds me of someone I can't place, until I realize it's the tapir in Doña Clara's painting, listening with his whole body for a noise in the jungle.

"Surprise!" I say, because it's the only thing I can think of, and it must not be a bad choice, because everyone laughs.

Madre says she's tired and needs to find a place to stay, and I find myself telling her that my hotel is nice and that the captain will be back in an hour if she wants to return with me. She pays her own captain and waves good-bye so vigorously that I wonder if he's an old friend, too, and what exactly went on during the Revolución that they're all so nostalgic for it, because when Madre talks about it, it just sounds like a lot of making speeches and slogging through mud. Back inside, they tell me stories about that time while we drink more instant coffee, stories about Ernesto Cardenal, and Don Alejandro's first few paintings, and Doña Clara passing secret messages between guerrillas who would sail past in canoes and imitate birdcalls to let her know they were there. Normally, these tales would fascinate me; I would store them away to tell Allen later, to impress him with the wonders of my country, the bravery of my mother. But although I'm nodding, and even laughing, as they speak, I'm not really listening to the Posadas and to Madre at all. I'm too surprised, shocked, really, to find that I'm not angry. For a minute I was furious, not at Madre for having found me but at myself for having invited her to my hotel. At myself for being so infantile, so easy to please, so delighted that she noticed I'd run away. I ran away once or twice when I was little in Managua, but just next door to the neighbors, and I always wandered back by dinnertime because I knew that my Bela would take me for an Eskimo afterward if I ate all my mashed potatoes. At the time it seemed that I sat on the neighbor's tufted sofa for hours without anyone realizing I'd left home, but I'm probably misremembering.

It's the child in me hoping to be discovered that feels almost giddy at the thought that Madre is here. But the adult is glad, too. Because if there's one thing Madre is good at, it's strategic planning. And that's exactly what I need right now. My Bela would be a comfort, she would rub my hair and order me tea. But Madre may be able to tell me what I actually need to do.

At first the hour can't pass fast enough, and I find myself wishing, for the first time since I got to Nicaragua, that I hadn't left my watch on the table in Allen's studio. It has two faces stacked one above the other—one is on New York time, the other, Nica—but that's not doing me any good now as it ticks away in Chelsea and I sit in this wooden box on stilts above the shore. But then, as I hear the captain motor up to us, I feel my stomach rising and dropping again, and the glee at having a mother who will actually chase me when I flee is eroding, being eaten away at the corners by the anger that's always with me whenever Madre is, the resentment that she's finally showing up now, when I'm thirty-three, rather than when I was nine, or eleven, or eighteen. I'm angry at myself, too, that now that I've finally gotten what I wanted—my mother dropped everything and came to be with me—I'm still too bitter, too much of a baby just to enjoy the fact of her being here. And there's another emotion that's keeping me from being nothing but happy to see her, besides bitterness and anger. I'm afraid of what she'll say, or what she'll expect me to do.

The captain has told me that he's trying to learn English, but I'm not in the mood to practice, so I take a seat in the back of the boat, as far from him as I can, and I put my bag in the chair next to mine, so Madre will sit in the row in front of me. I want to hear what she thinks I should do, but I'm not sure I'm ready to face her as she tells me.

"So you know, then," I say to the back of her head. "Allen told you." She turns her head so I can see her profile while the captain busies himself with ropes and her bag, and says, "He's very worried about you. We were all worried."

"Sorry," I say. "I should have left you a note. And him, too, I guess. I wasn't trying to be dramatic, I just wanted to figure things out on my own. But now that you're here, I'm ready to listen to what you have to say."

"Me?" She's still for a few seconds before twisting in her seat so that I can see three-quarters of her face. "I can understand what you like about Allen. I mean, I wouldn't have picked him, an older man, with teenaged kids. But I like how just when you think you know everything you need to about him, he opens his mouth and says the last thing you'd expect."

The captain turns on the motor and we start chugging across the lake. Madre turns back to watch the scenery.

"That's it?" I say. I know it's her way to be cool under pressure, controlled at all times. But I thought she'd have an opinion. Fear. Anxiety. Disappointment. Or maybe joy.

"No," Madre says. "And yes. I mean, I'd love to talk to you about how you're feeling, but in terms of what you decide about your future? It's really not any of my business."

I can't speak. It's such a cold thing to say, even for someone as buttoned-up as she is. If Madre's so uninterested in my life, then why come all this way to find me? It's only when the dock to Mancarron comes into sight that I realize she must be here because my Bela sent her to bring me back. My Bela's too old to come herself, Allen's too angry, and so it fell to Madre to clean up the mess I've made, to bring the runaway home.

In a way, she's right. The decision is mine. I'm as alone as I ever was. I had been worried about my Bela's shame, Madre's disappointment that I've now made it even less likely that I'll ever pull myself together and do something great, and Allen's resentment that he can't just concentrate on his painting. I had been worried about all of them. But really, none of their opinions matter—if, unlike Madre, they even have an opinion at all. It's funny, but after days of ruminating, hearing Madre say that it's none of her business does help me articulate what I want. Just as she turns her head and opens her mouth, I speak into her ear, louder than a whisper so I can be heard over the dying motor, but softer than a shout so that the captain can't listen.

"You're right; it's not your business," I say. "It's just mine. I'm the one who made this mess, I'm the one who should have to deal with it. But, on the off chance that you're at all curious, I've decided I'm going to have this baby."

32

Isabela

Soon I will go back to Managua. To a house without Ignacio. With so much empty space that I'm not sure where I'll fit anymore. Ninexin was going to pack me off today; she was in full comandante mode, giving the orders. But Mariana's young man—or man, anyway—gave me a reprieve. He wants to stay here until he's heard from Mariana, until he knows what happens next, where she wants to see him. He didn't say, "*if* she wants to see me," but he has to be thinking it. She hasn't called him, not once, since she's been gone. Of course, she hasn't called me, either, and I like to think I'm the person she loves most in the world. I'm not worried, I know she will come back to me soon; she always does. Even when she was very little and angry at her mother, she would run away next door, and when Doña Auxiliadora would call to tell me she was there, I didn't rush over and drag her back. I let her have her flight, her freedom. When your mother is a soldier, it's important to feel like you can disobey orders sometimes. And Mariana always came back to me, in time for dinner and our walk to the Eskimo store afterward. That is how you make someone love you so that they will never leave, with affection, with amusement, with ice cream and attention.

I'm not worried about Mariana, but I do need her back now. I'm so desperate to talk to someone about Mauricio's letter that I almost crumbled and told Ninexin about it several times before she left. I've read it so many times that I could recite it by memory, like we used to do poems in school. But, it would have been a huge mistake to take Ninexin into my confidence. She is her father's daughter, after all, a father she has just lost. It wouldn't do to tell her there was another man I loved, truly loved, even more.

The miracle of the letter is that he loved me, too. He still does. It proves I'm not just a silly old woman giving herself airs, embellishing stories, embroidering the truth as we did pillowcases for our dowries. It was real. I was loved, I am loved.

But now that I have this proof, this delicious knowledge, what do I do about it? I'm approaching eighty. What would be the point of meeting with Mauricio, besides satisfying my curiosity? It's not as if we'll build a life together, start a family. Perhaps it's better to let him remember me as I was, the smooth-skinned girl he loved, whom he crossed oceans for, than to have him see me as I am now, when even my wrists have wrinkles. I protected my hands so vigilantly, wearing the gloves Papa's factory made long after it was fashionable. And still these hands betray me now. I've used the creams, I've rubbed the salves into my skin as if I were a fine leather bag worth protecting, but there's only so much you can do to outrun time. My heart looks exactly the same as when I was eighteen, I'm sure of it. But there are so many more inches between my heart and the outside world now; you could fit two of me then in one of the skirts I wear now, with room to spare.

Mauricio will be different, too, of course. But I wouldn't care. It doesn't seem to matter as much to women, does it? Ignacio grew a belly, one that was bigger than mine when I was pregnant with either of our daughters, and I never cared. I never thought he looked silly or weak, like less of a man.

Am I underestimating Mauricio? Isn't it possible that a man who could write a letter like his, after all these years, could look past the sagging skin and wobbly flesh to see the girl he loved, and love her still? If any man could do it, it would be him.

It's not only what I look like now that concerns me. I was beautiful once, and you never really lose that completely. Even the gringo can tell, when he looks at me, that I was once a woman who would have made him stop and stare.

What worries me isn't just my own ruin; it's that Mauricio's letter is so perfect as it is. His love for me is so strong, without him having so much as glimpsed me on a street corner for decades. And my memories of him are so golden, my thoughts of him so precious. Memories are always much prettier than the present. Just watching Granada from the balcony of the hotel has taught me that; the city is so much cleaner in my mind, the people so much better dressed, in hats and gloves and shoes made of leather, not rubber, each of them with a familiar face under his or her hat brim. I thought my memories of Mauricio were like diamonds, clear and so hard as to be unbreakable. But I see now that they could be crystal, as fragile as they are beautiful. What if we meet and feel the disappointment of returning to a place you once loved, to a city that has changed without you? What if we realize that the reality we have now is just a fading echo of the love we kept and polished in our minds? What if seeing each other somehow ruins the dream, the beauty, all that we already have at this moment?

I have so many thoughts! I should see him; I shouldn't, but I should at least write to him; no, not even that, what on earth would I say? And there is no one I can talk to about it, with Mariana away. If Connie were here—but then, I don't even know where she lives now. I sent a Christmas card to the last address I had for her, but have yet to receive a response. Maybe there is a card, full of pictures of her grandchildren and her behind sunglasses so large I can barely tell what she looks like anymore, waiting for me on the table in the entry of the house in Managua. The quiet, empty house. But even if it's there, and she's written her phone number in her swollen, bubble-like numbers at the bottom, it's not doing me any good here in Granada. There's not a soul here to talk to at all. Except for the gringo. Mariana's youngish man. And now he is knocking on the door and it's time for lunch, and what will I find to say to him for the hour it will take to eat?

"So, Mr. Allen," I start, once we have ordered; I suggested the guapote, telling him it's the specialty of the house, caught fresh from the lake daily, and after that, he had no choice in the matter, did he? But he cuts me off and says, "Just Allen, please, Bela," even though I haven't told him he could dispense with the Doña, or Señora, or Mrs., even, to use Mariana's name for me. How could I have told him to drop a title when he never tried one out to begin with?

"Allen." I smile, and the New Orleans schoolgirl must not be buried as deeply as I thought behind wrinkles and kilos, because he looks down at the table before picking up his water glass to drink. A decade or two ago, I might have even been able to cause him to blush.

But now that I've got his attention, what do I say? I have nothing in common with this tall, youngish gringo. Nothing except Mariana.

"What are your intensives toward my granddaughter?" I cock my head to look as stern as possible, but I smile, too, because it's always better to smile when you ask a serious question. And because I'm proud that I've thought of the perfect thing to say and that my English is coming back so fluidly; I've been dreaming of Sacred Heart since I got Mauricio's letter, so I've been hearing the language in my sleep, but it feels good to use it after all this time, to speak it out loud and hear it in my own voice.

He sips again, and makes his fork and knife trade positions, even though the table was set properly in the first place. "I want to marry her, Bela." He stares at me as if daring me to look away. "I didn't think I'd ever want to get married again; after the divorce, I didn't see the point."

He keeps talking, but I'm not listening anymore. "Divorce?" It's not that I'm shocked, many of my friends' daughters are divorced, and those are some of the best families in Nicaragua. This man, he might not even be Catholic; now that I know about the divorce, I'm not about to ask. No, what's shocking is that Mariana didn't mention this to me. I'm beginning to realize that in all our conversations, she never mentioned anything of importance about him.

"Marriage, kids, I thought that was all in my past, which wasn't so bad, because it allows me to concentrate on other things, my work, mainly, but also on my relationships. I still see my college roommates once a week—crazy, right? And Maria. She's incredible. You know how she gets when she's excited, all quiet and intense, taking every-thing in. I get so focused on what I'm doing, especially when I'm paint-ing, that I don't see the world around me. Usually I think that's a good thing. But Mariana, she notices everything. We take a cab and she looks at the driver's name, figures out where he's from. Sometimes she'll strike up a conversation, sometimes she doesn't, but when we get out she'll have a whole theory about his life before he came to New York, like, this one used to be a professor, because he was wearing a tweed jacket and tie in the photo, or that one's got a wife he longs for at home, which is why he's listening to Serbian love songs on the radio. Everywhere she turns she sees a story. It might end up in a painting, it might not, but she always finds a story. Now, when she's not with me, I try to notice things, too. In the cab on the way to the airport, I didn't look at my phone or watch the taxi TV. I turned off the sound so I could hear the music the driver was listening to. But it was just a regular oldies station. ABBA. When I was talking to Ninexin yesterday, all that was running through my head was, 'Can you hear the drums, Fernando?' It's about some revolution. Maybe Ninexin's, right?"

I don't answer. He's not making any sense, but it doesn't matter; he's not talking to me any longer, he's talking to himself. It's not that I don't understand the words—I do, or at least I think I do. It's that he's not really giving me any information. "You asked Mariana to marry you?"

He nods.

"What was her answer?"

He looks down as the fish is placed in front of him. I always like to watch a visitor see a guapote for the first time; they're the ugliest fish I've looked upon in my three-quarters of a century, with teeth that would benefit from underwater orthodontia, and big, fat, delicious cheeks. Mariana's friend, Beth, actually gave a little scream the first time a guapote was set down in front of her. But Allen, for all his talk about noticing things, he doesn't even seem to see it. There's a giant, prehistoric-looking fish on his plate, staring him in the eye; he just glanced at it as if it were a hamburger and went back to his drink.

"She didn't really answer, not at the time. Then when she wanted to talk about it again, I was really into this painting. It sounds terrible, I know, but when you paint . . ." He picks up his knife, looks at the fish, and puts it down again. "The next thing I knew she was in Miami, on her way to Managua."

"You did not run behind her?"

"I thought it was best to give her time to cool off."

I take a sip of my water; they've put in too much ice, as usual. "I see now why the divorce."

I could hear Mariana gasping inside my head when I said that, but I think it helps a man to let him know when he's behaved like an idiot; perhaps it will keep him from doing so the next time. The gringo just laughs; he's an agreeable sort, really. Now he's cutting into the fish and not doing such a bad job at it.

"It's raising teenagers that does it. They run off in a rage and a couple hours later, they're fine." He chews appreciatively. His table manners are not bad, for an American. "Of course, I know Maria's not a teenager. But by the time I realized that grown women like her don't cool off, they just spend the time between incident and apology marinating in anger, thinking up even more reasons why you're a massive jerk, it was too late to call. So I texted her that I was sorry—"

My snort of derision stops him, but not for long.

"I called as soon as I woke up the next morning." He takes a sip of his drink. "It took fourteen messages to get a reply, and even that was just a text telling me that she'd be in Managua for longer than just the funeral, she had some thinking to do."

"I might necessitate a drink," I say, although the only alcohol I've consumed in years is ronpopo at Christmas. But I can tell it's going to take him some time to eat that guapote, and something about having luncheon with a young man who's made a mess of love and is telling his sad tale in English reminds me of New Orleans. I ask the waitress for a Tom Collins, hoping that she won't ask what's in one because I have no idea. I just remember the name after all these years; it sounds so glamorous and yet reassuring, as if it would be attached to a handsome man, like Gary Cooper.

"I knew that was ominous—the needing-to-think part—so I followed her here, on the theory that we could think together. We've talked a lot about me coming to Nicaragua; it didn't seem out of the realm of possibility that she'd want me here." He stops and looks down at his half-eaten fish, as if he is wondering how it got there. I'm starting to think that I should say something reassuring, something to make him forget that it's possible—or even probable—that Mariana wouldn't want him here. But then he looks straight at me and grins. "Plus, I thought it was time for a grand gesture. Cinematic."

"Of course," I say, because I like the sound of the words. He looks back at his fish, forlorn, and pity flutters in my stomach, so I refrain from pointing out that it's only really a grand gesture if there's a ring involved.

Now I wish Mariana were here not just for me, but for this poor, sad man, who is looking more like a little boy than any father of teenagers has a right to, and it can't be the alcohol making me sympathetic because my Tom Collins only just arrived. But feeling sorry for a man is no reason to marry him. And I'm still not convinced that he's really good enough for my Mariana, this divorced gringo.

"I tell you a story, Mr. Allen," I say, and I don't want him to talk with his mouth full, so I add, "Allen, disculpe; I mean, I tell you a story, Allen." And then I take the first sip of my Tom Collins to prepare myself and I can feel New Orleans sliding down my throat and spreading through my body, bringing me back to life. "When I was first married and we live with my husband here, en Granada, my husband, she was a very important lawyer. After two, three years, she—"

"Your husband?"

"Yes, she hire a young clerk to work with him. I see this clerk when I stop in to find Ignacio, get money, bring the childrens, but never I see the clerk outside of the office, though I do walk in front to the window many times each day. Many years pass and the young clerk, he fall sick." I raise my hand and shake it at the wrist to indicate that the poor boy drank too much and was dying of cirrhosis, because I don't want to explain this out loud and speak ill of the dead. "And when she is nearing the end, his doctor call for me and she say, 'Doña Isabela, this boy refuse to leave to go to the hospital. He says he only leave his room if you come see him.'" Here I pause so that Allen can make an appropriate comment, but he just nods to indicate he's listening and keeps right on chewing his guapote.

"I say, 'Doctor, I am a married woman, I cannot go to a young man's room,' and the doctor, she say, 'Doña Isabela, do it as a work of charity.' So I go, of course I go, and this young man, he see me and ask for a pen and start writing something, and when he is done she hand me the paper, only it's not a paper but a photo of him like we used to make in those days, black-and-white, and she is wearing a jacket and tie. And he kiss my hand when I take the photo and then she say to his nurse, 'I can go now.'"

I stop to take a bite, but also to make Mr. Allen wait just a little while. It's always a good idea to make a man wait.

"What had he written on the back?"

I keep chewing, like a lady; I read in *Vanidades* about an actress who chews each bite thirty-seven times, and she has a lovely figure, still, although she's no longer young. She's not as old as I am, though, maybe Ninexin's age. Mr. Allen doesn't even move, he keeps his knife and fork in the air until I reveal, "On the back, he write, 'To Isabela, the lover of my dreams, with gratefulness for making beautiful my unhappy life.'"

The gringo puts down his knife and fork. I lean forward and ask him, "Allen, do you love my granddaughter like that?"

At first I think he is so moved by my story that he is crying. But then he tilts his head back and I realize that he is laughing, most unbecomingly; I can see the fillings in his teeth, the old, cheap American fillings that are black instead of white or silver or gold.

"I don't mean any disrespect, Bela, but, hell, no!" He stops to laugh some more. "I absolutely do not love your granddaughter like that." He takes a sip of water before he can continue. "I'm sure you were very attractive, and that's a lovely story," he says, but the compliments come too late after his unseemly display of laughter. It's not that his laughter embarrasses me; he's the one who should be ashamed of his behavior. It enrages me: he's not just insulting me, he's belittling Mariana by his laughter and his words. If only he understood Spanish I could tell him exactly how unsuited he is for Mariana, how lucky he is even to have been in the same room with her. But I'm too unsettled to find the words in English, so I just sit in icy silence, and I'm glad, for the first time, that Mariana is far away. I would even hope that she'd stay a day longer if I didn't need to see her so badly, just so that she could teach this rude gringo a lesson.

"Bela, that boy with the Parkinson's, or whatever made his hands shake, he wasn't in love with you—he loved the idea of you." Mr. Allen has quieted down now, he's starting to speak calmly. "I'm sure it gave him great comfort, the idea of you. But I really know Maria. I know what makes her laugh. I know which movies she would never see because she can't quite convince herself that they're not real and she knows they'd keep her up all night crying. She's a person to me, Bela, not an idea. I know her and I want to spend my life with her. That's got to matter."

"Perhaps." I like the way the word sounds, so I say it again after taking a rather long sip of my Tom Collins. "Perhaps." He hasn't quite convinced me that his version of love matters so much. Not after his laughing fit. "We shall see when Mariana return," I say. "We shall see."

Allen reaches across the table to grab my wrist, moving so fast that I don't have time to take my hand away. "Bela, I don't think that these days anyone loves anyone the way that clerk loved you. Maria does make my life beautiful, and it's very likely that I'll have an unhappy life if she doesn't come home with me," he says, and it's the first time I've heard him admit that this is in fact a possibility, that she might not return with him, or to him. "But that's where my similarities to your clerk end."

He lays his knife and fork across his plate aslant, and I find myself pleased to see that someone raised him properly, which makes me think that I may not be quite as offended by his presence as I should be.

"I know you were married for fifty-something years, and I was only married for ten—although, believe me, it felt like a hundred," Allen says. "I have no business telling you my theories on love. But I think when you love an idea like that clerk cherished the idea of you, that can't last. I mean, not unless you die young. For love to last, it has to be based on something real, not timing, or circumstance, or imagination, or even beauty, however stunning that beauty may be." He nods at me again, just a small tilt of his head, but this time I like it. "And I'm sure, in this case, it was staggering."

He's right about the last part. I was something to look at back then. But is he right about the rest of it, about love and reality and imagination? Or does he just think the way he does because he lacks any imagination at all?

My Mariana, she deserves to be adored. I'm not saying I want depressed, drunken boys, God rest their souls, dying with her name on their lips. But this gringo, who had a wife he must have once thought he'd spend his life with, could he ever consider Mariana his one true love? Because that's exactly what I want for her, exactly the kind of love she deserves.

It's the kind of love I had. I wonder, for Mariana's sake, and, I'll admit, for my own curiosity, too, if Allen is even capable of that kind of emotion. I even wonder, what would this gringo leaning back in his chair, calmly assessing the skeleton of his decimated guapote, think about Mauricio and his letter? Would he consider that kind of love real?

33

Ninexin

I think maybe I imagined it, or misheard because of the sound of the motor and the captain's voice saying, "We're here!" But she definitely said the word "baby." Mariana gets up from her seat behind mine, walks to the front of the boat, and takes the captain's hand to hop out onto the dock, smiling at him with her usual radiance, as if the world hadn't just hushed to a stop.

"Señora?" the captain says, and he takes my hand and leads me to the edge of the boat as if I'm my mother. Only when I'm safely on the dock does he let me go and nod toward the island. Mariana is on the land already, walking steadily, a few yards ahead of me. As I follow her onto the island I can hear the birds in the trees shaking the leaves, and, somewhere, a far-off monkey. The dusk blurs the green of the land and the gray of the lake, and the only thing I can still see sharply is Mariana, her slim body swaying slightly as she walks ahead of me. Even when she stops and turns to open the door of the last cabin, and I see her in profile, she looks the same as always. Her breasts—were they always that full? But then it wasn't until the fourth month that I started to show. I wonder how far along she is, but when I walk into the cabin and open my mouth to ask, I realize the room is empty. There's an open blue door in the corner that takes me to a concrete porch looking out onto the lake where Mariana is sitting in a rocking chair, which is painted the same ridiculously calm blue as the door, watching a flock of birds showing off. There's another rocker next to hers, so I sit down in it and watch the birds, too, hoping that she will be more likely to talk to me if we don't have to look at each other.

"I didn't know," I say, because it's true, but when I hear the words I realize it's completely the wrong thing; it makes this all about me. I should have gone with my first instinct and asked how far along she was.

When she asks, "Allen didn't tell you?" Mariana's voice has lost the hard edge it had on the boat. She sounds lost.

"No." Maybe I should feel hurt that he didn't assume Mariana had told me right away, but I don't. He let me think she was simply angry at him, so that she could tell me herself. It shows how well he knows Mariana, and I'm glad that he's turning out to be such an adult, grateful that he's watching out for my daughter, especially now.

"I guess he wanted me to be the one to spread the good news." She laughs, but it's more of a snort.

"But it is good news, Mariana!"

I turn to her so she can hear the force of my words, see me say them and understand how deeply I mean them. Mariana is crying when she says, "Do you really think so, Mama?"

I want to seize her, to pick her up like I used to when she was a toddler and she'd wrap her arms around my neck and her legs around my back. But it's been three decades since I cradled her like that, so instead I get up from my chair, sit at her feet, and grab one of her ankles, because I need something of her to hold.

"Of course! A baby!" Saying the words keeps me from blurting out what I'm really thinking, what I was thinking on the walk from the boat, which seemed so long ago, although it must have been only a few minutes. That her life is about to become infinitely more complicated. And so much better! I have done things I'm proud of: I have fought for my country, and then helped it heal from the fight. And I've done little, practical things, too: lived in villages where women can work to support their families because I caused a well to be built that saved them having to spend all day getting clean water. Seen Doña Olga's daughter become a teacher after I paid for her school uniform and helped her with her homework because her mother can't read. Convinced representatives of superpowers to support environmental programs in my own small country. But none of it has been as exciting or as important, nothing has changed me as much as having Mariana. Now it's her turn. And she will never have to choose like I did. She can have her work and her home and her child. It still won't be easy. And it will be even harder if Allen isn't a part of their lives. But it will be amazing. It's a new beginning for her.

And for me! Maybe it's selfish to think about it this way, but for me, Mariana's child is a second chance. With this baby, I won't be preoccupied, or nervous all the time. I won't have to share her child with my mother, just with Mariana, and the best part is, it's an opportunity for me to love Mariana more openly, too. I want to offer to baby-sit, I want to invite Mariana to move in with me so I can support them both. But I don't, because I know it's possible that she will make that huffing noise again and ask me why I would want to live with my grandchild when I couldn't be bothered to live with my own daughter.

"I'm so glad!" Mariana is still crying, not even bothering to wipe away her tears, but she seems more excited than sad, rocking back and forth so that I have to, finally, release her ankle. But I stay sitting at her feet, looking up at her, because I don't want to disrupt anything by moving. "I thought you would tell me to forget it, to make something of myself, not to spend the rest of my life atoning for one mistake."

I know I need to say something, but it's all so precarious. How could she think I'd be anything but delighted? She's not a child. She can support this baby. And if she can't, I can. Is this really how she sees me, as someone who has a plan for her life that has to be followed as strictly as a prison sentence?

"You can still make something of yourself!" I say finally. And even though I know there's a chance that my imagined disapproval is part of what made her decide she wants to raise this baby in the first place, I add, "You *are* making something of yourself. And now, you'll be making yourself a mother, too. You'll be a wonderful mother, Mariana!"

She's still crying, but now she's laughing, too, not the snort but a real laugh. She has to stop for breath between the words as she says, "Come on, Madre!" She gasps again. "You don't know that! I'll probably be a terrible mother! I've never even had a pet. I killed the orchid Beth sent to the gallery when I got promoted." Now she's not crying anymore, just laughing. "You don't get to be a great mom just by watching reruns of *The Cosby Show*. Beth says it's instinctive, biologically coded in us. But what about genetics? I mean, the women in our family, we're not going to win any prizes in the motherhood department. No offense." The laughing fit has passed but she forces out one more so that I know she's joking. I've seen enough American TV, read enough English books to know that this is where I'm supposed to say, "None taken!" But I don't. And she rushes to fill the void of my silence.

"I mean, look at us," she continues, her breath steadier now. "It took both you and my Bela to raise me, and my Bela never had anything important going on but me, and you always had everything else going on but me. What do I have? A job that will keep me away from the baby all day?"

"A job you love!"

"A job that, you're right, really makes no difference in the world. A job I love that has me spending all day talking up everyone else's art but my own. And I'm already so exhausted all the time I don't have the energy to talk, much less paint, and the baby's only the size of a kidney bean!"

What about Allen? Surely he would help support the child, pay for a nanny so you can keep working? I want to ask, but it doesn't seem like the right time, she's rocking so fast now that I wouldn't be surprised if she were propelled out of her chair and ended up floating over the lake like the bride in that Chagall painting. Oh. Will they get married now? I can't ask that either, I'll sound like my mother.

"So, then I think, okay, maybe I'll never set the world on fire with my art; maybe I never would have anyway. The baby won't care."

"Of course not! She'll love you no matter what you do. And she'll respect you for doing it."

Mariana looks at me as if I've just said that the Metropolitan Museum of Art had called to ask about purchasing her latest painting, only I forgot to mention it to her.

"Right, Mama. Because kids are always so loving and respectful of their parents' work. Just like I was," she says. "You know, Beth once told me that whatever headaches you caused your parents, your kids give them back to you three times worse. It's karma."

I want to tell her that I don't care what she thinks about my work, that I wish I'd done a better job letting her know I was thinking of her, always, even as I was working. But that's not the kind of thing we say to each other, and I don't want to disrupt the flow of the conversation. We've been getting along so well, talking about the baby.

"In any case, he or she will already have one parent who's a famous artist," Mariana continues. "And see, that just makes me feel worse, because it makes me think of Allen, and how shocked he was. I just know he must think that I did this on purpose—I mean, who gets pregnant by accident anymore? And in their thirties?"

That gringo giant should thank God and the Virgen and Papachu on his knees, every day, that he even met my daughter, much less was able to date her. "He said that?"

"No, of course not. I mean, he knows I didn't want this any more than he did. Not yet. Maybe not ever. I wanted to travel and paint and watch him do the same, because watching him is like doing everything amazing twice, multiplying it to the second power."

Math was never my strength, but I know how it felt to see the future, and the country, and even the muddy villages around me, through Manuel's eyes, so I have a sense of what she means.

"It's Abuelo's fault," she rushes in. "I mean it's mine, of course, but when I came to Miami for Abuelo's last round of doctor's appointments, I forgot to bring my pills. I didn't even realize it until after I got back and saw the pack next to the sink where I'd left it. But it had only been three or four days! Do you know how hard Beth had to try to get pregnant? I mean, at my last checkup the gynecologist asked if I'd ever considered freezing my eggs!"

I laugh before I can stop myself and she laughs, too. Then she's silent, staring at her hands in her lap.

"Allen doesn't want the baby?"

Her hands come to life, flying into the air near her face. "Allen! Allen wants whatever I want, Allen respects my decision, Allen's been in so much therapy since the divorce he doesn't know what he thinks until he talks to Dr. Leitner." She looks back at her hands, which have settled in her lap again. "He proposed. He said we were probably going to get married anyway, we might as well do so now, he just had to figure out a way to break it to his kids."

"Pendejo!" I say and she looks at me and laughs even harder than before.

"I know, right? What an idiot. As if that's what was worrying me this whole time, not how I'm going to raise this kid on my salary, not whether I'm ready or even fit to be a mom, not whether the wine I drank before I knew I was pregnant has doomed this baby to a life of mediocrity, but whether or not two teenagers would decide that I get to be Mrs. Allen the Second. And then, when I tried to explain why this maybe wasn't the proposal of my dreams, why I maybe wasn't sure I even wanted to get married, to him or anyone, now or ever, he said the most horrible thing."

"What?" I'm ready to swim back to Granada and use the gringo giant for target practice.

Mariana takes a deep breath, shuddering as she exhales, a sound I haven't heard in decades. "The night before I left, a few days after we found out about the baby, I thought we should talk about things, make some decisions before I came down here. But he was in the middle of painting, and it's a great painting, sure, an important painting, but he was so distracted by the canvas calling to him from the back of the studio that he couldn't speak, or even listen to me. And I just kept getting madder and madder, and finally I said he should go back to the painting if it was so much more important to him."

She stops speaking but keeps rocking, slowly, so that the only sound is the birds in the trees and the wood on the cement. "And he stood up, smiling, he was so relieved, and said that I was right, he'd have a much clearer mind once he finished, and that he was sorry he was so preoccupied, but that he felt this painting might be a departure for him." She stops rocking altogether. "He said he felt he was doing something revolutionary."

Now Mariana is crying again and I give in to my body and stand up so that I can take her damp face into my hands. "Oh, mi amor! You're worried about what your Bela says? About revolutionaries making bad husbands? I'm not sure how much you know about your grandparents' marriage, but I've seen enough to be sure that Mama is not in a position to give advice. Not that it ever stops her."

Mariana smiles, but I can tell it's out of kindness more than anything else. She stands up, gently shaking off my hands, and walks over to the railing of the porch, then leans against a post that holds up the roof as if she's decided she needs to help it do its job.

"I'm not worried about Allen being a good husband." She's staring at the lake again. "He would be, I think, he's learned from experience. But I don't know if I want to marry him, or at least not yet."

I step up behind her. I want to put my arms around her waist, to press my hands against her stomach and imagine my grandchild growing inside her. I want to lean my chin against the back of her head and smell her hair like I used to when she was a child. "What is it then, hija?" I ask, softly, because even though I haven't taken the step toward her, my mouth is still quite close to her ear.

At first I think that she's not going to answer. But then she says, "I'm worried about how he'll be as a father. He's great with his kids, but when we first started dating he was really honest about saying he'd had children young and he wasn't sure he wanted any more. So when I first found out, before I told Allen, before I even went to the doctor to confirm the pregnancy test, I tried to imagine raising this baby alone."

"You wouldn't be alone."

"I know. Allen would at least provide child support."

That's not what I meant, but I don't correct her.

"And I decided that I could do the heavy lifting, the day-to-day, I could raise my daughter on my own if I had to, without disrupting Allen's life, his revolution. I even started to get excited about it. And then I thought—what if it's a boy?"

I laugh softly, but she hears me.

"No, really. I don't know anything about boys. And the more I thought about it, the more I realized, whether it's a boy or a girl, I think it would be . . . important, and, I don't know, nice, I guess, for the baby to have a father." A cormorant sticks his beak into the lake, then raises it back up to the sky. The movement catches Mariana's attention and she turns her head to be able to watch him more easily. "That's such a lame word, but it's all I can come up with: I always thought it would be nice to have a father. But the thing is, I don't have such a great track record with fathers. Or much of one at all."

Now I do step forward and envelop her, my arms around her waist, my chin resting above her shoulder. "I'm sorry," I say, so quietly that I'm not sure she can hear it even though I'm so close to her.

"Why wasn't I enough?" She's still looking out at the water although it's almost too dark to see the crane diving its beak into the lake. "He had a new baby. Why wasn't that reason enough to opt out of the action?"

"Oh, hija—" I start but she interrupts before I can finish.

"I know, it was an important mission. And I know, you all had ideals and this was his way to help change things. And I appreciate that, I really do. But all the other guerrillas, they got out alive. It was just that fat rich guy who died, just him and Papi, who wasn't fat, and who had spent years in the jungle learning how not to get killed. It's just too crazy."

"Mariana, in a situation like that—" I begin, hugging her so tightly that my face is almost past her ear, and I can imagine my words floating past her shoulder and down to the shore, until they drown in Lake Cocibolca.

"Thank you, Mama, I know what you're going to say: these things happen and it's unpredictable and he died fighting for something he believed in. But you don't know what he was thinking at the time, when he walked up to that fat man with his gun. You don't know if maybe, just in that moment, he wanted to die." She shrugs her shoulders to wriggle free of my grip, then turns to look at me. "We'll never know. But I can't help thinking about it. Sometimes I wonder why I wasn't enough. And sometimes I wonder if I was too much. If he felt trapped by having a baby, someone he needed to put ahead of the greater good."

Mariana shrugs again, a movement that should seem light and fluid, but she moves slowly as she starts walking across the porch, as if she's wading neck deep in the lake. Before she can go too far I grab her hand. "You can't possibly think that Allen would feel so trapped that he would do something drastic?"

"No." She smiles again and this time I can tell she's genuinely amused instead of trying to make me feel better. Her smile should make me feel calmer, lighter, but it doesn't. "Allen may think of himself as a revolutionary, but he's just an artist, even if he's a pretty big one. He's not going to try to take any generals hostage or run toward any loaded guns." She looks down at her free hand. No. At her stomach, which is behind her hand. "But I don't want him to do whatever the Allen equivalent is: run toward bottles of loaded scotch, or stop painting, or paint furiously, recklessly, so that he never has to wipe up the vomit or smell the poop or dab at the drool. I just don't want to make anyone feel trapped if I can help it. I've already done that. I know you'll swear this wasn't the case, but how could Papa not have felt stuck with a baby that interfered with his great adventure, all his good work? And you, too, Mama."

"Never, Mariana," I whisper. "I never felt trapped. Just torn." Maybe I shouldn't have said that last part, but we're being honest with each other now. And I want her to know it's normal: she'll feel torn, too, between her child and everything else she loves. I want to tell her that this dilemma is a gift, an embarrassment of riches. But I also know it's going to be hard, maybe the hardest thing she'll do, so I stay quiet. I don't want to scare her or upset her, I just want to reassure her. But I'm not very good at doing that, so it may be safer to say nothing at all.

She's kept her hand in mine this whole time, and now she tightens her grip and steps forward to hug me. This sweet and unexpected embrace is more than I let myself wish for, normally, but now that I'm in her arms, I don't feel comforted, just hot and short of breath. I pat her on the back and break the hold.

"I'm going to lie down a little before dinner." Mariana starts walking to the door, but before she enters the cabin she turns to say, "Thanks for being excited, Mama. I'm glad you know."

I think I smile at her. Maybe I even say something. But I don't follow her inside. Instead, I sit in the chair she just left, which is still warm from her body.

I'd never realized until now how little she knows. How much she's invented to make up for that lack of information about her father's death. But I know that I can't let her live in her own imagination anymore. It was her I was trying to protect, not me. It was always her, I promise. And me a little, too. But I can't protect either of us anymore.

The sun is long gone and the world has deepened from pink to light blue to navy. And I will sit here, rocking, until everything around me is black. That's one of the advantages of an island without electricity: it's much easier to hide, even from yourself.

But soon Mariana will wake up, and we'll go to the dining room to eat. And then we'll sleep and sometime tomorrow after breakfast, we'll sail back to San Carlos, where a driver from the office will meet us to take us to Managua. It should all be lovely, this mother-daughter road trip. Except for the fact that at some point I'm going to have to do what I've put off for too long. What I hoped I might be able to get away with avoiding forever. I'm going to have to tell Mariana what only one other living person knows: that I'm the one who killed her father.

34

❧

Maria

On the bedside table, there's a balsa-wood angel, painted white with blue flowers trailing down its gown. The hotel is full of these decorations, showcasing the handicraft of the island; even the chain you pull to flush the toilet has a wooden turtle at the end. It's like living in a children's book.

Maybe I will name the baby Marisol, for Solentiname. But that sounds too much like my name and she deserves her own. Or he, I suppose. Maybe if it's a boy I can call him Ernesto and he can claim Ernesto Cardenal as his spiritual father, and live in a world as vibrant and lush as this archipelago. I've actually teared up at the thought; at least it's dark, so Madre can't see me.

It's the hormones. Oh, Wooden Bedside Angel, let it be the hormones! Because if they're not responsible for the shifts in my mood then I am truly going insane. In New York my overriding emotion was anxiety—a ferocious need to be over this precarious stage in my life, to know what happens next. I told myself that whatever happened, I could deal with it; it was the not knowing that made things seem so vast, so overwhelming. I tried to prepare myself to imagine all potential scenarios. Me in a studio apartment with a baby sleeping in a Moses basket, a baby Allen never sees. Me and Allen, hand in hand at his mother's house in the Berkshires, watching a toddler run through the wildflowers. Me acting as godmother to Beth's second child, the baby they've adopted and love with more stability and security than I could ever offer. Me, without Allen, without a baby, traveling to Switzerland for the first Art Basel that will show my work, trying to keep from doing the math to figure out how old my child would have been at this point.

By the time I got to Nicaragua, I was so angry there was no room for anxiety anymore. I'm starting to think it's myself I was most mad at it, for adding more stress and drama to my overly dramatic family at such a difficult time. But it was easier to believe I was angry with everyone else. I was furious at my mother for not being the kind of mom Beth's was, for not giving me a model of a working mother that seemed positive or even feasible. The fact that I always blamed her for abandoning me when I wanted her to stay made it that much harder to decide what to do with my own child, especially since I was considering abandoning this baby with much more finality than Madre ever did, by giving it up for adoption. Or not having it at all.

I was also mad at Abuelo, for dying and taking away the one stable male presence in my life, and erasing the possibility of my imagined life in Nicaragua, with him teaching the baby to ride a bike or play baseball. The truth is, even if Abuelo had lived, that scenario was unlikely. I couldn't really see myself dropping my career and moving to Nicaragua to live off my mother. And I wasn't about to follow Madre's example by staying in New York and sending my baby to Nicaragua to be raised by great-grandparents. They'd already done more than their fair share by raising me, and at their age, they wouldn't have had the energy to bring up another child. Still, I had thought, perhaps if I could move to Miami, to open a gallery in Wynwood and have my baby grow up near Beth and her kids, maybe then Abuelo and my Bela would come to spend six months of the year with us, and he and I could take the kid for watermelon juice and bike rides on weekends and my Bela could enjoy her great-grandchild in the glorious anonymity of a big, American city without worrying about what all her Nicaraguan lady friends would say about the poor little bastard, how the whispers would boil over the minute she walked out of Mass on Sundays.

With Abuelo gone, that compromise world is lost, too. And even though it's crazy and selfish and narcissistic, I've felt as mad at him as I have sad about his loss. Just telling my Bela would have been easier with him here to remind her that it doesn't matter what other people think, what matters is that you do what you know is right. He would have been surprised to learn I was pregnant, of course. And disappointed. But he was a man who absorbed the shocks life threw his way and tried to make the best of them without complaining, whether it was rebuilding his life outside his beloved country to keep his family safe, or parenting another child long after retirement age. Abuelo would have taken a deep breath, stared down at the tiled floor, and then looked up and said something that made me feel everything would be okay. Something like, "Every baby is a blessing."

In the end, it was Madre who suggested that this baby could be a good thing. And when she did, I felt more than relief. I felt joy. I had made her happy. And hope, that maybe I can make myself happy, and this baby, too.

I shouldn't be so surprised that it was Madre who made me feel better. She is Abuelo's daughter, after all. She's great under pressure:

calm, and clear-thinking. But ever since I arrived in Nicaragua, I've slipped back into the way I used to see Madre when I was a hurt, hormonal teenager. It's immature, and so unfair, but from the minute I spotted her staring at her iPhone in the airport in Managua, I felt the old irritation rise up in me. If I had been able to see her with an open mind, if I had thought to confide in her from the beginning, maybe I wouldn't have been so eaten alive with my own fear and anger that I felt the need to flee from everyone I love.

Including, of course, Allen. Has he come to rescind the proposal, having spoken to his children? Or was he so shocked, and his pride so hurt, when I wasn't delighted with his grudging offer of marriage, that he had to rush to my side to lock this down?

I know, I know it's possible that he's just worried about me, that he's come to support me. He knows how much I loved Abuelo, how much I still do. And until now Allen was the one person who knew about the baby, knew that my future, and my life, has never been less certain. I like certainty. I'm the planner. I make the reservations, I book the hotels, I arrange the dinners with friends. Allen shows up and sees what happens. But when I saw him standing there in the funeral home, I knew things were different now, that he had a plan and I was the one just crossing my fingers. And I knew I had to get far away from him before his own easy confidence took over and I ended up floating along in the current of his desires, letting myself get washed into a life that is his creation, where I'm just an acolyte to the Artist and, if he so desires, the Baby, and what's left of me swirls away down some cosmic drain.

In the end it wasn't Allen or the storybook setting of Solentiname that made me decide I'm going to raise this baby somehow. It wasn't even Madre. It was Clara Posada. I was looking at her husband's paintings, and her daughters' work, and her granddaughter's, and at her own unexpected canvases. And I found myself thinking, I wonder what my baby's paintings will look like.

It wasn't a decision even, but more of an epiphany. I had already decided. I'm still not sure it's the right thing. It would be kinder, more sensible, maybe, to arrange a private adoption with Beth, to magically provide the sibling she's longing to give to Olivia, and at the same time to give my child a life free from my neuroses, a life with a father whom I already know is giving and loving and ready to be there always, so eager to raise children, as opposed to willing to do it again, if he's forced to, because he feels like he should. I didn't mention this plan to Beth; I didn't want to get her hopes up. I didn't tell her about the pregnancy at all, didn't tell anyone except Allen. And I hadn't gotten around to bringing up the idea of adoption to Allen yet; I thought I should wait until we had a chance to discuss things further, to come to an agreement together—or a rupture that would make it clear this baby's future was mine to decide alone. But when I saw the Posadas' paintings all lined up, so similar to each other and yet distinct enough to be immediately identifiable, I knew I was going to keep this baby. When Madre said "It's not really my business," and I thought she was referring to the pregnancy, it just confirmed what I'd already decided looking at the Posadas' artwork: that everyone else—Allen, Madre, Bela—is a supporting character in this situation; I'll just have to see where they fit in. All I'm sure of right now is that the baby is going to grow up with me.

I know that's simplistic. I know I'll have to figure out how to support this child and where to raise her. Or him. I know I'll be exploding some lives in the process. Allen's daughter will be mortified and his ex-wife will be livid and I can't even imagine how my Bela will react without Abuelo to calm her down, to make her realize that the gossip of the chirping ladies in her tiny world doesn't matter as much as she thinks it does.

Since yesterday at the Posadas', my mood has been swinging wildly between relief at having decided, mixed with strange surges of joy and a weird urge to run—me! Running!—and a violent desire to punch something or someone, to fight anyone who doesn't agree with my decision to keep the baby. I was convinced that once Madre found out, she would want me to give up the baby and get on with my life, to finally do something important like she does every day. She's always dropping suggestions that I should come run an orphanage or at least develop a project that teaches art to street children, something that will make me move back and help her rebuild Nicaragua. It seemed only natural that she would want me to put the interests of all of Nicaragua's children ahead of a selfish desire to manage my own life as I pleased, to raise my own child; that's what she did with me, after all.

It never occurred to me that Madre would be happy, thrilled, even, for me and the baby. I know it's narcissistic and petty to feel sibling rivalry with all of humanity, with an entire nation, but I'll admit it: it felt so good to know that Madre was thinking of just me tonight. Me and the baby. When I saw her face on the porch, the way it softened and smoothed and glowed, I knew I was watching her in a moment of uncomplicated joy. I don't think I've ever seen her look that way before. Madre's joy was contagious; seeing it infected me with the belief that everything is going to work out, somehow.

Now I've lost all desire to fight, or to run, I'm just tired, so tired. I know I should call Allen and tell him we can talk tomorrow, in person, then I should figure out what it is that I want to do with him, with the baby, with all of our lives, and present that scenario to him as a fact, not an option.

That's what I should do. But I'm not going to. Because all I want to do is sleep for a few hours and then wake up, eat something, and sleep some more. I want to sleep for hours before I think about anything rational or logical, before I start wondering if my mother's unconditional joy will last or if she'll start thinking of plans to mold me into the kind of mother she was; if nurture is destiny and I am doomed to raise a child without a father, like she did; and if my baby will judge me as harshly as I have her.

Just for this evening—no, all the way until tomorrow morning—I want to forget about all the things that I lack: a father of my own, a father for my child. I want to concentrate instead on what I have: a brief, divinely sleepy moment of peace.

I know it's a hormone-borne illusion, a chemically induced calm. But I'm going to curl up in it and try to pretend that it's real, and not just cosmic payback for the nausea and the fatigue and the painfully swollen breasts. I'm going to stare at this wooden picture-book angel until my eyes drift shut and I fall asleep to the sound of my mother breathing in the next bed, and hope that when I drift off, I'll dream of a life in which this feeling can last.

35

Isabela

I'm not the strongest of women. Sometimes I think it's ironic that I've gotten this far, that I've outlived my husband, virtually all of his friends, and even a few of mine. Apparently, I have staying power.

But while I may have stamina, I know I don't have much strength. I can never turn down the dessert I shouldn't eat, the way Ninexin does. And I always do what I'm told, which sounds like obedience, but which I'm old enough and honest enough to know is just a form of laziness. There are so many ways my life would be different if I were stronger. Perhaps I would have turned my back on Papa that day in the church in New Orleans, nodded at Father Antony to continue, and I'd be married to Mauricio right now. Or maybe I would have fled when I had the chance. On the morning of my wedding, Papa came to my room as Dolly was pinning my veil into my hair and asked her to leave us. I thought he was going to give me his blessing or some advice, maybe even a little spending money for the honeymoon. I was doing what he wanted; this had to prove that I was, in the end, a good daughter. Whatever he had to say, I wanted to know that I had made up for disappointing him so in New Orleans. To know that he still loved me as much as he always had. I started to turn away from the mirror, toward him, but he put his hands on my shoulders, held me in place, and said, "Look at yourself. Look how beautiful you are." I tried to smile at my reflection but I couldn't; I looked down at the silver brush and comb set on my vanity so that I wouldn't have to watch my own eyes fill with tears.

"I thought," my father said, and let his hands fall off my shoulders. "I hoped . . ." He walked over to the window that faced the street behind our house. "There's a carriage and driver waiting downstairs. I was going to send him to the station to get your tía Gabriela; her driver took ill. But he'll go wherever I tell him. You'll be safe if you go to the Poor Clares; the nuns will take you in and I won't tell anyone where you are until we figure out what comes next." He crossed the room to my side. I could hear his footsteps and then sensed him next to me but I couldn't look up, I felt frozen in place. "You shouldn't have to do this if you don't want to, hija," he said. "You don't have to do this."

Maybe Dolly would have let me live with her in Matagalpa, which was far enough away that the shame might not reach, and where a spinster sister could be useful in running her household, raising her children. Or perhaps if I prayed hard enough, I would have felt a calling and stayed with the nuns indefinitely. But I knew I wasn't strong enough to face the shame of humiliating my family, breaking my engagement to Ignacio, and none of the alternative futures running through my head changed that. So I turned to my father and said, "Thank you, Papa, but Tía Gabriela must be waiting at the station. And you look so handsome; I'll be proud to have you walk me down the aisle."

Did my life turn out so badly as a result of my weakness? Not really. Yes, I'm a widow, and the effects of the too-many desserts are immediately visible. But I have my daughters, my grandchildren. Perhaps weakness isn't the worst defect a woman can have. I'm still here, aren't I? And I'm still receiving love letters from a person who can't forget me, although he hasn't seen me in over half a century. How many people can say that?

I'm boasting now. I know that. But I'm also making excuses. Because the same lack of resolve that has me eating Pio Quinto when I'm already bursting with churrasco and puré de papa is the same defect of character that caused me to show Mariana's gringo Mauricio's letter tonight at dinner.

I shouldn't have, I know I shouldn't have. Now he knows secrets that Mariana doesn't, that Ninexin could never imagine, things about me that Ignacio never got to know, thank heaven. If sharing those confidences with a virtual stranger is not a betrayal of the people who love me most, then I don't know what is.

But I couldn't help it. Mauricio's words keep floating around in my mind, which suddenly seems empty of everything else. I have become a living embodiment of one of Mariana's paintings, all words and blank space, with some hazy images scurrying around the edges. I needed to talk about it with somebody. And after Allen's honesty at lunch, it was my turn to offer a confidence. Besides, I do so hate a silence at the dinner table.

I had ordered a Tom Collins right away, and then, once our salads were cleared and before they brought the soup, I gave him the letter. I made no explanation, offered no context. I just handed it to him and said, "Read this."

He looked at it so intensely I felt he could see through the words to Mauricio's soul. And then he handed it back and said, "It's in Spanish."

I had to laugh then. I'm afraid I must have caused a bit of a scene, because the waiter rushed over to ask if everything was all right. But I shooed him away and once I regained my composure, I took the letter back and translated it for the gringo giant.

I won't pretend I didn't enjoy doing so. Hearing Mauricio's words out loud, in almost-whispered English because you never know who is listening, made them even more romantic somehow, as if I were watching a movie in the cinema on Canal Street with him by my side.

By the time I said, "I remain, your Mauricio," our soup had been on the table for several minutes and Allen hadn't taken a bite. I lifted my purse off the little stool the restaurant had provided for it, put the letter away, and said, "Your soup is getting cold." I didn't want to seem too eager to hear his thoughts.

But Allen didn't start eating. Instead he looked at me and said, "That's some letter." Only then did he finally lift a spoonful to his mouth.

I was feeling pleased with myself, thinking that I had made the right decision to share my secret with him, when he put down his spoon, reached for a roll, and said, "So you two never slept together?"

I dropped my spoon to the ground; luckily, it was empty, so broth didn't fly all over the restaurant, although I had to stop myself from spitting out what was in my mouth.

"Sorry, I've offended you," the gringo said. "I shouldn't have even asked; it's clear from the letter that you didn't. It's full of the mystery relationships had back then. We've lost that."

I probably should have gotten up and stormed out of the restaurant so that he would know how inappropriate his comment had been, so that he would realize how a gentleman should act, the kinds of things he should say and the kinds he shouldn't. But La Gran Francia makes the best French onion soup in Nicaragua, probably in Central America. So I took another bite, not dignifying his comment with a response.

He didn't notice that I was no longer speaking to him. He just kept right on talking. "Now the mystery isn't will we or won't we, so much as what will I do after? In the beginning it's all fun. But when things get serious, you can't help but start wondering, how will this end? Will I bungle it all somehow?"

"Most probably." I took a sip of my Tom Collins. "I would not be surprised if you often said or did the wrong thing, Mr. Allen." I emphasized the "mister," so he would know how frosty our relationship was now.

"That's the thing with me and Maria." I raised my hand to stop him from speaking; I don't want to know the bedroom details of this stranger's life, or my granddaughter's, for that matter. But he didn't seem to notice, even though he was looking straight at me. "I've never doubted her, not for a minute. She's an amazing person, she'll be a great wife someday—and probably a pathologically terrific mother, even if it's just to spite her mom."

It almost seemed as if he were talking to himself, so I didn't say anything when he paused. In any case, I was back to not speaking to him. But he was so oblivious, he reached across the table and put his hand on top of mine. "It's me, Bela. I know I want to be with Maria forever, but I'm not 100 percent sure I'm up to being married again. The last one was such a spectacular failure."

He took his hand back and I immediately placed mine in my lap, where it should have been in the first place, to diminish the risk of any further inappropriate displays.

"It didn't need to be. With women like Taylor—my ex—it's clear what they want. They need a man who makes a certain amount of money, who can give them a particular lifestyle. You know that go-ing in, that's the bargain you're striking. In a way, it's a relief, because there's a clear agreement in place, a bar you can reach. You can de-liver on that promise. Maybe there will be times when you'll want more of a partnership. But at least you know you won't disappoint them when it comes to what matters most to them. With someone like Maria—I couldn't tell you what it is she wants. And that scares me."

I opened my mouth but he wasn't waiting for an answer. "But what if fearing the potential for failure just guarantees that I ruin everything anyway? What if I end up like Mauricio?"

I refrained from saying that I highly doubted he and Mauricio have anything in common.

"What if I lose the woman I love and fifty years from now—who'm I kidding? More like fifteen, or even five—what if five years pass and I spend all that time wishing I had done things differently, wishing I could be with her? The way this Mauricio wishes he could be with you. His one true love."

The gringo pays attention, even if he is a bit self-centered. I have to give him that.

"You like the letter, then?"

"It's the saddest thing I've ever heard. It crushed me when he said that as soon as Castro dies, he wants to take you to the place he grew up."

"Camagüey."

"He wants you to come away to Camagüey," Allen says. "It would sound like a song if it weren't so poignant. He wants to bring the woman he loved and lost to the place he loved and lost."

I didn't know what to say to that. Then the waiter came and asked if he could take our plates and Allen nodded, although his soup bowl was still half full. "It's a cautionary tale," he continued. "The man wants another chance to do everything over again, to set things right now that he's at the end of his life."

"Mauricio is very fit!" I informed Allen. "When he was in New Orleans he rode and played tennis and he never ate or drank overmuch. I'm sure he has many good years ahead of him."

"Of course!" The gringo grinned as if I'd said something amusing. "I never meant to imply any different."

The waiter returned and Allen asked for the check, then thought the better of it. "Dessert, Bela?"

I shook my head, so as not to give him the satisfaction, but he said, "Let's share something; you'll be giving me an excuse to try a local specialty."

We ate our Pio Quinto mostly in silence as I tried to decide whether I should write to Mauricio, and if so, what would I say? Perhaps I should even figure out a way to try to see him if it's possible? Especially if the gringo isn't wrong about Mauricio reaching the end of his life. There are so many logistics to consider, and, besides those, emotions. But I already felt a little lighter, just having shared my secret.

Allen paid for the check, and gave me his arm to escort me back to my room. As he unlocked the door for me, I thanked him for dinner. He grabbed my hands again and said, "No, thank you for reading me the letter and making this lovely night in this grand old city even more beautiful."

The words were pretty, and he seemed sad, so I let him bend over and kiss my cheek. Then he leaned a little farther forward and whispered, "You know, Bela, I've been to Cuba, on a junket with a museum that shows my work. And at least one of the cabbies there told me that the locals haven't seen Fidel in years. You know he's not in charge anymore; Raul Castro is the president now. Maybe Fidel's already dead."

He straightened up but I held on to his arm, steadying myself. "Even the Cuban government could not keep so big a secret," I said, dropping my hand and turning to cross the threshold into my room. "You are making yourself ridiculous."

"That may be true," Allen said, helping me with the heavy door by pulling it toward him. "But either way, why leave it up to Castro to decide whether or not you get to see each other again after all these years?"

36

Ninexin

I thought about telling her at dinner, but that seemed too much like a setup, waiting until we were in public so that she'd have to modulate her reaction because of the waiter or the eight Costa Ricans at the table next to ours. But when she got up from the table and gave a satisfied little sigh, I wished I had already told her, that it was over and I was already weathering her reaction, whatever it turned out to be. Rage. Fear. Disgust.

She seemed fatigued, but in a happy way, a feeling I remember so well from being pregnant with her: when the idea of keeping your eyes open seems like an impossibility, but you can't bring yourself to care. I hated to snatch this sweet, sleepy calm away from her.

I told her I was going to take a cup of tea to the little gazebo in the middle of the hotel lawn. "Why don't you sit with me a bit?" I asked, and I was already promising myself that when she said no, she was too tired, I would let her go and tell her before breakfast, in the morning when we were both fresh.

But she said, "Sure, Mama," and asked the waiter for a mug of chamomile. I had no choice but to turn the little flashlight he lent us out toward the lawn, to do what it could to illuminate the vast darkness. I didn't want her to see me as I tried to fix this memory into my brain, of the last time she called me Mama. As I wondered whether it would be the last time, for a long time, that she called me anything at all.

I turn the flashlight off once we are settled in our sloping wooden chairs. The moon is hiding behind the clouds; there will never be a better setting than this. Nature is on my side, although I don't deserve it.

"I was trying to protect you," I say, starting with excuses, already trying to justify myself, my choices.

"What, Mama?"

"I never told you about the night your father died because I thought no good could come from you knowing the details."

Mariana's soft laughter floats over to my chair. She doesn't seem to be understanding what I'm saying. "Madre, there's this thing called the Internet now," she says, and her voice sounds less sleepy with each word that follows. "You and Bela always shut down the conversation when I asked about my dad, but I know everything about how Papi died; I have since grad school. I know he was the one guerrilla killed in the takeover of Memo Paredes's house, the one casualty besides fat Memo himself. I've seen floor plans of the mansion. The list of demands the guerrillas made in return for releasing everyone safely. Pictures of them boarding the flight to Cuba after the siege ended, all smiles and sideburns. I'm filled with so much information about that night, I used to dream about the takeover, as if I were there. Such clear, specific dreams that I'm sometimes convinced I was there, in a weird way, that a memory of that night is floating through my veins, a legacy from Papi."

She stops speaking and I'm trying to figure out how to begin again when her voice floats through the darkness, a little softer than before, as if she worries someone is listening. "It used to bother me that those other guys were so happy when Papi had just been killed. But I think I understand now. They were young and vital and working to overthrow a dictator, and it was starting to look like they might actually succeed. They really were changing the world. One compañero down, even one who left an infant behind, is pretty minor in the scheme of history."

I picture Mariana at twenty-two, pushing thick bangs off of her forehead to stare at a computer screen, at the faces of all the young men, and the few young women, who survived when her father didn't, carrying hate for them around with her among Miami and Managua and New York, a heavy, unwieldy inheritance, and one that I unwittingly gave her. I should have told her long ago. I thought I was protecting her by not burdening her with this horrible legacy, but now I'm starting to suspect that anything would have been better than not knowing.

"He didn't suffer." I can give her that comfort, anyway, and it's true.

"Mama," she says softly. "I know he was shot in the stomach. It must have been awful: such a protracted, messy way to die."

"Not at close enough range like that. Your papi died instantly. Almost."

I can hear Mariana's breath, slow and heavy, over the sound of the geckos shrieking at each other. "I don't want to be cynical," she says, "but that's the kind of thing you tell a young widow with a baby. That her husband died instantly, with her name and the name of their baby daughter on his lips. That he felt no pain." She's been carrying her vision of Manuel's death with her for so long, she isn't ready to let it go yet. But I have to make sure she does, even if the reality is more painful than the gruesome end she'd envisioned. She's been living in her imagination long enough, with a distorted image of a father who ran from her straight into waiting gunfire.

"He didn't say anyone's name, not yours, not mine. He just lay where he had fallen, looking so, so shocked."

"Mama," she says in a too-patient voice.

"I know what I'm saying is true, Mariana. I know because I was there."

Even the geckos are silent. I hear the grass rustle as something hops or slithers or crawls through it, and then there is quiet again.

"No," Mariana says, not bothering to add the "Mama" anymore. "You're not in the pictures of them boarding the plane to Cuba. Your name isn't on any list."

"But I was there in Memo Paredes's house, hija. I couldn't go to Cuba—I had a husband to bury and a daughter to raise."

"That's even less believable." Her voice sounds less shaky, stronger than before. "That you'd stop playing soldier long enough to take care of me."

I can tell from the sharp edges of her words that she's starting to believe me now, even as she insists she doesn't. And even though it's what I hoped for, what I undoubtedly deserve, I wish I could take back the last few minutes and return to where we were before, with her pitying my naïveté and calling me "Mama." My tea is cold now but I drink it anyway, in one gulp, as if it is medicine that might somehow save me.

"I wish I hadn't been there. It's why I asked that my name not be released to the press. The compañeros had reasons to agree; I wasn't the only one being protected. And the truth is, no one wanted me there, least of all Manuel. You turned four months old two days before, you didn't even sleep through the night yet. The comandantes, they said women and men were equal, but we still ended up doing the soft jobs, mostly, community-building, literacy. Cooking for the male soldiers. Manuel said you needed me more than the commando unit taking over the house did. But I insisted on coming. And he died because he let me."

Mariana moves in her chair and I hear a thud. Her mug must have fallen off of her lap.

"He died because he was there," Mariana said. "And you could have, too, and I wouldn't have even had you."

Her voice is soft but shaky; I've already hurt her by revealing that both of us chose to leave her that night. And there's so much more I still have to tell her. "Listen to me, hija." I turn toward her in my chair, although it is too dark for me to make out anything but the outline of her face. "I insisted that they let me come, and they agreed. They had to, because I was the one who got them that floor plan in the first place. Memo's daughter, Brigida, had gone to school at La Asuncion. We had been friends since third grade, when I invited her to my birthday party after Mama said I had to. She felt bad for Brigida, growing up without a mother; hers had died, it was rumored of alcoholism, when we were just little kids. Also, she said I had to invite all the girls in the class, because that's what nice young ladies did."

"That sounds like my Bela." At least she is listening. If Mariana understands I am telling the truth about Brigida and my birthday party, maybe she will let me get the rest of it out.

"We were never that close; Brigida always made me a little nervous. She had these stunning green eyes that somehow made her look sneaky, like a cat. But, I included her, which most people didn't."

"Because my Bela raised you to be a nice young lady."

"Also because, eventually, I felt sorry for her, too. By high school, she used to spend most of her lunch hours in the library. One day I was walking behind her on the way to check out a book, when she tripped on a step and fell forward. Her skirt flipped up; they made us wear these itchy blue pleated skirts which looked demure but blew up like balloons every time there was a strong wind. Anyway, when I helped her with her skirt I saw the backs of her legs were covered in welts. I gasped—I couldn't help it—and she said, 'Don't worry; he doesn't usually notice me much.'

"I asked what happened. Maybe it wasn't polite, but I asked before I could think about it, and Brigida said her father didn't like her report card. I knew she got good grades; they published the class rankings at the end of each term. 'But not the best,' Brigida said. 'My dad's pretty competitive.'"

"What a jerk."

My eyes have gotten used to the dark and I can see that Mariana has pulled her feet up onto the chair and is rubbing the backs of her own thighs. I had the same reaction when I saw Brigida's legs; I felt the skin on the backs of my own legs rise, and I wanted to reach out and try to soothe her welts. I felt I owed Brigida something, because at that point, violence was still so shocking to me and clearly so commonplace to her.

"More like a monster," I say. "He was a general in Somoza's army. Everyone knew that if Somoza—or anyone in the dictator's family, really—hated someone, that person disappeared. But what we weren't sure was true or not was the rumor that our president for life had them dropped into the lava-filled mouth of the Volcan Masaya from one of his helicopters. When people whispered about this, they said that Brigida's father did the dropping. That's why most of the other parents were afraid to have his daughter in their homes; it was safer just to avoid notice, and to avoid her, too."

Mariana wraps her arms around her knees and I start to wonder if I hadn't been right in the first place, to keep this story from her. What I've told her so far is nothing, really, compared to what she still has to hear, things she might later wish she still didn't know.

When I was pregnant with Mariana, Manuel used to sing to my belly, describing anything beautiful we saw—an orchid twining around a tree, a parrot flying out of a cliff side. To make up for all the brutality in the world around us, he said, and so that the baby would hear happy thoughts and sounds, not just talk of war. I'm sure Mariana wants the same for her baby, an atmosphere of calm and security, of beauty. And now I'm ruining all that.

"I lost touch with Brigida after graduation," I press on; it's too late to stop now. "I was dating your father, and caught up in the Movimiento; Brigida didn't move in the same circles we did. But one night when I was pregnant with you, Rigoberto and Celia had a party, and there was Brigida, home from the University of Houston, where her father had sent her to study, 'at least until things calm down,' she said. The school was only a couple of years old, and she liked her classes, art history, mostly. But she felt bad being so far away, she said, when she really wanted to help with the struggle. I was shocked at first; her father's job was to prop up the corrupt government Manuel and I were working to destroy. But she wasn't the only compañero in the Movimiento who had relatives who worked for Somoza. And I knew—maybe I was the only person who did—that she had every reason to disrespect her father, to hate him, even. She had seen the depravity and decadence of the regime up close, she said.

"Brigida was home for the summer, and we became close. Closer than we ever had been in school, really. Manuel didn't want me involved in any dangerous operations as my due date approached, and I was bored. Brigida would stop by almost daily to visit. Talking to her gave me something to do."

"Something like planning an attack on her father?"

"It was her idea, Mariana." I can hear how defensive my voice sounds. "At first she just gave me money from her dress allowance to pass on to the compañeros to support our efforts. It was the least she could do to help Nicaragua, she said. She couldn't risk working with the poor herself—what if someone saw her and told her father? After she went back to school in August, I got a letter, maybe two. But when she was home for Thanksgiving, she came by to see you—she brought a pink baby blanket printed with ballerinas. And when I unrolled it, there were the plans for her father's new home inside. 'He's having his usual Christmas party early this year, on the twenty-first, to break in the new place,' she told me. I knew what she was suggesting, even though she didn't say the words. If we were able to capture him, her father would make an irresistible bargaining point: we could use him to get amnesty for our condemned leaders, rights for our prisoners, whatever we wanted, really. On top of that, he was a bully, and I'd seen enough of his kind to know that bullies tend to flail when they're put in a position of weakness. He might fold and tell us things about Somoza that would prove invaluable, insider information that could help us do so much good.

"Still, kidnapping Memo was a best-case-scenario situation, it was what would happen if everything went smoothly, and no one was harmed. But there was no guarantee that would be the case. I didn't want to be responsible for Brigida putting things in motion that might end in tragedy, things that she might later regret. I told her that although we tried to work as nonviolently as possible, there was always a chance that her father would get hurt. And she said that she knew that was a risk, but she couldn't prioritize the comfort of one man over the good of society. 'Besides, my father never had any issue with hurting me,' she said. 'Ninexin, there were times when I thought he'd kill me. I still have nightmares that he does.'

"I didn't like to think of how much Brigida had suffered, so I changed the subject from her father and asked if she would be there. She said the young people usually left by eleven to go to a disco. I wasn't sure what to do. I believed in our cause so much. I knew Somoza's henchmen had caused so much suffering. In theory, I had no problem with them meeting a little karmic retribution. But in practice, we were talking about a man I had met, the father of a person I cared about, someone who might later regret causing him harm, or, at best, humiliation. But Brigida said to me, 'I risked a lot to sneak those out of my papa's office and make a copy; I'm not taking them back with me. Give the plans to Manuel. He'll think of something that will help the most people with the least amount of violence.' And she dropped them on the table and went home.

"The next day Manuel and I went to my parents' for lunch and I brought the plans with me; I thought I might hide them in my old closet for a few days while I thought things over, that they'd be safer there. Two police goons had started standing across the street from our house, watching me and your father come and go. But just as we were about to leave, I had a vision of the National Guard searching Papa and Mama's house, which they knew we frequented, of course. If those plans were found it would be enough to throw them into one of Somoza's torture dungeons. I couldn't expose them to even more risk than I had just by joining the Movimiento. I thought about destroying the plans, but that would be a betrayal of all I had done so far. Brigida was right: Manuel would know what to do. I couldn't rob him of this opportunity to affect real change, to become a star in the Movement as he had always been in my eyes."

"Brigida hated her father," Mariana interrupts. And she's right, of course.

"Manuel and the others did all the planning. He tried to keep me out of it. But I insisted that this was something I could still be involved in; there would only be a month of training, and they could give me the least dangerous jobs. I could be the one who let the maids and waiters go, for example, or went through the coats to collect the guests' IDs. I didn't care what I did, but now that I had passed on the plans and put the mission in motion, I wanted to be a part of it. I needed to feel that way again—the way I had in Matagalpa when Manuel and I each had our missions and he'd go off to train or do whatever it is the men did that was kept top secret, and I'd give lectures or teach the women how to read, and afterwards we'd meet to swim in the River of Dreams. I wanted us to share something like that again, to be working on something important together."

"More important than taking care of me?"

It takes me a minute to answer. A year from now, I hope, Mariana will understand, will judge me less harshly. But if I say the wrong thing now, she might walk away from me for good, and I'll lose the chance to have her understand me. And worse than losing her will be knowing that in her eyes, I was the one who ended our relationship. If I make a mistake now, she'll feel that I rejected her all over again.

"Not more important. Never more important. Just different," I say finally, hearing how weak the words sound, especially after all the time it takes me to summon them. "You were only four months old, I hadn't slept through the night since you were born; my life was breast-feeding and burping. Being involved in this—being instrumental in this—reminded me of who I was, of who your father and I were before. I missed you every minute we weren't together. But I missed him, too. He got to play with you and wonder at you and still go off to training and meetings. He was still a revolutionary and I didn't feel like one anymore. It felt like Manuel was changing the world and I was just changing diapers. Like he was leaving me behind."

There is silence.

"Do you understand what I'm saying?" My voice is so small I don't even recognize it.

"Why don't you just tell me about the night my father was killed." In the darkness, Mariana's disembodied voice is unnaturally even, devoid of all inflection.

And so I do. I tell her about how we came up through the back patio, because Brigida promised us that she'd convince the guard stationed there to go meet her at a nearby disco. I tell her how we dispersed through the house, how I went straight past the pool area and through the living room, where the rest of our team had already disarmed the startled guards and were organizing the partygoers into groups, men on one side, women on the other, hands visible at all times. I tell her that I was banished to the spare bedroom behind the kitchen where guests' coats were kept, where I went through the pockets of the wraps, mostly silk opera coats the women had sauntered in wearing and then discarded; it was too warm for the men to need anything over their suits.

"I was separating the IDs of the wives of the most important guests when I heard a door slam shut," I hear myself say, but the voice sounds far away, as if I were listening to a radio program. "I felt something seep onto my shirt and for a minute I thought it was a gun I'd heard, and that I'd been shot, but it was just breast milk; it was almost midnight, when I would normally feed you. At his parties, the general always made a toast at midnight, Brigida told me, which was the signal that the event was winding down and the guests were free to leave. The plan was to ambush him during his toast, which would be any minute now. Then I heard another slamming noise, from the back of the house, where I knew Brigida's room was located. I had this terrible feeling that maybe she'd been waylaid for some reason and hadn't left for the disco by the appointed time. We hadn't given her any information about what would happen, so that there was no risk of her accidentally revealing anything to her father; the less she knew, the safer it was for her. That's what we'd thought, but maybe we were wrong, maybe we should have been in better communication with her. I hated the thought that we'd put her at risk. So I slipped out of the bedroom just to make sure she wasn't in danger."

I stop to take a sip of my tea, but there is none left. It doesn't matter; a parched tongue isn't going to make what I have to say any worse. "You know the floor plan of the house."

"Two big squares around interior courtyards, one for the public areas, where the party was held, the second the family's private apartments. Where Papi and Memo's bodies were found."

Mariana sounds as if she is reciting the times tables. When she speaks again, her voice has more urgency. "Memo had gone into his study to practice his speech, the articles said. That's why there were no guards around him—everyone was in the living room with the guests."

"I left the room to walk across the courtyard to Brigida's bedroom," I continue. "But when I stepped outside, I saw her arguing with a man in front of her door. She was blocking him from view, but when she shook her head, I caught enough of his face to realize that it was Manuel."

"Papi?"

I shiver, although it isn't cold. Mama would say someone walked over my grave, and normally I would mock her for it. But in the darkness, at that moment, it feels like Manuel is stepping out of his, called forth by his daughter to defend himself in death as he wasn't able to in life.

"They hadn't seen me—I was directly across the courtyard, and I was about to call out to them when Brigida stepped toward your father, put her hands on his chest, resting them on the ammunition he had strapped across himself, and kissed him. I was moving my mouth, trying to call to them, but no words came out. I heard a faint rolling noise to my left, turned and saw a fancy, Japanese-style door on the wall perpendicular to me slide open, and a fat hand holding a pistol stick out. Then the general peeked his head around the corner."

I haven't spoken of that night in years. No, I haven't spoken of it ever. But as I tell Mariana what happened, I can see it all so clearly, can feel the warm milk dripping down my stomach, can smell the yeasty, slightly sour smell. My voice is constant as I speak, and I realize that I'm crying only when a tear splashes onto my bottom lip, a moment of relief I don't deserve.

"Memo saw them and called his daughter's name. He wasn't screaming, but his regular speaking voice was chilling enough. Brigida turned to her father, breaking away from the kiss. I'm not sure exactly what happened next, because everything seemed to happen at once: the general rushing across the courtyard toward them, shooting, Brigida screaming, and Manuel collapsing. I closed my eyes! After all that training, all that target practice, still I closed my eyes. I heard another shot and when I forced my eyes open, I saw the general fallen on his side and Brigida holding Manuel's gun."

"But the article said Memo Paredes died of rounds of fire from machine guns," Mariana whispers, still trying not to believe, still using his full name as if we are talking not about a real person but a character in a film or a historical figure—although I suppose he is a historical figure, now.

"Two compañeros rushed in when they heard the gunshots and opened fire. Who's to say which killed him? The commandos wanted the credit. I suppose Brigida didn't want the blame. After the funeral, she returned to Houston. She got married later that year, to an American. We kept her name out of the papers. We even paid the guard she stood up to say she'd been at the disco with him."

"Did you ever see her again?"

"Brigida? No. She sent me a letter before her wedding saying that she'd been meeting with a priest in Houston as part of her Pre-Cana, and that she had forgiven herself for that night. She had been put in a difficult situation and gotten caught in the cross fire; she wrote that phrase in English, 'caught in the cross fire.' She said that she had forgiven herself for her part in what happened and was moving on, and she wanted me to know that she forgave me, too."

"Forgave you?" Mariana sits up in her chair and turns to face me. "How is her kissing your husband, murdering her fat father, and pretty much making sure mine got killed, too, your fault?"

She's so angry. And, for once, it isn't at me. I want to reach over and take her in my arms, I want to take advantage of this moment, of this absolution that I don't deserve, to start over, to build a new life with her and my grandchild. But I can't lie to her anymore.

"But she was right, Mariana." Somehow, now that I am done reliving all that violence, the steady voice that I've been so proud of is hiccupping, catching and gasping to match my tears. "The whole time I was standing there, watching everything that happened in the courtyard unfold in front of me as if it were a horror movie, I didn't say a word. Memo Paredes was a child abuser and a murderer, and still, that monster, he called out to Brigida before shooting. He saved the life of the person he loved most. And I just stood there, watching the whole thing, seeing Memo open the door and slither out of it. I should have screamed! I could have yelled and our compañeros would have come running, or at least Manuel would have heard me and reached for his gun or ducked or even run back into Brigida's room. I could have saved your father's life and I didn't. I'm the one who took your father from you, not Memo, not Brigida, and not Manuel himself. I should have screamed but I stayed silent. And I'm so, so sorry."

I stop to catch my breath and lean back into my chair in an attempt to calm myself; it seems a sacrilege to be disrupting the peaceful darkness of this archipelago, startling the parrots and the toucans and the lake sharks, if any still exist. "I never wrote back to Brigida," I say once my breath has regulated itself. "I have nothing to say to her. But I didn't deserve her forgiveness. And I don't expect yours either."

Once I stop speaking, I realize that the archipelago isn't silent at all. Birds are hooting in the distance and geckos are shrieking and even the grass seems alive, rustling and shaking. But there isn't a human sound to be heard.

37

María

When my Bela talks about her past I see crinolines and white gloves and the kind of little bouquets people called nosegays; her stories remind me of black-and-white movies. But until tonight, while I sat listening to Madre talk about secrets she's kept buried for over thirty years, I never really imagined her past. I knew certain stories about her privileged childhood, her bold youth—of course I did. But I thought of them as drawings or photographs, two-dimensional vignettes. I never imagined her in the world of the past, a place that looked, smelled, and felt differently. I never conjured her world up around me like I do when I start a painting. But tonight, it was as if she were still trapped in the realm of the past, as if she'd never left Memo Paredes's neo-Spanish-colonial house, and its walls were closing in on her, echoing with gunfire.

Unlike my Bela, Madre has always seemed like she exists only in the present; she's so vital, so strong. I always assumed that if she thought of the past at all it was with nothing but pride. Pride and, of course, sorrow at losing her husband, the father of her child, her partner in making history. I assumed that's why I never saw her with a boyfriend: because no one could live up to my heroic papi.

All this time I thought anything good in me came from him. My impatience, my defensiveness, even the fact that I'm a bit of a loner, they're all traits that were handed down by my mother. All my sharp edges are hers. But I thought—I hoped—they were balanced by something softer that could have only come from Papi. I examined every known image of him for clues, and then I secretly tried to cultivate Papi's optimism; in every photo of him, even the ones where he has bullets strapped across his chest and some massive weapon in his hand, his mouth curls up at the edges. Sometimes, when I'm walking through the city and I look west and catch a flash of sunset reflecting off the steel towers, something soars and leaps inside me like a bird, and I always thought that something was Papi's spirit. The good in him— the hope—it's what I wanted to pass on to my baby. And in the last few minutes I felt it dying, crumpling in on itself, dissolving.

"Are you sure that's what happened, Mama?" I ask. "Maybe you thought you saw Papi and Brigida kiss, but it was a trick of the light? Or she was scared and just hugging him?"

"I know what I saw, Mariana," she says. "Not that it matters."

I vault out of my chair to stand in front of her, speaking too loudly for the time of night. "Of course it matters! Did Papi cheat on you or not?"

She doesn't answer but I can hear her inhaling deeply, as if she's been asked a question at a press conference for which she's not sure she has a right answer.

"I wasn't trying to make excuses for what I did, Mariana," Madre says slowly. "Nothing about your father's behavior absolves me of any guilt. A stronger woman would have tackled Memo, saved her husband's life. But even a weak one, even Mama, she would have been screaming from the moment she saw Memo, no, from the moment she saw her husband in the hall, she would have created such a drama that he would have looked around, noticed the enemy approaching. In the end, my mother would have been the better soldier. I always thought I was so strong, but when it really mattered I froze. I froze and in doing so, I killed Manuel. It's my fault you don't have a father."

Apparently, all these years, I wasn't the only one living with a delusion about Papi, the only one blaming myself for his unnecessary death. It would never have occurred to me that all this time, Mama was suffering, too. I kneel down in front of her chair and take her hands in mine; it's the first time I notice that my mother's hands are smaller than my own. "Oh, Mama. You didn't kill Papi." I slide my calves out to the side so I can sit on the ground. "Anyone could have reacted that way; it all happened so fast. It's not your fault he's dead. And it's not your fault he turned out to be a jerk either."

Curling forward into her lap, I rest my head on top of our hands because I'm tired, so tired. And because I don't want her to realize that I'm crying, too. I'm crying for Madre, because her life has been so sad. I'm crying for Papi, because he died so young and so confused. And I'm crying for myself because I've spent my life missing my father. And now I've lost him all over again.

38

Isabela

Walking down the hall in my slippers, I remember the one other time I ever snuck out of my bed and tiptoed down a long corridor: the night I met Mauricio and Father Antony to plan our marriage. Our attempted marriage, I should say. I was so much more agile then, tripping down the passage, though it was fear of being caught that made me so fast, fear and youth.

Now I have nothing to be afraid of: I'm a paying guest in this hotel, I have a right to be in its public spaces, even if my housecoat is a questionable choice of attire. But I can't help but feel embarrassed, and that, along with my age, and, it has to be said, my weight, slow my pace, keep me shuffling down the hall. His room is only two doors down from mine and even now, as I'm standing in front of the brass knocker, my hand raised, it's not too late to turn around, return to my bed, wrap my dignity around myself like a blanket and go to sleep. I'm about to do just that when I hear a voice that isn't his. A woman's voice. Now it's not a question of my dignity but Mariana's happiness, so I thump the knocker as hard as I can, imagining the confusion, the shared horror on the other side of the door.

"Just a minute," Allen says, as I knew he would; he must be rushing the girl out onto the balcony. But her voice isn't getting any softer, and then the door's open and he's standing there, pulling a T-shirt down over the top of his baggy athletic pants.

My mouth is already open in outrage, but when I follow the sound of the incessant voice I realize it's coming from the television. And even though Allen can't know what I was thinking just now, it makes me feel all the more ridiculous, standing in the middle of a strange man's room in my housecoat, having barged in as if he were the housekeeper and I was going to ask him for a midnight snack. I'm not even wearing lipstick.

Luckily, Allen hasn't noticed my lips; his gaze has followed mine and we're both staring at the TV, where the chattering woman talking straight to the camera has been replaced by a harrowing live skeleton of a man with ragged dyed black hair and slits for eyes. "Who—what—do you watch?" I ask. I'm truly curious, but I also hope to deflect Allen's attention from me to this stranger on TV, who looks even worse than I do. Clearly, it was the wrong thing to say, because it has somehow inspired him to sit—plop!—at the foot of his unmade bed opposite the television. He is patting the mattress next to him; I do believe he intends for me to settle down there. There's a perfectly good armchair in the corner to the right of the bed; I make my way over to it and sit behind him so we can both look at the TV, not each other.

"Keith Richards, Bela!" Allen says, and the name does sound familiar although I can't quite place it. "I know, hard living, right? Makes me regret the scotch with dinner. Almost." He points the remote device at the television, making the sound stop although the picture keeps flickering, images of a past that is not my own I've always cared more for royalty than rock stars, even though, now that I see him standing next to Mick Jagger, I finally recognize the skeleton. Of course I do.

"The thing is, I can't sleep," Allen's saying now, as if it's an expected nocturnal occurrence for me to drop by for a chat. "I can't concentrate enough to read or answer work emails; the words start dancing around. I'm tired, I close my eyes, but without Mariana, it's impossible. Where is she? Why is she there? Nothing drowns out the questions, not even Keith Richards. The only time I managed to stop fixating on the fact that she's missing was when you were reading me Mauricio's letter. What a story."

Now I know I was right to creep down the hall like a common criminal; Allen wants to talk about this just as much as I do. I open my mouth but he's already yammering again. "So I turn on the TV, and who's on it but Bianca Jagger. I mean, she was only on for a minute or two, it's this Rolling Stones retrospective. But I had to watch, because I'm in Granada and Bianca Jagger's on TV. How can I not watch? She was the only Nicaraguan I'd heard of before I met Mariana. And, you know, seeing the pictures of her back in the day, she reminds me of Ninexin. I mean, they don't really look alike, except for that sort of defiant, observant stare."

I wish I could grab the remote out of his hand and turn off the images on the screen and his inane running commentary at the same time. "He's a beautiful woman, but she look nothing like Ninexin," I tell Allen. "His mother sold fruit on the steps of the court, but she manage to get out, to France, for an education."

"Wow."

I meant to shut Allen up by pointing out how ridiculous the comparison he'd made is, but he seems to have taken it as encouragement; he's shifted to sit at the side of the bed so he can face me, as if I'm here to entertain him with tales of rock stars' wives and assorted Nicaraguan arrivistes. I wish he'd stop it. I have to gaze up at the ceiling now, to avoid seeing his eyes staring at me; looking upward is making me dizzy.

"If you think Bianca's pretty, you should see his sister." I nod at the TV as if the sisters are likely to appear on it to allow us to compare their merits. It doesn't work; Allen's still looking at me.

"Really?"

"Oh yes, stunning. There were whisperings she was carrying on with Ignacio for a tiempito, but I am not so sure is this true or just it is idle chatter, wantful thinking for him."

Now I've succeeded; Allen is so flustered by my mentioning a mistress of Ignacio's, even if she's just, perhaps, an imaginary one, that he gets up and turns off the television. Now he's standing in front of me, looking at the door and then toward—but not at—me, and back at the door again.

"Well, it is becoming late." I lean forward in my chair, as if I mean to get up. "I just want to make sure you are feeling well; I see how nervous you feel for Mariana. You and me, too." I put my arms on the sides of the chair as if I'm going to raise myself up and out, and before I can sit down again and ask him what I came to ask, Allen is at my side, helping me stand. I didn't think he'd be so agile, at his age.

"One thing más, Allen," I say, taking tiny steps like a geriatric geisha. "What you say before?"

"About Bianca and Ninexin?"

How tiresome for Mariana to be with a man who can be so slow-witted! Handsome, but slow. "About how Fidel, how he should not decide." I take a step forward, and am careful to speak and walk slowly, as if I'm sleepy and distracted and what I'm about to say doesn't really matter, as if I didn't laboriously make my way to his room to solicit his opinion, but I'm just making pleasant in-the-middle-of-the-night conversation to pass our time as Allen walks me down the hall. "Did you mean I should consider to go to Cuba? You think I should write to him back, to Mauricio? After so much years?"

He's already got his hand on my door, but Allen stops turning the knob, stops walking, and looks down at me as if he's Padre Juan Cristobal and I'm sixteen again and confessing to having impure thoughts. "Bela," he says. "I'm divorced. The woman I love is hiding out somewhere in Central America to avoid seeing me, and I'm watching old Rolling Stones clips for solace. I'm hardly the person to ask."

He's right. It's ridiculous that I have come to him in the middle of the night like a ghost, wandering through public halls in my housecoat to beg for the advice of a middle-aged man who is as confused as any teenager. But Mariana's not here for me to talk to, and he's all I have. He's the only person who knows my secret. And now I have two important questions to resolve: What should I do about Mauricio? And what should Mariana do about this one in front of me? "But still, I ask," I say, because I don't want him to turn around and go back to his room and look for more interesting television programs before telling me what he thinks. "You have the good sense to be with Mariana. He is my granddaughter. Is it so strange I ask your thoughts on relations between men and women?"

He breathes hard through his nose, almost snorting like a bull in a ring, but it doesn't make him seem fierce. The breath actually seems to deflate him. "I know what they're thinking, when people see me walk into a gallery with Maria," he says, not answering my question about Mauricio and me. "That she gets to sit at my feet, taking in all my experience, basking in the reflected glory of my talent, while I suck the youth and vitality out of her, like a vampire. That, sure, we look good together now, but that it's really a race to the finish: either I'll deteriorate faster and she'll get tired of changing my diapers and amuse herself with lovers her own age while waiting for me to die, or she'll age quickly and I'll replace her with the next hungry young art history major who falls at my feet."

I have no idea why Allen is creating such an ugly picture, saying out loud things one shouldn't even let oneself think, but before I can defend Mariana he starts talking again. "Even my kids have said as much, although they're just passing on things they've heard their mother and her friends say at cocktail parties. And you know what? Let Taylor and her emaciated friends think it. If that makes them feel better, if that evens the score for them just a little bit, then I'm glad. Because every minute that I get to be with Maria is a minute I'm grateful and happy. I think it'll stay that way. But if it doesn't, and I end up paying for it later, I still come out a winner. I got all that joy before the pain, and those snide idiots just got the small satisfaction of making fun of me over mini–crab cakes."

I think I understand what he has said: that there are people who feel his relationship with Mariana is ridiculous, something to laugh at. And that he doesn't care who thinks he is an old fool. But he still hasn't told me what to do about Mauricio, and he's quiet as a church mouse all of a sudden. I can't ask again: a third time would be begging, and Isabela de la Torre does not beg.

I still don't know if Allen is the man for Mariana. But at least I know that he appreciates her. "Thank you for seeing me to my room, Allen," I say. He helps me with the door, and when the light from my room floods the dim hall he looks so tired, so forlorn, that I want to make him feel better. I open my mouth to tell him, "You know, I like you." But I get the English wrong, because I hear my voice saying, "You know, I envy you."

39

Ninexin

I can feel Mariana's head in my lap, its weight on my legs, her warm, flossy hair in my hands. At the funeral, when she bent over to drop the flowers into Papa's grave, I noticed a couple of gray strands sprouting from the middle of her crown. My baby. With gray hair. How is it possible? She still seems so young, so fragile. Especially now, crying in my lap.

Why didn't I say, "Yes, mi amor, it was a trick of the light, that's it, that's partly why I've felt so guilty all these years, for misunderstanding what I saw, for underestimating your father"? It's not like I'm under oath here. This confession was purely of my own volition. I wanted to free Mariana, to convince her that her father planned to live his life watching her grow up, that he had no intention of dying that night. But I just muddied the issue. And her image of him. When all she knew was that he put his country above everything, even his love for her, Manuel was a hero in Mariana's mind. But now that she knows what really happened that night, I've murdered his ghost, too.

It was selfish to tell her. I meant to free her, but on some level, I wanted to unburden myself. To have someone know what I did. And to know that person could love me despite my having done it.

But in telling Mariana, I took her father's death from her. I didn't let her have him, didn't let Nicaragua have him. I always worried what would happen if she found out the truth about his death, how it would change her opinion of me. It never occurred to me to think how my story would affect her relationship to Manuel. Because even though he's dead, they are linked. She's his daughter. It is a relationship. Or was.

I cost Manuel his life, regardless of whether Mariana sees it that way or not. It's why I've never had a serious relationship since, although I've been to dinners with men, to bed with a few. I even spent a week in Paris with an American who worked for the AP. But I refused to ever build my life around a man again. It wasn't because I was worried this American might betray me, that I might one day find him kissing another woman, the way I did Manuel in those last few moments he was alive. That was devastating, but it was nothing compared to what came next. The reason I left the American, and have cut off any man I've met before he becomes too important, is because I can't help but wonder how I will let him down, too, what I will take from him, the way I took everything from Manuel. I'm the reason Manuel didn't get to live the rest of his life. And now I've robbed him of his daughter as well.

I knew Mariana would be horrified by my story, but I didn't realize she'd be so shaken by the affair; she seems more disappointed in Manuel now than I was that night. I was angry, of course, in the moment when I saw them together. But more than that, I was hurt that he was sharing a moment of excitement, of electricity, with someone who wasn't me. There had been so many harrowing nights when we cried together after friends of ours had died in prison, or Manuel would visit someone who had made it out, and then have nightmares of the holes the guards' electroshock torture had burned into our compañero's skin. There were so many moments of fear. This takeover of Memo's house was going to be a turning point, one that would end so much suffering when we bartered one fat general for so many young, promising prisoners of conscience who had the passion and the skills to transform Nicaragua. We weren't just going to save our leaders from further torture; we were going to save our country, too. Beyond my desire to help the movement, and the country, I knew that this operation was a shining opportunity for Manuel, the most exciting thing to happen to him since the birth of Mariana; that was why I insisted on being there, to share in his triumph. And Brigida had provided Manuel with this brilliant opportunity, she was the one who asked me to give him the plans. Maybe it was all part of a scheme to get rid of the man who made her life miserable and get closer to the man she wanted in one, patriotic move.

Whatever Brigida's plan was, it wouldn't have worked. That's what I told myself, anyway, through all the events that followed. At Manuel's funeral when his supporters clogged the streets of Managua sobbing as I passed by them, dry-eyed, holding his crying baby. And every time since I have thought of that night, although I've tried my utmost not to. I've always told myself that Manuel may have gotten caught up in the excitement of the takeover of Memo Paredes's house, but he never would have left me. I had his child. And I think I had his heart, too. Brigida just had his attention momentarily.

Maybe that's wishful thinking. Maybe I'm underestimating Brigida, or overestimating how well I knew Manuel, or how well he knew himself at that point. Maybe Manuel would have left me and Mariana for her, who knows? We were so young then, practically children; I see that now. Manuel had been out with girls before me, but he was my first kiss. I know I was the first girl he told he loved.

It turns out, I was the last girl, too. The one time I saw Brigida again was in the airport two years after Manuel's death. I was on my way to Mexico, to do some recruiting for the Frente. She must have been visiting from Houston. She saw me; I know she did. But then she raised an American magazine up high so that it hid her face. That was my cue to keep heading straight to my gate, and maybe it's because I knew that was what she wanted that I surprised myself by walking up to her and saying hello, sitting right down in the empty seat next to her. Still she didn't acknowledge me. Finally, I said her name. And when she turned to look at me, I saw that her eyes were wet, threatening to spill over. For a minute I thought she was afraid of me.

"You never wrote back," she said. And just when I thought there was nothing she could say or do to shock me, I realized it wasn't fear that was making her emotional. She was angry. "I wrote to you. I forgave you. And you never wrote back."

If life were the way it is in Mama's telenovelas I would have thought of something witty to say. But I just blurted, "You had an affair with my husband!"

"Is that it?" Brigida laughed, once. "It was hardly an affair. A few stolen kisses here or there after a planning meeting—which they wouldn't even let me attend. It was always, 'Oh, Brigida, it's safer if you just go away and let us save the world.' You all took the plans and just brushed me aside."

"Not Manuel," I said. "Not from what I saw."

"They let me stay for the meetings once or twice and I asked him to drive me home. We got caught up in it all, the thrill of changing the world. It was intoxicating."

"But why him?"

"Who else would drive me home? Most of the other compañeros were strangers. And not all of them from nice families; half of them didn't even have a car."

"That's not what I'm talking about!" I grabbed her arm and she shook my hand off. "He was my husband," I said more softly.

She looked at the magazine in her lap. "When we were little, I always wished I was part of your family," she said. "I think Manuel was my attempt at trying on something of yours. But even when I was with him, I knew it was just playing pretend. The whole time he talked about nothing but the Movimiento. And you."

As I heard her say the words, I waited to feel happy. Brigida was too self-centered and too awkward to make things up to please me. Hearing that my husband wasn't in love with her should have made me feel better. But it didn't. It just reminded me how much I'd lost. So much of what matters to me, what defines me, I shared with Manuel: my passion for justice, my love for my country. And Mariana. When I met Manuel I was a girl. It's because of him I became an adult, a revolutionary. It's thanks to him I became a mother.

"He's not a jerk, Mariana," I say.

"What?"

"Your father. He's not a jerk; I mean, he wasn't one."

Mariana raises herself up on her knees so that her face almost reaches mine. "You said you know what you saw."

"I saw Brigida kiss him, and I didn't see him push her away, that's true." I'm talking slowly, determined to make sure that, strictly speaking, I'm telling the truth. "But it was all so shocking, I have no idea how much time passed between Brigida kissing Manuel and Memo calling out to her. Was it ten seconds? Or half a second? Maybe there wasn't time for your father to push Brigida away, or maybe he was just so confused, he didn't want to cause trouble. Brigida was the one who gave us the plans, after all."

"Right!" Mariana is standing now, pulling me up to stand with her. "And you said she specifically told you to give them to Papi, didn't you? Maybe that's why she stayed behind when she was supposed to go to the disco, so she could be alone with him. I mean, it's possible he didn't want her to kiss him at all. He could have been totally taken by surprise when she hurled herself at him."

"I guess it's a possibility," I say.

"Of course it is." Mariana looks straight into my eyes. And I make sure I'm looking back at her when I say, "Yes, it's entirely possible."

40

❧

Maria

Mama's been asleep for hours and still I just keep dozing, coming in and out of consciousness, but never falling asleep long enough to rest. I have to pee but I'm so tired and the little bathroom with the toilet pull seems so far, all the way across the pitch-black room. There's something so complete about this darkness.

Poor Mama. I can hear her breathing. There's still a catch each time she breathes out, a catch I remember from being little and crying so hard that my breath was interrupted long after I stopped sobbing over the lost toy, the unexpected scrape on the knee, or the vast injustice that adults seemed incapable of understanding.

I didn't find it easy to be a child. I'm not complaining; my childhood was fine, I knew Abuelo and my Bela loved me like crazy. There were birthday parties and field trips, many indulgences, and more than a few moments of real happiness: riding a bike for the first time with Abuelo cheering me on, pointing out his granddaughter to the old Cuban men sitting on their park bench; or afternoons at the public library on Key Biscayne, which had square cushions on the floor in the children's area where you could sit all day reading as the sun streamed in from the window, and no one would bother you to go outside and play. But I remember feeling on edge all the time, as if I had to be alert to every subtle shift in the unfamiliar world around me. I was painfully aware that there was so much I didn't know, that I couldn't control. Like where my mother was. Or when I'd see her again. Half the time I wondered if we'd ever go back to Managua, which my Bela and Abuelo missed every day, and where it might be possible to see Mama all the time. And the other half I prayed that we wouldn't, because I liked my school, my friends, and even though Rigobertito called me a baby and always beat me at checkers, I didn't want him to die in the army like my Bela said he would have if we'd stayed. I only prayed on the inside. I didn't put my hands together or anything, except in church or at bedtime. My Bela, Abuelo, Tía Celia, they were always watching me, trying to keep me safe and happy. It was almost a relief to grow up, go away to college, and be able to make my own mistakes without worrying anyone but myself.

Madre never had the luxury of screwing up with no one watching or caring. First it was her parents who had to be considered, then her compañeros and their cause, and then me. I have always admired how self-sufficient Madre is, how in control. She didn't seem to worry about pleasing people, not even me; she just went where she was needed and got done whatever job it was she wanted to do, even if it made my Bela lie down for days, saying she was sick with worry, or me whimper that I wanted her to stay longer. There were wars to fight and peace treaties to negotiate and rights to guarantee, and they weren't going to get done right without her. It never occurred to me that the downside of acting as if you control the world is that you might actually believe that you are, in fact, responsible for everything that happens, the good and the bad.

All these years Madre thought that she was the one who took my father from me. Not Memo Paredes, maker of who knows how many widows and orphans. Not the cause that Papi devoted himself to. Not Brigida, who, although her life was not a cakewalk, seems like a royal bitch, as far as I'm concerned. Not even Papi himself, with his rash choices and unlucky stars. It wasn't Madre who lured Papi into the wrong hall, where Memo surprised him after holing up in his study to practice his toast. He got there himself, with Brigida's help.

I believe in everything Madre was fighting for, but I still wish she had been more interested in watching me than in making history that night; I wish Papi had been, too. But what Madre told me to-night makes me see how flawed and rushed and risky the whole evening—their whole life—was at that point. Papi wasn't just a hero. He was also a confused, excited kid. Someone who was still easily flustered enough not to push away the wrong girl when she threw her arms around him.

There are so many questions I'm tempted to ask Mama: Does anyone else know what really happened? Has she ever confided in another one of the compañeros? Is this why she always happens to be out of town when the commemoration of the takeover of Memo Paredes's house is celebrated? Has *she* ever killed anyone, in combat?

I don't think I want to know the answer to that one. I wouldn't want to bring up any more painful memories. I hate it that the last moment Madre saw Papi alive, it was in the arms of another woman, even if it wasn't a real kiss, even if they weren't fooling around be-hind her back. I wish Papi had died with his name on her lips. And my name, too. But I can't make that happen. I can't bring him back or make it so that my mother never saw him and Brigida together. All I can do is tell Mama that what happened wasn't her fault.

I did tell her that, in the dark, once we got back to our room. I brushed my teeth first, and she drank the cold tea that was left in my cup. She held the mug to her forehead, shielding her face for several minutes, but I could tell she was crying. Even though she tried to do it soundlessly, I could see the white T-shirt that covered her shoulders rising up and down, as they glowed a bit in the darkness.

I thought about hugging her, but then she would have realized that I could see she was crying. Instead I said I was tired, and unsteady on my feet, and could I lean on her arm to walk back across the room now that I was done in the bathroom? By the time we got to the edge of my bed, her eyes were dry, so I was able to kiss her good night on the cheek. Once we were both lying in our separate beds, I said, "I'm glad I know."

"I should have told you sooner." Her voice in the darkness sounded like she was lying in the bed next to me, but I knew she was against the wall, in the other bed, where the balsa-wood figurine on the side table wasn't an angel but a toucan.

"No. You were right to wait." I turned on my side, rustling the sheets so that she could hear the sound, to indicate that the conversation was over and I was drifting off to sleep. I didn't want to have to say that if she had told me sooner, I would have blamed her. I would have thought that she told me about the kiss, or whatever it was, so that I'd think less of my father. Or at least that she was trying to justify her choice to devote most of her time to carrying on Papi's mission because she felt responsible for his death, even though she knew I wanted her to spend most of her time raising me, loving me back.

Blaming her would have been ridiculous. Still, I would have done it. I would have armed myself with any ammunition possible to justify my resentment that she wasn't the kind of mother I wanted to have, that she never gave me the chance to be the kind of daughter I wanted to be, as sweet and loving and involved as Beth. But I would have been wrong.

Talking in the darkness offered safe cover; the blackness kept us from looking at each other too closely, from judging each other too harshly. It softened the edges. But when I closed my eyes, the words took shape in front of me and I saw everything that Mama had described instead of just hearing it. Now I keep waking up in the dark room in an attempt to banish the images that appear in my sleep. First, red welts forming on the backs of Brigida's thighs as Memo Paredes's thick belt hits them with rhythmic slaps that, once I woke up, I realized were actually the sound of the ceiling fan clacking as it rotates. Then Mama, in a soggy shirt, with an open mouth out of which words won't come as she watches Memo Paredes's gun, then his leg, emerge out of his study door.

This time I woke to the sound of a gunshot. I knew it had to be a boat engine backfiring somewhere out on the lake, but still I grabbed my stomach, thinking of my father. The difference is, Papi fell forward, at least in the scenario I envisioned outside in the dark. And I'm lying on my back, which I guess makes me Memo, bleeding as his daughter's face blurs, then disappears, above him. The thought makes me feel cold and damp, as if I'm lying in something wet.

I can't believe this happened. I was never a bed wetter, not even as a child. It must have been the chamomile, and my ridiculous refusal to get up in the dark. Or is this something that happens all the time to pregnant women? No, that would be too awful. But then, I hadn't really realized that your boobs leak either, until Madre got graphic with her story. There's no use wondering why; I should just try to mop this up as best as I can without waking her.

I keep my hands out in front of me as I cross the bedroom in the dark. I make it successfully, but in the bathroom it happens again, a rush of liquid I have no control over. I don't even know if it all hit the toilet. I can't possibly clean all this up in the dark; I'll have to get the little flashlight the waiter gave us, which is lying next to the balsa-wood toucan on Madre's bedside table.

When I open the door, she's standing there, with her mouth open and moving, but no sounds coming out. Her cell phone is in her left hand, the flashlight is in her right, and the weak circle of light it offers is trained on the trail of blood I've left, marking my path from the bed to the bathroom.

41

Isabela

WEDNESDAY, JANUARY 14, 2009

We didn't even wait for Don Pedro to arrive. When Allen burst into my room at half past seven, he had already hired a car and driver from the tourist agency across the street. I can't imagine how he got them to open the shop that early. He probably banged on their door, which is what he claims he did to mine. He says he pounded for several minutes before convincing the girl at the desk— it's the one with the smooth forehead again, she must be back from her days off—that there was an emergency and he needed the housekeeping key to my room. Poor girl must have thought I had expired in my bed, died of grief.

I was mortified, of course, when he shook me awake. I screamed, "Díos mio! Que pasó?" before my brain woke up and I realized whom I was talking to. When I saw it was Allen, and he looked perfectly fine, I managed to say, "You could have killed me," in English. "A woman my age, his heart is weak. And I have the emphysema from all the smoking of Ignacio."

He apologized, of course, and said he'd been knocking hard but I hadn't heard him. It's possible he's telling the truth; my hearing isn't what it used to be, but I want to grow my hair out a bit more so that it covers my ears before I start using a hearing aid, like all of my girl-friends.

I didn't tell that to Allen; it's not his business, and he wasn't in my room to talk about hairstyles. "Now that you're up, hurry and get ready, Bela," he barked, as if he's in a position to be giving me orders. "We're going to Managua. Ninexin called. Maria's sick and she got a helicopter to bring them to the Metropolitano hospital."

He thrust his arm at me, to help me out of bed, and I grabbed on but didn't start inching out toward the floor although he was practi-cally dragging me. "Sick? My Mariana? With what? And why?"

I meant, why had Ninexin called him first, not me? But he didn't give me time to express all that.

"The connection wasn't very good; Ninexin said she couldn't talk long but they were in the hospital, the doctors are working on Mariana, and she'll call as soon as she has more information. All I really know is, I'm leaving in fifteen minutes whether you're with me or not. I'm going to finish packing and check out. I'll see you in the lobby." I crossed my arms over my chest, but then he said, "Bela, it's our girl," and offered me his other arm. This time I did slide my feet to the floor. What did it matter if he saw me *en déshabillé*? My night-wear is as modest as you can buy these days, what with all the over-night nurses we've had staying at the house since Ignacio's heart started failing.

Ignacio! Thank God he isn't here with me now, getting ready to go see our granddaughter in the hospital, suffering. The anxiety would have killed him. He loved Mariana more than anything or anyone, and he hated situations that he couldn't control. To think of her flying through the air in a bumpy, whirring toy of a plane, sick, and with God knows what! Ninexin went to collect Mariana in Solentiname. Maybe she got jungle leprosy there. Or food poisoning. She probably has the stomach of a gringa now and is susceptible to that sort of thing.

Those thoughts were buzzing through my brain like a plague of locusts, but I didn't stop to call Ninexin. There would be time for that from the car. Even as my mind was busy, my body was calmly gathering my things—thank goodness for Mother Dauphinais, who checked our drawers for neatness; having everything arranged in piles makes short work of packing, even for a slow-moving old woman on an unfair deadline. I was packed and dressed and drinking coffee in the courtyard when Allen came running down the hall twenty minutes later. I didn't even want the coffee, although I enjoyed the croissant that came with it. I just wanted to show him that even in a crisis, there's nothing to be gained by acting like animals.

"Nice work, Bela," he said. As if I had asked for his evaluation or approval. "Can you get that to go?"

"I have dined sufficiently." I rose without the help of the hand he offered. I hoped he saw the red imprint my lips left on the coffee cup, that he noticed I had managed to put on lipstick. This is the caliber of women in the family he aspires to marry into.

I called Ninexin three times before we even left the outskirts of Granada, but each time I got her recorded message; Allen told me her phone must have been turned off. The bouncing of the van on the highway made my hollow stomach ache with nausea as well as hunger. I took out my rosary and closed my eyes so that Allen wouldn't interrupt me. But when he put his hand on my shoulder, I didn't shrug it off. I thought it might be his ignorant way of joining in my prayers.

We were ten minutes from the hospital when Allen's cell phone rang. He picked up, nodded a bit, then said, "Oh, thank God!"

"Give me the phone!" I demanded and he handed it over before running both his hands through his hair, as if he were making space for the stupid grin spreading across his face.

"Que pasó?" I demanded, and Ninexin told me that Mariana was fine, she was in with the doctor now, it turns out she had a blood clot on her pancreas, which was not unheard of in these situations. "Oh, Dios mio!" I said, and Ninexin, who must have ice water in her veins, replied, "I know, Mama, but I promise it's nothing to worry about." I was about to tell her of course I was worried when she started right in again: "Listen, Mariana's going to be with the doctor for a while. Drop Allen off here, go home, shower and change, and come back when you're fresh," Ninexin said, and it was a command, not a suggestion, as if I were one of her subordinates and she were my co-mandante.

"Absolutely not!" I told her. "Not even if God wanted me to. I have every right to be there, I raised that girl when you were too busy looking after this ungrateful country instead of your own daughter. And now you think she'd rather see this—foreigner—instead of me? I think not." I used the word "foreigner" because I thought Allen would hear "gringo" and understand that we were talking about him. And just because this was a crisis, and I had been offended beyond all reason, was no excuse to go around making people feel badly.

"Calm yourself, Mama. Mariana *asked* that you go to the house first, she wants you to bring a clean nightgown and the large sketch-book she left in the guest room. She may be here a few days and sketching will make her feel better."

"Why does she need to be in the hospital for a few days if there's nothing to worry about?" I demanded.

"She'll rest better here, and the doctors can observe her. It's just a precaution, Mama, and she really wants her sketchbook."

I knew what was going on. Ninexin wanted Mariana to herself. She's always been jealous of all the time we had together, as if she weren't the one who had chosen to be busy elsewhere. But I wasn't going to remind her of that now; there was no need for a scene. "One of the maids can bring it, they've had nothing to do for days," I pointed out. But Ninexin said that Mariana didn't want anyone else snooping through the paintings, that some of them showed subjects she preferred to keep private. "She said you'd understand. You're the only person she trusts, Mama."

"Of course I am," I said. "And with good reason!"

"Great. Now please put Allen on," Ninexin instructed, without so much as a good-bye for me, the woman who brought her into this world.

I left Allen in front of the hospital—he, at least, had the decency to kiss me good-bye before leaping from the van. I went home to take a shower and run a comb through my hair, change into a navy suit, and throw on a bright scarf, even if I am in mourning, because people in a hospital need cheering up. And I had a proper breakfast, too, so that I'd be at my best when I saw my Mariana.

She looks so pale, lying in the hospital bed with her father's dark hair spread all around her. I can't help sobbing when I walk in. "Oh, Mariana!" I manage to choke out. "Oh, mi hija!"

"I'm starved." Allen rises from the chair at her side. "I'm going to go grab lunch, now that you're in such capable hands." He extends his arm to help me settle into the chair but I stay leaning over my Mariana for a moment, touching her cheeks, her eyes, her throat, her hands, just to make sure she's all right. She giggles, squirming away from me.

"Is it painful, mi corazón? Where does it hurt?"

"I'm fine, Bela. Nothing hurts. It didn't even when I was bleeding. I had no cramps, no pain, nothing. I was just scared more than anything."

"And what caused it, this clot on your pancreas?" Mariana starts laughing again, only much harder this time, as if I'm just the funniest comedienne she's ever heard, a regular Lucille Ball. A great eruption of honking behind me means that Ninexin is apparently in on the joke.

"Not pancreas, Bela, *placenta*! I have a blood clot on my placenta."

"Well, your mother said pancreas." I turn to Ninexin so she can admit that she's the one being made a fool of here. But Ninexin just glides to the foot of Mariana's bed and sits down at her feet.

"Did not, Mama; I never said 'pancreas.'" The word makes them both fall about laughing all over again, although there is nothing humorous about the pancreas.

"Well, of course you did. And it can't be 'placenta' anyway, because only pregnant women have placentas to speak of."

Now they're laughing harder than before, Mariana's sheeplike bleats and Ninexin's unbecoming honks making a barnyard symphony. I drop into the chair.

She's pregnant. My unmarried granddaughter is pregnant. And laughing. It's not that I expected her to be a virgin, not really. I know it's not like that for girls anymore; half of my friends' daughters walked down the aisle with a baby under their white gowns and no one batted an eye, unless it was one of the bride's girlfriends winking at her, thinking how clever she was to trap whatever slippery man she had been dating into marrying her.

Speaking of slippery men, this is why Allen ran out for lunch, the coward! He was afraid to face me. A grown man like him should know better, taking advantage of my sweet Mariana. He should at least know how to prevent such things from happening. He's not a teenager! "Ay, Dios mio!" I whisper, and the two of them start laughing again.

"This is not funny!" I shout, but that only makes them laugh more.

"Maybe not, but it is joyous." Ninexin inches farther up the bed, closer to where I am sitting. She grabs my hand. "Think of it, Mama! A baby!"

"The next generation." Mariana looks happy, for the first time since she showed me the painting whose photo she had hidden for me on her phone. It's a very similar expression to the one she wore when the little screen lit up with that image: joyful and shy and a little bit proud. Even Ninexin is beaming at her.

"A baby!" I say. And then, because I'm not one to sit around guffawing like an idiot when there's work to be done, I reach into my purse for the little leather notebook with the gold-tipped pen Ignacio gave me every year at Christmas; this year's was bright pink. Even though it's the last gift I'll ever receive from him, I was considering giving it away; it's hardly the right color for a woman in mourning. But it is the perfect shade for planning a wedding.

"Xalteva, like your abuelo and me," I say. "Definitely Xalteva. We'll have to wait at least three months from your grandfather's death, to show respect, but we can't wait any longer than that, you'll be showing. How far along are you?"

"Eight weeks; in three months I will be showing. But, listen—"

"Well, that's not so bad, we'll find a dress that makes the best of it. I don't think I'm up to making the trip to New York, but as soon as the doctor says it's okay, we can fly to Miami and shop in Coral Gables. It's where all the girls get their gowns, anyway. And you won't be the first bride showing a bit of a stomach at her wedding, even Maria Leonora's granddaughter—"

"'Bela, I'm not getting married!" Mariana grabs my hand. "Not any time soon, anyway."

"But why don't you want to get married?" I'm trying to understand, to be pleased for her, because she's obviously happy herself, but none of this is making any sense.

"It's not that we definitely don't want to get married," she says. "Allen and I want to see how things go, to concentrate on the baby first. The doctor said the blood clot will likely disappear on its own, but right now this is still a high-risk pregnancy."

"Pendejo!"

"Mama!" Ninexin jumps to her feet. "Please!"

"He wants to wait to make sure the baby's actually born first? That is not how a gentleman behaves!" I stand up again; Allen couldn't have made it that far. I'll get him to behave responsibly.

"Sit down, Bela!" Mariana shouts. "Sit down and listen!" She never yells at me. And she must be thinking the same thing, because then she adds, in a softer voice, "Sit down and relax. Please."

As I settle into my chair, even more slowly than I need to, as a show of protest, Mariana takes a breath so deep it seems she's drawing in all the air in the room before she finally speaks. "Allen would get married now, today, if I wanted to. I just think we have other things to concentrate on, under the circumstances, besides finding a dress to flatter my impending gut. If and when we have a wedding, I want to be able to drink champagne and wear a gown I love. And maybe the baby will dance, too."

"Now you're the one saying things we should all laugh at! Why would you have a child out of wedlock when the father wants to give the baby his name?"

"The baby can have his name—"

"You're just being foolish now."

"Madre, it's Mariana's life, she can get married when she chooses, if she chooses," Ninexin says, again using her comandante voice.

"I would expect you to say that." I turn back to Mariana and the conversation that matters. "You think you're being modern or smart, but you're just being selfish. Think of the baby. Think of Allen."

"Mama!" Ninexin huffs, but Mariana says, "No, Bela's right. I guess I am being selfish."

I lean back now that my point has been made.

"But maybe this is my last chance to be selfish for a while. I need to know I'm making the right decisions, and if it takes me a little longer than most people, maybe it's a good thing. The baby will learn early on not to expect perfection from me." Ninexin pats Mariana's leg, but I, for one, am not about to let her get away with that ludicrous little speech.

"This must be the side of you that scares Allen."

Mariana makes a one-syllable noise that isn't very attractive. "Oh yes, Allen is scared of you," I continue. "But he still wants to marry you. He told me so."

Mariana pulls the white hospital blanket up to her shoulders and curls into the shape of a seashell, turning her face toward me. "Did he, Bela? Well, I guess each of us is full of surprises these days." She closes her eyes, and if she weren't in a hospital bed, I could almost convince myself we were back on Key Biscayne, and she was turning in early because she has a big exam tomorrow.

I can't be sure what Mariana meant by that, each of us being full of surprises. Mauricio's letter was sealed, so there's no way she could know I'm considering replying to him. Unless, of course, Allen told her. Which is entirely possible; you should never trust a man with a confidence, their constitutions aren't strong enough to keep secrets. That's why God gives us girlfriends.

But it's just as possible that Mariana's simply referring to Allen confiding in me, and to her pregnancy, although that's more of a shock than a surprise. Even perhaps to Ninexin's odd mood; she is so happy she almost seems giddy. The pregnancy, the emergency, it's making everyone act strange. It makes sense that it's all that Ninexin and Mariana can think of. But Mariana's right, I am full of surprises, because to my shock, even though my heart and head are full with this news—jumbled, and confused, happy, and outraged, but definitely full—I still find myself thinking about Mauricio, wondering what I should do. All those days in Granada, I thought that when I finally saw Mariana, I'd have the chance to show her the letter, that we could read it together. But now, she has her own upheaval to react to, her own decisions to make, although, with the brashness of youth, she seems to have decided everything and won't be swayed by common sense. It's not the right time to talk to Mariana about Mauricio. It might never be anymore. And that's disappointing but also a bit of a relief; just the thought of bringing up his letter makes me feel shaky. But if I'm too nervous to even speak of Mauricio, then how can I entertain the idea of one day seeing him? And if I decide not to see him, how can I reject him again after all these years? I don't know what to do or say. Before I can come up with anything, Ninexin looks up from the phone she's been glancing at, then slaps it shut and leans over to kiss Mariana's forehead. "Allen texted he's on his way back, so your Bela and I will go get something to eat, too, and let you sleep."

"Okay, Mama." Mariana closes her eyes but opens them again as Ninexin starts toward the door, and smiles at me. "See you later, Bela."

I lean in to kiss her and she smells as she always has, of violets and soap. She still looks as lost, as swallowed up by the hospital bed as she did when she was sixteen and her appendix almost burst and we all slept at Mt. Sinai overnight. How can this little girl become a mother?

But as I think the words, I picture her holding a baby, and a wave of excitement breaks over me, so strongly that it almost knocks me over. A week ago everything seemed to be ending and now it's just beginning. I feel unwell all of a sudden, but then I realize that there's nothing physically wrong with me; it's just that I'm missing Ignacio more sharply than I have since the day he died. I wish he were here to see this, his great-grandchild on the way.

I give Mariana a kiss on each eyelid, like I used to when she was a little girl, and before I leave, I lean over and whisper, "Maybe just a civil ceremony in three months—and you can have the party with the dress and the champagne later, after the baby is born?"

42

Ninexin

Every Christmas and Easter, every time the three of us are together, really, I've watched Mama rattling on and Mariana laughing and patting her on the arm, and chattering back, and I always wondered what she found so fascinating about Mama's patter that my attempts at conversation lacked. Although most of the time Mama and I get along well enough, I have to admit that there were times when she would begin her stream-of-consciousness soliloquies with me, and the waterfall of inconsequential thoughts would infuriate me as I wondered, this is what Mariana calls several times a week to hear? For this she found an international calling plan?

But today Mama's as loquacious as ever and, while I'm not exactly entranced by her commentary, I'm not bothered either. Maybe it's because I've got such happy topics to think about as she chatters, or because I enjoyed my fair share of meaningful conversation on Solentiname. Or maybe I've just discovered Mariana's secret: if you let Mama's words wash over you without paying too much attention, she's really a delightful companion, or at least an effortless one. If that's the case, I wish Mariana had tipped me off long ago. I have no idea what Mama's rattling on about now. First it was Maria Leonora's daughter, who got married seven months pregnant in a gorgeous gown and the priest didn't even blink, then she moved on to the horrid state of nurses' uniforms today, and just now it was about how healthy Jell-O is for you, a fact she no doubt picked up in *Vanidades*, where she does most of her scientific research.

Now she's talking about how she wants to die at home—hospitals always have this effect on her—which means that soon she'll be planning her funeral, dictating lists of hymns that should be sung and the ensemble in which she'd like to be buried. The clothes change, but the music remains pretty static. And it usually drives me crazy, makes me yell, "For God's sake, Mama, you're not dying yet," which gets her all teary and huffy, so she'll say something like, "Only God knows whether that's true or not, and the last time I checked He hadn't appointed you His spokesperson."

But today, I don't say anything at all, I just roll along on the Ferris wheel of her conversation, up and down, swinging all around. Maybe we'll never argue again now that I've learned the trick of turning Mama into white noise, like what emanates from the expensive alarm clocks you find in fancy hotel rooms, with tropical frogs croaking or waves crashing to the shore, sounds that are equal parts pleasant and irrelevant.

The funny thing is, I think Mariana actually listens to what Mama says, and still they get along perfectly. It could be that my absence, although they both always complained about it, gave them the gift of all that time together, time in which they learned to understand what each of them was saying underneath their words. Or maybe it's just the distance the extra generation offers that somehow renders

Mama charming and funny and poignant and wise in Mariana's eyes instead of wildly annoying, and that everyone holds their mothers—the person responsible for their existence—to a higher standard. Maybe that alchemy will benefit me with Mariana's baby?

I was so sure I was responsible for the death of that baby, too. I heard noise in the bathroom, the sound of Mariana bumping around in the dark, and when I stood up and turned on the flashlight and saw the trail of blood, I knew that it was my fault, as sure as if I had kicked Mariana in the stomach. It was telling her about her father, the kiss, and the murder that did it, expecting her to take in all that violence, when her body and mind were already full with new life, and had no room to absorb old deaths. I know that sounds crazier than any health advice in *Vanidades*, it's the opposite of scientific, but that doesn't mean it's not true.

By the time Mariana opened the bathroom door, I already had my cell phone in my hand. After I helped her to the bed, I sat there stroking her back while I called Hector Flores and arranged for his helicopter to retrieve us and take us to the Metropolitano. I could have called Managua's chief of police and sent for their helicopter, but this wasn't a crime, and the truth is, I thought Hector's would arrive faster. He's an almost maniacally efficient man; he just edged past Camilo Lopez to become the single largest coffee producer in the country. But he's also a genuinely nice person who won't make inquiries or expect favors, he'll just accept my payment of eight hundred dollars—the friends-and-family rate for use of the helicopter—with no questions asked.

By the time it was arranged and the hospital knew to expect us, Mariana had stopped crying and was starting to rock forward. I thought she must be in pain, but she was trying to get out of bed, moving toward the bloodstains on the floor, saying, "We can't leave this mess. It looks like a crime scene." I managed to carry her back to bed, and pulled out some clean clothes for her to put on while I wiped the floor with the bathroom towels.

"Leave some cords so they can replace the linens," Mariana said, stepping around me on her way to the bathroom. I wanted to tell her to stop worrying about the linens, no one cared about the damn sheets. But I didn't. I just pulled out one thousand córdobas and slipped them under the little wooden angel. I know that in times of crisis, it's comforting to think of anything other than what's happened, to focus on details that can be controlled. I wasn't going to say anything about the baby Mariana was clearly losing if she didn't. But then she stepped out of the bathroom in clean clothes, with a toothbrush still in her hand, and said, "I'm not bleeding anymore, Mama. Does that mean it's over?"

I didn't know. It's moments like that when I realize how few useful things I really do know. So I just grabbed her and held her while she cried. I had nothing helpful to say.

"Do you think it's because in the beginning I wasn't sure—" she whispered into my ear, and I grabbed her tighter and promised, "No, of course not."

It wasn't until we were in the helicopter, holding hands in the last row, the farthest away from the pilot, who was trying his best to be invisible and leave the shaken women in the back of his vehicle to their grief, that I said, "I shouldn't have told you."

This was my punishment. I was responsible for Manuel's death, and now this new life was being taken from us in exchange. And we didn't even know what was going on; was this simply a miscarriage or did the hemorrhage mean that something was horribly wrong with Mariana, too? Would she be able to conceive again? Or could the situation be even graver than that? Was there a chance she might be taken from me, as well? "I shouldn't have told you," I said again, and I gripped her hand even tighter. She pulled it away, using the back of her palm to wipe tears off her face as she laughed.

"Mariana?" I asked with such force that the pilot glanced back at us for a minute before turning back to the controls.

"Mama, this has nothing to do with what you said or did. Can we just agree that this is happening to me, not you?"

Then I started laughing, too, because Mariana sounded just like herself, which made me feel that she might be okay after all.

When we got to the hospital, the on-duty doctor—so young, younger than Mariana—was overly solicitous the way they only ever are when something terrible has happened. He said he was going to perform a pelvic ultrasound and nodded at me to indicate that I should leave the room. But Mariana said, "She can stay, can't she?" And then, "Mama, please stay."

I stood beside her and held her hand but I couldn't look at her; she seemed so small, so scared. I felt the same way I had when she was napping as a toddler and looked so peaceful and fragile that I had to rest my hand on her chest to make sure that she was still breathing. If I kept looking at Mariana I knew I would start crying, but if she wasn't going to, I couldn't let myself crumble. I didn't want to look at the screen, either, to see the emptiness there, so I focused on the doctor, who had a slight beard, which I found disrespectful: he works in a hospital in Managua, not a Red Cross camp in the jungle, the least he could do is shave for his patients. It was a thought that belonged more to my mother than to me, but I needed someone to be angry at and he was going to have to do. And then he smiled, breaking up his bristled face. When I saw that, I finally looked at the terrifying machine.

I hadn't realized that Mariana was keeping her eyes trained on me, not the screen with its blurs of black and gray, until she whispered, "What, Mama? Why are you smiling?"

"You have a good eye, señora," the doctor said. Then he turned his bristly smile to Mariana. "Your mother has recognized her grandchild. There's the embryo, see?" He pointed to a pulsing blob on the screen.

"But the blood?" Mariana was crying now, so it would have been all right if I did, too, but all I could do was grin so hard that my cheeks hurt. I moved to press my hands against them, and when I realized I was still holding Mariana's hand in mine, pulling her arm up into the air, I didn't let go, I just dropped down to sit on her bed so we were on the same level and I could see my own feet, swinging like a little girl's.

"There are two subchorionic hematomas, blood clots, on your placenta; a larger one and a small one that looks like it might be dissolving," the doctor said. "That's probably what caused the hemorrhage. In the majority of cases, the clots simply resolve themselves. But it does make this a high-risk pregnancy; we'll have to watch you."

"Fine," Mariana said. "That's fine. But the baby's okay?"

"The heart is beating away. Do you want to hear it?" the doctor asked, and I stopped trying to puzzle out the word before "hematoma" and laughed out loud because it's such a ridiculous question—does anyone ever say no? Are there parents who respond, "Oh, thank you, but I'd rather not hear my child's heartbeat?"

Mariana looked at me and laughed, too. "Of course we do."

"Wait!" I yelled as the doctor reached for a switch on the side of the ultrasound machine. He raised his hands as if he were the victim of a holdup, and I blushed a little before asking Mariana, "Shouldn't we wait until Allen gets here?" I had called him from the helicopter, I knew they were on their way.

"Probably," Mariana said. "But I don't want to wait! I don't think I'll believe the baby's okay until I hear it."

"I'll have to check on the clot again," the doctor said. "There'll be more ultrasounds, plenty of chances to hear the heartbeat."

"See! Win-win!" Mariana grabbed my hand, the doctor flipped a switch, and the sound of our baby filled the room, stronger, more rhythmic, and more powerful than anything else I've heard. If I could, I would have these three noises programmed into every alarm in every hotel room in the world, so that I would always have a choice among the chattering of my mother, the deep breathing of Mariana as she sleeps, and the thumping heart of my grandchild.

43

Maria

THURSDAY, JANUARY 15

When I first found out about the baby, I kept listing all the reasons why this pregnancy was a disaster. It complicated things with Allen, when we had such a nice situation, just the two of us grown-ups. The pregnancy—the baby—could very likely stall my career, derail my relationship, suck me away from my art. I would no longer be the protagonist of my own story, the subject of my own painting. In the first few days after taking the at-home test, before my doctor's appointment, I didn't tell anyone—not even Allen— because it seemed so unlikely, so ludicrous, that I kept thinking that maybe this would just go away. Not just thinking. Hoping. Wishing, even.

But I spent most of the terrifying time on the helicopter praying in Spanish, the language of all my most serious supplications, that everything would be all right, that my baby would live. Every now and then one of the items on that early list of fears would float up into my consciousness and shock me with how quickly, and how completely, my feelings had changed. The baby could spell the end of me and Allen, or of my career, or both. All of this was still true. And yet, each time I thought of one of these reasons, which had relentlessly laid siege to my brain in those first few weeks, I now wanted to scream, "I don't care!" The facts were still true but the feelings weren't anymore. And then the shock and fear would subside, making room for guilt, which kept whispering that maybe I deserved to lose what I now wanted most. Maybe that's what you get for changing your mind.

That's what I was telling myself, that I was just getting what I deserved, yesterday when Dr. Alvarez discovered the baby's heartbeat. I make him sound like an explorer, landing in a new country. But that's what it felt like to me, like he was breaking new ground, changing the very geography of the world in which I live.

I've heard the baby's heart twice now: once with Mama, once with Allen. Both times I cried, the first time because the sound was so strong, so real, it made me understand that I hadn't lost what had somehow become the most salient feature of who I am right now.

And the second time because I was watching Allen. Mama had told him I was okay, and so was the baby, but that was all he knew, so when he arrived at the hospital he swooped in, trying to take control, for once, to be the planner, the person who fixed things. He'd spent the car ride to Managua manning his phone, and when he arrived, he was erupting with names of doctors at high-risk pregnancy practices in New York, dates of how soon we could get on a flight out of Managua, agencies with private nurses who could move in with us overnight—because, of course, I couldn't live alone at my place anymore and would have to move into his apartment.

I just laughed until he finally shut up and sat down, kissing my fingers, my wrist, my palm until I got so embarrassed I had to do something, so I turned to Dr. Alvarez and said, "This is Allen. He's very worried about me. And he has a very efficient assistant who, it appears, has been rather busy this morning."

I had spoken in English, so that Allen could hear me making fun of him, and so that he'd understand that the doctor spoke the language perfectly. Allen extended his hand and said, "I'm Maria's fiancé." I didn't correct him; maybe after spending so much time with my Bela, Allen had transformed into a social conservative, and he felt the doctor would give me better care if we were about to be married. Or, he was just taking advantage of my ridiculously good—no, giddy—mood, to try to settle everything to his liking. It's a smart tactical move, to force the issue when I'm feeling amenable. Mother would be impressed. Whatever his motive, I decided to let him identify himself, and our relationship, to the doctor however he liked. No one was writing this on our permanent records. And it didn't really matter, certainly not to Dr. Alvarez. To him—and to me—what is more important than the question of what Allen is to me is the fact that he's the father of this baby.

I asked the doctor if he could please repeat the ultrasound. Allen watched the blob on the screen pulsing before the sound was turned on, and when it was, he closed his eyes and all the worry slid off his face, leaving his contorted forehead smooth.

Dr. Alvarez is a miracle worker—he managed both Allen and my Bela. He informed them that I'd be going home with neither of them, that he wanted to observe me for a week to see if the smaller clot dissolved completely. And that I wouldn't be flying to New York, or anywhere, until he and his colleagues had a better sense of the larger clot, as flying can make clotting worse.

Dr. Alvarez is also the gatekeeper. He's instructed the nurse as to when my Bela and Allen are allowed in the room and when they need to leave so that I can sleep. He seems to have a soft spot for Mama when she pops over from the office, because I've woken up to find her sitting in the chair next to my bed, staring at me in a way that makes me a little nervous. And happy. When I was in grade school, about twice a month I would dream that Mama was with me, rubbing my shoulder to wake me up the way she did when she visited. Sometimes the dreams were so vivid that I'd actually see her until my sleepy eyes focused and I realized it was my Bela or the housekeeper, and I would turn away so that they couldn't see my disappointment and realize that they weren't the person I wanted to see first when I woke up. Now, when my eyes blink open and I see Mama, I always roll over so that I'm not facing her; it's a reflex. But then I stretch and twist and turn back to her once I'm fully awake, glad that she's still there, that she was willing to gaze quietly at the back of my head for a moment.

Allen and my Bela have plenty to do when they're not here. She's busy thinking of names and digging through boxes to find Abuelo's old christening gown, the one Mama, Tía Celia, Rigobertito, and I were baptized wearing. I think she feels that if she has the outfit for the baby, there's no way we'll omit the ritual, and we'd have to be married before we stand before a priest to baptize our child—at least according to Bela's rules, if not the priest's.

And Allen's making arrangements. He called the gallery and set up for my short-term disability leave, telling them I had internal bleeding. No one has asked for more information so far, and no one's gotten any. And he's flying home on Monday; he was reluctant, but I insisted. He has work to do and I'm in good hands; if I need to stay much longer, he can always come back.

Sometimes Allen and my Bela visit together—apparently they spend hours gossiping like old ladies. Given the somewhat risky nature of my pregnancy, I want to keep it quiet. And given the illegitimate nature of it, so does my Bela. Which means that she has no one but me, Mama, and Allen to talk to about the baby. And Allen says he knows no one else in Managua, and no one in New York who tells such good stories as my Bela. I'm not one hundred percent convinced that they actually have a fully functioning language in common, but when I asked Allen how they manage to communicate so well, he said that after a few Tom Collinses, my Bela sounds just like Scarlett O'Hara.

As for me, I've been sleeping a lot, which is the point of bed rest, I guess. And when I'm awake and alone I draw in the sketchbook my Bela brought me. I have a new painting in mind. There's a woman who takes up one entire edge of the canvas, but you can't see her head, just her arms and breasts and swollen belly. And on the other edge there's a man with graying hair, gesturing toward the middle. I'm not sure exactly what's going to go there; it hasn't come to me yet. But I know it will. I keep playing the sound over and over in my mind and I know that one of these days I'll come up with a visual representation of our baby's heartbeat.

44

Isabela

FRIDAY, JANUARY 16, 2009

It wasn't until this morning that I was able to shake off Allen. He's a lovely person, if a bit crass at times, and I did just begin a novena to pray that he'll become my grandson-in-law, and sooner, rather than later, now that we're going to be related by blood, if not marriage. But I've never met a needier man in my entire life. All he wants to do is talk about how well Mariana looks—except he calls her Maria—how much ruddier her coloring is, how her mood gets brighter with each passing day. And then he wants to discuss all the articles he's been reading about prenatal blood clots, which is even worse. He attacks me with percentages, how many resolve themselves within the first trimester, within the second, and how many go on to pose serious problems. It's enough to make me wish that his hotel didn't have the Internet floating around everywhere, enabling him to pull up charts and numbers on his phone and thrust it in my face while I'm trying to enjoy the darling basket of tiny *pains aux chocolat* they serve with coffee in the lobby café.

I understand what he's doing, of course: he wants a guarantee, a promise that everything is going to turn out all right and that a year from now he'll be a married man again and a new father with a healthy, happy baby and a healthy, even happier young bride. I give him every reassurance I can. Mariana has the best doctor in Managua, Ninexin saw to that, and Dr. Alvarez raves about the practice he recommends for her in New York. He's not the kind of man who says things just to make women happy, or because he knows what it is they want to hear; he looked right at me, bold as brass, when he said that Mariana didn't need any added pressure right now, just pleasant distraction, and that I wasn't to bring up any topics that might cause her stress. So when he assures us that we have every reason to hope for, and expect, a positive outcome, I know we can believe him.

I used to be offended when doctors said things like that, "positive outcome," as if we were talking about science experiments and not the lives of two people who are among the most important in the world, as far as I'm concerned. But during Ignacio's illness, I became used to how they speak—and they're much worse in the States, where they want you actually to tell terminal patients that they're dying. It's so rude, like telling fat people they've put on weight; is it really possible they haven't noticed? You should have seen the doctor's face in Miami when I asked for his cell phone in case Ignacio had an episode late at night! You would have thought I asked for his number so that we could make a date to go out dancing!

The older I get, the more experience I'm gaining with the men in white; they're almost as familiar to me as their black-dressed counterparts, the priests. And I've got several of those at work on Mariana, too: I've sponsored a Mass each week from now until her due date, as a show of faith and gratitude for the luck we've had so far.

When I thanked him at the end of the last service, Padre Juan Bautista told me he kept my granddaughter and her husband and their unborn child in his prayers every day. I just thanked him. What he doesn't know won't hurt him, Allen says, and he taught me the most wonderful English phrase: "Need-to-Know Basis." I am keeping everyone on a Need-to-Know Basis as far as Mariana and the baby are concerned. And I know Padre Juan Bautista well enough to know that he uses his resonant voice to great effect to say Masses and keeps quiet the rest of the time; I won't have everyone in the congregation sidling up to me asking why they're the last to hear the good news of Mariana's marriage and the impending arrival. I told him, "Padre, Mariana doesn't want to worry anyone so we aren't saying a word about the pregnancy. Not unless someone has a demonstrated Need to Know."

He just smiled and nodded at the phrase, which I said in English; pobrecito, his English isn't as good as mine. But he's a lovely priest, just the same.

I've told Allen that if Dr. Alvarez and Padre Juan Bautista and God Himself are in charge of Mariana and the baby, which they are, mother and child are in good hands and I am confident everything will be fine. Every morning since we arrived in Managua I've told him that, over breakfast at his hotel, and most afternoons and evenings at the hospital, too. I am as sincere and reassuring as I can be. But there are just some things that should not be discussed at the breakfast table.

Allen acts like he's modern. Too modern, if you ask me; he can't even say the rosary—"wouldn't begin to know what to do," he told me when I asked him if he wanted to borrow my beads. But he seems to have a deep-seated belief in the power of repetition, of incantation, because he wants to hear me say it, again and again: "I promise

Mariana will be fine. And the baby, too." He prompts me if I don't remember to add the last part.

I appreciate his faith in me, but I'm starting to get hoarse. I can tell the poor boy—man, I should say, he's hardly a boy—is desperate to take some action, to do something with all his nervous energy, to help somehow. So, since he wasn't willing to try the rosary, this morning after coffee at his hotel I sent him to a restaurant on the other side of Managua where they make the rice pudding that Mariana loved when she was a girl. I even told him that, here in Nicaragua, we believe rice pudding is good for expectant mothers. That's not necessarily true, but we Nicaragüense should believe it; why not? It's just milk and rice and what could be healthier than that? The poor man set off with such energy, as if he had wings on his feet. Don Pedro even let him drive.

I'll admit I didn't remember the rice pudding just for Allen's sake. Or even for Mariana's. I needed to see her alone. The worry over Mariana, the shock about the baby, it made the question of how I should answer Mauricio feel less urgent. But, once I began to believe what I'd been telling Allen—that all that could be done for Mariana and the baby is being done, and all that is left for us to do is pray—I thought it might be all right to consider my life again, and what I plan to do next. The letter still requires a reply. In the cacophony of the last several days, the question of whether or not I should write back was drowned out. But now everything else has quieted down, and Mauricio is still awaiting my answer.

I've already written it. I wrote it on Wednesday night, after I was convinced that Mariana was going to be okay. And, truth be told, after I stopped worrying about what everyone would say about the baby. "If people want to talk about us, they'll find a reason to do so, Mama," Ninexin told me when she brought me my evening chamomile. "What matters is that Mariana's healthy and happy. She's too strong to let the gossip of ladies with empty minds and empty lives, who have nothing better to do than talk about her, ruin her happiness. You could learn something from her."

I know Ninexin was talking about my attitude toward the baby. And I know that she is right, and not just about the baby. I've spent my life doing what everyone thought I should. It worked out, in its way. But there may not be much life left. You'd think I would have realized that my time on earth was getting short years ago, at my seventieth birthday, perhaps. But even though intellectually I knew that the end was coming nearer every day, and that I should make the most of the years that remain, I didn't really feel it. I didn't believe it until now, not in my soul. Ignacio gave me that knowledge. It was his parting gift, along with the fuchsia datebook. And I want to fill that little calendar with events that are worthy of its cover, bright and bold. Maybe even shocking.

I wrote the letter after Ninexin left, in an old notebook that I use for shopping lists and phone messages. But I won't copy it over until I know that what I've written is possible. I can't know that until I see Mariana alone. And that couldn't happen until today, when I managed to get Allen to leave my side for a few hours.

As soon as Dr. Alvarez is done with Mariana, it's my turn to go in. Ninexin has meetings all morning, she said, she'll stop by at lunch. But we'll be done by then. Allen will be back with the rice pudding, and if I've gotten the answer I want, I'll tell them I need to lie down. I'll leave them to enjoy the sweet and I'll go home and copy over my draft on my nice stationery, which is so thick you have to use the right pen so it doesn't get stuck in the weave of the paper, so thick that it takes some effort to fold it, and then I'll ask Don Pedro to take me to the post office. I won't send it off with the housekeeper's daughter or give it to Ninexin to mail from her office. I will post the letter myself.

Dr. Alvarez is taking longer than I expected, and as each minute passes, my anxiety increases. I'm not worried anything's gone wrong with Mariana; I can hear them laughing. That Dr. Alvarez is too chatty and charming for his own good.

He's always running behind, showing off for the mothers-to-be with his little funnel for hearing the baby's heart and his anecdotes about his own little boy at home who is just learning to speak and whom the nanny has taught to yell, "Doctor!" when he wants his papi's attention.

It's me I'm nervous for; what if Mariana doesn't approve? What if she's disappointed? Or worse, disgusted?

I can't even imagine such a reaction from her. The one time she told me she was disgusted with me, when I complained to her over the phone that I realized the housekeeper was washing Don Pedro's uniform along with our household clothes, she could barely stop laughing long enough to admonish me. She's never really angry with me; she saves that for her mother. I'd like to think that's a privilege of age, but I'm starting to suspect that, really, she thinks I'm too silly to scold.

The thing is, I don't want her to laugh at me this time. Or to think I'm silly. I don't want her to think this is a trivial little matter I'm bringing up at a time when she's experiencing something truly life-changing. And I don't want her to think it's adorable, either, like Dr. Alvarez's son's escapades. This whole time I've been waiting for her to come back, not just to Managua, but to return to her old self, so that I can confide in her. But maybe the right moment still hasn't arrived.

"Abuela, you're next." Dr. Alvarez helps me into the room, and I let him, although I'm tempted to remind him that I'm not his abuela.

"I sent Allen for the rice pudding you love, mi corazón," I say. "I hope you still like rice pudding; it's probably been years since you had it."

"Decades." Mariana says. "Shut the door, please."

I do, although the doctor should have taken care to do that, instead of making an old woman like me exert herself. He's too busy with his jokes, that one. But I'm not here to complain. "He's a good person, he was happy to go get it," I say as I make my way to the door, and I'm talking about Allen, not the doctor. "But so talkative for a man! Every morning we have a coffee at his hotel before coming here and it's always Maria this and Maria—"

"When he's not painting Allen's just like a gossipy old biddy. It's as if, without a particular canvas to work on, he's got nothing serious to fill his mind, so he becomes obsessed with all sorts of things that are none of his business: local political scandals, the doorman's budding romance, the latest paperback thriller," Mariana says as the door shuts and I make my way to the chair at the side of her bed. "But enough about Allen. Look, we don't know how much time we have." She adjusts the movable bed and squeezes the pillows behind her so she can sit up straighter. "Did you bring the letter? You don't know how many times I held it up to the light to see if I could make out any words through the envelope! I've been dying to read it, but there's always someone else around. Tell me it's in that massive purse!"

I don't say anything, I just busy myself going through my handbag, because of course I do have the letter, hidden in the pages of an old *Vanidades*, and also so that she can't see how relieved I am.

"I can't *believe* you showed Allen before you showed me! I mean, I know, I was indisposed, otherwise engaged." Mariana laughs. "See, I get all old-fashioned just thinking about it. Tell me Mauricio used a fountain pen! I asked Allen to describe the handwriting but he said he couldn't remember what it looked like. Men are useless sometimes."

"He shouldn't have told you anything about the letter!" I have it in my hand now, holding it in my lap.

"Ha!" Mariana sits up even further; I hope she's not straining herself. "Of course he should have told me! I need something to think about while I lie here all day. I only brought one book with me, and there's just so much TV a person can watch. You're the one who shouldn't go around showing everyone if you don't want them to talk about your business."

"*Everyone!*" I'm so horrified I put the letter right back in my purse. "I like that! Everyone!"

"Bela! Give it to me!" Mariana begs. And then, as I'm reaching back in the bag for it, she adds, "Have you already shown Madre?"

"Mariana!" I sit up straight and hang my handbag on the arm of the chair; I never put it on the floor because a Colombian girl at Sacred Heart told me that if you put your wallet on the ground, that's where your money will go, too. "Only Allen has seen the letter, and only because you were unavailable, as you said, and I needed to tell *someone.*"

"Of course, Bela, to make sure it was real," Mariana says, and I'm already relieved; she has always understood me. "I'm just teasing you."

"I am only showing people on a Need-to-Know Basis," I tell her. "And your mother has no Need to Know." Now it's Mariana's turn to respond to some questioning. "How much did Allen tell you?"

"Well." She grins and I have to admit that Allen is right: she does get brighter, and ruddier, and even more beautiful every day. It's as if her soul is expanding along with her stomach. "Just that you're Mauricio's one true love, that his wife left him years ago, and that he wants you to come away to Camagüey when Castro dies, but Allen thinks Castro is dead already and they're never going to admit it. And he might be right, Bela. You know Beth told me that some of the Cubans in Miami think he's a santero and that he's going to live forever."

"That sounds right."

"You think Castro's going to live forever?"

"No, that's ridiculous, I wasn't even going to acknowledge that remark. I meant that's right, what Allen told you about the letter."

"But I still want to see it!" Mariana leans forward. "I need to! I have a Need to Know!"

And she does, she's just not aware of it yet. So I stop torturing the poor, sick girl, and I hand her the letter. Mariana has always been a fast reader; I watch her eyes slide across each line and start again at the other side, alighting on each word. Occasionally she breathes in, too deeply for a regular breath but not long enough or forceful enough to be a sigh. She doesn't smile, she doesn't frown, but she has the thumbnail of her free hand in her mouth as she reads. I'm so absorbed in watching her that I don't register this disgusting habit until she's almost done with the letter. I pull her hand from her mouth as she drops the paper onto the blanket covering her legs.

"Oh, Bela!" She clasps my hand as if I had meant to reach out and hold hers rather than yank her nail out of her teeth. "It's amazing. And his penmanship—it's just as beautiful as I imagined! I do think it's an ink pen. Did you see that the letters blur a little toward the left of the page, as if he's dragging his hand over the wet words as he writes?"

Mariana starts to bring her thumb back to her mouth before catching herself and stopping it in front of her face, reaching out to point at me instead. "Okay, here's what I think you should say to him. Do you have a pen and paper?"

"I do. But I don't care."

"You're not going to respond! But, Bela—"

"Of course I'm going to respond! I just meant that I don't care what you think I should say."

Mariana just looks confused, not properly taken aback or impressed. "I mean, I do care what you think, of course, mi reina," I reassure her. "But I've already written a draft of a response, and I'd rather hear your thoughts about that."

"Bela!" I can tell from Mariana's voice that she's smiling at me, even though I can't see her face because I'm engaged in the complicated process of untangling my bag's straps from the chair, thanks to that Colombian girl whose name I can't even remember right now. "Good for you! Can I see it?" She sounds almost shy, she's so eager. I extract the notebook paper from the back of my stealth *Vanidades*. It was sandwiched between a starlet's diet and a perfume advertisement, so it smells of heaven. But it doesn't look anywhere near as elegant as it smells, or as nice as Mauricio's letter. You can tell I used a ballpoint. I start tearing off the little chits of paper that remained when I pulled out the notebook pages, but Mariana yells, "Stop! You're going to rewrite it later, right? Just give me that thing."

So I do.

Mauricio, it begins:

When you wrote your letter, you couldn't have known that it would serve as a beacon in the darkest days of my life since the ones I suffered when I first left New Orleans and you. Even as I did so, even as I convinced myself that leaving meant upholding everything that was right, I knew it was wrong. Nothing in my life has ever felt like more of a sin.

And when, reading your letter, I realized that you followed me, that you came to Granada to find me, that we had a second chance to be together which was ruined by circumstance, by a chance interaction in the park I've always loved, for a moment I thought I was dying, the pain of that revelation was so strong. I closed my eyes fully expecting that I would never open them again.

But when I closed them, an image arose in my mind. It's a painting my granddaughter made—she's a very talented artist—and it shows a girl, me, dropping her schoolbook at the foot of a man who looms over the upper right corner of the canvas like an angel or a demigod of pagan mythology. And I stopped thinking of the loss I suffered—we suffered—in our parting, and realized all that had been gained. If I hadn't left, the painting wouldn't exist. Mariana would have never been born. And I can't imagine a world without her, or my grandson, or my daughters, or even my late husband any more than you could envision one without your children.

I wasn't getting married on the day you came to Granada. But I did marry, several months later, and had two girls, both lovely but otherwise more different from each other than you can imagine. My husband, Ignacio, was a man you would have liked. He was a man I liked, and admired, most of the time. I did not feel about him as I had for you, and I don't flatter myself to think that I was his one true love. I know I wasn't. But we gave each other our daughters, and also over a half century of our lives. And our daughters gave us our grandchildren, a boy, Rigoberto, and a girl, Mariana, whom Cristian Hidalgo met at Mt. Sinai.

If God had a hand in keeping us apart, it was so that Celia and her son Rigobertito and Ninexin and her daughter Mariana could be born, along with the children who were born to you and your wife. And I have no doubt that God also brought Cristian and Mariana to the same waiting room at Mt. Sinai, where they would meet. Mariana was there with Ignacio, and I like to think that, in this way, he too played a part in our finding each other again, knowing that he was about to leave this world and my side. He was a responsible man, it would have been like him to see that I had some joy to make up for the sorrow his loss would cause me.

Perhaps that meeting in Miami was ordained by God, knowing that He was about to take my husband from me. Or perhaps it's sacrilege to think that God bothers with lives as trivial as my own. In any case, if He had a hand in Cristian and Mariana finding each other, I believe that, after that, God stepped back to see what we would do with the gift he had given us.

You wrote me that brave and beautiful letter. Mariana kept it until her grandfather died. She knew all my stories about Sacred Heart, knew how much you had meant to me; maybe she felt giving it to me sooner would have been disrespectful of him. And I'm glad she waited, because if Ignacio had been alive when I read your letter, it would have been a definite betrayal of him, and of our life together, if I answered the way I am writing to you now. I cannot express myself better than you did in your letter to me, so I will use the same words in writing to you. Mauricio, you are my one true love.

But I am not the same girl I was when I left you. I am not young and beautiful. And I am not scared and shy. I don't know how long I have left, how long anyone does. And I don't know how we will feel if we meet, or how it will change our lives. All I know is that I want to see you again.

The greatest sins of my life have been sins of omission, borne of passivity, fear, or even politeness. Leaving you is chief among them. If seeing you after all these years is some sort of sin, then it is one I propose to commit knowingly, even if foolishly.

I am sure that Camagüey has changed since you last saw it, that it is not the city you remember. But if you still want to rediscover it, I would be honored to be at your side when you do. As for Castro, I don't know how long he has left either. But I am tired of waiting for other people to decide the events of my life. I am no longer willing to live according to others' schedules or rules.

Those are bold words for a woman who is approaching eighty. For all my brave talk, I am too nervous, and, perhaps, too slow-moving, to travel alone. My granddaughter is the one who brought me your letter. She is the one person to whom I've spoken of you all these years. She let me keep my love for you alive. I would like her to be the one to bring me to you as she brought your letter to me.

However, Mariana is expecting my great-grandchild. It is a great blessing, but there have been some complications in her pregnancy. I don't know when she will be able to travel. But if she is willing to accompany me, I propose that we meet as soon as that time comes.

If you agree, the where can be decided later. Should you prefer not to share Camagüey with Castro, why not New Orleans? We could meet in the lobby of the Roosevelt Hotel, where you took me and Miss Birdie to see the Christmas lights one December. We could meet at

Antoine's, where you ordered the Baked Alaska on your birthday and it
was so large we had to share it with the next table. We could meet in
Audubon Park or the lunch counter at Walgreens, or under the clock
at D. H. Holmes, or even in the courtyard of Sacred Heart, where I
first looked up and saw you standing under the archway, laughing at
me. You had a date with Silvia Contreras that night but you said you
would see me tomorrow. And I was ready.

I am ready again. My address is at the top of this stationery; my
phone number, I will write below. I will understand if you find this
letter too eager, if the idea of meeting was more pleasant than the
reality. But if you are prepared to start making plans, then let us begin
again.

Whatever happens, I thank you for the joy your letter brought into
my life in this time of loss, and for the joy you brought into my life
long ago. I, too, remain Your,

Isa

I did not watch Mariana as she read; I couldn't. Instead I read the
Vanidades again, or, at least, stared at the pictures and smelled
the perfume. But I know how quickly she reads, and it seemed to take
her far too long to finish my letter. When I could stand it no longer, I looked up to see that the notebook pages had fallen on the
blanket, too, on top of Mauricio's stationery, and that Mariana was
crying.

"Mariana?" Even though I'd spoken softly, when she heard me
she started crying harder. I waited for her to tell me why—was she
weeping for the years Mauricio and I had lost? Or were the tears
sorrow for Ignacio, since I had never fully given him my heart?
Perhaps she was crying because she knew she couldn't come with

me, wouldn't be a part of this, and she hated to disappoint an old woman.

I waited for her to explain, but she didn't, not even when I reached over and lifted the letters from her lap. Then I took her hand, so that she'd feel safer when she answered me. Because I couldn't not ask. "Mariana," I said finally. "Will you come with me?"

45

Ninexin

MAY 18, 2009

They invited me to come with them to New Orleans. It was a sweet gesture, and I don't know whose idea it was, Mama's or Mariana's. I like to think they both wanted me to feel included in this little adventure. But I told them no, thank you, that they should have a lovely time and text me photos all weekend, but that I need to save my vacation for August, when the baby is due, as I'll want to stay in New York as long as possible.

It's all arranged: in a few months, Mariana will move into Allen's apartment, which has plenty of room for her and the baby, and, just before she's due, I will come to stay in hers. If everyone likes the arrangement, Mariana says, maybe we'll keep it that way, and she'll hang on to her place so that Mama and I can visit as often as we like. I thought Mama would insist that she come for the birth, too, but I think having this trip to New Orleans, this shared romance, with Mariana and Allen makes her feel as if she's had enough alone time with her granddaughter. Maybe in her old age, Mama's becoming less competitive, less possessive of Mariana's love. Maybe Mauricio's constant letters and phone calls have distracted her, and, if so, I'm grateful to him for that. Or maybe I'm overthinking it, and that what she said is true: tiny little infants scare her and she'd rather wait until the baby can at least hold its head up. Mariana and Allen have promised to come to Managua for Christmas, so she'll get to meet the baby then. Mama has half of the old ladies in Granada busy smocking miniature dresses since we found out the gender.

It's a girl. Of course. The next generation, just like Mariana said. When she called to tell us the baby is a girl, standing on a street corner outside her obstetrician's, I burst into tears. I can't remember the last time I sobbed that violently. Not when my father died, which was sad, but not shocking, and made bearable by the fact that he had given me so much of the best of himself while he was alive. Not when Mariana was hemorrhaging; there was too much to do. Not even at Manuel's funeral. I was too numb then. Mariana was crying on the phone, too, but she, at least, has the excuse of hormones. I had no such explanation, I was just so happy. I didn't think I cared about the baby's gender, just that he or she continued to grow healthy and safe in Mariana's belly. But when I heard it was a girl, it felt exactly the same as when the doctor held Mariana, slick with blood, up in front of me, as Manuel squeezed my hand and said, "It's a girl! Our baby girl."

I think that's part of the reason I was crying, too. That Manuel isn't here to see this. That he never got the chance to see the world he left behind, to see his country, the country he died for, grow, sometimes with his party in power, sometimes not, but freed from the dictator he fought to topple. That he never got to see his baby grow into a girl and then a woman. That he'll never get to meet his granddaughter. Manuel died for what he believed in; his death can never be called a waste. But I think this was the first time I let myself feel it as a personal loss. I missed him that day. For the first time in over thirty years, I missed him, not as a comrade or a national hero but as my husband.

I even suggested to Mariana that they name the baby Manuela. "It's a nice idea, Mama," she said. "But I just don't think it's a very pretty name."

I didn't say anything; I didn't want to press the issue. "Besides," she added, "Allen and I have already picked out a name."

"Oh?" I tried to make the syllable sound as unobtrusive, as non-judgmental, as possible.

"Yes, but we're not telling anyone until she's born. And don't worry, I won't let my Bela drag it out of me in New Orleans no matter how hard she tries. But I'll give you a clue: it's continuing a family tradition."

"Ay, Dios!" I said, before I could help it. "Please tell me you're not naming her after a Mayan warrior princess!"

I don't care what they name the baby. I suppose they might name her after Mama, which would thrill her, of course. But it's their decision. I already pushed the one baby-related matter I felt strongly about, that their little trip down Memory Lane take place in New Orleans rather than Cuba. The blood clots on Mariana's placenta have both disappeared; her pregnancy is no longer classified as high-risk, gracias a Dios. And she's having a wonderful second trimester, as every pregnant woman should, to make up for the fear and worry and nausea of the first trimester and the discomfort and bloating of the third. But I just feel better having all of them in the U.S., near a major medical center, than in Cuba, no matter how good Cuban medical schools are, no matter how many wonderful Cuban doctors I've seen here in Nicaragua.

Mauricio preferred the idea of New Orleans, anyway. He's

old-school anti-Castro; in his mind, the two of them are engaged in a personal vendetta to see who can outlive whom. I can't wait to hear what he thinks of my career as a Sandinista; should make for interesting dinner-table conversation if we ever meet. Although that generation, I suppose, was raised not to bring up politics at the table. Lucky for me. Lucky for him is more like it.

But if Mauricio was pro-New Orleans, Mariana was voting for Cuba. She said the trip was also meant to be a babymoon—whatever that is—for her and Allen, and she so wanted to see Havana. I promised that they could go after the baby was born; they can leave her with me and go alone on a post-babymoon (although, apparently, that's not how the concept works). Or, I suggested, we can all go together. I could even get them in to see Castro, I promised, dangling the old man as bait in front of Mariana; everyone loves to meet a legend, especially one not long for this world. Everyone except Mauricio, I guess.

"Really, Mama?" she teased. "You could arrange that? You're that important in the world of Latin American politics?"

"Hija," I told her, "last time I saw Castro, at a Nicaraguan-Cuban Friendship Summit, miniskirts were in fashion, and he kept wrapping his arm around me during photo ops, and trying to get me to join him for dinner."

"No!"

"It wasn't easy turning down Castro without letting down the Revolución. I had to keep reminding him I was a war widow, faithful to a fallen soldier."

It was all true. I don't know why she found it so hard to believe; I was a fetching twenty-something comrade, and Castro was an older man with good taste and a habit of getting what he wanted. But it was also a convenient truth to recall at this point; Mariana's as gossipy as her grandmother in some ways, and the story put her in such a good mood, she agreed to my request. She even said she'd like us to have a trip together, since I couldn't make it on this one.

I felt a little guilty then; I could make it if I wanted to, could join them for the weekend, only taking Friday and Monday off. But it wouldn't feel right. I was worried Mama would fall into a depression after Papa died, and Mauricio, and Mariana's baby, have kept her from that. Oh, and her new best girlfriend, Allen. He bought her an iPhone so that they can Skype, but of course she can never figure out how to use it if I'm not there. Still, I wouldn't be surprised if she learned sooner rather than later; Mama's life is so full now that she seems to be growing younger each day.

I'm thankful for that. But it's barely been four months since Papa died. I'm not ready to watch Mama meet the man she might have married instead. It all seems a bit sudden, and to be there would feel disrespectful. I would never tell her that; she deserves this late-in-life happiness. And if I did tell her, I know what she'd say: that she's never regretted marrying Papa because doing so gave her me and Celia, and Rigobertito and Mariana, and we are her world. And she'd mean it, too.

But I don't like to think of Papa as being a means to an end. I like to remember them not as two old people who'd grown used to each other, but as they were when they used to go out to the country club at night, and would tuck me and Celia in before leaving, Papa in his dark blue suit and slicked-back hair, Mama in long gloves and the jewelry from each of our births.

Mariana said that Mauricio wrote Mama that she was his one true love. I don't know what would have happened to me and Manuel, if our marriage would have survived Brigida, outlasted the Revolution. But I do know there was a time when I was his one true love, and he was mine. I think everyone deserves to feel that they were someone's. And I don't like to think that Papa may have lived and died without having that.

I know that's a narrow way to view the world. Love comes in so many forms. Mariana may have been Papa's one true love, or Rigobertito. Or even me. And he was loved in return, by all of us, even Mama. Mauricio coming back into her life doesn't take that away from Papa.

Still, I'm not ready to watch him return and romance my mother, this seventy-something Casanova. And they don't need me there. So I will let them have New Orleans. I will leave it to the lovers, Mariana and Allen, Mama and Mauricio. A couple figuring out their future, and another revisiting their past. Maybe I'm even a little jealous, not overly eager to be the odd woman out, the fifth wheel. Or perhaps the real reason I didn't accept their invitation was cowardice. It makes me a little nervous just thinking about it, all the expectations that are on this trip. The weight of half a century of memories.

Mama prays in the morning when she wakes up, at night when she goes to bed, when she's happy, when she's sad, when she loses her pen and wants help finding it. I prefer to save my supplications for moments of great importance. So I will pray that they all have an amazing time, that the city, and their feelings for each other, are as light-filled and sparkling as they remember. It's easy to wish for the best for others when you know you have a great love awaiting you, and mine is due in August. So I can pray with an open heart. I think my father would approve.

46

❧

Mariana

MAY 22, 2009

I've created a monster. My Bela felt none of her vast wardrobe was worthy of New Orleans, and she asked me to pick up some things for her to wear in New York. It wasn't too much trouble; I know her taste, we spent half of my childhood together in a Loehmann's dressing room. And it's not like I was overburdened with choices; Manhattan isn't exactly overflowing with stores that carry "women's" sizes. But I persevered, and she loved everything I brought. Until she caught sight of herself in a picture I was texting to Mama, of us eating beignets at the Café du Monde, and hated how she looked—she actually accused me of picking out the blouse she was wearing in order to make her look fat. Which would be a heinous crime if it were true; as soon as my Bela heard back from Mauricio, agreeing to meet, she put herself on a strict diet of her own devising. She decided she would eat only grilled cheese or pasta de pollo sandwiches, with the crusts cut off for added caloric savings, but she allowed herself as many of those as she craved in a day. I tried to warn her that this hardly qualified as smart nutrition, but she didn't care, and I couldn't even rope Beth into supporting me. She's a nurse practitioner, but she thought the diet sounded like the work of a genius, since no one would want to eat more than one of those super-rich sandwiches in one sitting. And maybe my Bela knows what she's doing: she's lost sixteen pounds since I last saw her.

"Bela, por favor!" I huffed when accused. Since I look like I've swallowed a small watermelon myself these days, I'm sensitive to the plight of the Buddha-bellied. But I didn't tell her that. I just pointed out that of course I want her to look her best, and that if she didn't like her new clothes, she was not required to keep them, she was welcome to send them on to her housekeeper with my compliments. That suggestion quieted her right down. It wasn't very nice of me, I suppose, but God bless Allen, who saved the day by telling my Bela that she looked infinitely slimmer, and even more beautiful, than she had in Managua. That finally put a smile back on her face.

My Bela's always been high-strung, bless her heart, but I've never seen her so nervous as she's been since she joined us here yesterday. Rigobertito flew with her to Miami then New Orleans—he's on his way to New York for work, and he'll pick her up on his way back, too—and Allen and I met her at the airport. Her first words when she got off the plane were "I think I'm having a heart attack."

She wasn't, of course. It was just the emotion of arriving back in the city that belonged to her youth. Once we'd collected her bags and stepped out into the haze, she reached in front of her as if shaking hands with the thick, moist air, and said, "This is what New Orleans feels like."

We booked at the Roosevelt Hotel because it's where my great-grandparents used to stay when they would visit my Bela and Gran-tía Dolores on their way to Paris, and once, when my Bela was seventeen and sitting cross-legged on a bench waiting for her parents to come down to the lobby, the actor Robert Taylor passed by and told her she had beautiful ankles. Gran-tía Dolores refused to speak to her for the rest of the day, she was so choked by jealousy.

That's one of my Bela's favorite stories, so I told it to Allen as we entered the lobby, and halfway through her whole blushing and giggling routine my Bela stopped walking and said, "Oh. Just look at my ankles now."

It's been like that nonstop, like watching a tennis match played by Elation and Horror. One minute she's as blithe and delighted as only an eighteen-year-old in love can be and the next she's a scared old woman. The hotel thrilled her; the state of Canal Street, without Maison Blanche, without D. H. Holmes and its glorious clock, had her practically in tears. I'm beginning to think Mama knew what she was doing when she opted out of coming.

Except for the fact that the city is amazing. Allen and I spent all yesterday strolling the French Quarter and it was like walking through the past, my Bela's past, specifically. New Orleans is the perfect city for a pregnant woman; you wouldn't think so, with the heat and the bars, the dubious smells of the streets in the morning. But the food is so glorious. I told Allen that I wanted to name our baby Almond, in homage to the almond croissant at the Croissant d'Or.

I was joking, of course. The truth is, we already have a name picked out. I knew it as soon as I came across it, reading a guidebook to Cuba. Before we decided to meet in New Orleans, for reasons both practical, on my part, and political, on Mauricio's, we were looking into staging this big reunion in Cuba. Mauricio insisted he could never return to Cuba while Castro was alive; the island, apparently, isn't big enough for the two of them. But I was so eager to go; when I see pictures of Havana, there are parts of it I feel I recognize from paintings I have yet to start. And I fantasized that Allen and I might stay on after the long-lost-lovers' reunion, now that I'm feeling better, and travel around the country ourselves, a last trip, just the two of us. I was sure I could talk Mauricio into a temporary détente, but my doctors nixed the idea of a Cuban adventure: no unnecessary flying for me, given my history of subchorionic hemorrhages. So we drove down here, instead. Still, Mama promises we can all go to Cuba at some point, and she'll even introduce us to Castro, who, it turns out, is a bit of a butt-pincher, or at least was in his heyday. Or maybe that was Mama's heyday?

I have no desire to get my butt pinched by Castro—although it would make a pretty great anecdote at cocktail parties for decades to come. But, having read a few guidebooks before our plans changed, I'm more determined to get to Cuba than ever; I've vowed to go on a pilgrimage to the Virgen de la Caridad del Cobre. I'd seen Her before in Cuban art, a Madonna floating over three black boys in a boat; those are los tres Juanes, three slaves named Juan whom She saved when they were lost at sea. That miracle made Her so many things in the eyes of the Cubans—a protector of the underdog, a patron of children, an ally in times of great fear—and the faithful who come to Her church in Cobre leave ex-votos for Her in exchange for miracles already executed or not yet performed.

The guidebook I read said that there's a gold talisman of a guerrilla there, left by Lina, Fidel Castro's mother, when he and his brother returned safely from a covert mission. I'd never really thought of Fidel as having a mother, but the fact that this woman had wished so fervently for her children's safety that she felt the need to give her desire a physical form made me feel as if I knew her. So I did a little research, and it turns out she was decades younger than Castro's father, and was his maid and mistress; they didn't marry until Fidel was in junior high, and the Jesuits wouldn't let him into the good Catholic school if his parents weren't legitimately wed.

Even more fascinating, there were rumors that Lina's mother was a celebrated Santería priestess, that she came from a long line of strong, strange women. Maybe that's why I feel a sort of kinship to her. It's not the having-children-out-of-wedlock thing; when she did it, it actually carried some stigma, whereas with me, the only person who can manage to drum up any righteous indignation is my Bela. But even though my baby is not born yet, I know that if I ever felt she were in danger, I couldn't sit by just waiting and hoping that she'd be okay. I'd need to do something to work toward her safety, even if it was impractical, as spiritual, as praying to another mother, as mystical as re-creating my child in gold.

And did her son thank Lina for her intercessions on his behalf? How could he when he banned religious holidays after coming to power? At the same time, he can't have been surprised by her actions. After all, she named him "faithful." I wonder if Fidel was embarrassed by his name, by her devotion, by the little gold guerrilla. I know that I am destined to embarrass my daughter with the force of my love, too, fated to do it wrong, to be judged by her just as I watched my own mother all these years and found her wanting.

When I read about the shrine Lina visited, I knew it contained my daughter's name. We will call her Caridad, after the Virgen de la Caridad del Cobre. Allen agrees it's perfect for our baby. Not that he had much of a choice. How could he not agree when I pointed out that it follows family tradition of naming baby girls for the Virgin Mary? My mother named me Mariana, which means "of the Virgen," but when I was in sixth grade I decided the name sounded too elegant for me; I wanted to be just another Maria like the three others in my class. Now I like to think that, as my belly expands and my feet outgrow my shoes, maybe I'm growing into the name, maybe I'll return to being Mariana. And soon there will be another generation named for the original Maria.

Allen said he feels like Caridad has a touch of the revolutionary in it, too, the warrior princess. And I would like it if my daughter took that from Mama: her strength. Her fearlessness.

Or maybe I'm just hedging my bets, hoping that my daughter will live up to her name, which means "charity" in English, and show a little charity when she thinks of her mother. We could all use a little more *caridad*. Although, when she's in sixth grade, if she wants everyone to call her Carrie, I'll have to be fine with that, too.

It's a high-risk, high-reward situation, motherhood. That's part of why I felt I had to be here this weekend, with my swollen belly and ringless finger. Because my Bela is putting herself in a similarly high stakes position by looking straight at the most precious part of her past and knowing that it might be found wanting in the harsh, low-energy light of the present. Allen is downstairs in the bar with her now; they're each having a Bloody Mary for courage before we get on the streetcar and take it up St. Charles to Sacred Heart, where she and Mauricio agreed to meet. I suggested that she carry a copy of the *Elements of Style* so that he'll recognize her, but she told me I was being ridiculous. And that I didn't even have the title right: apparently, in her day, it was *The Elements of Practice and Composition*.

I wish she had let me find the book for her. I wish I had some lucky charm I could give her to ensure that this meeting will go as well as I hope, to guarantee that her life will be full of so much happiness that there's never any room for pain or disappointment. It's the same feeling I have when I imagine Caridad being born, coming outside of my body and into the world, where I can no longer surround and protect her.

I know this is the wrong wish, not one worth incarnating in gold. Because love, I'm learning, is laced with pain. The joy and the sadness are too intertwined to be separated. If Caridad never felt sorrow or fear, she could never love anyone as deeply as I do her great-grandmother, as complexly as I do her grandmother, as profoundly as I do her, already.

It's time to go and I'm so nervous that I've gotten Caridad overexcited: she's swirling and kicking and shimmying like a modern dance impresario. Allen and I are going to drop my Bela off with our best wishes and Allen's cell phone, and then stroll around the neighborhood, maybe stopping for a pastry at an Italian place a block away from the school that the concierge recommended. And then we'll wait for my Bela's call. We haven't made any plans for the evening. This is one of those moments where you can't plan what comes next: you just have to wait and see what happens and hope for the best. You have to have faith.

Last night, while Allen was in the shower, my Bela showed me some of her souvenirs of her years in New Orleans, a lifetime ago. She had a sky-blue *Très Bien* ribbon from Sacred Heart, a black-and-white photo of herself and my tía Dolores in gloves and hats posed under the raised hoof of Andrew Jackson's horse in Jackson Square, and a tiny little spoon she stole from the Court of the Two Sisters, where Mauricio took her for tea on her seventeenth birthday. On my way downstairs, I'll use the extra key to slip into my Bela's room and borrow the spoon from her bedside table, where she put it away last night. I want this piece of my Bela, and her past, with me. While Allen and I share our pastry, I can rub the cold metal between my fingers and feel it warming to my touch. Maybe it will bring us all luck.

47

Isabela

Mariana keeps saying I'm nervous. As if I didn't know. As if it would be possible not to be. She keeps reminding me of the phone calls Mauricio and I have exchanged over the past four months, of all the plans he made to come here. One of his daughters took vacation from her job at the bank to travel with him. Even though her mother lives in the city, she doesn't know they're here. Mauricio and his daughter are staying uptown, with an old friend of the girl's. Woman's, I suppose: Mauricio's daughter must be in her mid-fifties by now. He wouldn't have gone to such effort, Mariana says, involved so many people, if he weren't as eager to see me as I am to find him again after all these years. "Remember," she's said two dozen times at least, "you're his one true love."

She's just making things worse. Right now, I'm his one true love. After he sees me, I might be just an anecdote, an uplifting tale to tell his grandsons when some girl breaks their hearts. "Hijo, you're devastated now, but in fifty years, she'll just be another fat old lady like the rest of them. Trust me, I found out the hard way."

What if it turns out not to have been worth the expense, the energy, the effort? Maybe we were better off with our phone calls, with just the dream of reuniting. What if the possibility of meeting turns out to have been so much richer than the reality?

"Prepare yourself for the worst, but hope for the best," Ignacio used to say. He had his faults, but he was a wise man. A good husband. So, as cold-blooded as it may seem, I've been trying to do that, to imagine meeting Mauricio and realizing that whatever existed between us died a long, slow death, wasted away while we refused to acknowledge what was happening. We're both adults. We both grew up in nice families. We're both well educated. Neither of us is going to gasp in horror if we see the other and is disappointed. Suppose we meet and are polite and then part and try to enjoy the rest of the weekend with our respective families: we'll be no worse off than we were five months ago, before Mariana brought me Mauricio's letter.

Except that, if that happens, I will cease to be anyone's one true love. I will officially become just another silly old woman, talking about men who once admired her and how tiny her waist used to be, recalling old triumphs with a coquettish wave of her head even as too-bright lipstick is stuck to her discolored front teeth. The kind of woman who aggrandizes and mythologizes her past, and then when you see a photo of her in her prime, you realize that she was never really breathtaking, except in her own mind. That's not entirely fair, because photos don't capture the spark, the flair, that character and personality give to a vibrant young girl. But what if I'm misremembering that, too? Then I'll be the kind of old woman who lives in the past, where love existed, because the present is just too empty, as sterile as an operating room.

When I think about that, I close my eyes, hoping for a minute that I'll feel faint, that I'll stumble and Mariana will say, "Have a seat, Bela," and decide that I'm not well enough to go uptown to Sacred Heart, that they have to get me back to Managua, and my doctors, as soon as possible.

But then there are moments when I forget to prepare myself for the worst, and the air wraps around me exactly as it did when I was a young girl with bare arms and gloved hands, and it's no longer nerves that I feel but excitement, that youthful sense that everything is about to happen, that your real life, the life you knew you were destined for, is about to start in the very next minute. How can your mind prepare for the worst when your body betrays you and is readying itself for the best?

I try to pray, to leave this in God's hands. But I'm not sure what to pray for. What's the best outcome? That I won't have to go and I can return to my quiet life in Managua, with my old *Très Bien* ribbons and black-and-white photos? That Mauricio and I will feel the same way we did half a century ago? I'm not sure that's possible. And, really, wouldn't God's loyalty, under the circumstances, belong with Ignacio?

I'm already a silly old woman; I can't even pray rationally anymore. The best I can do is clear my mind and let Allen and Mariana lead me along like a child on the way to her terrifying first day of school.

"Maybe we should take a cab," Mariana frets as we stand in the crush of people waiting for the streetcar on St. Charles. When I lived in New Orleans, there were streetcar lines on North Carrollton,

Napoleon, South Claiborne, maybe more; it seemed like the whole city clattered with their sound. Now it appears that there's just this last rickety track and we're being jostled by tourists awaiting the car. And local people, too. There's a young black woman in a nurse's uniform; she must live in town. I hope she'll stay on until we get to Sacred Heart, in case I collapse.

"One of the things Bela wanted to do was take a streetcar, babe," Allen says. "It's part of the sentimental journey, right, Bela?" Now Allen has started singing, and I don't want people to think he's a panhandler; he could be, with his wrinkled trousers and paint-stained hands. These two are supposed to be here to support me, but in the end he's a gringo pretending to be a human saxophone, and she's a pregnant woman who's wound up to the point of hysteria.

"We'll be fine, Mariana; half of these people are men and, you'll see, a gentleman always gives up his seat for a lady."

I'm right, of course. As soon as we board, a man who seems to belong to the nurse clears a path for me and Mariana to walk straight to one of the wooden seats, which look just like I remember. It was the same when I was a student: all the gentlemen would stand to let the pretty girls take a seat.

"Can I sit next to the window, Bela?" Mariana asks. "I might make some quick sketches."

I nod and she slides past me. I would have liked to have felt the breeze coming in through the window, but it's better this way; I had my hair set this morning in the hotel salon, which cost six times what it does in Managua, and I don't want the wind to ruin it. And Allen is standing in the aisle, at the edge of my seat, so I can tap him if he starts singing again; Mariana never controls him, she just grins, and, if she sees me glaring, shrugs as if Allen's behavior is not her affair. Whose affair is it, then? Mine? I didn't make him the father of her child.

It's helping, thinking about the present, about Allen and Mariana and the baby. The baby's a girl, and I think they want to name her for me, although I'll have to tell Mariana not to, it might seem like a slight to Ninexin. I have to make an effort to keep my mind in the here and now because after we pass a few office buildings, St. Charles looks so much like it did when I was a girl. The cars are different. When I was young, cars looked like shoes or boats; now they look like large, shiny insects or prettied-up tanks. But the massive trees are there, branches swaying. And I feel the past grow so large inside me that I think I can't contain it, I might burst right here on this streetcar and the poor young nurse will be of no help at all; they're not trained to heal the past.

So I stop looking out the window and focus on Mariana's hands: one is holding her little book and the other a pencil, which is moving furiously as images take shape under it. An ornate church steeple manifests in a matter of seconds. Then she flips the page and it's gone. A porch filled with hanging flowers appears, then it, too, is brushed away.

"So fast!" I say.

"They're just sketches, Bela. Things I might go back to later, if I decide I really want to draw them."

She sketches a mother pushing a stroller, a young woman in practically no clothes being dragged by four large dogs. Now she's drawing a hunched old man, crouching over a park bench, and Allen taps my shoulder and says, "It's go time, Bela," as the streetcar shudders to a stop.

But it's impossible. The image on her paper can have nothing to do with the Mauricio I know, so I refuse to look out the window. Allen is dragging me up from my seat, thinking he's being helpful, but I stop still, I refuse to move. They think I've simply stopped in order to let Mariana pass in front of me. She's the first one to step out of the back door of the streetcar and then Allen is gently pushing me forward. As Mariana descends, I catch sight of him: white hair flopping down to reveal a patch of scalp. He's slumped over, doubled almost in half, and I know this is all a mistake, I should never have come, I should never have seen him in such a weakened state, I should have remembered him as he was in his youth and in his letter and on the phone, strong and bold. The tall, skinny woman sitting next to him taps him, and he gives his pants a final tug and straightens up. And suddenly, it really is him. Mauricio. Just as I remembered. He now has the mustache I once recommended, a white one, and his hair is white, too, but his eyes are exactly the same, and as he stands up and pulls on a navy jacket that had been folded in his lap, I can see him becoming himself, as if his soul is settling back into his body.

"You should have warned me!" he says to his daughter in Spanish as Allen pushes me off the streetcar.

"I told you to stop fussing, you just didn't hear me." She turns to Allen and says, in English, "Apparently, I haven't ironed the creases in my father's pants to his liking."

Allen looks at the pants in question and says, "I'd hire you," and the woman laughs and puts out her hand. "Paloma. Pleased to meet you."

"Allen." He shakes her hand. "I'm Maria's husband."

Mariana is laughing at that white lie but she doesn't contradict him, and I'm so grateful to them both. Until, Dios mio, I notice that she's also crying, although I can't imagine why. "I'm sorry." Mariana hugs Paloma and even poor, startled Mauricio. "It's just so beautiful, the school, like in my Bela's pictures." She wipes her face and adds, "It's the hormones. I cry all the time."

"I remember," says Paloma. "Crying and peeing."

"Hija!" Mauricio whispers, but Paloma is unconcerned. She appears to have a lot in common with Ninexin.

"Don't worry, Papa. We'll stop embarrassing you and take ourselves around the corner for coffee. Sit on the porch so you don't get too hot; the lady in the office said it was fine. School doesn't get out until three; we'll be back long before then."

Everyone says hello and good-bye but I can't hear them, I can just see their lips moving. I make myself say something, too, and it must be the right kind of thing people say in situations like this, because Paloma is kissing me on the cheek, and Mariana is hugging me as close as her belly allows, and Allen winks and, from the looks of it, starts singing again as he follows Paloma down the street, holding Mariana's hand.

A girl in a uniform comes running out of the gate—if I had ever run like that a nun would have stuck her head out of a window to admonish me—and Mauricio grabs it and holds it open, offering me his other arm. I take it and neither of us speaks as we walk across this courtyard, which we crossed together so many times, so long ago. It looks so much the same, with the fountain in the middle and the brick building stretching out around it on three sides. Mauricio helps me up the small steps to the porch and then follows, so we're both standing there, under the sky-blue ceiling. There's a bench right behind us, but I'm not ready to sit down yet. I lean against a white pillar to look at the courtyard and breathe it in, to let it match up with the courtyard I remember, and settle into my mind and body so that I'll believe that we're really here, together.

Something is missing. Not in the real courtyard, but in Mariana's painting of it, of our meeting. Here, there's a fountain in the middle, and her painting needs it, she should add it in. In real life I was worried that my book was going to fall into the fountain, but on her canvas, there's just blank space with the letters of the title floating across it.

"*The Elements of Practice and Composition*," I say.

"Isa?" Mauricio is standing behind me, so I turn toward him to explain.

"The book? The one I dropped when I met you. Mariana said I should carry a copy of it today, so that you'd recognize me."

"Recognize you?" He puts one hand on my shoulder and brings the other to settle on my cheek. "But, Isa, you're exactly the same as you always were."

Acknowledgments

They say you don't just marry the man, you marry his whole family. Sometimes you get an entire country in the bargain. If I had never met Emilio, I might never have gone to Nicaragua. And I almost certainly wouldn't have an entire flock of Nicaraguan relatives who were instrumental in the writing of this book. I won't name all of the Oyangurens and Baltodanos who shared their homes, time, and stories with me, for lack of space. But I am grateful to all of them, and would especially like to mention Mamina, Emilio's grandmother, who was educated in New Orleans back in what for most people would have been called their glory days. The beauty of Mamina is that every day continues to be one of her glory days; her exuberant perspective and the amount of change she has seen in her life inspired the character of Isabela.

My mother-in-law, Carmen, could not be more different from Ninexin, which is probably a good thing; neither a guerrilla fighter nor the mother of daughters, she was nonetheless instrumental in the writing of the book, chatting with me for hours and exposing me to locales ranging from the Huembes market in Managua, to the house of the pastelito seller in Granada, to the private homes of many of her friends.

José Oyanguren and Maria Isabel Rivas were among my earliest readers and fact-checkers, and invaluable resources for everything from Catholic ritual to Nicaraguan naming conventions to national history.

And my deepest thanks to Emilio, who traveled with me to Ometepe and Solentiname, lived with me in Granada and Managua, and never complained about my poor conjugation of Spanish verbs or pampered need for hot water in the shower. I look forward to many more journeys together.

I'm living proof that the most fun way to learn about another culture is to marry into it. Traveling the country is a close second. But another indispensible path to getting to know a place is reading about it. The following books on Nicaragua informed this novel, and would be useful to anyone interested in the country: virtually all of Gioconda Belli's oeuvre, but especially *The Country Under My Skin* and *The Inhabited Woman*; Omar Cabeza's *Fire from the Mountain*, which outlines the bravery of the Sandinista fighters but also makes it clear how difficult it must have been to be romantically involved with a guerrilla fighter; Shirley Christian's *Nicaragua: Revolution in the Family*; and Margaret Randall's oral histories, both *Sandino's Daughters* and *Sandino's Daughters Revisited*, which were useful in illuminating the struggle of female revolutionaries. For background on New Orleans in the middle of the last century, I turned to *Legacy of a Century: Academy of the Sacred Heart in New Orleans*, which was introduced to me by Liz Manthey, who gave me and Mamina an unforgettable tour of her alma mater; and to Mary

Lou Widmer's *New Orleans in the Forties,* and *New Orleans in the Fifties,* which were recommended to me by Britton Trice at the Garden District Bookshop. (Thanks, as always, to Kay Fausset, for introducing me to the people I just mentioned and to so much of that beloved city.) Obviously, any errors regarding Nicaragua or New Orleans are entirely my own.

Any book written by a parent would not be complete without a few words of gratitude for the people who watched the author's child while he or she wrote. Amalía has been blessed with the most loving caretakers, among them Catherine Wheeler-Baco in Miami, María José Bermudez in Granada, Jenny Zamora in Granada and New York, and Julia Ashley Simunek in New York.

I also want to thank early readers of the novel for their invaluable feedback, the ever-supportive Joan Paulson Gage and Katherine Fausset. Many thanks to Elizabeth Graves and everyone at *Martha Stewart Weddings* for the gainful, and gleeful, employment, which facilitates my expensive novel-writing habit. And my eternal gratitude belongs to Stéphanie Abou, a revolutionary at heart (but the most glamorous one you'll ever meet), and Nichole Argyres, life partner and coparent of this, our third child together. And many thanks to Laura Chasen at St. Martin's Press and Tanya Farrell at Wunderkind PR for their invaluable help and support.

Thanks to my friends for listening patiently to way too much detail about the writing process. And to my own family for child care, literary advice, and friendly conversation. I didn't think it was possible for my parents, Nicholas and Joan Gage, to be more loving, until I had a child and our worlds multiplied. One of the lessons Mariana learns in this book is that there's no greater blessing than having multiple mothers; I knew that already thanks to Eleni Nikolaides, who helped raise me. And perhaps the greatest lack in

Mariana's life is that she doesn't have a sister, or a female cousin, to provide moral (and tech!) support. Happily for me, I do. Thank you to Marina Gage, Efrosini Nikolaides, and to Efro's husband, Sy Suire, who got swept up in the joyous chaos of our own family. Finally to Amalía, thank you for allowing me to experience firsthand the struggles and joys of motherhood, and for helping me, and the characters in the book, to understand how the latter will always outweigh the former.